Grant called, and at first it wasn't that much fun. He told me how he likes his roommate, Matt, and how he's sending me pictures of his dorm room and how he got a job at a pet store this afternoon, only it's one of those giant corporate chains—not what he wanted. He went on and on. He sounded so good, so happy . . . I almost really hated him for a minute. How dare he?

Told him I couldn't do this, that I missed him too much and was coming home immediately. That I hated everything here and felt completely out of place.

"Hello? Is this Courtney Von Dragen Smith?" he said, tapping the phone. "Operator? I thought I was talking to Courtney V.D. Smith."

"Will you quit saying that?" I started laughing even though I was still crying. Nobody was allowed to use my middle initials except Grant. "Why are you saying that?"

"Because this isn't you. This really doesn't sound like you."

"The crying part? Or the whining, complaining part?"

"The giving up part. You don't give up that easily. On like, anything."

"I don't?" I asked. Shoot. Because this throwing-in-the-college-towel thing was something I felt I could be a real natural at.

Love and Other Things I'm Bad At

Love and
Other Things
I'm Bad At

Rocky Road Trip

Sundae My Prince Will Come

CATHERINE CLARK

HARPER TEEN
An Imprint of HarperCollinsPublishers

HarperTeen is an imprint of HarperCollins Publishers.

Library of Congress catalog card number: 2009941831
ISBN 978-0-06-177863-6
Typography by Sasha Illingworth
11 12 13 14 15   LP/BV   10 9 8 7 6 5 4 3 2 1
❖
First Edition

For Erica, Chris, and Andrew.
You'll know why.

CONTENTS

Rocky
Road
Trip

8/18 FRIDAY NIGHT

Can I even explain the weirdness that is my life right now?

My new college roommate, the person I have to spend the next 9 months living with, Mary Jo Johannsen, is sleeping now. Went to bed at 10. Set alarm for 5 but said she'd probably wake up before it went off. What? Who wakes up before 5?

Her straw-blond hair is spread out on the pillow. She has baby-blue flannel pajamas with little black-and-white Holstein cows on them. Which she is wearing even though it is about 90 degrees in our room. 3rd floor. Hot, humid. No A/C.

Mary Jo is the type of person you might hate if she weren't so nice. Too nice, actually. Highly suspect. Has perfect body, perfect hair, and no clue of this. Wears unflattering clothes that end up looking good anyway—orange corduroy pants, the kind you see for $1.99 at Old Navy, only hers are legitimately vintage, plus white T-shirt with green John Deere tractor logo. She's tan, she has muscles. She looks healthy, strong, *normal*. Sort of like Drew Barrymore.

Me, I feel like the heifer in the photo at the end of her bed. Could be the fact I ate cheese in addition to sour cream today, however. In spite of being a vegan. Okay, a semi-vegan. Mary Jo's mom brought snacks and sandwiches and cubed cheese and kept insisting I have some, wouldn't take no for an answer. Realized I had to take something or she would never stop asking. Opted for the lesser of 27 evils and had cheddar cubes. Mom was in heaven, bonding with other mom over advantages of having large cooler stocked with bite-size items in Ziploc.

Anyway, now my stomach is as bloated as my college

application was, which is the reason I ended up with mega-size scholarship and grants to this supposedly "top-notch" Cornwall Falls College in the first place. It is *way* out in the country. Thought I would like that for some reason. Now it seems crazy as I am too far from major airports. Where is my escape route?

Never should have listened to Mom. Or guidance counselor. Or Gerry, the ex-guidance counselor. They all told me to volunteer, like being the student council VP and then P wasn't enough. End result: I cleaned out streams. I collected donated books. I tutored at elementary school. I nearly joined the Girl Scouts to get into a good college. Insane concept, as I am too old to wear uniforms and badges, not that I had any badges yet, which would have been really embarrassing. Would have been oldest living Brownie, and though I have a few camping skills, like rolling up my sleeping bag, and gathering firewood, I am lousy at camp songs and cannot cook a marshmallow without singeing my hair.

What was I thinking when I decided to go away to college? What was I thinking when I said, "Hey, okay, Wisconsin!" I even went for a tour, which should have given me time to think. But no. Must have been in a dairy-induced daze. Just because they served free Starbucks Frappuccinos on the plane and got my vegan/vegetarian/non-chicken meal right, I took that as a sign. A flight attendant with frosted blond hair and an attitude about me having a special request meal gives me a stupid egg-free, gluten-free cookie . . . and I make a major life decision based on that? Am I *that* insane?

Anyway, that's beside the point. It's all beside the

point. The point is that I am here at Cornwall Falls College.

Getting here was *so weird*. Little sign outside; Rankin Hall. Crowded parking lot. We walked up the stairs and I was wondering if Mary Jo would be here yet. Nervous about meeting her. Have never had a roommate except for Alison, and sisters don't count. Wondered if I'd filled out my housing questionnaire right, if there was such a thing as a right answer to "Hobbies You Enjoy."

What about "Hobbies You *Don't* Enjoy"? Why don't they ever ask the important questions?

Anyway, we wandered down the hall looking for 326. Very crowded. Lots of parents, lots of microwaves and computer boxes and trunks, lots of girls looking either ecstatic or terrified. I kept saying "Hi," like an automaton. Hi, hi, hi. Then suddenly we were at room 326.

I peeked around the corner. Mary Jo was standing on her bed, putting up a Faith Hill poster. Which would add to the 10 million other things she already had on the wall: barn print, family portrait, Leann Rimes calendar, and 3 different "Precious Moments" posters with uplifting sayings and supposedly cute photos of kittens and puppies.

Agh!

Mrs. Johannsen was scrubbing built-in dresser and closet with toxic cleaning product. No oxygen in room.

Mr. Johannsen was creating new furniture, putting up shelves, hammering nails into concrete, with plaster pieces crumbling to the floor which was covered with giant red University of Wisconsin rug.

"Um. Hi?" I said.

Everyone totally dropped what they were doing and

turned around. Mary Jo smiled as Mom and her parents shook hands and exchanged fascinating news of trip, highway route, weather. Mary Jo said she hoped I didn't mind if she kind of got the place settled—she left all this wall space for me, and if I wanted to change beds or anything, that was completely fine, etc. Very sweet and polite. I was looking around this tiny room trying to imagine how I could make it look remotely like a place I lived when suddenly this crowd of tall blond boys came rushing at me. Thought it was some fraternity reference when Mary Jo mentioned "brothers." Then I remembered there are no frats here, and realized these were her actual brothers. 6 of them, all over age 20. Was introduced but forgot each name instantaneously as they all wore similar T-shirts and jeans and boots. They all work on the family dairy farm. They all have the blondest hair I've ever seen. They all insisted on bringing up my stuff (which was very, very cool). Only took them 5 minutes.

Mrs. Johannsen then served a huge lunch. Their giant cooler was used as a table. 6 boys perched on Mary Jo's bed; me, Mom sat on my bed across from them; Mary Jo, Mr. and Mrs. J insisted on sitting on empty cardboard boxes, which they were practically falling into. Very bizarre meal. Kept having to say I wasn't that hungry as everyone else devoured ham and cheese on white, cold fried chicken, macaroni salad, some sort of Jell-O salad made with cottage cheese and marshmallows. Bluck.

Realized boys were staring at my "Meat is Murder" anti-animal-abuse poster and my framed "Vegetarians Make Better Lovers" bumper sticker (a joke gift! It's a joke, guys!), and old "Truth or Dairy" sign from the original store (Gerry's going-away gift). Very embarrassing.

But is it my fault they were gnawing on drumsticks at the time?

"Colorado! *Wow*. That's *so* far away! So how did you end up here?" Mary Jo asked. 6 brothers stared at me, awaiting answer.

I launched into the story of how Grandma and Grandpa went here, and how I was interested in environmental law, and how Cornwall Falls kept calling and adding more stuff to my financial package just to get me to accept, so it seemed like they really wanted me to come, and I told Mary Jo how at the same time I was waitlisted at Colorado College, and how it seemed like I should go somewhere where they wanted me. Etc. Too depressing to remember faulty chain of events right now.

At the same time, I was thinking about how Grandma told me I'd be a better person for accepting the challenge of moving away from home, and how Grant and I would be a better couple for it, etc., etc., blah blah blah. She snowed me. I can see that now. Don't want to see Grandma tomorrow when she and Grandpa are supposed to visit. Hate her for giving me that speech.

I'm beginning to feel very, very sorry for myself. I miss Grant so intensely right now.

Okay, so I'm going to take a deep breath and think calming thoughts. Repeat after me, Courtney: Grant and I will stay together, we are going to make this long-distance relationship work. I'm picturing happy places. Sun, mountains, gurgling streams.

What a bunch of crap. This isn't working at all.

Anyway, Mary Jo and her family were really into what I said about deciding to go to CFC. Her mother started talking about how Cornwall Falls launches this major recruitment drive to bring in students from all over the country, and how they're committed to a diverse population, which is great considering it's a small college in a rural area.

"It's known for being a microcosm of society," Mary Jo said.

"Yeah, that sounds familiar," I said. It was straight out of their shiny, misleading brochure with photos of cornstalks. So far all I've seen are tall blond people. Microcosm of Norway, *maybe*.

Mary Jo is from a small town about two hours from here. She's going to study science and math, and she likes country-western music. I'm living with a brainy Faith Hill. Who goes to bed way earlier than me and snores, I just found out a minute ago.

It's so strange, because they did make us fill out those really long questionnaires. There are like 2,000 other students here, and Mary Jo and I are supposed to be the most compatible out of all the other people I could have been matched with? Based on what? The fact we're both 18?

I am looking around our room. It is as polarized as a plug-in. Her side: country. My side: rock 'n' roll. Her side: cows. My side: leave cows alone.

She has a serious number of knickknacks on all open surfaces. We're talking a clock shaped like a potato, and tiny porcelain lambs, and other crap like that. She put about 18 different editions of *Chicken Soup for the Soul* on her new dad-installed bookshelves (he built me some, too, which is very cool). What is the deal with those books? Souls don't need *soup*. And chicken? Definitely not. My soul wants miso soup, if anything.

Also, my soul wants to get out of here and move back home. To be with Grant. But I guess it's too soon to bail. When *would* be a good time? Must check Leann Rimes calendar.

Grandma and Grandpa came today, stopping by on their way home from 2-week tour of the Great Lakes. They were on some senior excursion where they drive around hauling trailers and all hook up at the same spot. Hook up their trailers that is. Though with my grandparents you never know. Ever since Viagra was invented, their lifestyle's gotten a lot more, shall we say, active. The less I know about it, the better.

Grandpa insisted on coming to town because he loved going to school here and wanted to show me the sights and give me the tour of town. Which took all of 10 minutes. I must have been in *such* a daze when we drove into town for our campus tour last March that I didn't really notice. Perhaps I was too out of it due to multiple Frappuccinos. Perhaps they distracted me at crucial town-viewing moments by asking me all about myself. They kept doing that. Very tricky.

First of all, when you get down to Main Street from campus (which is only about a 5-minute walk), there's a sign that says, "You're in the One and Only Wonderful Wauzataukie!" Like I wasn't painfully aware of that.

The place is like a shrine to Dairiness.

I mean it. There's a bronze statue of a guy called His Royal Dairiness in the center of town, in the park. (Cute park. Very green. Little healthy-looking kids running around, high on calcium.) The founder of the town was a dairy god, I guess. He invented the udder or something. I also learned that the town's name is ancient—it comes from a Native American tribe's language and means "land of standing water," or something like that. Nice connection, but not exactly inspiring—sort of mildewy-sounding.

Grandpa kept joking that the town is the nation's largest breeding ground for the state bird: the mosquito. Then Grandma said no, that was Minnesota's state bird. Ha ha ha. Funny. Except that right now I have too many red welts on my legs to count.

There also was a cow sculpture representing different breeds, with some bronzed goats running around the base. I don't know why cow sculptures are necessary, when cows are never out of sight and certainly never out of smell here.

Grandpa and Grandma kept lamenting the stores that have closed since they went here 100 years ago. The missing "five and dime," the vanished Bert's Dairy Bar. (Since when do you order milk at a bar? No wonder the concept failed.)

"At least good old Brat Wurstenburger's still around. If you ever want the perfect brat, that's the place to go," Grandpa said. "You can get it boiled or grilled, made with cheese or beer, you can get weisswurst and knockwurst. . . ." And he was off on another lecture about the wonders and virtues of sausage casing.

Naturally we ended up at Brat Wurstenburger for lunch. It's incredibly popular—all the tables were full of other parents and their unsuspecting children. I had a lemonade and some pickles and then afterward a slice of apple cake.

"Worried about gaining the freshman fifteen?" Grandma patted my knee. "Well, sure. And you're smart to be."

"I'm not worried about that!" I snapped. They were all really getting on my nerves. Couldn't they tell I was going through the most painful day of my existence? And that watching them eat pork while I smelled sauerkraut wasn't helping? Also, seeing all those hot dogs made me miss Oscar, world's strangest dog. And thinking of Oscar made me miss Grant, the only person who understands Oscar. And we were all separated now. Got so upset I had to go into the bathroom and cry for a while. Very embarrassing, because girls who will probably be in my classes kept coming in and there I was sniffling into a paper towel.

Then we were back out, exploring the town. It seemed to me that *all* the stores advertised "Cheese" and "Sausage" and "Bratwurst" in their windows. Like they *wouldn't* have them. Where was the sign for "Organics Sold Here" or "Meat-Free Zone"?

"Grandpa, I *told* you," I had to say before he nearly dragged me into Karl's House of Meat. "I don't eat meat."

"Well, no, not at every meal, of course," Grandpa said.

"Not ever!" Unless you counted the random times I slipped, but those were only 2 or 3 times a year, or maybe a month, at most. Only when I got really stressed out. "How many times do I have to tell you guys? I'm a vegetarian. I'm practically verging on being a vegan."

"A what?" Grandma asked. Her ears turned red. I think she thought I said I was a virgin. Not exactly.

"Nonsense," Grandpa said. "There's no such thing as not eating meat."

I think he has mad-pig disease from all the pork he eats.

"She's just tired from the long drive," Grandma said.

No I'm not! I just want everyone to leave me alone for 2 seconds and quit hovering and let me just cry my eyes out in private, if that's OKAY with everyone.

"Bagle Finagle. What's *that*?" Grandpa turned up his

nose as we stopped outside yet another brick building. "Didn't they spell bagel wrong?"

"It's cute," I said, peering inside. To me, it looked like the only cool place in town. It figures that Grandpa wouldn't be able to see that. He was too busy complaining about bagels, and what was wrong with a good old piece of toast, and how toast went so well with bacon and eggs, it was God's food.

I can't *wait* until they all leave tomorrow. I just want classes to start. The sooner classes start, the sooner the semester ends, the sooner I'll be home with Grant.

Did I mention the worst part of the trip?

When we were driving through Nebraska, I saw this evil road sign on the highway: "Exit 126. Ogallala. Grant."

Total conspiracy to make me burst out crying and regret decision to be in a mini-van leaving Grant behind. "They should really put more thought into those signs," I told Mom. "It's not very considerate of them."

"It's a town, Courtney," Mom said. "Grant's been here for years and years. It's not a conspiracy."

Sure it isn't. That town's name never *used* to be on the sign, okay?

Then we had to drive through Grant County when we got to Wisconsin. And then I studied the map and realized there is also a Superior, WI, way up north (spent way too much time bonding with AAA maps on the drive). This is in addition to Grant and Superior in Colorado.

Grant Superior is everywhere. Just not here with me, where he should be.

Mom just left, caravanning in Caravan behind Grandpa and Grandma and giant trailer, which Grandma and Grandpa and Mom all slept in last night, in the dorm parking lot. Completely embarrassing when they marched upstairs this morning with towels around their necks, ready for showers. I love her and them. I do. But I was dying for a second of time by myself. All day yesterday, Mom wouldn't stop talking. Probably sensed that I was miserable and was trying to fill the empty, sad aura around my head. Instead she just annoyed me. My aura became irate at one point.

"Look at the trees, Courtney!" Mom kept saying as we drove around. "Have you ever seen anything so beautiful?"

That's Mom. Psyched about the trees, living for foliage, while I'm completely miserable over leaving home.

"These trees are okay, but the aspen back home are more beautiful," I said. "The mountains are beautiful. Living in the same state as my boyfriend is beautiful. *Was* beautiful."

"I know you miss Grant. How about we get some nice, crisp, tart apples and some nice Wisconsin cheddar," she suggested.

How would that fix anything? She *knows* I don't eat cheese. And why did everything have to be so beautiful and *nice* in her world? I was dying inside.

"Mom, *no*," I said. I was talking about the "nice" cheddar, but she thought I was rebuffing her in general and got upset. Then I had to make it up to her by being extra nice the rest of the day. If I were a cheddar, I'd be an extra sharp.

Listen to me! I'm going insane. I have got to drop out

of this college immediately. I haven't been in the state for even 48 hours and I'm already using cheese terms to describe myself.

Roommate Alert: Did I mention that Mary Jo got up at 5? On a Sunday? She put headphones on and was listening to music and smiling and reading her bio textbook. Classes haven't even started yet. I haven't even located the *bookstore* yet.

I've got to talk to Grant.

Just tried calling him. Grant is not home. How can he not be home? I need him.

This is going to suck, isn't it?

LATER . . .

Just discovered that Mary Jo's mini-fridge is not stocked with soda, as I hoped. The thing is packed full of meat and cheese. It's like a deli case. Filled with meats I don't recognize, like this reddish ham-looking thing with white pieces of something (fat? flesh? bones?) in it. Mary Jo's lucky. If my grandfather had seen this, he would have totally feasted and cleaned the place out.

So I got a glass of water from the drinking fountain. But you know what? Even the water here tastes like milk. It's like some science fiction universe. A World Made Entirely of Milk. The question is not "Got milk?" but rather, "Got anything *but* milk?" I honestly don't think I can make it here.

Tried to be optimistic. Decided to decorate my side of the room. I put up my animal rights poster. It looks sort of strange next to the picture of Mary Jo from 4-H showing her champion cow Sophie, which is next to the photo of her gold-medal goat Chipper, but, oh well.

Then I hung up my favorite pictures of Grant, and me and Grant. And me and Beth and Jane. And Grant. Pretty soon I had this major collage going, so I finished it.

Then R.A., Krystyne (yes, that's how she spells it), walked by and saw me holding the glue gun. "Uff da!" she yelled.

"Um . . . what?" I said. "Is that a compliment?"

"No, it's Norwegian for 'Whoa, Courtney!'" She started laughing. She was really cracking herself up.

Meanwhile, I was staring at her annoying, red "Cornwall Falls into Your Heart" sweatshirt.

"What did you do? You're not supposed to use that stuff. It's a fire hazard." She said glue wasn't on the list of "approved mounting materials" (what?!). So I had to take down all the photos. She said I had to get a bulletin board, and that they sold some really nice ones at the bookstore.

I was so mad. All the work I'd done. I was just trying to make this place look like mine. And the pictures were already stuck to the wall; they didn't come off easily. I got so frustrated, I just yanked at one. I ripped in half one of the pictures of me and Grant with our arms around each other.

NOT AN OMEN NOT AN OMEN NOT AN OMEN

I grabbed the Scotch tape and put about 6 layers on. You can't even tell it's me and Grant anymore.

NOT AN OMEN NOT AN OMEN NOT AN OMEN

Need to email Grant now and ask him to send more pictures of us.

LATER STILL . . .

Obviously I will be writing in here constantly, as I am too lonely here and have nothing else to do.

Went into town this afternoon in search of natural foods store, or at the very least some foods more natural than pimento loaf. Mary Jo went to a meeting for the Biology–Chemistry–Pre-med Club. "The program here is incredibly respected," Mary Jo told me before she left.

"So is the political science department," I said. All of a sudden, we were like competing for being smart, discussing GPAs and SAT scores. She got a 780(!!!) on the math part. I immediately changed the subject and told her about my cool work-study job. Which I've got to find more out about tomorrow.

On the way to town, I stopped this guy to ask where the closest grocery store was. "Take a left at the stop sign," he said. "Then turn right at Hertzmann's Implement."

What? What is an implement? Sounds scary, like something out of a Stephen King novel. Like this whole *experience* so far. *Misery.*

Anyway, when I got to town, I thought I must have fallen asleep and dreamt I was Heidi. These people walked by me on Main Street wearing lederhosen, and the women had their blond hair in cute little wired braids, like Pippi Longstocking.

"*Willkommen!*" one of the men said with this hearty wave.

That's when I realized it wasn't a dream. Oh my God, I thought. What next? I have got to get out of this place.

I found out they were having this festival to celebrate the end of summer, and also to welcome us to campus. They called it the Fall Alpen Fest.

More like Late-Summer Dork Fest. There are no Alps around here, in case no one's noticed. There are a few hills and these things called "mounds" that I read about in Mom's AAA book, but you couldn't ski down one unless you were being towed by a helicopter. Besides, they're sacred, ancient Native American sites, and you shouldn't even be on them, so quit it.

Anyway. Swiss Miss, I'm not. I guess there are lederhosen in my Von Dragen ancestral line, but I'd rather not know about it.

The only people who looked like they were having fun were the ones in the beer tent, but I wasn't allowed inside since I'm not 21. No all-ages tent anywhere. Completely thoughtless Swiss-German welcome to town.

There was a polka band playing on this little wooden stage that looked more like a gazebo whose walls had blown off. Accordions were flashing in the sunlight. People started to dance. *Oom pah pah* HELP.

I decided I'd sit down and write Grant a letter describing the whole scene. I'd make him laugh, and also realize how lucky he was to still be close to home. I found a spot on the grass that hadn't had mustard spilled on it yet and sat down.

But before I could think of anything brilliant to write to Grant, I noticed this girl sitting a few feet away, writing in a blank book. She was holding a pencil that looked like a whittled tree branch, and her brown hair was tied into about a hundred tiny braids.

She caught me looking at her and she smiled. "Hey, Courtney."

I stared at her. Was I still wearing one of those heinous nametags they'd tried to hand out? No. So how did she know my name? I asked. I'd never seen her before.

"I studied the book," she said. "The freshman book they posted on the website this summer? And I have this photographic memory, so when I saw you I knew. Courtney Smith, Denver, Colorado, Bugling Elk High School."

"Wow," I said, impressed. She was like Raymond in *Rain Man*. If I dropped my value-pack of cinnamon Trident she'd probably instantly be able to tell how many pieces were on the ground. "So, um, what's your name?"

"It's time," she said.

"Time?" I said. "For what?" I looked at the stage, wondering if a new polka was about to start up.

"My name. It's time," she said. "T-h-y-m-e. Like the spice? Parsley, sage, rosemary, and me."

"Are those your sisters?" I asked.

"No," she said, laughing. "I was just trying to explain what I meant."

"Oops. *Sorry*," I said. "Thyme's a really cool name." I didn't know anyone with a name like that back home. Well, maybe—there were a Meadow and a Rain in my class. Not to mention a Hope and a Faith. But this is different. This is herbal.

"Yeah, I picked it out myself." Thyme scratched at something on her arm. That's when I realized she didn't shave her underarms. Or her legs.

I really respect that in a woman, but I just can't do it myself. It wouldn't work with my red hair. Also, Mom would have a fit. On top of not shaving, Thyme has about 5 tattoos: 3 on her legs, 1 on her arm, even 1 on her neck. Various goddesses and symbols. Wonder why she doesn't shave, because if she did her tattoos would show up better. But won't mention that until we're closer friends.

I looked around the town square, thinking: if I felt out of place here, how did Thyme feel? Anyway, turns out that Thyme lives 2 doors down, just across the hall. And she and her roommate have already gotten into 3 fights in 2 days.

"Can you believe this cow town? And isn't the dorm a complete nightmare? I can't *wait* until I can move off campus," Thyme said. "Those awful, unhealthy fluorescent lights in the bathroom, plus the hall carpet's made out of like asbestos or dioxin or something—I can't even smell it without sneezing. I mean, it's amazing we're not dead yet."

"Oh, yeah," I said, "I know." I hadn't noticed that yet, but I told myself it's because I've been too upset. "Well, um . . . I like your scarf," I said.

"Thanks! All my clothes are made of natural fibers. Even my shoes."

"Cool." I nodded. Cotton shoes aren't exactly my style, I'm shamefully more of a leather girl, but I did admire her for being so dedicated.

"So anyway, my roommate is like from the Stone Age. She was putting up these shelves for her Treasure Troll collection. Trolls! So I told her I wanted to fung-sway our room, and she was like . . . 'Thyme, what are you talking about?'"

What *was* Thyme talking about? I still don't know.

But she's nice. She's from Chicago, went to an alternative high school, seems interesting. At least I have a lot more in common with her than I do with Mary Jo.

We went off to find the grocery store together. They have some organic vegetables that cost about $3 each and vegetarian baked beans and that's about it. Thyme said since we have to be on the school cafeteria meal plan anyway, and we already paid for that, what we should do is just eat there and scavenge for things that seem remotely healthy.

I told her how I helped get more vegetarian items on the Bugling Elk menu rotation when I was student council VP. She said something about how easy it was to get things done when you "went establishment." Thought it was rude of her to slam me like that, but forgave her when she invited me up to her room to snack on soy-yogurt-covered raisins and nuts. She's probably just stressed out about being here, like I am.

Grant is the best person ever. Best best best best. True to his name. Superior.

He called, and at first it wasn't that much fun. He told me how he likes his roommate, Matt, and how he's sending me pictures of his dorm room and how he got a job at a pet store this afternoon, only it's one of those giant corporate chains—not what he wanted. He went on and on. He sounded so good, so happy . . . I almost really hated him for a minute. How dare he?

Told him I couldn't do this, that I missed him too much and was coming home immediately. That I hated everything here and felt completely out of place.

"Hello? Is this Courtney Von Dragen Smith?" he said, tapping the phone. "Operator? I thought I was talking to Courtney V.D. Smith."

"Will you quit saying that?" I started laughing even though I was still crying. Nobody was allowed to use my middle initials except Grant. "Why are you saying that?"

"Because this isn't you. This really doesn't sound like you."

"The crying part? Or the whining, complaining part?"

"The giving up part. You don't give up that easily. On like, anything."

"I don't?" I asked. Shoot. Because this throwing-in-the-college-towel thing was something I felt I could be a real natural at.

"No." Then he launched into this long laundry list of things I've pursued that supposedly showed my perseverance. "And it's one of the things that I really love about you." Grant paused. "Does that help?"

Does it *help*? Grant is like this incredibly hot first-aid

kit. When I got back to my room I wrote him a very gushy long letter, which I must take to post office and mail immediately. Perhaps for overnight delivery.

Sweetest thing he has ever done, unless you count the I.D. tag he made for me at Pet Me for Valentine's Day with his phone number on it.

Or the day he called and said he was going to give me a ride to school, but he took me hiking instead.

Or the way he signed my yearbook and wrote "I Love You, Courtney." None of the other boyfriends did that. I took an informal poll. It confirmed what I already knew: Grant is the best boyfriend ever. Superior.

He said it was a zoo the day I left, with everyone showing up to say good-bye to me. "And not the good kind of zoo, either," he said. "The kind where they don't let the animals out."

Not sure what he meant by that. All I remember is pulling out of the driveway in the Caravan. I thought I was going to crumble into a hundred pieces, like those stale egg-less, flour-less muffins they sell at Earthen Fare way beyond their "best if sold by" dates. If they're ever at their best, which I seriously doubt.

I looked at Grant. He looked at me. Mom hit reverse. We nearly knocked over a couple of trash cans because she burst out crying while she was driving.

"Mom, you're not leaving," I said, sobbing. "You get to come back!"

"But—you'll—be—gone," she said, tears almost blinding her from the 4-way stop at the end of our block.

It all seemed so tragic, like I was shipping off to war.

Still and all. A really, really dumb idea to come this

far. But it can't be that dumb, because Jane's in Wisconsin, too. And I sort of only agreed to come here because she was leaving home, too, and it seemed like the cool thing to do. Must call her now and compare cheese stories.

LATER...

Just had our first official 3rd floor meeting. It was called "The Settling-In Shindig," and was supposedly happening on every floor of every dorm here tonight at the same time. Eerie. Freaky Friday. Except it's Monday.

At the meeting, R.A. Krystyne *actually said* that "Alone" is just "Baloney" without the B and Y! Baloney metaphors. For people in college. *Meat* metaphors. It's like . . . way to make us vegetarians feel welcome. Couldn't she come up with something else? Like: alone is just . . . soybean. Without the s,y,b, and with an l, and if you rearrange all the letters? Sure, it's a lot *harder*. Like everything is if you decide not to eat meat.

She made us all sit in a circle, introduce ourselves, and say something about what we did over the summer and why we chose to come to Cornwall Falls—what influenced our decisions.

"I worked at this smoothie and ice cream café called Truth or Dairy, and I came here due to temporary insanity," were my comments.

Everyone laughed and then Krystyne said, "No, *really*, Courtney."

Really. It's true, I wanted to say. But I came up with something about how I wanted to explore the world beyond in order to better understand the universe. Sounded sort of astronaut-like. Courtney In Space.

Here is my tally so far of the girls on the 3rd floor: Not a complete tally as 3 or 4 girls failed to show for the mandatory meeting. Krystyne went ballistic in a friendly sort of way about that. "Of course it doesn't really matter," she said. "But they definitely ought to be here and there's no acceptable excuse."

- 4 very brainy girls; spent the summer doing very impressive things like working at Wisconsin State Senate and internships at the U.N.; made me feel like a complete idiot
- 3 girls who talked about their boyfriends non-stop; what they did all summer was follow their boyfriends around; they came here because their boyfriends are going here; bluck
- 1 girl who said she came to Cornwall "under duress" because her parents went here and her grandparents went here (hey, I can relate, sister)
- 1 skateboard champion who did tricks on lounge furniture
- 6 girls from the soccer team; we're like the Soccer Block
- 1 girl from Milwaukee
- 1 girl who wouldn't talk, period
- me
- Mary Jo
- Thyme

After we all introduced ourselves, there was a talk from the student health service about not doing drugs and about having safe sex. Like we haven't had the same talk since 6th grade, or 2nd, or whenever it was they started badgering us. (I know it's important and everyone says it can't be said often enough, but trust me, it can.) It went pretty quickly because nobody asked any questions. Nobody *had* any questions.

I caught Thyme's eye a couple of times across the lounge and shook my head. "What are we doing here?" I mouthed.

She rolled her eyes. Later in the talk she interrupted to tell everyone about some new kind of natural-fiber 36-hour tampon that was better for the environment. Everyone looked at her sort of strangely, like you didn't bring up stuff like that in polite conversation. But we were talking about really impolite stuff, like certain types of lubricating gels, so I don't know what their problem was.

Afterward, we all dispersed and went back to our rooms. Which was good because I wanted to finish my package for Grant.

"What are you doing?" Mary Jo asked when I started filling an envelope with a bunch of different things for Grant: a goofy postcard of a cheese factory, a copy of my class schedule, a list of things that seemed weird about Mary Jo. Like the fact she used health and beauty products originally intended for horses or cows. (Grant would probably know all about them: Mane 'n Tail? Udder Butter? Bag Balm? Am I living with a girl or a thorough-bred?) I use stuff not tested on animals. She uses stuff *created for* animals. Which means they have to test it on them, don't they? How can you tell if a horse shampoo is bad, anyway? If its tail has split ends? Who cares?

"I'm putting together a letter for Grant," I told Mary Jo. "My boyfriend, remember?"

"Tell me more about Grant," she said. "What's he like?"

I just sat there and stared at all the pictures of him on the bulletin board. "He's great."

"He's really good-looking," she said. "Are you going to get married?"

"What? I don't know!" I laughed. "How would I know that? I'm only eighteen."

28

Mary Jo shrugged. "Most people back home know. That's all. My parents got married when *they* were eighteen."

"Oh. Well, see . . . mine didn't," I said. I actually didn't know how old they were, off the top of my head, but I did know they hadn't *stayed* married. Which reminded me. Dad was way behind with his monthly check.

I started writing another letter. *Dear Dad . . . Hello? Do you expect me to live on Saltines and tap water?*

"So, um, do you and Grant have a commitment?" Mary Jo asked. "Like a promise ring?"

I raised my eyebrow. "What? No." I did, however, have the faux rabies tag necklace, which was almost the same thing. And he bought me a new hoop for my belly button, and if that isn't commitment I don't know what is.

"Oh. So you're not serious," Mary Jo said.

"Yes we are!" I protested. What was her problem? "We're *extremely* serious. But we've only been together for about nine months."

Which would mean, if you were my stepsister Angelina, that you'd have a baby by now, but still no commitment.

Getting engaged at 18? I mean, I love Grant and all. But that really hadn't crossed my mind. Should it have? Am I weird for not thinking about it? Does Grant think about it?

8/22

So much for cool on-campus work-study job. I was supposed to be a research assistant. I was supposed to be in the law dept. Pictured myself writing legal briefs, wearing suits, appearing in court. Perhaps got a little carried away by watching too much *Law & Order* and *Ally McBeal*. Okay, I admit that. But do I deserve this?

I just called the work-study office to find out about my research-assistant job. The woman on the phone looked up my name, then she sounded nervous and flustered and told me to look in my "welcome packet" for my assignment—I must have missed it.

There was this letter stuffed in there, right underneath the list of Mental Health Resources (which I immediately stashed in my top desk drawer for easy access). It said that due to "changes in funding," my work-study job in the political science/law department had been eliminated.

ELIMINATED. Like something in a James Bond movie.

And it had been replaced by a job in the Cornwall Falls Fun-Times Funders. What is *that*? Sounds like some sort of horrid barbershop quartet. Help me!

LATER . . .

Okay, I'm back from the Student Administration building. (Quit administering us already! You're doing a really bad job.)

I now have a job as a glorified telemarketer. Must not tell Mom. She will be furious, since she is obsessed with running all telemarketers out of business, after she settles her lawsuit against the phone company.

Went down to find out what on earth they were talking about. They said my one job had been cut, which was kind of serious because it was lots of hours a week, and this new job was only going to be 5 hours a week. Which is going to amount to like $25 a week at minimum wage, which I can't possibly *live* on, not happily anyway. But they were still giving me all this GRANT money, of course, so not to worry, I should be okey-dokey here at Cornwall Falls. I could either get a job in town. Or I could get loans to make up the rest. Or I could rely on my family's trust fund, or I could start playing the lottery regularly, or I might want to start standing outside the student union, holding an empty coffee can and a placard that says: "Will Take Your Exams for Food."

Okay, those last parts they didn't say.

But the woman I was talking to was acting all bubbly about it, like this was *good* news and I should not be upset.

Excuse me, but that work-study job is part of why I came to this tofu-forsaken town in the first place! I wanted to scream, but didn't, due to the fact there was a line of 50 students behind me. Instead I asked who I should talk to about my assignment. They said I could talk to the Dean of Student Affairs, Dean Robert Sobransky.

I found his office and knocked on the door. In the

catalog, they kept bragging about this "open-door" policy they had when it came to teachers and students. So why was it closed?

He opened the door. Apparently he had just finished getting changed for a tennis match. He asked if he could help me. Which was funny coming from someone wearing too-short white shorts against pale white legs with curly black hair and a bright green polo shirt with the collar turned up. If anything, he needed help. Fashion Emergency.

I introduced myself, calmly. Professionally. Then I went into a slight tirade and said I really had to have an explanation for this. I said I had specifically come to Cornwall Falls because I was promised a chance to work in the law department, and now I find out, after I get here, it's all a ruse, a sham to lure me and innocent other people from Colorado—

"Whoa there, Courtney." He sat on the edge of his desk. "Are you a conspiracy theorist?"

"No, of course not," I said. Though the whole thing was incredibly fishy.

"Good. We have enough of those in our political science department already," he said. "Ha ha ha."

Ha. So hilarious.

He went on to explain that the school learned they had to make budget cuts over the summer, and they cut as few jobs as possible, and I shouldn't take it personally, blah blah blah. . . . But he'd sure be happy to recommend me for anything I found in town, and next semester we could see about getting another work-study job for me, obviously I was in need. I should come talk to him anytime, and if I faced any hardships because of this he'd see what he could do, etc.

32

The whole time he was talking, he kept tossing a tennis ball up to the ceiling and catching it, over and over, sort of obsessively watching it and trying to get it as close to the ceiling as he could without hitting it. Very weird guy.

"So what is this job I have now?" I finally asked.

He checked out my paperwork and smiled. "You'll be a key member of our Cornwall Falls Funding Team!"

"And that means . . . ?"

"Ah! I keep forgetting you're a freshman," he said. "You seem so much more ma-toor." (That's how he pronounced it.) (What the hell did he mean by that?) (Adults who say this to me always highly suspect.)

"It's in our alumni relations office. You'll be working with our gift programs, contacting alumni, and asking them to donate money, stock, land, what have you."

I guess I must have looked sort of upset, because then he said, "Don't worry, Courtney, I'll work with you every step of the way." At which point he walked into the desk, hit his knee, and started swearing profusely.

Afterward when I left the building, I was so mad I was walking really fast and not paying attention. I crashed right into this kiosk with a million flyers stapled onto it.

There was this girl from my hall standing there, drinking a Mountain Dew and smoking a clove cigarette, and she caught my arm. "Watch out, Courtney!"

"Hey . . ." I said really slowly, as I tried to remember her name. "Annemarie!" She is the one who didn't say a word at our hall meeting except to keep reminding everyone her name was 1 *word* and not 2, and her last name was Gustafsen with an e, not an o. She has one of the few single rooms on our hall. Her days so far seem to consist of coming home, slamming her door, putting on loud music like Garbage, Violent Femmes, Beastie Boys. She's never even made eye contact with me, not even in the bathroom when we were both brushing our teeth at neighboring sinks. But now she was actually talking to me. It was so cool.

"You look upset. What's wrong?"

"I just found out my work-study job," I told her. "I have to call alumni and ask them to donate money."

"That sucks. Hey, you know that chick on our hall who doesn't wear deodorant and has that Eve Goddess tattoo? Call her parents," Annemarie said.

"Thyme?" I said. "Why should I call her parents?"

She pointed to a brick building across the quad. "That's theirs. I mean, she told me it's named after them," she said. "The Newell Hall of Economics. Maybe they can cough up some cash for a new dorm and knock ours down."

Thyme's parents are stinking rich? Huh. I'm surprised.

"I could never call former students and ask them for money," Annemarie said. "Aren't we paying this place enough? I mean, I haven't even been here a week and it's like they want eighteen thousand dollars before I can even sign up for my gym card. Not that I want one." She took a drag of her clove cigarette, then offered it to me. "My work-study job is working in the *library*. I can't stand libraries. They're too quiet. I don't know how I ended up here, but I'm transferring."

Annemarie is completely right. I should transfer, too.

Why am *I* here? So I want a degree in environmental law. So my grandfather went here and says it's a great school. Since when have I trusted his opinion? The man thinks pork rinds are a food group. So they came after me and promised me enough financial aid to support me for 4 years and a work-study job. Which they already pretty much took away. Didn't they?

Isn't there more to life? Like . . . a *life*?

Why can't I be getting a scholarship like Grant to study veterinary medicine? Why can't I be any good at the same subjects he is? Grant and I could study side by side. We could open our own practice together. We'd call it Superior Animal Hospital. Brilliant, perfect name.

Except I am afraid of blood. Seeing animals in pain also freaks me out. Could be a problem.

Then I'll be the receptionist. I'll sit in the outer room, away from surgical procedures, and schedule appointments on environmentally friendly 100 percent recycled paper without thinking too long about what they're for. I'll be oblivious. Negligent. Whatever.

Mary Jo and I are *not* getting along.

I was getting dressed this morning and all of a sudden Mary Jo shrieked and said, "What's that on your stomach? Oh my God!"

She was referring to my pierced navel.

I explained that this was a piece of jewelry. She still seemed really confused about the whole thing.

"Well, I just think that's, um, I don't know. Wrong?"

"What's wrong about it? People pierce their ears. And lots of other things," I reminded her.

"Yeah, but—I don't know. It makes me think of the way that our cows have to get tags stapled to their ears to tell them apart," Mary Jo said.

She was comparing my navel to a cow's ear?

"Yeah, but that probably hurts them," I said. "This didn't." Not much, anyway. Except for the way it swelled up whenever I didn't use enough Hibiclens on it. "And besides, I *chose* to mutilate myself. I mean decorate myself. Whatever. Cows don't have that choice." Ha! So there for getting all self-righteous on me. At least I never stapled a cow.

Maybe people argue so much here because of the crappy weather. It's so hot. There's like 97 percent humidity. My hair is a frizz pile. Rain came in through the window and soaked the granola fruit bars I left on the windowsill, and now they're oatmeal. All the photos on my bulletin board are curled up at the corners. My towel smells like mildew. *I* smell like mildew.

"This is nothing," Mary Jo said. "Last spring it rained so much, our basement flooded. And outside? The cows

36

kept falling in the mud and a couple of them broke their legs."

"How long is this going to last? I really need some sun," I said.

"Don't worry, Courtney—you'll get used to it," Mary Jo told me when I kept staring out the window.

"I don't *want* to get used to it," I said. "I want to get away from it. The weather back home is so much better."

Mary Jo got insulted and left for the cafeteria without waiting for me or anyone else. Like she's responsible for the rain?

LATER...

Back from my new, exciting job.

Had to phone people today and remind them what a great place "Cornball" Falls is.

Hello? Does anyone see a problem here?

So far I haven't even been here a week, and I hate it. But there I was with my canned lines, reading them off a script that's so worn it looks as if it's been used by students every year since 1915.

"Your donation provides valuable support for students like me."

"Would you consider increasing your gift this year?"

"Would you like to donate a building?"

"Would you like fries with that?"

There's this ear-of-corn Velcro poster-thing on the wall that measures how well we're doing on the fund drive, like a thermometer filled with corn kernels instead of mercury. It looks like a project for a day-care center. And everyone has these signs up on their cubicle walls in front of them, to prod them into pushing for more money, like a reward system. "Way to Go, Rachel! $250!" and "$1,000—You Rule, Wittenauer!" Those are for the upperclassmen.

And then there's me. "Courtney. Keep Improving. $20."

Hey, is it my fault I get the losers' cards?

We have these index cards we have to use for each alum, with all this personal info, like what dorm they lived in, and what their major was, and what they do now, and how many kids they have. We have weekly goals, total amounts. So far I'm several hundred dollars short. Okay, thousands. I know—I'll flip through the cards, find the person with the largest donation ever, hit them up. Is there a chance in hell that Bill Gates went to Cornball Falls?

This afternoon was fun. Thyme and I went to the bagel place for coffee. I asked her about the Newell Hall of Economics. She launched into their entire family history. "It's—it's not my dad, it was my grandfather, because he went here," she said.

Are we all just here because of grandparents? *Must* we pay for their generation's mistakes?

Her grandfather gave the money a long time ago when he made a ton of money by inventing something or other. Then he got pushed out of the company, and Thyme said he was "a victim of evil downsizing corporate warfare." Is that typical or what? So they did have a lot of money, but they don't anymore. How sad. Whereas I don't have any money now, and never really had any, although I did all right working at T or D.

After coffee we went to the bank so I could open an account with my last few paychecks. Thyme already had an account but she came with me. Which was funny, because there were all these signs all over the bank: "Tyme is money," plastered on the cash machines. Turns out Tyme is the name of the ATM network here. I asked Thyme if that was embarrassing and she said she liked the juxtaposition of a free spirit and a corporate establishment. "Because it's so untrue, you know. Me, Thyme? I'm not money. I'm so *anti*-money. So it's so ironic."

The customer service person totally gave me the 3rd degree. She made me fill out a dozen forms, sign in 18 places. She practically wanted a sample of my blood. She was so suspicious of me, it was ridiculous. I was going to leave and open an account at another bank, but I'd filled out so many forms I felt like I couldn't move.

"Von . . . what does that say? Van Dragon?" the woman asked.

"Your middle initials are V.D.?" Thyme asked. "Ooh. How rude."

"Tell me about it," I said.

"It's better than STD though. I guess." Thyme started laughing, and then told me if I thought my middle name was bad, *hers* was Penelope. So I guess things could be worse. Maybe. Thyme Penelope equals T.P. Not good at all.

I got this big lecture on how not to bounce checks and customer service woman said they had problems with new students every fall, blah blah blah, and she hoped they wouldn't have trouble with *me*, Courtney Von Dragoon Smith. Like we're small children and can't take care of ourselves or something without *her* telling us how to add and subtract? It was so insulting.

"I've never bounced a check in my life," I said.

She smiled, sort of. "Oh, I'm sure you haven't, Ms. Smith. But if you have, we'll find out about it."

"What a witch," I said to Thyme as we left. "She's out to get me or something."

"It's clear-cut ageism," Thyme agreed. "You could file a complaint. *I* would."

"Maybe I should switch banks," I said.

"Don't bother. They're all the same." Thyme flipped her skinny braids over her shoulder. "I don't even believe in banks, but they're a necessary evil."

"Like coffee?" I joked.

We laughed and went over to the student center for another 3 cups. After that we were so wired we went to gym to work out. Thyme did yoga; I sprinted on LifeCycle.

Felt like a real athlete until actual cycling club walked into gym. Very fit. Sleek. Me, sweating out coffee, face red from exertion. Thyme walked up cool and refreshed from basically lying on foam pad for an hour. Guys in club checked her out, ignored me.

Must give up coffee. Must also invest in sleeker workout clothes.

I got a package from Grant!!! Yes! Good karma, because I tried so hard today to get settled here. I went to classes and bought my books.

Inside Grant's package was a Colorado State notebook and baseball cap. Plus an old T-shirt of his I'd been pestering him for. I'm putting it in my book bag and carrying it everywhere and when I miss him, I'll take it out and smell it.

People will look at me strangely, but I don't care. They probably already do, because I'm not Norwegian or Swedish or whatever everyone is here. (I'm not tall, I'm not blond. What am I, anyway?) (Too philosophical a question for me right now.)

Grant's package gave me a burst of energy, and then I realized how much I miss him and started to cry. Why didn't I go to CSU? What's wrong with me? Why do I make such bad choices?

I needed to calm myself. If I were back home, I'd drive to the buffalo overlook and check out the herd. But no such luck. No buffalo here. No car.

But we are out in the country, and it was actually a sunny afternoon, so I got on my bike, hoped it wouldn't rain, and rode out of town. The road I was on was curvy and pretty. Not to mention bumpy. Green trees, wildflowers everywhere. Reminded me of a picture in the CF catalog. The one they used to shamelessly lure me here.

Anyway, there I was, riding on scenic country road, feeling really happy for once, except for constant rolling hills that all went straight up, and the fact I'm not in the best shape of my life. Then I went past this sign that said BUCK'S TAXIDERMY—i.e., e.g., turning dead animals into living statues/monuments to hunting skill. Then beneath the "Buck's" part, like I wasn't getting a graphic enough picture of exactly what he was talking about, the sign said FUR, FOWL, ETC.

"Etc."? What does that mean? People? Reptiles? Swine? Disgusting.

When I got to the cows, they were marching single file along this path to the barn. I put down my bike and walked over to look at them. They were so orderly, they looked like soldiers. Milk soldiers. Fighting for dairy. Fighting for their lives, no doubt. Do dairy cows get to retire to green(er) pastures? Or when they're milked out, are they turned into burgers? Poor cows. They'd be cute if they weren't full of gallons of milk.

I went back to my bike and realized I'd set it down in world's largest cow chip. Spent an hour scraping off the seat with a stick. Bluck.

8/26

My first "real" weekend here, without relatives! Yes!

There was a major catastrophe here this morning: everyone realized there was no home football game and no home *anything* games this weekend. Girls (except soccer players who were at practice) drifted aimlessly until everyone paired off into different cars to head to the outlet mall.

Okay, not everyone. Annemarie stayed in dorm, music blaring. Mary Jo got irritated and went to science library so she could study in peace and quiet. Thyme went on hike with CF Nature Club. Kept trying to convince me to go with her, but I couldn't.

Last night I figured out I have to get a job in town right away. My money is running out very quickly.

Job search really sucked. Everything's already taken, or I'm not qualified, or I don't *want* to dress up like Helga and wear horns on my head and serve German potato salad on roller skates at the Vivacious Viking.

For some reason in this town, employers only want kids who are 14 and 15 to scoop ice cream. Even though it's totally clear I have the muscle for it from working at T or D and could outscoop them, *plus* I know about smoothies and wheatgrass, which they're going to have to make the transition to sometime. But no. Looked at me as if I were speaking foreign language.

Plus half of the places served frozen custard, and I don't even know what that is. Who eats frozen pudding? I thought that was like . . . British or something. Or is that flan? What *is* flan?

There are the 6 or 7 identical-looking souvenir shops, where you can buy trolls, German beer steins, and any

Cornwall Falls College T-shirt your heart desires. (Which would be none, so far.) In one of the stores, this man kept offering me fudge and cheese samples. In another, the women working there kept giving me dirty looks, like I was going to steal a bronzed badger or a cuckoo clock or something. No thank you. I have enough crap in my room, thanks to Mary Jo.

I was sitting outside on the brick wall by the dorm, thinking about whether there was a plasma bank nearby, whether I could finance my higher education *that* way, or maybe an egg bank, after all I'm in the prime of my reproductive life, aren't I? And aren't you supposed to be able to get a few thousand bucks for some prime eggs? I've got several dozen to spare.

I had totally given up hope when Tricia came by. She's the bubbly one who said during our drugs 'n' sex talk that she'd organized a rally to keep *every single kid in her neighborhood* off crack, and it worked, gosh darn it.

Like they have crack in Walla Walla, Idaho, or whatever small town she said she was from. Like they even have neighborhoods.

"Courtney! What are you *doing* up there?" she asked. As if no one had ever sat on a wall before. She had this giant pink Cornwall sweatshirt on and a matching hair ribbon. Her hair is the color of corn, just like Mary Jo's, but also has many, many faux shiny highlights. If this place had sororities she'd be all over them. But that's one of the reasons I liked this place—or thought I liked this place, anyway—no exclusive Greek societies. No "rushing," except maybe to class when I'm late because I'm riding my bike through snowdrifts.

Anyway, I told Tricia how I have to find a job, and

she excitedly started shrieking how the place where she worked was hiring. "Um, and where's that?" I asked, expecting her to say the Hallmark store. Which wouldn't be so bad, actually, because I'll be buying lots of cards this year to send to Grant.

"Bagle Finagle!" she said. "It's so cool, and so fun. And I know Jennifer would hire you in a second? Because she's the manager? And she's really cool?" Tricia says everything like a question.

I thought about what Gerry said to me on my last day of work at T or D as he toasted me with a Coconut Fantasy Supreme. "Any employer would be lucky to have you. But don't bowl them over with your individuality." Whatever *that* meant.

So she took me over there and I filled out an application. Everyone working there seems nice. Jennifer seems sort of like a tyrant, but who cares? I need money.

"It would be so great if we could get the same shifts?" Tricia said after we left to walk back to the dorm together.

"Um . . . yeah," I said, thinking, *Um, no. Not really. Not at all, actually.* She would probably try to organize a rally to keep me off caffeine.

Very funny thing happened this morning for brunch. We were all traipsing off to the cafeteria together, en masse, that's how we've been doing everything. (Is the 3rd floor hungry? Does the 3rd floor need to go to the post office? We must do everything in groups of no less than 15.)

So we were going down the stairs and I was between Mary Jo and Thyme. Mary Jo was asking Thyme about her tattoos and how much it hurt to get a tattoo. Girl is obsessed with pain of body art—why? Is she considering getting Sophie memorialized? Where?

"Well, MJ," Thyme said. She paused. "Is it okay if I call you MJ?"

"Um, well . . ." Mary Jo tried to be polite at first.

"Well, MJ, the thing about tattoos is—"

"Please, um, don't . . . call me MJ," Mary Jo said.

"Oh? But it's so natural. And it's sort of more, you know, twenty-first century, when you think about it—"

"Not really. And besides, nobody calls me that."

"But it could be a nickname—"

"*No*," Mary Jo said. "It couldn't." Then she moved ahead and started walking next to other people. Completely blowing us off!!!

Surprising amount of backbone considering everyone has been doing everything humanly possible just to get along for the past 4 days and has been clinging to each other like the way we desperately grasp trays in the cafeteria. Not me. Of course. Them.

LATER—GREAT NEWS!

I got the job!!! Yes!!! I'll make $6.75 an hour plus get 2 free bagels with every shift (toppings not included, but who needs toppings?). No need to waste time at horrid cafeteria eating oyster crackers for lunch anymore.

First I called Beth. She was hungover, but very happy for me. Then I called Grant. He was out so I left a hyper message on his answering machine. His roommate's voice is on the machine, which bugs me, because I want to at least hear Grant saying he isn't home. It's so unsatisfying to call and not hear him say *anything*.

Then I called Mom but she wasn't home, so I talked to Bryan. He said he was doing okay in cross-country. I knew that was an understatement because Mom told me the newspaper did a big article on him. When you talk to him, though, he doesn't mention it. Nothing about paces, or splits, or meets he's won by a minute. I asked if he was hungover, too, like Beth. He said no. He said she's been going kind of wild and was going to parties every night of the week.

Somehow that didn't sound too good to me. I don't know why, I mean, I know I've only been gone for a week so things can't have changed too much. Maybe I'm just jealous. So far I haven't been to any parties. Thyme and I went to the movies last night. Afterward we went to this little café near campus and drank herbal tea. Which sounds like something Grandma would do with *her* friends.

Question: What is it like for Thyme to drink thyme tea?

Anyway, went across hall to tell Thyme about my new job. She was sort of happy at first, but then she got this glum look.

"Have you checked into their investments?" she asked. "I think I heard they get their flour from some country that's on an Amnesty International watch list. And aren't they owned by some major oil corporation?"

"Um, I don't know," I said. "I think they just have stores in the upper Midwest."

"Yeah, okay. But you should really check out their investment background."

"Sure, of course," I said. But if the place is good enough for her to buy coffee from, isn't it okay for me to work there? I mean, if you're going to boycott a place, you have to be a *little* more consistent.

"I get free bagels, so you know, if you ever want some, just come by during my shift," I offered.

"I can't. Bagels plague my harmonic system," she said.

Okay. Whatever. You're welcome.

Fortunately Mary Jo knocked on the door then, looking for me. Grant was on the phone. Yes! Spent an hour talking to him. The whole time, Mary Jo was getting ready for bed, then going off to brush her teeth with her little horse-product bucket (horse toothpaste?), and then she came back, and then she was reading in bed, and then she turned out her light, etc.

When I got off the phone, she said, "I really don't want to make a big deal out of this. But do you think you could maybe call Grant, like, during the day sometimes?"

What? "It's pretty hard. It's expensive during the day, plus he has class, and then he works, and—anyway, I didn't call him. He called *me*."

"It's just that my schedule this semester is going to be really hard," Mary Jo said. "I'm sorry."

So then I had to feel like a real jerk. "No, I'm sorry," I

said. "I'll try not to be on the phone so late." But if Grant calls? I am not *not* going to talk to him.

I wish Beth were my roommate, not Mary Jo. Beth would be *fun*. We'd stay up late, listen to good music, fridge would be stocked with Frappuccinos and fresh-squeezed juice; we'd probably even buy a juicer and share it. Maybe she wants to transfer. No, wait. I want to transfer.

My training for Bagle Finagle was tonight from 5–8. 3 long hours involving history of company, history of bagels, history of flour and cream cheese. Yawn.

"We have fifty-six Bagle Finagles across the upper Midwest, and we're rising like dough!" Jennifer is definitely a little on the annoying side. Okay, a lot. There were 9 other people in training, but after we took a bathroom break there were only 5 of us left. 1 was this very funny guy named Mark, a freshperson like me, who wore 3 earrings in one ear, had a bleached crewcut, and club look.

They're introducing some new bakery items, so Jennifer gave us each samples. There was a cinnamon roll with inch-high frosting, and something called the Muller's Cruller, which looked like a hot dog bun that had fallen into a vat of glue.

"Who the hell is Muller?" one guy asked.

Mark nudged me and said, "Check this thing out. It's like glazed to within an inch of its life." He took a bite, then tossed the rest into the trash can. It made such a loud clang that we cracked up laughing and then got a dirty look from Jennifer. She does that a lot. Glares at people.

I kept staring at this obnoxious sign by the cash register (right under the giant NO CHECKS sign; people are obsessed with bad checks in this town, there are signs at every cash register I've seen so far):

OUR NAME MIGHT BE **BAGLE FINAGLE,**
BUT DON'T FINAGLE THE BAGELS!

There was a set of handcuffs hanging down, like they'd actually handcuff someone for stealing a bagel? Maybe they save those for the more violent crimes. Like stealing scallion-chive cream cheese.

Speaking of cheese. What is their number-one seller? Cheese bagels. With cheddar-cheese-flavored cream cheese. Bluck.

There are regulations regarding how to stack napkins on the counter so the logo always faces out. We had tests regarding how many ounces of cream cheese make up a slather, and how many make up a super slather. If a customer asks for extra pickles on their bagel sandwich, they get 2 more than standard. Personal phone calls can last only 30 seconds. Etc. Mark asked about smoke breaks and that started a whole debate about whether the rest of us should get breaks even though we don't smoke, and then 1 more girl quit because she said she didn't want to work with anyone who smoked, period.

"Give me a break," Mark said. "Does she think I'm going to blow secondhand smoke in her face? Well, who cares. I'm glad she's gone, because *I* don't want to work with anyone who wears a Packers T-shirt."

I asked Mark how he felt about wearing the goofy BF aprons. He said he'd find a way to make it work for him. "Or I'll find a way to work it," he said. "Period."

Jennifer overheard us and asked Mark what he meant by that, and then reminded us about the strict dress and hair codes.

I thought about Gerry wanting to start a little chain of his ice cream and smoothie shops. So far he has 2 locations for Truth or Dairy. Really on a roll there.

But maybe Gerry has the right idea. This place is a bit on the rigid side. No room for individualism or self-expression. In other words, you have to ask the same questions in the same tone of every single customer. The first one is the killer. I can't picture these words coming out of my mouth, but I guess they will: "What kind of bagel can I finagle for you?"

And if I can say that without dying of embarrassment, I get to run through the "Option Board": "Sliced? Toasted? Would you like cream cheese with that? Anything to drink with that? Would you like to make this a steal deal?" Why do I sound like a Fembot? Ugh. But this won't be so bad. From wheatgrass juice to wheat 'n' honey bagels. Same healthy principle, but better tasting.

When I got back to the dorm I was feeling very outgoing as a result of our "Bagle-Bonding" exercises. We each had to pretend to fall into a boiling vat of water and have our team catch us, also did the same thing pretending to fall into the oven. Seemed sort of sadistic or at the very least a rip-off of "Hansel and Gretel." I stopped by Thyme's room to see if she wanted to go out. She told me how she finally feng-shui-ed the room, and then she showed me a book on feng shui, so now I know what she's talking about.

We went to the student center. It was really dead, not surprising because it is Monday night. Ended up going into the pool hall/video game/bowling alley area. Neither of us is very good at pool, but we met some guys who kept challenging us to another game, even though they kept winning.

I had an okay time, but Thyme was annoyed because they kept making fun of her name. First they compared her to the Tyme machine on the wall and kept calling her "Money." Then, when that got old, they started calling us "Parsley" and "Sage" and saying things like, "Hey, Rosemary, it's your turn," and humming that Simon & Garfunkel song about the spices.

"People are so closed-minded," she muttered on our way back to the dorm. "Haven't they ever heard of originality? Haven't they ever heard of being an individual? They were so paternalistic and *standardized*."

I don't know. I thought they were actually sort of fun. Reminded me of guys from home. Like Grant. Sigh. Only 10.5 weeks until Thanksgiving.

Sitting in student center with Thyme. Since neither one of us really loves being in our rooms, this is like our home now. She's using photographic memory to help me memorize everything for my first shift tomorrow at BF. We get an actual report written up with things we need to work on. I hate those kind of reports. I've hated "Needs Improvement" since kindergarten.

The thing is that Thyme should be the one who goes to work at BF because she's looked at the setup there all of *once* and has it down cold. She has even drawn me a map of all the bagel bins. This is something I could hate her for if she weren't so nice about it. But nice in a condescending way, because she doesn't understand what it's like to have faulty, real-time memory and confuse sesame seed with poppy seed.

Anyway, we were sitting there drinking coffee and working on this when Tricia came by. She said it was a really good idea for me to be so prepared? And that she'd mention it to Jennifer? She said that Jennifer was this incredibly wonderful manager who might insist on the rules a lot? But was only doing that for our benefit, and I shouldn't take it personally if she yelled at me; she yelled at everyone?

Great. I am so looking forward to my first day.

8/30

Scored big points on several levels today. I'd celebrate but I have a ton of homework to do.

Spoke up in my sociology class.

Actually got someone to donate some money tonight. Thank you, Mrs. Benson of Chippewa Falls, for increasing your gift this year. No thank you for the long story detailing the history of the grain elevator.

This morning, aced my first shift at BF. Mostly because of coworker named Ben. Incredibly nice, English major, sophomore, fishitarian. He took about 90 percent of the orders and let me work slowly until I got things straight.

I asked all the right preformulated questions, didn't mess up the cream cheese types. One error, though: forgot my hairnet. Okay, pretended to forget it. Was hoping no one would notice. Jennifer scolded me. I put it on and as soon as I did, who walked in but the one cute guy who came in all day.

Not that I care what random guy thinks, but still. Felt like lunch lady about to dish up Sloppy Joes. Need cat-eye glasses on a chain to complete the look.

Went online to do research for my poli sci paper tonight. After Mary Jo *finally* finished writing her paper and got off the computer. So rude. I had so much work of my own to do, and she really should be using the computer lab, only I'm so nice I offered to let her use my computer because she wasn't feeling very well. Well, who *would* if they insisted on eating the cafeteria's all-beef chili?

Ended up getting 9 Tarot card readings, 6 different horoscopes, and spent 2 hours in an LDR chat room. Everyone was pouring out their tales of woe. There were like 5 people out of 100 who said they'd managed to make it work.

"Agree to see other people" was the major advice. There were also a lot of angry "It'll never work!" comments and "You'll break up," so "See other people." I know it was all coming from guys. I could just tell. But after I read all that, I couldn't concentrate. I kept wondering if Grant thought anything like that. I emailed Grant, but he didn't write back within a few minutes. Called Grant. Not home. Left message. Then Mary Jo asked me to please be quiet. It's 9:30!!!

This *isn't* going to work.

Thank God tomorrow's the last day of August. Almost September, but that's not good enough. Please let it be October soon, so we'll be closer to November and Thanksgiving and me going home or at least getting out of here for a few days.

Can't believe what happened today. I'm writing this in the first-floor lounge while other people watch TV because I can't be in my room right now. I'm not welcome. Also it just feels really really awkward and uncomfortable. Maybe it's all my fault, but I don't think so.

Thyme and I had this brilliant insight over lunch, as we surveyed the salad bar for edibles: The Great Roommate Switch. It would be so easy for me just to move across the hall. And Mary Jo and Kirsten get along as well as Thyme and I do, right?

So we went to the housing office to plead our case. We immediately got to see 2 housing counselors. But they wouldn't even "entertain" the idea. I pointed out how different me and Mary Jo are, and how they were supposed to match us with someone compatible. Not someone who eats rolled slices of ham and Swiss for breakfast.

They said that part of college was learning people skills and how to get along with others who were different. They said they'd evaluated all the applications with "personal growth" in mind. And anyway, the semester was already 2 weeks old, they'd done their best, and there was nothing they could do about it now. Thyme started going on a rant about how she was being forced to listen to pop music and it was stunting her personal growth. But it didn't help. Actually, I think she sort of hurt our cause. We left feeling utterly defeated.

So we walk out to the front desk, and who's standing there, waiting to talk to the same counselors? MARY JO AND KIRSTEN!!! How rude. I mean, it's one thing for me and Thyme to want to switch. We have *reasons*.

So we all got really embarrassed and uncomfortable

and everyone started mumbling about how we were just reporting the fact that the showers need more water pressure, and how there's this girl on our floor who's drunk every night and we're very concerned about her, etc.

Does Mary Jo hate me that much? What's up with that? Am I so hard to live with? My family never had a problem with me.

Entire hall went to big pro–Cornwall Falls rally tonight. Mary Jo and Kirsten were hovering together, avoiding me and Thyme. Like Thyme and I wanted to hang out with them. Like we wanted to even go to the rally. But Krystyne insisted that this was a fun, all-campus event and we'd be sorry if we missed our first one, and of course she couldn't force anyone, but it would look really bad and it wouldn't be "in the spirit of team spirit"—

At which point Annemarie slammed the door in her face and turned up the new Green Day CD.

Thyme and I went to the rally for about 3 minutes, then ditched it. Thyme insisted on going to a workers' rights rally outside the student center instead. Only about 20 people there. Couldn't hear the speaker because the marching band was blaring jock hits of the 1980s and the crowd was singing/yelling along. Also, we were downwind from the big bonfire. Smoke kept getting in my eyes and making me cough.

Go Cornwall Falls, though. Really. Win win win.

"You should have come," Mary Jo said, when we met up back at the room.

For once I think maybe she was right about something.

9/2

Got off work at noon. Had to be there at 6 to open. Grueling. Anyway, turned out to be fun, because I got to work with Mark and Ben (and also Tricia, who we assigned to be money finagler and therefore got to mostly ignore all morning). Place was really crowded, but we handled it. When we were getting off work, Ben asked me whether I was going to the big football game. I told him that I had other plans. "Oh, well, that's cool. What are your plans?" he asked.

"Um, well, I was thinking of maybe, um, reading," I said. "Either that or sitting around missing my boyfriend."

"Are you insane? Come on, you've got to go to the game. Everyone goes. You can't call yourself a Cornwaller Faller until you do."

"And I'd *want* to call myself that?" I asked.

He laughed. Somehow, 5 minutes later, Ben, Mark, and I were heading over to the field. I didn't think I should go because Thyme and I pledged we'd never do anything as stupid as attend a football game. Even though I did it a lot in high school, that was a long time ago. I'm older now. More mature. "Besides, the human violence that game promotes is just unthinkable," Thyme said, and she's right, helmets bashing, concussions and separated shoulders all over the field. She was going to spend the day searching for wildflowers and then collecting evidence of harmful chemicals in the dorm drinking water.

So Mark, Ben, and I got there and the game had already started. It was true: everyone was there, and it didn't seem to have much to do with the actual game. I heard someone yelling my name and looked up in the bleachers and saw a bunch of girls from my floor sitting in a row. Mary Jo was waving at me and gesturing for me to come join her. I waved back. I felt important for a second, being recognized. "My roommate," I explained to Mark and Ben. "My whole *floor*, actually."

"Who's the leather chick?" Mark asked. "I dig her."

I couldn't believe it. Annemarie was sitting next to Krystyne and wearing her black motorcycle jacket. She had probably been dragged there, under duress. She had her Walkman on. I was explaining her to Mark when there was some big play on the field, and Cornwall Falls got the ball. All of a sudden the cheerleaders, who had been sitting in front of us, sprang to their feet. They started chanting the school's initials and thrusting their arms into the air.

"C—F—C! C—F—C!"

It sounded so familiar. Then, for the first time ever, it dawned on me. I stared at their sweaters, at the guy cheer-leader's megaphones. CFC. It's not just Cornwall Falls College. It's chlorofluorocarbon. It's a harmful chemical. It's been *banned* because it's responsible for the destruc-tion of the ozone layer. And this is the school I ended up at? And they have the nerve to stand around and *chant* that—like it's a good thing?

A running back got knocked out of bounds just then and nearly knocked us down, so we had to move. I ended up sitting with Ben and some of his friends for a while, then at halftime went to sit with Annemarie, who kept making me wear her headphones to check out new songs, which was more fun than listening to people chant "C—F—C." At one point I could have sworn I saw Thyme sitting across field in opposing team bleachers.

"Is that Thyme over there?" I asked.

Annemarie laughed. "Are you *high*? If she was here, it would be because she was organizing a protest for cheerleaders' rights or the exploitation of hot dog vendors."

"True," I said. "Well, they *are* exploited. The cheerleaders, I mean. But I can think of a few things I'd rather protest." I was talking for a while before I realized Annemarie had her headphones back on and wasn't listening to me anymore. Rest of crowd was on its feet cheering wildly for C—F—C.

Very embarrassing moment today in front of entire college. Might need to think about transferring sooner than planned.

There was this big party outside on the quad today—the Fall Semester Kickoff. It didn't rain. Amazing. Unheard of. There were 3 bands that played, plus a giant cookout, corn on the cob, etc. Thyme and I started out sitting with everyone on our hall, but after a while took off to wander around and check out the crowd. Everyone was in a really good mood. I was having fun. We went out and started dancing.

Then I thought I heard someone calling my name. I had no idea who it would be—thought maybe it was Mark. I kept looking around while I danced. The music got softer and I realized it wasn't just one person shouting my name, it was several. "Courtney, Courtney!"

What? I was thinking. I'm not *that* good—or bad—of a dancer. And I only know like 12 people here.

"Courtney, Courtney!"

So I yelled, "What?"

Then I heard a bunch of people laughing. Someone tapped me on the shoulder, someone with really long hair that tickled my neck. I turned around.

That's when I saw the giant cob of corn dancing behind me.

First I thought there must have been drugs in the brownies I'd just eaten. Then I realized they weren't yelling "Courtney" at all, they were yelling "Corny!" Because I was standing face-to-face with *Corny*, the Cornwall Falls mascot. An ear of corn. With long, fake blond hair sticking out of its neck, a giant yellow helmet, a bright green peeling-off costume on its body.

He/she/it took my hand and started twirling me around.

Why are school mascots drawn to me? Why? I was mauled by the Bugling Elk in high school, and in middle school I was kissed by some guy in a tiger suit from the opposing team.

Is it because I love animals so much, that people who dress up as animals feel this overpowering need to get close to me? But wait. That doesn't explain Corny guy. Unless vegetables can feel the love?

"Hey, how's it going?" he said.

"Come on, Thyme. Let's go," I said.

"Cool. We can get back to the dorm in time for that PBS special on communism," Thyme said.

That wasn't exactly my idea of alternative fun, but, oh, well. Maybe now I can skip that chapter in my poli sci textbook.

Spent all morning on the phone with Grant. Mary Jo was off at her 9:10 class and then her 10:10 and after that I lost track. It was great to have the room to myself. Of course it meant that I missed my 11:10, but, oh, well.

Anyway, I told Grant all about my weekend. He said it sounded like fun.

"Grant, I think we're growing apart," I said.

"What?" He sounded panicked. "What do you mean by that?"

"It wasn't fun. It was awful."

"Oh. Well, okay." He laughed. "In that case, my weekend was awful, too."

"What did *you* mean by that?" I asked.

I was worried that we weren't communicating very well. First sign of trouble, according to everyone in LDR chat room.

But then our conversation went on for 2 more hours and involved many goofy romantic comments, so I think we're okay. Not to worry. Grant loves me. I love Grant. I can't wait to see him at Thanksgiving, even if it must be at Grandma and Grandpa's in Nebraska, surrounded by relatives and turkeys.

Is that redundant?

We haven't figured out the plan yet, but he might hitch a ride with Mom and Bryan just so he can see me. Hurrah!

Made major gaffe today at work. It was a slow time and I was studying the sandwich cards. I still don't have them all memorized and I hate looking stupid and checking the cards when people come in, and if I *don't* get them right, Jennifer gets mad. So anyway, Ben and I were talking about what an adjustment it was, living in a small town like Wauzataukie, going to what he calls "Cowpie Falls." We were joking about the Cornwall Falls and how we've never actually *seen* the falls, and maybe it's just another catalog ruse to get people to campus. And how it would be nice to have at least one place where we could buy clothes we liked.

"So where do you get your clothes?" I asked. Because they were very cool, except of course for the standard BF apron.

"Online," he said. "You know, you could order your whole life online if you needed to."

"Really? There's a website for that?" I asked. "Give me a password. Like, now."

Ben laughed. "It's definitely weird being here," he said. "I mean, I feel like such an outsider."

"Oh, I know!" I said. "I *totally* understand." (Only I didn't.)

"You do?" Ben asked.

"Sure. I'm from Colorado and nobody really gets that. I mean, they don't even really know where that *is*. Half the people here can't find it on a map."

Ben looked a little confused, like we weren't having the same conversation anymore. He took off his gold-wire glasses and rubbed a spot off them. "Okay, but you couldn't tell the difference between Illinois and Indiana the other day," he reminded me. Jennifer had quizzed us on other Bagle Finagle locations, because that's the kind of thing she does for fun.

"That's different—they're smaller and they both start with I. But who confuses Colorado and Wyoming?" I asked. "Anyway, everyone just thinks that all I ever did was *ski* all day, and they expect me to be a certain way, and they expect me to know what a hot dish is, and they expect me to love meat and cheese and milk and have blond hair, and I just *don't*."

Ben looked at me and sighed. "Courtney, I'm sure that's sort of frustrating and all. But actually, I was talking about being African-American? And how we're only like five percent of the student population?"

"Oh." I felt like *such* an idiot. "Sorry," I said. I couldn't apologize enough. I think I said it 100 times.

"It's okay, you didn't know," Ben said.

"Well, I did kind of have an idea," I said.

Then we both cracked up laughing. Ended on a good note. But still. How insulting was that, talking about *ski-ing* and not being Scandinavian?

I think I probably have overestimated how hard this is for me. It's probably much harder for other people. I'm probably being self-involved to the point of absurdity. All I really have to deal with is a lack of sun, mild heartbreak, and 5,000-foot altitude change. If I can't handle that, then I'm really pathetic. But then I knew that already, sort of.

Must make a bigger and better effort to get settled here. Must find groups to join. But then I think of that

Groucho Marx line that Woody Allen quotes at the beginning of *Annie Hall*, Mom's favorite movie, about never wanting to belong to a club that would have me as a member. And what sort of club could I join, anyway?

I realized the big benefit of my dumb work-study job today. Am I that dense that Annemarie had to point it out to me? *Free long distance.*

First I called Jane to invite her up for this weekend, next weekend, any weekend. She has a car and I don't, but then she lives in a cool place—Madison—and I don't, so who knows when we'll actually get together. Besides, she has a new boyfriend, someone in a band who is writing songs about her already. I want Jane's life.

Then I called Beth, but she was too busy at work to talk.

Then I called Grant, totally thinking he wouldn't be home, was just going to leave a message. But he was *there*! I was complaining about feeling so left out and Grant gave me some great advice.

"Courtney, look. If you're that unhappy, *do* something about it."

I felt my heart start to do this little dance. "You mean, I can drop out and come home?"

"No. I mean . . . look, you used to be all involved in school. Back at Bugling Elk," Grant said. "So do something like that. Cornwall Falls must have dozens of groups, right?"

"No," I said. "It doesn't have anything." Yeah, okay, so I sounded like a 5-year-old.

"Yes, it does," Grant said with a laugh. "You just *said* that you wanted to join a group. I want you to promise me that you'll check out a bunch of them." He said I can't keep not getting settled into the place; if I'm going to be here 4 years, I should work on changing the things that aren't working for me.

"Okay, so transfer, because what isn't working is you being there and me being here," I said. Then I told him all the things I really miss about him, and I was really getting kind of mushy about it, about how much I love being with him—

And then all of a sudden I realized Dean Sobransky was standing right next to me. Listening to the whole thing.

I was *so* busted.

I got off the phone really quickly by saying something loud about how it was always nice to catch up with old classmates. Then I turned to Dean S. with a hopeful smile.

"Well, er, and how is it going, Courtney?" he asked. "Making contact with some alumni you know?"

"Yes," I said. But not as much contact as I'd like.

He said he often dropped by to check on us, since his office was just upstairs (we work in a large basement room). He said he'd like to sit in on my next call, see if he could offer some helpful tips since I'm new at this. Nightmare!

I changed the subject and told him I wanted to get involved in some campus groups and could he tell me about some? He asked me what my interests were. The whole time I talked, he kept opening the file cabinet beside my desk, then closing it. Very weird guy. Has to have something near him in perpetual motion.

"We have the nature club, of course," he said. "And there's the faculty-student birding society."

"Well, I'm not necessarily interested in just watching nature. I'm more interested in *saving* it," I said. "Is there anything about, um, I don't know. Saving the cows?"

"Why do the cows need to be saved? Or, wait—do you

mean in a religious sense?"

The guy in my neighboring cubicle wheeled over. "I've got a suggestion." His voice sounded familiar, but I couldn't place it at first. Probably I'd overheard him begging for donations, and since he actually got quite a few, maybe he talked more than most.

"Wittenauer. My favorite fund-raiser! What do you know?" Dean S. asked.

Wittenauer is the guy who pulls in huge donations seemingly without trying. He started talking about a group he's in to protest this hormone that is used campus-wide. Dean S. looked very embarrassed, then Wittenauer explained it wasn't a male or female or sex hormone. It's something in the milk that's served in the cafeteria, student center, etc. He explained that he was talking about RBGH.

I couldn't believe it. "You mean the date rape drug? They put that in the *milk* here? What sort of place is this, what sort of society—" I was sputtering irately when Wittenauer put his hand on my arm and told me I was confusing RBGH with GHB.

"No, no. Courtney, is it?" He smiled. "No, they don't put that in the milk." Like that wasn't a mistake anyone could make!

"RBGH isn't as bad as GHB," he said. "I mean, we're not talking about men drugging drinks with sedatives to get women to sleep with them."

Dean Sobransky was so embarrassed he could barely talk. "I'm sure nothing like that goes on here," he said. "I, have to . . . have to . . . have to check my messages." He bolted from the room.

Wittenauer went on to explain that RBGH was

something like Repulsive Bovine Growth Hormone. It makes cows produce more milk, which is definitely not a good idea. Anyway, isn't milk gross enough on its own, without additives? But then additives are in everything, so why am I surprised? "That sounds disgusting," I said.

"You should come to the next meeting," he said. "It's the RBGH Action Group. We meet on Sunday nights. We're always looking for more members."

Yes! I have found my first group.

Mom called tonight so we could start planning Thanksgiving. Big surprise. She has planned Thanksgiving in early September for as long as I can remember. I told her I couldn't be in charge of anything this year because it's going to be hard enough for me to just get there. I played the travel hardship card. So ha! Bryan can bake "all the breads" this year. Which means we'll see many canned Pillsbury products. Then I asked if she could bring Grant with her, and she said of course.

So after I talked to her, I called Grant. He was home but said he couldn't talk long because the guys were waiting for him to go out. I could hear them talking loudly and laughing in the background. Grant kept asking what my weekend plans are. He has a bunch. I don't.

"I'm like . . . a loser all of a sudden, Grant," I said.

"Come on, Court. You can definitely find parties to go to," Grant said, laughing. "You and Oregano—"

"Hey, *don't* make fun of her. She's my best friend here!" I said.

"So you and Thyme should pick some parties to go to. Okay?" Grant said. "Read your student newspaper. Read every flyer you see. Listen to your campus radio station."

He sounded like a public-service announcement. He sounded so *smug*, him with his roomful of friends, me with my roomful of . . . knickknacks.

In a way, I'm getting kind of sick of these pep talks. Like Grant knows how to adjust to a new environment and I *don't*, or something. Like I'm not evolving. I know more about adjusting than he does. It's really very insulting. Did *he* go 1,000 miles from home? I don't think so.

I'll go out and party all weekend. Then I'll go to that milk meeting. I'll show him that I can adapt as well as anyone.

Mary Jo asked if I wanted to go shopping this afternoon. Which was *really* nice of her. She has this old yellow beater pickup truck that her parents are lending her so she can get settled, but she has to return it to them tonight when she goes home for a weekend visit. (Yay! Weekend of solitude in the room! But I won't really be alone. *Baloney*. Because I'll have Mary Jo's baloney in the fridge to keep me company. Hope it doesn't spoil over the weekend.)

So anyway, she invited me to come along to this place called Farm Supply to stock up on stuff like shampoo and crackers. Even though I didn't need anything for my farm, I thought I should make the effort to be friends. Thinking that she doesn't like me is really upsetting. Ever since the housing-switch fiasco, we've been avoiding each other, except for 9–10 each night, when we both end up here.

So back to the excursion. (Mary Jo is a very good driver. Said she learned how when she was 10, driving around the farm.) The store was like a giant department store with tons of hardware instead of underwear. This is shopping? I thought, as I wandered past aisles of wrenches and drills and chainsaws. Many industrial cleaning products. Snow throwers. Appliances. Candy. There were some semi-interesting canvas overalls and flannel-lined jeans. That and a ton of bright orange and camouflage clothing under the HUNTER'S PARADISE sign.

Mary Jo really knew her way around the place. I stayed with her because I was afraid of getting lost. She has some very helpful skills, it turns out. Like figuring out what size picture hangers we need for our room.

"How far would we have to drive to reach an actual mall?" I asked as we stood in line. There was a special on

Twizzlers so I bought 8 or 9 family-size packages, since I didn't want to leave empty-handed. They looked sort of massive as I watched them go down the conveyor belt. But, oh well, Super Size Me.

"Hm. To reach any mall?" she asked. "Or a good mall?"

"Good," I said. "As in not the lame outlets on the edge of town."

"Well, probably about two hours," Mary Jo said, putting all her horse hairstyling and skin care products on the belt. "Why?"

WHY? Wasn't it obvious?

Emailed Grant after Mary Jo left for the weekend and told him that Mary Jo is a bit weird but basically nice. He emailed back that she seemed nice whenever he talked to her and that I was lucky to have a good roommate. I guess he's right. Especially if she goes home on random weekends.

FRIDAY NIGHT . . .

Do they have to put bar code stickers on pens like this? You can't pull them off or it leaves a sticky film. But then you have to stare at the bar code as you write. Not very inspiring. Yes, I am just 1 of a billion humans writing in a journal today. Not even the best journal or best writer. A speck, a UPC code.

Sorry. Tonight wasn't *that* bad, really. And I do have the room to myself, so maybe I should be doing something more fun than writing in here about the sorry decline of fountain pens and the increasing depersonalization of our society. (Yes, I've been reading too much poli sci.)

Thyme and I hung out at the student center listening to bad student jazz in the bad student coffeehouse, a section in the center that they've roped off and tried to make hip. But it has bad coffee, all of which tastes like hazelnut whether you order hazelnut or not, and bright lighting. I guess it might work in the morning if you were trying to wake up. And liked hazelnut. Maybe.

But our pain and suffering was all worth it, because we met some girls who told us about a party tomorrow night. It's at a big house off campus that is known for having great parties. These girls said it's like considered a failure if the police don't show up. What? They have parties like that here?

SATURDAY NIGHT . . . DATE? NO THANK YOU. I MEAN I DON'T KNOW.

Got home about 10 hours ago. 10 minutes I mean. Whatever. Can't think straight can't walk straight.

Party was sooooo fun. Talked with a billion people. Danced. Ate hummus. Yes!

Some guys wanted to dance with me but I said no. No because I love Grant. The guys from pool table also there. Kept slamming into us and spilling beer on me. Suede coat is ruined but oh well.

Okay so Thyme is dragging her sleeping bag into the room because MJ "Don't Call Me MJ!" is away for weekend. While she is gone I called Grant and this is what I said on his machine I think:

"If you were a pen I'd be the bar code sticker."

Couldn't stop laughing when I hung up. I hope he gets home before his roomie.

Wait. Why is he not home? It's middle of the night.

Oops. Different time zone. I'm waiting an hour then calling him. He has a right to be out as late as me.

1:10 A.M. Sleepy.

1:30 A.M. Thyme is putting horse hair products on her face. "Be careful, or you'll grow a tail," I said and we are laughing so loud that Krystyne told us to be quiet. Rules against laughing at this dumb place.

2:10 A.M. Called him again. Told him to call me no matter when he gets in.

So far I have spent the morning doing 5 things:

1. Trying not to puke.
2. Remembering embarrassing things I did and said last night and cringing and then wanting to puke.
3. Waiting for Grant to call.
4. Waiting for ibuprofen to work so this god-awful headache goes away. (Am writing this with one eye closed. Ow.)
5. Waiting for Thyme to stop telling me what's wrong with patriarchal society.

"Hey, I wasn't even *raised* by my dad, so why are you lecturing me?" I said, wanting to annoy her so much that she'd just realize I was in pain and didn't want to chat. Especially not, with feeling so embarrassed over being blown off by my boyfriend and dancing with people I don't know and discussing the meaning of life and the relation of animals to God in between shouting out song lyrics. But I guess that was sort of sucking up to the patriarchal society in her eyes to even care about a boy (like she doesn't have a crush on Ben, she only comes in every day to see me at work so she can see him, and she wanted to dance with him last night when he showed up, but he didn't want to dance, he only wanted to talk to me about the concept of alienation not being so alienating when you've had a few beers).

"Courtney, it goes much, much deeper than you real-ize," she said.

"I know," I said. "I was just joking."

"Well, it's not something to joke about. Remember, no one is truly free when others are oppressed."

She says that about every situation that bothers her. Which is every situation.

Now she's examining everything on my dresser for environmental correctness. Maybe having Thyme for a roommate would not be such a good idea.

"You know, the binge drinking that goes on in today's college society is just awful," she said. "We never would have gotten so plowed last night if those guys hadn't kept filling our glasses with beer. That was so *patronizing* of them, to just assume we wanted more, like *we* didn't know how much we wanted."

"Maybe if we hadn't kept drinking it," I said. "They wouldn't have refilled . . . um . . ." Really vivid memories of keg beer were flooding my stomach. If a stomach has memories. Which I think it does.

LATER THAT SAME DAY. MUCH TOO MUCH LATER, IN MY OPINION . . .

Grant finally called. Let's just say that it did not go well. I needed him to tell me he was home visiting his parents and grandmother in Denver and that's why he wasn't home at 1 and 2 A.M. That's what I thought he was going to say. The only explanation. But that wasn't it.

He was at a party. He had fun. He went out to breakfast at 2 A.M. He wouldn't stop talking about how much *fun* it was.

"So how was your night?" he asked after he'd finished telling me the details of his late-night donut selection. "You sounded kind of wild. What did you mean about the pen thing?"

I didn't know what he was talking about. "You must be talking about someone else's message," I said, sounding hopelessly and pathetically jealous. "I wasn't wild and I never mentioned a pen." Although as soon as I said that, I remembered.

"Whatever you say, Court." Then I heard him yawning. It made me miss him so much that I burst out crying. Why couldn't I be there to lie around on a Sunday with him?

Ended up with him spending 10 minutes trying to cheer me up. The whole time I could hear a football game playing in the background. How could he listen to Broncos and console me from darkest depths of depression at the same time? How rude.

Major mistake tonight. Very embarrassing. Did I leave my brain in Colorado?

I thought I was at the anti-growth-hormones-in-milk meeting. Didn't see Wittenauer (what is his first name?), but decided he must be running late. Meeting started. A lot of people had been there before, but a lot hadn't, according to the group leader. So we went around the circle and everyone was supposed to say something about themselves. Knew something was odd when the 6 people before me all stated their sexual preferences. Didn't understand how that related to dairy products. I didn't want to state mine because it seemed like I might be the only hetero there, but I did say, "Hi, I'm Courtney, and I think I'm at the wrong meeting."

"It's okay, Courtney," the group leader said. "Everyone feels shy at first. It's normal to be uncomfortable, but no one's going to judge you here."

The woman sitting next to me reached over and put her hand on my knee. "We're all friends, and nothing you say will go beyond this room."

"Okay, but um . . . is this about milk?"

16 blank faces stared at me.

"I'm supposed to be at a meeting protesting hormonal supplements," I said.

The group leader, Jay, cleared his throat. "This is the meeting for Bisexual and Gay Republican Hearts. We try to introduce students who have something in common?"

Agh! I was at dating club for non-hetero non-Democrats! Stupid me got initials confused.

"You're not here to infiltrate our group, are you?" one paranoid guy asked.

"You're not here to find out our names?" someone else asked.

"You're not free on Saturday night, are you?" the girl next to me asked.

"My sister's a lesbian," I said. "But um . . . I don't know if she votes Republican or Democrat. Excuse me."

How embarrassing!

Sunday nights. Not *Monday* nights.

When I told Thyme about it, she said, "Well, of course. I could have told you that." Then she rattled off every campus group's meeting time, place, agenda. So why *didn't* she tell me that when I mentioned I was dashing off to the meeting? Does she *want* me to fail? Does she *want* hormones in milk?

If I had a photographic memory, I wouldn't go through life constantly embarrassing myself. I would also be nicer to my friends.

Sitting at BF on my break. It's raining. I should be study-ing, but, oh well. Ben is studying and isn't that enough for both of us? I should also be writing Grant a letter (we decided not to call this week in order to save $$). But I'm not in the mood. Can't tell him how I blew first attempt to get involved in community.

Mark seems to be walking a tightrope. Business is slow but instead of cleaning and refilling bins, he is touch-ing up his nails by the register.

"I don't know. I don't like the double coat so much." He just held out his hand, admiring the nail polish. Jennifer went by, saw him, and told him to check the bagels baking in the back, and not to get any Revlon on them.

Prediction: Mark will be getting a burned bagel sticker next to his name on the schedule.

Systems of pluses and minuses she uses is really asinine. Good service = cute little muffin sticker and nick-name "muffin" all week. Mark would probably like that.

LATER. DUDE . . .

Work deteriorated majorly after I wrote the above.

Hate this job. Hate how it makes me spell everything wrong.

"Jennifer?" I asked as I anti-bacterialized the slicer. "Why does bagel have to be spelled wrong in the store names? I mean, it would rhyme even if we spelled it right. It's a homonym. You know, like um . . . time? And thyme, the herb?"

She patted me on the shoulder. "I think we know what we're doing, McCartney."

I had a *name tag* on. "It's Courtney," I said.

"Oh my gosh, what was I thinking?" Jennifer laughed. "You remind me of this girl who used to work here, last year. *Sorry*," she said in this incredibly phony voice.

Later on, Ben told me that McCartney was a really good friend of his. But she hated working at BF and she hated CF and she and Jennifer got into a huge fight. She quit and after freshman year she transferred to another school.

"So do I remind you of McCartney? And were her parents Beatles freaks? I mean, did she have a brother named Lennon or Ringo?" I asked.

Ben laughed. "Harrison and Lennon, I think. Twins. You do remind me of her a little. But I think when Jennifer says it, it's not a compliment, so look out."

Does this mean I get to quit and transfer, too?

Oh joy oh joy oh joy. When?

Got home from phoning unsuspecting alumni and received very disturbing emails from naïve Mom. She has suddenly gone from not dating to being romanced by a chat-room guy.

She forwarded me a couple of emails he wrote and asked my opinion. Didn't he seem like a great guy to me? she asked. SEEM being the operative word here. Here's our email exchange:

Mom—
I'm slightly worried about this Internet Romance Idea of yours. What about meeting guys in person? What about that guy in your book club? You said he was nice and sweet and you liked the same books. You really need to be careful. Haven't you told me a hundred billion times not to do risky things like this? Promise me you won't agree to meet this guy in person!!! —C

Bryan—
You have got to keep an eye on Mom! She's getting swept away by guy in chat room who is at best a psycho and at worst a serial killer. Don't let her make any dates, and keep track of her, wherever she goes. —C

Courtney—
She's already met the chat-room guy. He's fine, harmless, bald, boring as hell. Don't worry.
—Bryan

Like I trust Bryan's opinion on anything involving romance, the heart, etc.? He pined after Beth for 5 years and then somehow convinced her to date him. Still don't understand that, 1 year later.

Anyway, I should be glad Mom is at least showing interest in the dating thing. If she finds someone she really likes, that will be great. I just don't want him to be the kind of person who turns out to be—well, just like Dad.

Must call Alison now and ask her to intervene. Mom will listen to Alison because she's the oldest and because she's—well—better at this stuff than me. Has had stable relationship with Jessie for almost a year. Of course, they go to the same *college*, so that helps.

I really do need to stop resenting everyone else on the planet. Especially when they're my siblings.

You know how sometimes your friends don't get along? And you're the link and you feel really awkward because of it? Tried to hang out with Mark and Thyme today. I had already planned on lunch with Thyme, and Mark invited himself along. Mark had already told me he thought Thyme's hair was cool but that he hated the rest of her neo-hippie look. Since he comments on everyone's hair and clothes, I didn't think much of it—until they got into a raging argument while we waited for a table. Thyme insisted we wait so we could sit in non-smoking; Mark insisted we sit at the counter so he could smoke. Since I'm used to hanging out with Beth, who used to smoke, it didn't really matter one way or the other to me. Thyme thought I was taking Mark's side and stormed out. I thought maybe I should go after her but just then one of the waitresses walked by with a yummy-looking giant salad on her tray and I decided not to.

"You're not having a malt?" Mark asked after we ordered. "Are you high?"

(Why does everyone keep asking me that?)

I laughed. "No, actually, I'm LI."

"You're from Long Island? I thought you were from Denver."

I hit his arm. "No, it's my stomach. It's a condition."

Mark unwrapped his straw as he thought this over. Then his nose wrinkled, like he'd just thought something sort of gross. "You have a problem with your large intestine?"

I couldn't stop laughing. "No! Well, sort of. I'm lactose intolerant."

"Oh. What a drag. That's kind of like me and cheap

hair products." He shivered. "I break out in hives if it's not salon quality."

Mark slurped his chocolate malt when it came, topped with this perfect pinnacle of whipped cream. My mouth watered. Of course it was impossible for me to tell him that I really wanted a sip now. Have to wait until we're better friends.

Thyme came in to visit me at work today—she said it was to make up for being so crabby yesterday, and because she always needs to drink extra coffee when it's raining steadily, but I think it's only because she's obsessed with Ben. He's a great guy and she's my best friend here, so I'll do what I can, but I think she pretty much blew it today.

She came in and tried to start this in-depth conversation with Ben, telling him her opinions on men, women, world peace, harmony, life after death, etc.

I mean, all she really had to do was ask him questions about himself or tell him the onion bagels were good, or something simple like that. But no. She got into the concepts of how you need to open yourself up and be Zenlike and how the Bagle Finagle stores could really use some feng shui.

"So where are you from? California?" Ben asked her.

"Um, no, outside Chicago," Thyme said.

"Really? Where? I grew up in Chicago," Ben said.

"Oh, um." Thyme looked sort of uncomfortable all of a sudden. "Are those tomatoes organic?"

I put my hands on my hips. "What do *you* think?"

"Is that margarine or unsalted butter?" she asked next.

Ben gave me this sideways glance, like: what's up with that? "So where did you say you were from?" he asked.

"Well, technically I was born a little north of Chicago. On the lake," Thyme said.

"Uh huh. Where exactly?" Ben asked.

"Ummmmm . . . in Sheboygan," Thyme finally said.

"But that's in Wisconsin," Ben said. "You said you were from Chicago. It's not really all that close."

"Okay, well maybe technically I guess you could say I lived there my whole life. But inside, I always considered myself a *Chicagoan*," Thyme said, sounding really lame to me all of a sudden. Who lies about where they're from? What's the point?

Just then Jennifer came up and told us our break was over, and had been over for 5 minutes, didn't we pay attention to the clock? It was like getting caught talking in class. But to be honest, I was sort of relieved.

"The phony Buddhist from Sheboygan. Now I've seen everything," Ben muttered as we slid sheets of hot bagels into baskets. "How do you know her exactly?"

"Oh, um, she lives across the hall from me," I said. Not getting into the fact that she was the closest thing to a friend I had on campus. If she's a phony, I guess it's better to know now. But I thought she had passionate ideas about fibers and fabrics and free-range animals. I don't think she has a chance in hell with Ben. I wonder if she knows that now.

What a weird, great day. Still trying to absorb everything that happened. Like soggy ground, I can only absorb so much more at this point.

Last night's rah-rah bonfire was rained out, literally—the rain put out the fire. Does not smell like team spirit. Smells like mildew. Even outside. Today was still drizzling and soggy; everyone showing off latest umbrella styles and rain gear at the football game.

When we got there, it turned out that it was "Highlighting Student Activities Day." And all these different groups, from dancers to backgammon clubs, etc., had booths set up with paper banners that had been highlighted with neon green, pink, orange, etc. Very colorful, except the rain had gotten the banners wet and the letters were all runny and streaked and it was hard to determine what each group was, unless you stopped, made eye contact, collected handout.

We circulated: me, Thyme, Mary Jo, Tricia, Annemarie, Peña. Everyone. It was funny because we were all moving at different speeds; some of us raced by certain booths, while others stopped to sign up. And vice versa. I was thinking maybe this place wasn't so bad. There really is something for everyone here. It truly is a microcosm or macrocosm or, at the very least, cosmic. In the background, football was going on. Mud flying through the air. Random cheers and sounds of helmets crushing into pads.

We were standing by this booth that was the only one smart enough to have a banner not written in highlighter—they had a real sewn banner made of cloth, as if the group has been here forever. Students for Change. And they had signs up that said QUESTION AUTHORITY and

"Have you heard about the Campus Badicals?" this really nice girl asked me. She handed me a brochure.

"These people are like, so on the fringe?" Tricia said when the girl started talking to someone else. "Everything's going really well here, everything's *fine*? But they have to change everything or complain about it or whatever?"

"I don't know—there's always room for improvement," Annemarie said. "Don't you think, Courtney?"

"Definitely," I said. "Like, *lots* of room." Everyone sort of moved ahead, but I was still checking out the stuff on the table.

Just then the cheerleaders started up with their "C—F—C! C—F—C!" chant. I joked to the girl behind the table how it was really distressing to hear that our college initials represented a harmful chemical. And that we were all supposed to chant along, like we were cheering for the destruction of the ozone layer, like CFCs hadn't been phased out, or as if they should be phased back *in* or something.

Suddenly everyone at the booth was gazing at me like I had just invented tofu.

"Finally. A fresh voice," the girl said.

Like I was the new Dalai Lama. A freshperson born in the wilderness, the 7th child of . . . well, whatever. They all jumped up and introduced themselves and shook my hand and insisted I come to a meeting tomorrow.

"Cool," Annemarie said. "Maybe I'll go with you."

"I don't even know what you were talking about." Mary Jo was looking at me with some sort of newfound respect, or maybe just bafflement. Impressed that I could impress someone, I guess.

"So what do they want you to, like, *do*?" Tricia asked. "I don't know what you guys were talking about. But that group is always in the campus newspaper?"

Thyme was suddenly nowhere to be found. Odd, because this was totally her kind of group, too. I'll ask her to go with me and Annemarie tomorrow.

Tonight we all rented multiple movies, and I must go because next showing is starting.

9/17

Went to the Campus Badicals meeting today. Annemarie went with me, also Thyme. We were kind of intimidated, so it was good to go as a group. We had tried to check out the group's history beforehand, but Krystyne didn't know much except that they got arrested once. Thyme said she wouldn't mind getting arrested; the weekends had been sort of boring lately, right? We laughed nervously as we entered the basement of the student union.

Room was half full. It turned out my idea to revise the college initials was the topic of the meeting. Someone mentioned that I had a brilliant insight and could I share it? So I did, and all of sudden it was the main and only issue of the group. Someone insisted a focus/splinter group be formed immediately, then everyone joined the focus group.

It was so exciting I completely forgot about the RBGH meeting afterward, came running home to call Grant. But then remembered our pledge not to call this week. Then called anyway. He wasn't home, so I hung up quickly so as not to be busted on breaking the not-calling pledge.

I want to tell him everything. It feels very weird to go through a weekend without him. How can I be going through the most exciting stuff yet and not call him? Okay, so I've been emailing 3, 4 times a day. Maybe that's enough, but it's still not the same.

Came home after work and Mary Jo was on the phone. Which was lousy because I really wanted to call Grant. Our 1-week break was over and I was dying to talk to him. I sat on the edge of the bed and waited. She was laughing and talking about cows and then about how helpful a good dog can be on the farm, and how much she missed her dogs, and what the best kind of dogs are, etc.

So then Mary Jo says, "Well, it's been fun talking to you, but Courtney just got home, so . . ." I expected her to say, "'Bye, Mom," or "'Bye, Aunt Peggy" or whatever. Then she said, "So here she is, Grant. Good luck in biology!" She handed the phone to me as I nearly fell off the bed. Grant and Mary Jo are hitting it off, sounding like old buds? They're having better phone conversations than we do, and we haven't even *talked* for a week, and now somehow Mary Jo has an in with him and I don't?

How can I be jealous of Mary Jo? But I am. She and Grant have so much in common. She probably knows tons about being a vet; has probably delivered baby cows before, the way they do on those prairie kids TV shows. She can talk to the animals. So can Grant.

I felt really sick to my stomach all of a sudden. There was so much I hadn't considered yet, so much to get really worried about. If there's a girl like this here, there's definitely a girl like that there. In Grant's classes. Horse-whispering girl from Colorado ranch. Rodeo-riding gal from Wyoming. Someone he'd been talking to all week when he *hadn't* been talking to me. Okay, so it was my idea to not call, to save money, but he didn't have to just go along with it, without a fight.

"Courtney? Are you there?" Grant asked when I didn't

say anything, because jealousy had commandeered my brain.

"Um, I don't feel very good. I'll call you back," I told him. I hung up the phone.

Mary Jo gave me this little innocent smile. "You're not feeling well? Is there anything I can get you?"

Fantasy reply: "How about a new roommate who isn't cute and knows nothing about vet science. That would be good."

Actual reply: "No, I'll be okay, but thanks." Returned little innocent smile. Ran to the bathroom, splashed cold water on my face. Tried to stop freaking out.

Will call Grant tomorrow morning when she's not here.

Working for Jennifer is killing me. Today she started this new stupid system where there's a board with our names on it, and we have to mark down where we are "at any given time." Like, even when we go to the bathroom. She has this board and when you leave your "post" you have to put a "code" on it, and a "time estimate." Like I'm telling people what I'm in the bathroom for? Is she insane?

"She needs more codes," Mark said after she explained the board to us and went back to her office. "What do I write down when I'm going to the bathroom to sneak a smoke?"

"And what do I write for 'went to bathroom to escape the sound of her *voice*?'" Ben asked.

"What is the code for 'I quit'?" I asked.

It's a good thing everyone I work with is so cool. Because it takes a village to counterbalance Jennifer's uncool.

Someone was trying to put up a flyer for a local band's concert, and then someone came by to post a sign for a meeting of Kids with Kids, a group that helps people like my stepsister. Jennifer came along and took them all off the bulletin board as soon as they had left.

"If you were going to do that, you should have told them," I said. "They could post them somewhere else and save paper."

"Not to mention the fact that there's such a thing as free speech," Ben said.

"And there's also such a thing as turning a profit," Jennifer said. "We can't afford to post all these flyers when we have wealthy advertisers who pay us to put up things."

She flounced around, picking up stray crumbs and straw wrappers.

"Yeah, and this campus needs more ad space for magazine subscription services," I told Ben as I scrubbed the cutting boards. "Because we all need to get *Ice Fishing* and *Wisconsin Brat Hunter*."

Ben started laughing. "You don't *hunt* brats, Courtney."

"Oh. Do they just come to you, then?" I asked.

Jennifer slammed down an empty napkin dispenser in front of me and nearly broke the glass counter. "There's nothing wrong with sausage. If you'd just try some, you'd know. Okay?"

"I know," I said. "I've had hot dogs."

"It's not the same at all," Jennifer scoffed.

Mark put his hand on my shoulder. "Don't get too mad at Courtney. She's led a sheltered life, you know. She's a brat virgin."

Brat Virgin. I love it. It's like the name of a band.

Mark, Ben, and I were laughing so hard we couldn't hear what Jennifer said. It was something like "You guys get back to work" blah blah blah. The usual. We ignored her.

Thyme sat down next to me on the quad today. Her tirade went something like this:

"I'm transferring. This place is a joke! Do you know there's only one women's studies course available next semester for freshpeople? I can't believe I didn't look into this before I got here. I just *assumed*. They told me the department needs more professors but there's a hiring freeze. So then I tried to find my adviser, but he changed his office hours, so I sat outside in the hall waiting for like an hour before someone bothered to tell me he wasn't coming in. They just want their paycheck and that's it. And the way they turned your work-study job from a law apprenticeship into groveling for money? It's unforgivable."

Why does she have to be so negative all the time? Why does she say out loud the things I'm thinking and trying to avoid?

"Thanks a lot," I told Thyme. "You really depressed the hell out of me." I got up and started to walk away.

She ran after me and apologized, then dragged me into the student center and insisted on buying me a smoothie. It was too runny and not cold enough and made with Kool-Aid and canned-tasting fruit instead of fresh frozen, but I didn't bother going into it. What's that saying about learning to accept the things you can't change? One of those 12 steps Beth hopped through on her way to becoming unaddicted to cigarettes. So I'll never have a good smoothie again. So . . . that's okay. I guess.

Then I thought, maybe it *isn't* okay. Maybe it *can* be changed. Screw acceptance. I'd get a business loan, open my own health food store, since there are a grand total of zero here. Or wait—Gerry, my old boss, was always talking about expanding. Gerry loved me. He could open a Truth or Dairy here, in Wauzataukie. I could manage it!

I called him as soon as I got back tonight from groveling for money. Now I'm groveling for a job. He wasn't in, but I left a message. It's just so obvious I don't belong at BF. I belong at a place like T or D.

Talked to Gerry today. It was so good to hear his voice. And that really almost freaks me out.

"Courtney! My favorite former employee!" he said when he answered the phone. Well, after he got past his trademark "Truth or Dairy, this is Gerry!" He gets so excited about it, like he's the first person who's ever rhymed before. Like he hasn't made the *same* rhyme year after year, day after day.

I told him how much I missed working with him and how working for BF was awful and then I begged him to think about opening a new store here. "There's nothing in town anything like T or D, you'd make so much money, and—"

"I don't know, Courtney." He was completely dragging his Birkenstocked feet.

"Come on, Gerry. We'll call it Truth or Dairyland! Or American Truth, or America's Dairyland!" I said. Total on-the-spot-new-state brainstorm.

Gerry wasn't impressed. He told me that sounded like a course title I must be taking. "Sorry, Courtney. But I really don't have the capital to expand right now. And even if I did . . . as much as I respect and trust you, Courtney, uh, Wauzataukie, Wisconsin, would not be my first choice." He made it sound like this town is a bad place or something just because of its tongue-twister name. "There are still Colorado cities I want to conquer. Wait, conquer isn't the right word, it's too violent. I'd never go in with the idea of starting anything. I don't want a smoothie war on my hands." He started laughing. "That would be quite a sticky mess!"

"My *life* is a sticky mess!" I interrupted him. "I'm

working for a corporate giant that chews up local competition and spits it out. They're like the Microsoft of bagel makers!"

"Oh. How unfortunate."

I started crying. In front of *Gerry*. (Okay, not in front technically, but close enough to be humiliating.) I told him all the problems I'd been having with the manager and how she kept comparing me to this "problem employee."

"Don't put up with that—quit!" Gerry said. "Isn't that what you usually do when you're trying to prove a point?" He reminded me of how I'd quit twice last fall when I was going through what he calls my "unstable senior-year period." (Once a guidance counselor, always insane.)

"I can't quit," I said, ignoring the way he was typecasting me as a quitter. "There aren't any other jobs here. That's why I'm asking you to create one."

"Sorry. I just can't," he said. He sounded really sincere about it. "I need to keep the business close to home."

Home. Yeah, I've heard of that place.

Then the conversation took a really weird turn.

"While I have you on the phone, Courtney, have you heard what happened to Beth?"

"No," I said slowly. I hadn't talked to her or gotten an email in the last week. "Why?"

"Well, she and your brother . . . they apparently got into a fight yesterday," Gerry said. "And Beth went out and bought some cigarettes on her way into work. And she was lighting one while she was driving, and I think a cell phone was involved, and, well—she crashed her car into the sign here."

The Shops at Canyon Boulevard sign? I couldn't

believe it. Why hadn't she told me? Called me in a panic? "Was she hurt?" I asked.

"No, not at all. But her parents are positively livid," Gerry said. "And the strip mall advisory board is none too happy with her. Business is down since yesterday. They want her banned from parking in our lot."

"That's ridiculous! Everyone has accidents," I said.

"Yes. But not everyone jumps out of their car and starts yelling at the sign in front of valuable patrons," Gerry said.

Beth sounds really stressed out. I have *got* to get in touch with her. Maybe she will transfer here after all.

Talked to Beth. She told me what happened and we laughed for a really long time. She said she went on a rant because she was mad at having to make that turn in all the traffic and the person behind her honked at her, etc. I could just picture it all *so clearly*. I probably would have been in the car with her, but then, if I had, she wouldn't have been smoking or talking on the phone, so maybe not. Anyway, she's fine, except that Gerry is asking her to go door-to-door and apologize to all the other businesses in the strip mall for her behavior.

She threw out the cigarettes as soon as it happened, and then called Bryan and they made up and life is hunky-dory and non-smoking again. She said she tried to call me but didn't get me, so she called Grant instead, and he calmed her down. Superior boyfriend even helps my friends.

Thyme and I went to the campus co-op house tonight for dinner. They were having an open house to recruit new members. We had to pay, but assumed we'd get awesome organic food. Probably our expectations were unreasonable. We're never going back.

Most disgusting meal ever. Mishmash of mush and tofu. Flavorless. Shapeless. Looked like prison food. Inedible.

Then afterward they said they had room for only *one* new member, so all the people there who were interested needed to write an essay with an application fee and then have an interview and then cook for all the existing members, just to get in so they could eat more crappy meals.

Thyme and I left before dessert. We were laughing so hard and still so hungry that she took me out for dinner at Koffee Kitchen. Drank too much coffee and now can't sleep.

Wonder what Grant is doing tonight. Probably has more fun things to do on Friday nights. Probably out.

Just called him, and his roommate said he hadn't seen him since 2.

Since 2? But it's 11 there. Doesn't he at least need to come home and, I don't know, *call me*?

Work this morning was very strange. Jennifer kept talk-ing about an exciting new menu addition, but wouldn't say what it actually was. She said we all needed to be "on board" for the "Bagle Brainstorm" that was coming our way on Monday.

Mark rolled his eyes. "We're so thrilled. What now? Blue cheese bagels?" I looked at his name tag. He had recently punched out a new one on the label maker, so it now said Marc.

"How about blue cheese and blueberry?" Ben asked.

"Or could we get goat cheese involved somehow?" I asked.

Jennifer shook her head. "You guys are *so* weird. Just be ready, that's all I'm saying. And what's with that?" She pointed to Mark/Marc's new name tag.

"It's called a name change," Marc said. "I'm exploring my identity. Do you *mind*?"

"No, but don't do it on company time," Jennifer said.

After work, I met Thyme back at the dorm. Mary Jo was hanging out with Kirsten in their room, so Thyme and I stayed in my room. Very awkward. The 4 of us kept run-ning back and forth to get stuff we all wanted. Reminded me of a fight I got into at a sleepover at Beth's house in junior high. We divided into 2 parties, except I left my sleeping bag, backpack, etc., in the wrong room. Ended up having to apologize just to get my pajamas. Why didn't I just go home? Not sure.

Shocking development at Badicals meeting today! We were all supposed to discuss ways to fight the college initials, or at least the chanting of them at football games. I didn't really have any big ideas, but since the major concept was mine, I didn't feel too much pressure. Thyme was going to do a presentation on how the school could easily become known as Feminist Falls or something like that (sounds like a product advertised by mothers and daughters); she was trying to come up with alternative names but had some really bad ones like that.

Anyway, we trekked into the meeting and this guy was already talking, doing his presentation. It was Wittenauer, the milk-hormone protester and champion fund-raiser! He's trying to undermine, change, revolutionize the place while simultaneously getting people to send in huge checks.

Wittenauer agrees with my idea to change the school name. He's also protesting the mascot, for promoting cruelty to corn and veggies in general. He said that to use their image to promote the college is just wrong.

"Okay, but not as bad as using an animal," I said. "Like the CU Buffaloes, when they run Ralphie out onto the field, or Cam the Ram at CSU—"

Everyone jumped all over me! They had like a dozen prepared arguments to shoot me down with. "It's *exactly* as bad!" Wittenauer started describing all the things that are done to harm defenseless crops—and defenseless mascots. I was wondering how he knew so much about it, and asked if he was an Ag major.

"No," he said, and his face got all red. "I'm Corny."

Agh! Top school fund-raiser is top Badical and also school mascot.

Corny believes in change from within. Which is why he's the mascot while simultaneously protesting the idea of the mascot. But no one can know Wittenauer is the mascot because "the position is secret and it's a Cornwall Falls tradition and only the people in this room know it's me," he insisted. "I only reveal my identity here because I think I can help our cause while remaining anonymous. The mascot gets chosen by the previous mascot by getting tapped on the shoulder. Nothing is ever spoken."

Wait a second, I thought. He tapped me on the shoulder at that outdoor party. Did that mean . . . ? But no, he's only a junior. I refuse the position anyway.

Afterward, Thyme and I went downstairs to play pool. Saw those guys who think Thyme's name is hilarious. When they saw us, one of them said, "Hey, look, it's Parsley and Sage!"

Thyme said she's heard this her whole life, and she's learned to just ignore it. But I couldn't ignore it because at first they were actually really funny. They kept calling me Oregano and the Un-named Spice Girl.

But then they totally turned on me and said, "Where did you go to high school again? Rutting Elk?" "No, I think it was Molting Elk," another one said.

"Bugling Elk," I said.

They started to make fun of it even more, and this weird feeling came over me, a feeling I'd only had a few times before, and usually only at assemblies or while signing yearbooks: intense pride in high school. Best place ever. Should never have left it and come to this place where guys roam student union looking for girls to pick on. I was V.P. there. I was *somebody*. I didn't hang around pool tables getting insulted by freshman boys in matching baseball caps.

Just wait until I change the school's name and their dumb caps are like *null and void.*

Why does everything have to happen at once? Just when I thought I was getting settled here, finding friends, feeling at home, blah blah blah, *wham!* How about *this* to ruin your life, Courtney?

Bagle Brainstorm: Bagle Finagle's meat license or whatever they needed finally came through. Now we don't just sell cold-cut sandwiches, which, okay, weren't that great to begin with. But now we're going to sell Bratwurst Bites, Bacon Bacles, Brat-in-a-Blanket, Knockwurst Knots, Sausage Snaps, ugh, all variation on the same theme, weird meats inside bagels.

Hello? Isn't one of the really great qualities about bagels that they *don't* have meat inside them???

And if that wasn't bad enough, Jennifer announced that she was putting me in charge of the "New Product Team."

"But I'm a vegetarian," I said. "Can't I be in charge of chopping the non-meat items? What about salad in a blanket?"

"Where does the dressing go?" Jennifer asked.

"In the blanket," I said.

"No way. Too soggy," she said.

She has an answer for everything.

"Courtney, life is change. You either accept that and move on, or, well, I don't know. Here." She handed me my new apron. Which says in big letters:

KNOCK KNOCK! (*right* across the chest)

WHO'S THERE?

KNOCKWURST KNOTS!

I am supposed to wear this thing? And have people

ask about my "knock knock" apron? The humiliation is going to be endless.

Jennifer only put me in charge because she knows I'd hate it and is trying to break my will, like something out of that Paul Newman movie involving a prisoner and eggs and a chain gang, only I'm not in "the hole," I'm in "the hell" of promoting pork-filled dough.

"Courtney, we've got to compete. We need to stay competitive. Brat Wurstenburger really cuts into our lunch business," Jennifer said, "and market studies in other Bagle Finagles show that there's a real need for these lunch items."

"But that place has been here for a hundred years. You're the one who's trying to cut into their business!" Found myself in the incredibly awkward position of standing up for Brat Wurstenburger. Grandpa might be proud, but my self-esteem was crumbling to the ground.

"I'm going to quit," I told Marc when the meeting broke up and we were standing there holding our new *brown* aprons.

"So am I," Marc said. "I refuse to wear this . . . this . . . whatever." His apron said MAKE MY BLT ON A BACLE! in big yellow letters.

"This is just her shameless attempt to like . . . dominate me," I said. "And she wants me to quit. But you know what? I'm not going to give her the satisfaction."

"Yeah. Neither am I," said Marc. And he grabbed the label maker and started making another new name tag for himself. At least I thought it was for him. Then he handed me the label. "Sucker."

Right now Mary Jo has soft music on, some country-western singer singing romantic crap . . . what's up with that? It's either just her bad taste in music, or she's in love.

"Why do you have to be so far away . . ." the song twangs, over and over, which only makes me think of Grant.

Does it make her think of him, too? Caught her yesterday staring closely at one of his photos. She said it was because she thought she saw a horse in the background—which was true, the picture was from when we visited a vet school—and wanted to know what kind it was, but now I'm not sure. Wasn't she really checking out Grant? And what was with those long phone conversations they have when he calls and I'm not home? Can't she just let the machine pick up?

Why did I have to get a roommate who communicates so well with animals and with my boyfriend?

I'm working at Funders right now. Have to write this down because it's very funny.

Corny/Wittenauer just came over and said, "So Courtney, it's all set for Saturday, right? The football game?"

We have big plans for our CFC protest. I'd ironed them out with Corny at the end of our meeting on Sunday and he was calling everyone to coordinate.

Anyway, the ever-present Dean Sobransky was hanging around. He thinks that just because he's our supervisor and we work downstairs from his office he should drop by constantly. He happened to overhear. "What's that?" he asked. "What's all set?"

"Oh, Courtney and I. We're uh, having breakfast," he said.

Dean S. raised his eyebrow. "I didn't mean to pry."

"No, of course you didn't," Wittenauer said, sort of winking at me.

"You're such a genius at this job. If you don't mind giving Courtney some tips. You know," Dean S. said in a tone I guess he thought was low enough for me not to hear. "Show her the way."

"Which way is that?" Wittenauer joked.

Out of town? I'm thinking. Really fast? Dean S. is way too nosey. He should not be in charge of Student Affairs, he should leave that to us. Not that I'm thinking of having one, just, you know. He's overinvolved. Needs his own life.

Nearly fainted from shock when I got home tonight. There was an actual boy in our room. I was wrong! Mary Jo isn't after Grant—she has a boyfriend of her own.

She'd been talking about someone named Joe for a while, but I honestly haven't been around much and I wasn't paying attention. I sort of thought it was one of her brothers.

Instead it's this freshman who is tall and skinny and has lots of nervous tics. But Mary Jo loves him.

Mary Jo and Joe. That's like a double Joe. (In other words, a large coffee?) If they have any kids, they can name him or her Jo-Joe Johannsen. If he lets her keep her name. Which he wouldn't. I can just tell.

But I'm hoping they don't get married, have kids, or even stay together for one more week, because even though Mary Jo and I have nothing in common and I can't wait to switch roommates and live off campus ASAP, I think she deserves way better than this guy. I guess he is her study partner, because they met in chemistry and got to know each other in class and while Mary Jo helped him with his homework. (Refuse to believe he could manage material on his own. Too stupid. Also, too much of an opinionated jerk.)

"Courtney's from Colorado," Mary Jo said when she introduced us. They were drinking giant Sprites and going through her CD collection, playing all the really awful stuff. Which is all of it.

"Oh." He almost glared at me. Like what is wrong with Colorado??? And even if there were something he didn't like about it, how is that *my* fault? Did I discover the state?

"What's that bumper sticker?" he grunted as he pointed at the T or D one on the wall.

I told him it was a place where I used to work. In the evil state of Colorado. I said it was a really popular place to hang out. He looked confused when I described the smoothies. "It's like Dairy Queen," I finally told him. Doofus.

"I hate Dairy Queen," he said. Idiot.

"Me too," Mary Jo said. "There's not enough butterfat in the ice cream, it tastes watered down or something."

"Well, it wasn't *like* DQ, really," I said. But there wasn't much point getting into it, not if they didn't know what I was talking about.

I left and went to the library, where I am now. If they keep dating, I will be spending a lot of time here. Which is just as well, I can ace all my classes and get my degree in 3 years.

GO AWAY. If you concentrate on something intensely enough, it will happen. Right?

Oops. Forgot crucial component of my thought.

GO AWAY, JOE.

I'm waiting. Nothing's happening. It's practically midnight, and Joe has been here since like 4:00. First he and Mary Jo were doing math homework together. So I went out for a while. When I came back, they were using my computer to look up favorite country singers' websites. Had to listen to bad songs filtered through my computer.

Went out again. Came back again.

Now he and Mary Jo are deciding what kind of pizza to order. Which means he'll be here waiting for pizza, then eating pizza . . . then I'll be listening to Joe talk about how Wisconsin pizza is so much better than Colorado pizza . . .

"So, um, Joe. Do you have a roommate?" I finally asked.

"Yeah. He's really loud, though," he said.

And you're not??? Go away!!!

Mary Jo just went to pay for pizza downstairs and I am stuck here with Joe.

"Are you writing a paper or something?" Joe grunted.

"This is my journal," I said.

"Journal?"

"Like . . . a diary," I explained. How long exactly *has* he been living in civilized society, anyway?

"Oh." He looked fairly bored. "My little sister keeps one of those. She writes all about boys. I stole it once and read the whole thing. Pretty boring."

Just as I thought, he's such a wonderful person.
JOE: If you are reading this right now?
You're too close.
GO AWAY!!!

"Maybe this isn't such a good idea," Thyme said as we marched toward the football field this morning. Her, me, the rest of the Badicals. Wittenauer couldn't be there as he was busy dancing in front of the crowd, sparring with opposing school's mascot, which was a cow, which could destroy ear of corn in seconds flat.

We set up at the CFC end of the field. I draped a banner from the uprights that said "Ozone End Zone." Yes, my brilliant idea. Thank you very much.

Whenever cheerleaders chanted "C—F—C!" we waited until they were done, then chanted, "No more C—F—C! No more C—F—C!" and "Change the name! Change the name!" Somebody had stolen some bullhorns from a gym office, so we were very loud. We interrupted the halftime show by charging across the field carrying flags and spray cans, wearing CFC sweatshirts with big circles and red lines through the initials. The one campus security guard that was working kept trying to chase us, but Corny/Wittenauer diverted her by chasing *her* instead—great comic relief, especially when she slipped on the field and fell in the mud. It was *so awesome.*

Except for one small problem.

Nobody knew what to make of us. Nobody got it.

Also, my floor seems totally split about the whole thing. Early in the game, before the football team forced us to get out of the end zone, Tricia and some other girls from the floor went by and glared at me. I heard Tricia mutter something like, "She doesn't even eat meat," and "*so* on the fringe."

But then Annemarie came over with the other half of our floor and they all high-fived me and Thyme, and said we were hilarious, so we felt better until Thyme pointed out that this wasn't supposed to be funny, it's a very, very serious issue. While she was talking, Mary Jo and Joe came walking up.

"Um, what are you guys doing?" Mary Jo asked. Like all our signs and banners didn't make it totally clear.

"This is a joke, right?" Joe asked. "Nice sweatshirts." He kept laughing at us.

"Some of us are less evolved than others," Thyme said.

"Why would I *want* to be involved in this?" Joe replied.

"Evolved. Not *involved*," I told him.

He looked at Mary Jo and they had some secret exchange and then they left. She's not home tonight. Ew.

Just got back from cafeteria. Have another protest group idea. They started this new "theme" meal-thing tonight, called Oktoberfest. Basically it's supposed to reflect German cuisine, so the bins are full of meat simmering in cabbage juice and there's potato salad with bacon bits.

Who invented bacon bits? Why do they seem like a good idea for any kind of salad? Wrong wrong wrong.

I asked how long this theme was going to go on and Larry, Caf. Supervisor, said "All month!" and I said, "Okay, but what Oktoberfest feature do you have for vegetarians?" and his smile disappeared and he said sauerkraut was a vegetable.

That's when I noticed that lots of people in the buffet line were staring at me. Pointing fingers. Should have gone to a bigger college, where no one would remember me. Should have colored my hair a boring brown, or should maybe wear large hats from now on. But that would be running away from my idea. I can't do that. I believe in what I'm doing. Even if it means that my floor is broken into factions and some people don't want me there.

When I got home, Joe was in our room. I didn't want to be there. Thyme was fighting with Kirsten. So I knocked on Annemarie's door. She turned down the music, told me to come in. I asked if I could hang for a while. She said sure, I slammed door behind me, she turned up music. Music is so loud I can barely think, let alone focus on completing sentences. It's perfect, actually.

10/2

Like dishing up glorified pigs in blankets is not bad enough! I got this ultimatum from Jennifer today re: the regimental hairnet. She found one hair in the cheddar spread and claimed it was mine because it was orange, and my hair is sort of reddish. Never mind that the cheddar is *orange*!!!

"Courtney, I'm not telling you again. Either wear your hairnet, or get your hair cut short. And don't forget to mop the ladies' restroom."

I felt like Cinderella. Mopping the ladies' while Mark/ Marc sat in a stall and smoked his Benson & Hedges 100. Only consolation is that everyone gets treated the same way. Very very poorly.

Thought I had a brilliant idea today.

Need to stop having those thoughts. Wrong every time.

Thyme convinced me to get my hair cut to avoid having to wear evil hairnet, to avoid Jennifer's constant reprimands. I thought about it for a while and decided I'd look okay with short hair. "Anyway, there's power in really short hair," Thyme said, throwing in some details about I wouldn't be oppressed by society's rigid standards of beauty, etc. She made it sound like she was going to shave my head, so maybe I should have stopped right there and then. But she was being so funny, pretending to run a real beauty salon. She gave me one of her roommate's magazines to read while I sat there waiting for her to chop it off. She was getting everything ready. She said she worked one summer at a hair salon. I trusted her. Why? Couldn't I just *look* at her hundred-braid hair and realize a short cut would not be her specialty?

But I was reading the magazine and having a great time until I came upon this article: "So You and Your Boyfriend Go to Different Colleges—Can It Work?"

They had all these stats about how few LDRs survive freshman year, and who cheats first, and all these way-too-easy-to-read pie charts that caught my eye when I tried to look away. The really big pieces of pie represented the couples that didn't make it.

"This is all a bunch of crap," I said as I threw the magazine across the room.

"Oh, I know, I *hate* those magazines," Thyme said. "I just thought you might see a short hairstyle you want."

I tried to smile. But then I saw what Thyme had done

to my hair, how much of it was on the floor, how little was left on my head.

If only I'd looked at the stupid celeb hair photos instead of the article that was far too relevant to my personal life. I'd still have good hair and wouldn't be depressed.

I called Grant to tell him about my new 'do. He couldn't talk for long because he has a bio exam tomorrow at 8. Quite obvious to me that his program is about 100 times more challenging than mine right now. I am stuck in Intro World. Everything's 101 and below.

Just got up to check my hair in the mirror again. "It's very, um, flattering," Mary Jo said. "It really shows off your ears."

I need new earrings. ASAP.

10/4

"Courtney, you certainly look . . . unique."

This is Dean Sobransky's idea of a compliment. Isn't he supposed to be making students feel okay about themselves?

Turned out his so-called small talk about hairstyles was just his way of stopping by my cubicle so he could ask me about what happened on Saturday. "Your little protest was, well, *unique*." Like that's the only word he knows how to use when he can't say anything nice.

"Thanks," I said. "We enjoyed it." I turned around to start dialing. Didn't even have a card ready for a person to call, but I didn't want to talk to him about my C—F—C ban idea.

He hovered by my cubicle, then actually put his hand over the thingy to hang up the phone. "But . . . er, well, of course you don't plan on continuing that," Dean S. said.

"Well . . ."

"Do you?"

"Umm . . ."

"Good. I'd hate to create such a diversion on campus . . . which could create division . . . which might lead to dissension . . ." Then he got to the real point. "Especially with Parents Weekend coming up! We need to put our best foot forward. Don't you agree?"

Totally forgot about Parents Weekend and the fact Dad has promised to come. Jotted down a note to call him before my shift was over to confirm.

Fortunately another Fun-Times Funder called Dean S. over to her cubicle just then. Wittenauer rushed over and asked if Sobransky was giving me a hard time.

"Parents Weekend is exactly why we have to keep it

up, be vigilant," Corny insisted.

"Yeah, but it's different for you," I whispered. "You're in costume. You're happy *corn*. No one knows you're in on the whole thing."

"Don't give up," Wittenauer said. "We're all in this together, and we're going to make things happen here. Okay? Trust me." He rubbed my shoulder and I felt this weird pang. First human contact in 6 weeks. Okay, first *boy* contact. Hugging all the members of the food co-op when I met them doesn't count.

Went to Wanda's Wauza Beauty Shoppe this afternoon. Wanda gave me this sad look and started telling me if I wore more makeup and maybe got one of those push-up bras, maybe people wouldn't look at my hair so much. And I should come back in 3–6 months for a trim. A *trim*. Like I'll need one.

When Joe came over and saw my hair today, he just laughed. And laughed. And started calling me "Truth or Hairless." Like that's even a joke. Certainly not funny. Mary Jo was laughing, too. Too afraid to stand up to him and explain that it wasn't my fault.

10/5

Tried to talk to Mary Jo today, about Joe. I think he is truly evil. Insists on calling me "Truth or Dairy Queen," which is not even a good name for a cross-dresser.

And also, I want our room back. Next thing you know he'll be sleeping over, and THAT CAN'T HAPPPEN.

So we went to breakfast together, and over dry bran cereal and a banana, I said, "Mary Jo, have you ever thought about . . . I don't know. Breaking up with Joe?"

She laughed. "Why would I want to do *that*?"

"Look at all the cute guys walking around," I said.

I should've looked up before I said that. I never realized that most hotties don't show up at the CF caf before 8 A.M. Lots of guys wearing sweats and carrying stacks of donuts do.

"Anyway, you could go out with any guy here you wanted to," I said.

"That's not true!" Mary Jo said. "Besides, I'm really happy with Joe. Why are you bringing this up? He didn't *do* anything to upset you, did he?" She looked very concerned as she buttered a butter roll.

"Oh, no. Not at all," I said. She's so sweet sometimes, it kills me. I can't just *demand* that she break up with her boyfriend. That wouldn't be fair. I can, however, continue to strongly suggest it.

Parents Weekend started tonight. Dad's coming tomorrow. Mary Jo's parents couldn't come because they're busy with a cow crisis, so 1 of her 6 brothers came—Ed. Mary Jo kept leaving us alone in the room while she went to look for Joe, who wasn't answering his phone. Joe was supposed to introduce her to his parents and then they'd all go out to dinner, but he never showed up. Mary Jo was completely devastated, not realizing that 1 meal without Joe wouldn't kill her and would only make her stronger. Maybe strong enough to dump him.

***ARE YOU READING THIS, JOE? I HOPE YOU ARE.

Anyway, Mr. Ed just sat there and stared at me, so I kept nervously talking. He kept smiling and nodding and laughing. He really needs to get out more, because I wasn't being very entertaining at all, plus I have a chopped pixie cut. I think they need to find 7 brides for 7 brothers. 6 brothers. Like, soon.

Later, after Ed finally convinced Mary Jo they should go to dinner without Joe, and after Ed made a dozen excuses for Joe in order to make MJ feel better (very sweet of him), I ran into Thyme in the hallway with her parents. She calls them "Mother" and "Father." Mother wears lots of plaid wool and expensive jewelry and calls Thyme "Morgan." Father wouldn't get off his cell phone, but did brusquely shake my hand. I think in their case the apple does fall far from the tree. Saw them pull away from dorm later in Jaguar, just as Dad was pulling up in rented mini-van. Mini-vans rule my life. Also ruin it.

Wait a second. Thyme said her family had lost all their money. So how can they drive a brand-new Jag?

Work today was insanely busy. You don't want to know how many visiting parents want Knockwurst Knots for *breakfast*. Bluck. Shudder. Etc.

"This place is making so much money, it's disgusting," Mark/Marc/now Marque said as he shoved a wad of twenties into the safe. "The register is like overflowing. And we're making six seventy-five an hour? I don't *think* so."

"Yeah, but we get these *aprons*," Ben pointed out. Marque has decorated his with a large button that says "Have a Day." "So Courtney, are you going to be doing your halftime show?" he teased me.

I've been trying to convince Ben and Marque to join our group, because we could use more members, especially ones that I'm already friends with. But they're not convinced yet. Marque won't wear heinous CFC sweatshirts, even if it's to protest them. Ben is more interested in his slightly more respectable Political Debate Union group, which I would probably check out were I not so deeply embroiled in the CFC protest already.

Anyway, we were completely thwarted at the football game today. Dean Sobransky, or someone else in charge, had hired multiple security guards to surround campus, ring off football field, and prevent us from making our point. No halftime show. No radical Badicals presence at the game, though most of our people did wear the sweatshirts with the red line through CFC.

"What we have here is a case of Protestus Interruptus," co-Badical Erik said when we all met under the goalposts before the game (I had told Dad a little about what was happening, but not much). "We might get a lot of publicity, but we might just look really, really bad."

Also, we all had to admit that the group was about ¼ the size it usually was, due to people hanging out with their parents.

I guess it was just as well, because I had my hands full with Dad. And then some. First off—he had to bring Angelina's baby with him, because Angelina has the flu and so does her mom, Dad's new wife, Sophia (not to be confused with Mary Jo's cow Sophie). (Can I get a *chart* with this?) Nobody where they live could baby-sit, and Dad's all of a sudden Mr. Grandparent of the Year, so he decided to bring her along, all the way from Arizona.

I have nothing against babies. I might have one, in like 10 or 15 years. But Bellarina isn't just any baby. She's the loudest baby in existence. And being away from her mom and grandma definitely wasn't helping. So far, Mary Jo is the only one here who can get Bellarina to calm down. Wanted her to come with us but of course she had to hang out with Ed and look for Joe, who had once again mysteriously disappeared.

Dad, Bellarina, and I sat in the bleachers. Started out next to Thyme and her parents. At first Bellarina was being cute. I sat there with her on my lap and watched Corny Wittenauer posing for photos in front of the bleachers, wrapping his cornstalk arms around students as moms and dads positioned cameras.

Then suddenly it all went horribly wrong: Bellarina screaming, Thyme's mom and dad casting many aggravated looks, people from different classes of mine scowling at me, Dad trying to put Bellarina's binky in her mouth, Bellarina throwing it at Thyme's mom with so much baby spit on it that it stuck to her blond coiffed hair. Thyme's parents insisting they move; Thyme insisting that

Bellarina simply needed a calming environment; taking Bellarina and leaving bleachers to sit under tree; Dad and I trying to ignore screams and cries becoming louder and louder.

End result: Thyme and her parents bought tickets and went to sit in the Preferred Parents' enclosed Plexiglas booths section.

Bellarina decided it was time to become stinky while sucking her binky. So it was off to the restroom to change her. But then Dad had to go back into the bathroom afterward, so he asked if I would hold her. Which I was doing, and she wasn't even screaming, so I thought things were looking up. Until Dean Sobransky came along. I thought he might be about to thank me for not staging a major protest, but his face turned all red when he saw me. Very embarrassed.

"Well, er, Courtney," he said. "How old is your, ah, she?"

"Oh, um . . ." I had to think. "About a year, I guess. No, wait. Ten months."

He seemed sort of surprised that I didn't know, exactly. Then he bolted into the men's room and that was the end of it. Very weird guy. Can't talk about much except "college's best interests."

Later on, Bellarina finally went to sleep in the hotel suite, so Dad and I ordered in calzones (mine without cheese), which is what we always do together, and sat around talking. Somehow, God help me, we got on the topic of "my relationship."

"Courtney, you'll find out a lot about Grant in the year you're apart."

"Years, Dad," I said. "It's going to be four *years*."

"Oh." He rubbed the side of his nose. "Well. That's a long time. Who knows what will happen." He made it sound incredibly tragic, like we were doomed. And maybe we are. And if we are, it's all my fault. I could have stayed home. Why was it so important for me to go 1,000 miles away? Just because Alison did it, in the opposite direction, and I must always copy her? Because I didn't want to live at home and knew Mom would make me? Because I was afraid I'd be stuck in same rut, with same job, same friends, forever?

Nothing wrong with ruts. Wagons would never have crossed plains without them.

Then again, if wagons hadn't crossed the plains, buffalo would still be around in the thousands and millions, not fighting for existence.

But then I might not exist.

Going to sleep now. Must stop this wagon train of thought immediately.

10/8

Finally got up the nerve to tell Dad over our good-bye brunch that I needed some extra spending money because my credit card limit wasn't very high and I might be getting sort of near it. I said it while Bellarina was screaming and banging her spoon and throwing food, so that I'd seem like the good child, the easy child. We visited a Tyme machine before they left for the airport. I came home with $200 and scrambled eggs in my hair.

Very exciting news in cafeteria tonight. The student association is chartering a bus to take anyone who wants to cough up $20 to Madison next weekend—we'll leave Saturday morning, come back Sunday at noon. Hurray! I'm going to see Jane! When I called to tell her, she was totally excited.

Grant called tonight. It was really fun because I kept making him laugh even though he doesn't really know Dad (except for hanging out at graduation party) or Thyme and her snooty parents or anyone in the Ozone End Zone group. At the end of our talk he said, "I'm really proud of you, Courtney. It sounds like things are going really well." Afterward I realized he hadn't said much about his weekend. Was it good? Bad? Indifferent? What did he do? I don't remember. Did he say? Did I monopolize the entire conversation? Maybe I should call back. But I have too much homework left to do before tomorrow.

Can't believe what happened at work today. First, a group of men from some office all came in at the same time to order meat rolls, kept asking me what my favorite menu item was, kept making "knock knock" jokes, asked me if I thought the Brat Blankets were as good as the bacon bit Bacles.

"Sure," I said. "They're . . . wonderful." If you like food involving casing, that makes you think of meat grinders, and slaughterhouses.

Oh God. Just realized something. Grandpa would be so happy if he knew I was in charge of the Best Wurst Bagels Ever team. All those years of lecturing me and showing me barbecue techniques for keeping burgers pink and juicy while at the same time killing *E. coli*. . . . Meanwhile I was trying not to spew on the lawn figurines. It was all actually paying off. Disgustingly.

Anyway, finally got the annoying guys through the line when Dean Sobransky came in. Either he'd just heard about our exciting new menu (and it's true, the line has gone out the door for these Brat Blankets) or he was continuing his plan to spy on me and watch my every move and turn me in to campus authorities before I succeed in changing the school name.

I guess Dean S. didn't know I worked there and was very surprised to see me. So he ordered a few items and started stammering something about how my BF job must help me "make ends meet," with "your little one at home to consider."

"What? You have a baby?" Mark/Marc/Marque asked. "How adorable."

"You never mentioned that. I thought you lived in the

dorm," Ben said. Looking totally shocked and defrauded.

My face burning. Me trying to pretend it was because I was standing too close to steam table. "I *do* live in the dorm," I said. "And I don't have a baby."

"But I saw you on Saturday. And you know, it's appropriate for students to be parents as well as children. And—oh, she's the spitting image of Courtney," Dean S. went on.

"That's because she's my dad's stepdaughter's—wait a second, we're not even related by blood. She doesn't look anything like me!"

"Courtney, what's this I hear? You're a single mom?" Jennifer asked as she rushed over to horn in on the conversation from hell. "You never mentioned that! You need family health insurance coverage, you need company-credit day care, you need some of our bagel teething rings—"

"No! My stepsister. *She* has a baby," I explained. "My dad brought her—the baby—for Parents Weekend, because my stepsister was home sick, and *that's* who you saw me holding."

Jennifer and Ben and Marque all stared at me, like they were trying to figure out if I was telling the truth or not.

"Guys! If I had a baby, don't you think I would have mentioned her by now?" I asked.

"Um. Well. No," Dean S. murmured.

"See, people here don't really, um, talk about stuff like that," Jennifer said. "Which is okay!"

People here are so weird.

Can I leave for Madison tonight? I am so embarrassed! There was an article about me in the school paper today, about the CFC protest last week (yes, the paper's notoriously slow about getting the word out) (or maybe Dean S. made them "hold the story" until now?). There was even a little picture of me, leading the chant. Why couldn't they use my school ID photo when I had hair, when I was vaguely attractive? Then again, real politicians don't think about these things. I should really be more serious about this.

"Next time you're getting your picture in the paper, you should really let me give you a makeover," said Julie, a girl on the hall, when I saw her in the cafeteria. "I used to work at a cosmetics counter."

"Oh?" My voice wavered as I realized she was really insulting me.

"I'm only saying that because I want you to win. I once set my sister's hair on fire by using hairspray in an aerosol can while I was smoking," she said. "Those cans are so dangerous, they definitely should be banned."

1. We clearly need to better explain what our cause is.
2. I won't ever let her give me a makeover.

LATER...

Just got back from taking a shower. When I went in, Tricia was standing at sink, brushing her teeth with battery-powered toothbrush. I said hi, trying to be civil. Which was useless. She gave me the cold shoulder, like I'm all of a sudden a terrible, horrible person, because I want to get rid of CFC sweatshirts. Oh yes. I really *should* do some jail time for that.

Then I had turned off the shower but I was still standing in the shower stall, drying off, when I heard Gretchen and Peña come in and discuss how the school was even more political than they'd hoped, how they admired me for taking a stand, and how everyone needs to get involved at a grassroots level. (Does that include a grass football-field level?)

Then I was walking down the hall when I heard Tricia telling Brittany and Kirsten how "It's like, I don't know how it's like where she's, like, from? But Courtney has no like *morals*?"

Never knew I could cause so much controversy.

Dean S. made his usual visit to our hallowed cubicles this afternoon. He was wearing giant snow boots and kept stopping to ask everyone if they'd taken precautions for the coming freak winter storm. Seemed in a holly-jolly mood to me. Or he was, until he saw me.

"Courtney, I forgot you worked on Wednesdays," he said, his face getting that purplish look again.

Does he have a crush on me or something? No, impossible. But that's how he acts sometimes. Too uncomfortable to be alive.

So he mentioned the *CF Courier* article about me and asked did I really mean what I said?

"Um, what did I say?" I asked. Because I barely remembered the reporter interviewing me. In fact I don't think she did. She's a member of the group and just sort of roughly quoted us.

"That no school today should be allowed to have the initials of a banned substance," Dean S. said. "Do you really believe that?"

"Well," I said, racking my brain. "You don't see schools with the initials DDT. Or TCE. Or even PCP."

"I think you mean PCB," Dean S. said.

"Right. Whatever," I said.

"No, but—but—" Dean S. sputtered as he tossed his leather gloves up to the ceiling and caught them. "We're talking about a reputation. We're talking about a hundred and thirty-seven years of history," he said.

"And we're talking about destroying the ozone layer and promoting things that contribute to that," I said.

Then it got ugly.

Dean S. shoved his gloves into his pocket and came

closer to me. "Weren't you interested in transferring at one point?" he asked. "Because I'm not sure you're going to be happy here, Courtney. And I could get you accepted at another college with a good reputation. I could find you a financial offer."

It was like getting threatened by the Mafia! "You mean, an offer I couldn't refuse?" I asked. I couldn't believe it. Dean S. wanted to get rid of me. I didn't know whether to be scared, or just damn impressed with myself. I was an instigator!

Then Wittenauer wheeled over in his chair. "You know, Dean Sobransky, you've always been so supportive of an open discussion of the issues. I'm really surprised to hear you talk that way. What's going on?" School mascot was completely coming to my rescue.

Dean S. cleared his throat. "Well, Walter, it's like this."

I nearly fell out of my cubicle. Walter Wittenauer? And I thought I had it bad with my V.D. initials? My life was *cake*. No wonder he was hiding under a mascot costume!

Dean S. and WW got into an in-depth discussion of issues facing Cornwall Falls, universities in general, the world. I joined in whenever it seemed appropriate. Ended with one of those famous statements that never made any sense to me, that we'd all "agree to disagree."

Still, have to look over my shoulder, make sure Dean S. isn't trying to boot me out of school.

I don't believe this. When I got back from class this morning, hiking through snowdrifts, Mary Jo, earliest riser of them all, was still in bed. She was crying. I asked her what was wrong. She said Joe broke up with her. That idiot! Joe, I mean. Like he can do better than Mary Jo! He should be grateful she spent even one day with him, let alone a month or so. And the worst part of all is the stuff he said to her when he did it. He told her that he wasn't attracted to her anymore, because she was sort of overweight. What?! She is not! And maybe he could have thought of that before ordering extra cheese and meat on every pizza they ever ordered. I'm so furious! I want to kill him. But I don't believe in killing, or at least I thought I didn't—until now. She's *not* overweight, and even if she were, she's a great person, if you like that kind of person, so who cares?

"I'm going to call Ed and your other brothers right now. They can come down tonight and kick Joe's butt." I grabbed the telephone. I also made Mary Jo look outside at the pretty snow and drink hot chocolate I made for her. "What's your home number?"

"What? Don't call them!" Mary Jo said.

"But you have to. Just imagine them showing up at his dorm room." I stared at her family portrait, all the tall, beef-raised guys perched on a giant tractor. "They'd stand in the doorway and he'd probably faint. It would be so perfect."

"But they wouldn't come just to do that," Mary Jo said.

"Sure they would!" I told her. "Big brothers are way into sticking up for their little sisters. Not that I know, but I've seen my little brother stand up for me. Anyway, all they'd have to do is carry something dangerous. Like a

141

farm knife or something."

"A *farm* knife? What's that?" Mary Jo laughed.

"That's not important. The key thing is to make him as miserable as he's making *you*," I said.

Mary Jo just sat there looking at me like a scared bunny rabbit. That's when I realized that she didn't have a sister or a best friend like Beth, and didn't understand how these things were done. You get furious together, you plot revenge, you talk about things you're never ever going to actually say or do.

"He's right, you know," she said, sounding pathetic. "I should probably go on a diet."

"What? But you're not overweight!" I said.

"I am," Mary Jo said. "Look, I've got farmer's flab." She pinched her waist. There was like one millionth of an inch of extra skin.

"Mary Jo. You're being ridiculous," I said. "He was trying to think of some dumb reason he could use to break up with you. That's what they always do."

"They do? How many guys have you gone out with?"

I was giving her the impression that I was quite the skank, I guess. I explained that I wasn't a skank, but that I'd gone through one bad breakup and had seen a bunch more.

Mary Jo looked at me blankly. "Skank? Is that like the past tense of skunk?" she asked, and we both cracked up laughing.

But then Mary Jo started crying again about 2 minutes later and I really needed to think of some way to cheer her up. Field trip to Farm Supply? Buy her a new mane comb? Kill Joe for her?

Grant called tonight and after I talked to him for a

while, he talked to Mary Jo for a couple of minutes. She told me what he said—he was being super-nice to Mary Jo on account of her heartache and the fact she's so blue. (She has been playing sad CDs all day, and I'm starting to talk like Martina McBride.)

He really can be so sweet. He can talk to anyone. While they were talking, I remembered when he helped me after Dave dumped me last year, how he listened to me babble about hating all guys and how they were all scum. And he didn't even take it personally.

7:00 P.M. Mom just called. Extremely frantic. Her book club is meeting at the house, and Oscar ran away when the house got too full of strangers. (He has set limits. 7 is fine; 8 is terrifying.) She hasn't found him yet, and Bryan isn't home because he's out with Beth, they're studying together.

I got so jealous of Beth and how she still gets to be with her boyfriend, even if it is my brother. I wonder how it would be if Grant and I got to study together. We probably wouldn't get enough done. So okay, we'd just hang together for an hour or so, like a sort of pre-study or post-study thing, and—

"Courtney!" Mom said. "Are you listening to me? What am I going to do about Oscar?"

"He'll come back," I predicted. "He's probably hiding under the bushes in Mr. Novotny's yard. Go check."

Mom walked outside with the phone and called him. Nothing. "Oh, I wish Grant were still around," she said. "I could really use him right now."

"Mom," I said. "Don't even tell *me* about needing Grant, okay?"

Well, at least I made her laugh.

I've got to leave for the movies now.

LATER...

Mom just called back. She found Oscar. Actually she and this guy Richard from her book club, the one who's in love with her, only Mom doesn't care, found him. Richard is this really, really nice guy who won't pick a book when it's his turn unless Mom also likes the book. And he insists on bringing food to the house whenever it's Mom's turn to host. Richard = total devotion. Mom = total insanity. The guy is good-looking, about 50, and as far as I can tell is bucks-up. What is the deal with that? Mom would rather get involved in a torrid chat-room affair. I sent her a clipping about a murder where a wife hooked up with a guy on the Internet; husband followed wife to the motel where they were meeting, shot everyone including himself. All Mom said was that it didn't apply to her because she wasn't married anymore.

Meanwhile, I went to this French film, part of on-campus foreign film series. Dreadful, depressing, sub-titles. Felt intelligent. Felt really bored, also. Afterward Thyme insisted on discussing it. I had to pretend I'd actually watched the whole thing instead of sitting there daydreaming about going to movies this past summer with Grant, and daydreaming about leaving town tomor-row for Madison. Can't wait to see Jane. Can't wait to be around other people.

"Courtney, you've lost weight! You're so skinny!"

That was the first thing Jane said when I got out of the van at the UW Student Union, staggering a little because I'd been scrunched up in the back.

"Look—you're not even strong enough to walk!" Jane said.

"I am, too," I said as I gave her a big hug. Then I explained what happened: the bus didn't show up like it was supposed to. We had 2 cargo vans, and that was it. People were literally fighting for seats, until they decided to have a lottery. I don't think I've ever prayed so hard for anything in my life, except maybe that they wouldn't serve chicken at my graduation party. So they'd given away almost all the seats except for this one in the way, way back—and that was mine. Practically under the luggage.

Jane said the first thing we had to do—after lunch—was go find some clothes in my actual size at the thrift shop. I guess I hadn't noticed, but now that I'm back in civilized society, and Jane has a full-length mirror, I guess I am looking sort of like a 14-year-old boy with my baggy look and short hair. "You're like a stick. Haven't you been eating?" Jane asked.

"Sure," I said. It was just that the cafeteria pickings for vegetarians are woefully slim. But I supplemented. Constantly. "Of course I've been eating, Jane, don't be ridiculous." But when I thought about it, not that much, really, except Twizzlers, plain bagels, and chocolate soy-milk. Hm. Maybe I am a 14-year-old boy.

Jane took me to an Indian restaurant. All delicious. All stuff that I absolutely couldn't get in Wauzataukie. Felt like I was in heaven, or at least a colder facsimile of

Boulder. We drank coffee, talked and talked, walked up and down State Street, bought cheap earrings and cool boots, and then Jane drove me to this place called Ella's, where she insisted I order something called the #1. Turned out to be a pound cake sundae, with vanilla ice cream and hot fudge and whipped cream. "Jane," I said. "You know I can't eat this."

"I saw you eat a banana split this summer at work," Jane reminded me. "So break your rules again—do it for me, Courtney. We have to fatten you up."

"I'm not a cow," I said. She made me sound like I was getting ready for the slaughterhouse and wouldn't fetch a good price at auction.

"You're not anorexic or something dumb like that, are you?" Jane asked as she stirred sugar into her coffee. "Because we all made a pledge to each other that we'd never go down that road." She hit her spoon against the table. "Oh, no. I forgot how bad you are at keeping your pledges."

"I am not," I protested, as my mouth literally watered.

But Jane looked really worried. And the sundae looked really good. But I couldn't, I told her. But then I did.

And it was delicious.

Perhaps it's time to reevaluate my survival strategy. Instead of being vegan, I could be a lacto-vegetarian. Let's face it, eggs and milk are easier to find around here than alfalfa and seaweed.

"Anyway, I'm not bad at pledges," I told Jane. "Grant and I pledged to make our relationship work, no matter what. And we're doing it."

"Mm." Jane took a sip of coffee but didn't say much else.

"What?" I asked. "Our relationship is surviving just fine."

She stared at these little Beatles marionette things that were dancing around, near the ceiling.

"Aren't we?" I asked, waving my spoon in front of her face. "Or do you know something I don't?"

"Hey, I don't know anything," Jane said. "I just think it's kind of unrealistic to assume you can be exclusive for an entire year when you're not together. Your relationship might be fine," she said. "But are *you*?"

I might have just been getting woozy from the sundae, but it sounded like she was being really critical. Of me and Grant. What's to criticize? Not me. Not Grant. So is there something else I should know about or worry about?

JANE HERE:

Hi, journal. Haven't talked to you lately, but want you to keep an eye on your owner/creator. Very worried about Courtney. Short hair, gaunt, looks pale. Wonder if it's because she misses Grant? Romantic, but stupid (sorry, Court, but *you* come first). Or it could just be major Vitamin D deficiency; no milk, no sun. Well, either way, Courtney, you need to put on some pounds. You're supposed to gain the freshman fifteen, not *lose* it. Very worried about Beth, also. She goes out almost every night, cracked up her mother's car that one time, is getting D's in her classes, and on top of all that is not being very nice to Bryan.

I never even saw Jane write in here. How funny.

Unfortunately I'm back from Madison. Had a great time with Jane and new bf Charles and saw his band and everything. But now I'm back in the land of total disasters.

While I was gone, Joe came over yesterday and brought Mary Jo flowers and told her she was beautiful and skinny, and I get the impression he spent the night, ew, and now they're off on a date at Il Fromaggio. Boy can tell her to lose weight and then take her out for lasagna and breadsticks. Like a couple of multicultural carnations make up for the way he insulted her and broke it off out of the blue. Multi*colored* carnations, whatever. I feel like going to the restaurant and spying on him, making sure he doesn't say something about he just realized what he was missing, blah blah blah. If I had his cell phone number I'd call it and tell him there was an emergency at home.

I just know he's only doing this because he misses her, or he needs something from her—not because he cares.

"Courtney, you don't know that," Grant said when I called him to complain. "He might have the best intentions."

"They have a giant midterm coming up," I said. "His intention is to pass bio. And Mary Jo can help him do it."

"You're shortchanging Mary Jo," Grant said. "Don't you think he might miss her? She seems like a really great person, and you said she's cute, so . . . why wouldn't he want her back?"

There it is again. That Mary Jo worship tone.

"The question isn't about Mary Jo," I said. "The thing is that Joe is a heinous individual and can't be trusted."

"You're too hard on people, you know that?" Grant

said. He sounded sort of critical. How dare he? He's not here, he doesn't know Joe. If he met him for even 2 seconds, he'd hate him. But suddenly I'm the one who's critical?

"Yeah, sure. Whatever. I have to go to the library," I said, and rushed off the phone. Stupid Joe is now ruining Mary Jo's life, and my life with Grant as well.

Mary Jo and I got into a huge fight this morning because I told her that Joe was only using her. She said he wasn't and that I was really mean to say that, and only someone as "jaded and skanky" as me would have such an evil thought.

Jaded and skanky? Sounds like a kids' show. 2 new dwarves have been added to "Snow White": Jaded and Skanky! Oh—don't forget Critical. I'm just getting so many compliments lately, I can hardly keep track of them all.

Can I help it if I've gone on a *few* more dates than Mary Jo? Which isn't her fault. And it isn't my fault. She should trust me when it comes to Joe.

Want him to drop out of this school and stop ruining Mary Jo's life, and, by transitive property, my life. I hope he flunks out. Soon. Sometimes I feel like I am more involved in their relationship than my own. But that's because theirs is in town and mine isn't. Where is mine, exactly?

Mary Jo and I are talking again. Or rather, we were, for about 3 minutes. Mary Jo aced her bio midterm yesterday; Joe didn't. So after they got their midterms back, he broke up with her again.

Mary Jo very upset. So upset that she mistakenly started talking to me again; forgot about silent treatment.

I tried not to say "I told you so," but I'm not very good at that. I have this thing where I just really really enjoy being right. Except that I wasn't enjoying it, because Mary Jo started crying again. Whatever I said came out totally wrong, and she went out of the room and slammed the door behind her.

"What was that all about?" Thyme asked, coming across the hall. Behind her, loud reggae music blared. "There is way too much hostility around here. I think it's because of the asbestos in the carpeting."

"No, it isn't," I said. "There's nothing wrong with this dorm! Except the people in it." Then I slammed the door in her face. I really don't know what came over me.

Oh crap. Now Thyme hates me. Mary Jo hates me. Krystyne came by, pretending she wanted to "chat," but was fishing for information to fill out her weekly "conflict report" to the housing office.

Mary Jo is on a hunger strike. I went to get a fruit juice from the fridge tonight, and discovered the cupboard is bare. Completely. "What happened to all the food in here?" I asked.

"Oh, I got rid of it all," she said.

For a split second I wondered if she ate it all. One of those breakup-induced binges. But she said she threw it out because her sponsor told her to remove temptation from her life.

"Sponsor?" I asked. "Temptation?"

She's joined some on-campus group that makes it sound like dieting is a religion.

"How about if you just sort of cut back?" I suggested. "You only have like five pounds to lose, at most. At most! And you look fine anyway and shouldn't worry about what Joe said."

"Easy for you to say," Mary Jo grumbled. "You've dropped at least ten pounds since we got here *and* you have a terrific guy back home waiting for you." She made it sound like we were off at war together, sharing a bunker.

Then she showed me all these brochures from this weight-loss group. Scary. She's convinced she'll get Joe back if she does this. Should I throw this stuff out so it can't work?

Meanwhile, I'm supposed to be organizing this giant rally for Saturday, have to meet with the group tomorrow. Need new ideas.

Where is Grant when I need him? Not home again. Left a message. Just got back from huge party at Mark/Marc/Marque's house. One of his roommates has it every fall, and it's called the "Oshkosh Slosh," because he's from Oshkosh and so are a bunch of people here. I didn't get sloshed, but I did dance a lot. Maybe a little sloshed, earlier, but switched over to water 3 glasses ago.

Funny thing happened. Was talking to Marque about Grant and how much I miss Grant and so he asked if I had a picture. Which I do in my wallet. Crumpled but still cute. So I was showing it to him and he was totally impressed. Marque and I sat on the stairs and talked for an hour about relationships and how hard they are and how great they are, etc.

Then Marque asked if I worry about Grant being with other women, because after all he is hot. Marque said if he dated Grant he wouldn't let him out of his sight. I thought that was very funny so I kept laughing. Then suddenly it wasn't funny and I was almost crying. Then Marque hugged me and said just because he was paranoid and insecure didn't mean I had to be.

Then a bunch of Badicals showed up and we all danced and I forgot about missing Grant. At one point I did tipsily harass Wittenauer about his first name, and he said as if his initials weren't bad enough, he was also a 3. What? I asked. He's a lot cuter than that, I thought. Why was he rating himself only a 3?

Then he cracked up laughing and said he had a 3 at the end of his name. Like Junior, but a III. So his initials are actually WW III. Can you even believe that?

"I'm surprised you can spend so much time trying to

change the college name," I said. "Don't you want to spend all your time changing your *own* initials?"

"Is there a group for that?" he asked. "Do you want to organize one?"

"Actually, yeah," I said. "But I'll tell you my middle initials some other time."

What a fun party. I really need to go to more parties.

I have decided not to drink at any more parties. Or drink anymore at parties. Or even go to parties. Not fun.

Have a major headache, still, and lost my wallet last night. I have no idea where. Completely irresponsible of me. I've retraced my steps—well, okay, so I can't remember every single step. I'm not Thyme. She did use her photographic memory to go through all the routes we walked together.

Funny how easy it was to make up with Mary Jo and Thyme. Perhaps Thyme's photographic memory is failing and she doesn't remember me shutting the door in her face?

I skimmed the Lost & Found section of the paper, and I've been to every Lost & Found desk there is.

"A wallet? Er, no," everyone said, trying not to laugh, as if everyone knows that no one ever turns in stolen wallets.

It's not like I had much in there.

Just my entire *life history*. My complete identity.

Feel very weird about hanging out and laughing with Corny last night. Like I did something wrong, had too much fun or something, and now must be punished.

Which is why Krystyne just came by and told me I had to go to a housing workshop tomorrow at 1 P.M. Mandatory.

Housing office called it "So You Got Off on the Wrong Foot: A Remedial Roommate Workshop."

I called it "Three Hours of My Life—Gone."

Mary Jo and I were there, along with Thyme and Kirsten and about 50 other miserable-looking students. Housing office won't let you move, but will spend time and money to force you to get along?

We had to do all these really stupid exercises to rebuild trust. Then we were supposed to turn to each other and each person got 2 minutes of "freestyle open expression." I went first, and I didn't even talk for 2 minutes, and if I did, it was all about Joe and what a bad choice he was for Mary Jo and how I wanted to protect her from him.

Mary Jo then started her rant and couldn't stop. She said, "No wonder you want to change the school's name. You don't agree with *anything*. You think everything should be one way, *your way*, and when it's not, you decide it's wrong," blah blah blah. I stopped listening, which was a mistake, because part of the exercise required repeating back what she had said.

"You never listen!" Mary Jo cried. "That's another thing that drives me crazy."

We left there with a giant 3-ring binder called "Cope, Don't Mope." And some extra credit that has to count *some*where.

There was some mail waiting for me today. Not the good kind. The kind that comes from the bank when your account is overdrawn. Well, of course it is, I thought—my *wallet* was stolen, my *Tyme card* was stolen—I'd already called the bank to report this, so I'm not responsible.

I went down to the bank to talk with a customer service rep. Unfortunately I got the same cranky woman who couldn't spell my middle name and lectured me on balancing my checkbook and not bouncing checks. "I was just about to call you, Ms. Vun Dragoon Smith," she said. Like I was about to make her day, because she could get all her bitchiness out in one customer transaction and then go home early. I tried to explain that the checks had bounced because someone stole my Tyme card. I told her I'd never actually written a bad check.

"Do you understand the *concept* of checking at all?" she said, as if I were 7 years old. "Listen, you are in big trouble here with us. And I warned you, didn't I?"

"But don't you see? We're dealing with a case of identity theft," I said. "Didn't you see that Sandra Bullock movie?" I explained how easy it was to have someone take your name, everything about you, and start acting like you, and start spending money like you—

Then she went to a file and came back with my signature card, and also photocopies of the bounced checks. They were all ones I'd written myself. A few of them while slightly impaired, apparently. Couldn't quite make out who they were to. It had nothing to do with my Tyme card.

"I'm sorry. Your account has been closed. Permanently," she said. "And you owe us two hundred dollars in fees."

Then she smiled. Yeah, she's so *sorry*. She lives for this.

10/25

Excellent news. Marque found my wallet at his house! Took him out to Koffee Kitchen to celebrate. After we ordered I realized I had no cash. Had to ask him to cover the meal. Very embarrassing. Now owe him 2 lunches.

Called Grant on the sly from Funders today. Told him about finding my wallet and joked how Marque was only keeping it because he thought Grant's photo was cute. He didn't even *laugh*. He was all preoccupied with something.

When I hung up the phone I felt vaguely insulted. Like it wasn't exciting to hear from me?

Went over to find Wittenauer, but he was wrapped up in a call to some former senator, discussing the needs of higher education.

What about *my* needs?

Mental breakdown. Sampled one of our Brat Blankets and a Knockwurst Knot today. I should have known it was only a matter of time, after all I do have this weakness for hot dogs. Also I'm completely broke and need free protein.

Anyway. They were actually almost yummy. Delicious. Way better than Oscar's cheapo hot dogs.

Sorry, body.

Sorry, PETA.

Sorry, cow somewhere, pig, whatever.

It's just that everyone was talking about how good they were, and they did smell good, and . . . well, there's no *excuse*, really. And I did pay for it afterward because my stomach went into a panic. So I don't think I should be criticized, especially not in my very own journal, so just *back off*.

Wow. Meat really brings out the testosterone in me. I'm yelling at a notebook.

Afterward I was hanging out with Thyme in student coffeehouse. She kept talking about how healthy she's felt ever since she purified her body, and I was sitting there listening to rumbling of digesting bratwurst.

Why do I have this capacity to just toss my convictions aside when a situation gets too difficult? I'm really not a credit to the cause. To *any* cause.

Must revise earlier statements about cows. Turns out they are much smarter than I thought. Also somewhat vindictive.

I went for a bike ride this afternoon. There's this bike path on the outskirts of town, so I thought I'd check it out now that weather has warmed up, snow has melted. Also I've been feeling very flabby from eating too much junk food, too much meat, not enough fruit unless you count fruit roll-ups.

So I was riding along—sunny afternoon, rapidly turning cloudy, but trying to ignore that. The path turned so that it was sandwiched between 2 cow pastures. Cows seemed cute to me. Lounging, gnawing on grass, etc. Then I turned a corner and a cow was standing right in front of me. It had somehow escaped from the pasture.

Decided to ride past; wasn't going to let 1 Holstein get in my way. Kept going. Suddenly 3 cows in front of me. Then 2 more. Farther ahead, cows standing in a line, barring bike path. Giant hole in barbed-wire fence suddenly very obvious.

Cows seeking revenge on me! Bad karma from eating meat yesterday.

"I'm sorry!" I yelled. "I'm really, really sorry. It won't happen again!"

Cows ignored apology. Well, of course they would—it was a bratwurst, not a hamburger. Started coming toward me. Turned and sprinted back past 1 lonely cow that started cantering beside me, hooves clicking on bike path, my heart pounding in my throat. Courtney vs. Cows. Felt like Lance Armstrong as I raced all the way back to campus. But much, much slower.

From now on, no eating meat. Or maybe no riding bike in the country. To get cow karma back, I will only say nice things about milk, cheese, cottage cheese, sour cream, ice cream. All dairy products are bright and beautiful. And dairy cows rule.

Next time I need to at least bring some carrots or hay or whatever it is cows like to eat. But that might make them chase me more. Probably not a good idea.

So to make amends, Thyme and I went to fish fry at Brat Wurstenburger tonight. I'd heard it was a popular Friday-night thing, but didn't realize—the place was *packed*. Thyme kept asking our server, named Dot, whether the fish had come from polluted waters and whether they were actually fresh. Dot got this little eye twitch as she listened to Thyme, but kept answering her politely, telling her the perch came from lakes nearby, she knew all the fishermen who caught them—

"Fisher*people*, you mean," Thyme said.

"I've known them for years, two of them are my sons, and they're named Steve, Eric, John, and Wayne," Dot said curtly.

"She didn't have to be so rude about it," Thyme complained after Dot left. Like Thyme hadn't been as rude as possible herself.

Ozone End Zone Rules!

We blew them away at Homecoming.

Thyme unfortunately missed the whole thing because she wasn't feeling well, or so she said. Later on, she wasn't home, so I don't know. Sometimes I think she is afraid of the spotlight. Anyway, not important. What's important is this: we got *applause*. We're starting to have people who *cheer* for us, we almost have a following.

It was really cool because Annemarie convinced a friend of hers from the campus radio station (she has her own DJ slot now) to blast music over the field speakers as we dashed through 35-member marching band's lame halftime routine, disrupting everything, drawing attention to the plight of our school being associated with, well, plight. Or do I mean blight?

Anyway, the crowd was *huge*. Several old fogies in plaid pants frowning at us. Several alumni heard reminiscing about life in the sixties. Meanwhile Corny was sprinting around trying to distract Dean S., president, football coach, marching band conductor, etc. Very busy mascot. His cornsilk was falling out all over the place; looked nearly bald at the end.

Just as I was leaving the field, Dean S. caught up with me. "Courtney, I thought you'd given up on all this," he said. "Don't you want to join a—a—team or something? You seem athletic. You could channel all that energy into, say, volleyball, or field hockey—or how about tennis? I'm the assistant coach, you know."

See, sometimes I think he does have a crush on me. Wants to be around me constantly. Very embarrassing because it looked to other Badicals like I was colluding with the enemy. "Let's agree to agree that I'm no good at tennis," I said, before running off to distribute flyers.

Shouldn't have run. He'll force me to be on the cross-country team now.

After the game we all got together to brainstorm ideas for final football game, 2 weeks from today. Everyone wants to do a dramatic scene, or okay, maybe that's just the people from the drama department who recently joined the group.

"So this would be Shakespeare in the parking lot?" Erik joked.

Looked for Wittenauer to laugh with, then remembered he had to go to various alumni functions, mingle, pose for more photos, pretend he wasn't in on this. Meeting very boring without him or Thyme there.

10/29

Forget CFC thing. Forget everything! Grant called this morning with the best news. He got me a plane ticket!!! I'm going to see him next weekend!!!

He's been working all these extra hours to save the money. Not telling me about it. And he kept asking me questions about my classes, like when my midterms were, and made me mail him a schedule, and all my dumb syllabuses. I thought he was just trying to be involved. Turns out he's been plotting this.

Best boyfriend ever. Confirmed yet again.

Ran across hall to tell Thyme the great news.

"Maybe I can come with you next weekend," Thyme said. "I have got to get out of here."

I smiled a little, hoping she wasn't serious. Don't really want to spend weekend with Grant *and* Thyme. With Grant and anyone, actually.

I've got the worst stomachache. I'm too excited about seeing Grant to do anything but think about seeing Grant. I know this is wrong because I need to get ahead on my schoolwork because I won't do any while I'm home. But instead I spent the afternoon shopping for perfect gift to bring. Ended up in Karl's House of Meat getting badgered by man behind the counter to sample latest cheese crop.

"The thing is, I don't really *like* cheese," I said. "This is a gift for a friend—"

"You'll love it after you try this!" He carved a giant chunk of something slightly stinky and handed it to me. "Now *that's* a cheese."

Well, it was either a cheese or a moldy ball of aged butter. Chunk after chunk kept coming over the counter on a wooden board. (Should really not think of chunks right now.) Ate some, stuffed some of it in my pockets, finally ended up buying a gift basket, which includes something called a "Nutted Three-Cheese Log." It's stuffed into our mini-fridge, and I hope Mary Jo won't get mad at me for sabotaging her diet.

10/31

It is sooooooooooo cold. Halloween, Wisconsin-style. You must sprint from house to house to collect hot chocolate instead of candy. Ended up working late (a few more weeks of this and I'll pay back the bank), then went to Halloween party in dorm. No costume for me. Everyone on floor yelling at me for not playing along. I'll probably start another faction war over this.

Mary Jo was in our room all night doing her best to avoid temptation of candy corn and candy in general. She looked completely miserable. Also a bit on the pale side.

"Have you been eating anything except that weird program food?" I asked her.

"No," she said. "And it's not weird!" She slammed down her chemistry book and grabbed the bottle of "Super Energetic Vitamin Boost" that goes with this diet, started shaking pills into her mouth with her shaky hand.

The woman is in desperate need of a good smoothie. She needs fruit and energy boosts. So do I.

7 P.M. At my Fun-Times Funders shift. Dying for it to be over so I can go home, write my poli sci paper. Just had very awkward conversation with WW III. He said, "So this weekend, I was thinking we could work on our next protest together. Maybe—"

"Actually, I can't," I said. "I'm going home."

"You are? All the way to Colorado? For a weekend?"

Felt my face turning red. "It's a long weekend. And it's, well, to see my boyfriend," I said. "He got me a ticket, and so . . . I'm going to visit him."

"Oh. I see." He went back to his cubicle.

Am I letting down the cause? But what about *my* cause: seeing Grant?

10:30 P.M. Here I am with 8 books, 3 legal pads, 4 pens, 43 index cards, 6 completely blank discs—like I'll need more than 1—and 1 computer, and . . . 1 very confused mind.

How am I ever going to finish my paper before I leave for the airport? Oh well. Where there's a will, there's a way.

Sure.

Thyme and I are in dorm lounge. Moved our computers down here.

4:27 A.M. Well, I made my point on the first page and it's followed by 6 pages of beating around the bush. Thyme's is the opposite.

Have to write 3 more pages to make it 10. Chugging iced tea. Trying to stay awake, but I think I got the caffeine-free kind by mistake.

6:24 A.M. Sunrise watching can be fun but in its appropriate time and place. Paper is almost finished. Thyme went to caf to get us donuts and coffee. Like we need coffee. Like we can even hold a cup.

7:30 A.M. Medical alert! I was staggering back to my room from the lounge, needing to print paper and get dressed for class. Mary Jo was walking toward me in robe and slippers. But she was weaving a little, as if following a line on the floor only she could see. Then she fainted! She totally keeled over! Her bucket dropped onto the carpet, and horsey shampoo and conditioner splattered on the walls. Waiting for Thyme to wake up Annemarie to borrow her car and then bring car around; taking MJ to campus health.

9:10 A.M. Have been waiting 2½ hours for someone to look at Mary Jo. Thyme left to go hand in our papers. Assistant gave Mary Jo a cursory glance and decided she was "non-emergencial," and promised to return. Have been up to the desk 6 times demanding help. Each time, Mary Jo tries to escape but is too weak, can't make it to the exit before I catch her.

Called her parents but got Ed instead. Told him that Mary Jo wasn't feeling well and it might be good if her family visited this weekend.

"Are *you* going to be there, Courtney?" Ed asked.

"No, that's why I thought you should come by," I said. "Because I have to go home to Denver for the weekend."

"Oh. Well, she'll probably be all right," Ed said. "Once she eats a decent meal."

So we're going to blow off the health center and go to Mary Jo's favorite breakfast place, Koffee Kitchen. My treat.

11/2 DENVER!

Same pen, different story.

I'm home! I can't believe it. I am actually about to go to sleep in my very own bed in my very own room with my very own psycho dog lying on the floor next to me.

Got in pretty late, so Grant and I could only hang out for an hour before Mom selfishly demanded he leave because it was after midnight. She said she wanted to talk to me. Our talk consisted of "What would you like for breakfast?" and "What are your plans?" and "Are you getting all A's or not?" But at least she did say she's definitely *not* seeing that chat room guy, or any other Internet guys.

Anyway, big news: Grant has a goatee now. Very weird when I saw him, but he does look even better than before. Typical Grant, he keeps it cut really short and neat. Discovered that I still love him to death even though he devoured the cheese basket I brought him within minutes, like a giant mouse, and didn't bring me anything.

Okay, so he bought the ticket. No problem there.

But not even 1 flower???

Mary Jo's stupid Joe even gave her bouquets. And isn't Grant a better person than that?

Okay. I am not going to spend the weekend thinking about that idiot Joe, or Mary Jo, or anything back at CF. Except maybe to hope that Mary Jo is eating real food.

I hate it here. I'm miserable. I wish I were in Wauzataukie.

Now that's a sentence I never thought I'd write.

Maybe I can catch an earlier flight back tomorrow. I could spend the weekend working on our ban-CFC act for next weekend. I am wasting my time here.

Can I really be saying this? Are things that bad? YES.

This was *supposed* to be a romantic trip. Grant and I were going to spend the weekend in each other's arms. We'd go to all our favorite places, cuddle, snuggle, etc.

So much for having a romantic weekend. I've ruined everything, or Grant's ruined everything, I don't know who's responsible. But tonight we got into the biggest fight we've ever had. (Maybe because we've never fought. Period.) It's because Grandmother Superior has bronchitis and sounds awful. Okay, I know that she has lived with Grant and his folks for the past couple of years since his grandfather died, and he's really close to her and she's really close to him, etc. But does she have to get bronchitis on the one weekend we can see each other?

So tonight he said he had to stay home and keep an eye on her because his parents had a business dinner thing. Hello! It's *Friday night*. I just got here last night, and this morning I had to hang out with my mom while he went to classes and then this afternoon he had to work for 4 hours, because he couldn't get anyone to cover that part of his shift.

So then he came down to meet me in Denver, and what does he want us to do? Not go out here. Not go back to Fort Collins so we can hang out in his room and I can meet his roommate and his friends and go to a party there. No. He wants to sit around holding Grandmother

Superior's hand! One of us on each side of her! It's *only* bronchitis, I told him. Even his grandmother told him not to be silly, that he should go out with me.

"You should," I said, trying to ignore her rattling cough. "I mean, Grant, you do see her all the time," I whispered.

"No, I don't," he said. "You don't know, Courtney. I haven't been down here at all lately. And she needs me, okay?" He really sort of snapped at me.

The unflappable Grant was actually very, very stressed out. It made me feel awful but I didn't know how to deal with him. So I came home. What else could I say? But now I feel worse.

Saturday afternoon, waiting for Grant to come over. Just had lunch with Beth. We spent like 3 hours going over everything and everyone new in our lives. I was afraid I was boring her with too many stories, but she was totally into it.

All in all, though, I didn't get a good feeling from her. I think she is failing out, though she didn't say that. And why aren't she and Bryan spending more time together?

I guess part of it is that I just can't help thinking that the only reason Bryan and Beth got together is because the dating pool at Bugling Elk had gotten a little shallow, esp. for Beth, who had a new fling every other weekend and had already dated a bunch of the seniors and juniors and had to seek out a sophomore. So I'm expecting her to want to break up with him, because she has a whole new pool of college guys.

Anyway, all through lunch, I couldn't stop staring at her hands. Her index finger was discolored. That's when I knew she was totally smoking again. "But it's different now. I'm only a social smoker," Beth said when I confronted her about it. "I only smoke at parties."

"You just told me that you go to parties almost every night! That means you're smoking *every day*."

"Oh," Beth said, like she hadn't realized that.

I grabbed her purse. She thought I was going for her smokes—which would have been easy, because there were like 2 or 3 packs inside—but I pulled out her wallet.

"Courtney, what are you doing? Stop that!" She lunged for the wallet.

Just as I suspected. Those charred-lung photos she used to carry around all the time to convince herself—and others—never to smoke again were gone. But why did she get so nervous when I picked up her wallet? "We used to share everything," I reminded her. "So why do you care if I look at your wallet?"

"It's private, that's all." She grabbed it back from me.

It took me all night to figure out why she didn't want me to look at her wallet. That's when I realized something I hadn't seen inside. Thyme's photographic memory must be growing on me. Bryan's picture wasn't in there anymore. And I can't stop thinking about what that means and what I'm supposed to say or do about it.

Oh well. At least things are good between me and Grant. I guess that sounds selfish, but last night turned out to be very romantic. Started out pathetic (see above) and I sat around being extremely unhappy for hours. No one else was home. Bryan was away for a cross-country meet and Mom was out with friends. It was me and Oscar. Together again. Not that I don't love him, but. So I decided there was only one way to repair the weekend. I took Oscar for a long walk. Thought this would create good karma for me, as spending quality time with pet with trauma-induced epilepsy only can.

Then the more I walked, the more I realized I wanted to make up with Grant—immediately. Actually half dragged Oscar all the way over to Grant's house.

While I was moping at home, Grant had gone to Safeway and bought cough drops for Grandmother Superior, flowers for me. When I got there we hugged for a really long time. He apologized for being selfish when it came to his grandmother. I apologized for being spoiled and unreasonable. But he said I wasn't unreasonable, the whole point of me coming to visit was for *us*.

I never realized that we hadn't actually had a fight before. I hated it, and don't want it to ever happen again. I was going to have us sign a pledge to that effect, but realized that would be childish and also like a prenuptial agreement or something.

So I just told him how I didn't want to leave on Sunday and how we only had 48 hours left.

"Then we'd better make the most of it," he said. So we went upstairs and did.

Hope Grandmother S. was really asleep, like Grant thought.

On plane now. Thyme and Annemarie will pick me up at airport. I should be studying but I'm not. I keep thinking about what a weird and good weekend it was.

Had wonderful Saturday night: Beth, Bryan, Grant, and I went out to dinner, then Grant and I hung out, then today we went to the zoo and walked around holding hands and being disgustingly romantic. At the airport when we were saying good-bye, I couldn't help crying, because I really didn't want to leave.

Grant gave me this gigantic Superior squeeze right before I was getting on the plane, when they started calling rows. "So what do you think of the goat? You never said." He took my hand and brushed his chin with my fingers.

"I like it," I told him. "What about my hair? *You* never said."

"Well, it shows off your gorgeous ears," he said.

Which is exactly what Mary Jo said! But then Grant started kissing my ears. So it wasn't really the same as Mary Jo saying it after all.

When I got on the plane, I was too flustered and in love to find my seat. Flight attendant asked if I was an unaccompanied minor. Very embarrassing.

Spent all morning lying in bed rehashing wonderful weekend with Grant. Then the day got worse all of a sudden. Realized I was going to be late for work. Sprinted to get ready. Still got there half an hour late and had to endure lecture from Jennifer. Endless blather about how I was letting down the New Product Team; never mind that the products aren't *new* anymore.

Then tonight, Beth called. She and Bryan broke up! "I can't believe you broke up with him," I said. Were they waiting for me to leave town or something?

"I didn't," she said.

"Oh, you mean it just sort of happened—it was mutual. Wow. You must be upset. I'm so sorry," I told her.

She muttered something about how they were holding it together for my visit but. . . . And then I couldn't understand the next couple of sentences. She was crying and smoking and crying and coughing.

"If you're that upset, maybe you guys shouldn't break up," I told her. "Are you sure it wasn't just a big fight, and you guys need to kiss and make up?"

"No . . . but . . . see . . ." And then the garbled gook again.

It was breaking my heart to hear her cry like that. "On the plus side?" I said. "It *was* the longest relationship you've ever had."

She started crying even harder and then she had to hang up. I don't know, I thought it was a valid point.

I waited a little while, then called Bryan. He seemed remarkably unfazed. "I really don't want to talk about it with you," he said.

"It's okay, B. You can open up to me. I won't tell her

anything you say, I promise."

"I just don't want to go into it. You wouldn't get it, anyway." He's always saying that, like he's Einstein and is dealing with the mysteries of the universe, and I'm not. "I'm fine," he said. "I'm actually relieved. I'll have a lot more time for training now."

Typical Bryan. Acting like nothing's wrong when his whole world's crumbling. Well okay, not whole world. Just the girlfriend part of it.

Anyway, Bryan and Beth were going out before me and Grant. So the fact they broke up now means . . . nothing. It has nothing to do with us. NOT AN OMEN. They only live a few miles from each other, so if they couldn't make things work, then their relationship must have been doomed.

I am a little peeved at Beth, though. I have to admit. But since she's the one who's upset, and Bryan sounds okay, I guess I won't be mad at her. It had to happen sooner or later. Now they're both "free and clear." Wonder if they'll get back together. Wonder if Bryan will find someone at Bugling Elk. Wonder who Beth will hook up with first, and how long it will take her.

Must call Jane now to place my bet. I give Beth until . . . let's say Thanksgiving. I bet she'll hook up with someone before then.

Thyme and I got into a huge HUGE argument in the hall today. We were trying to make plans and signs and stuff for our big final protest on Saturday and we kept disagreeing about everything. All of a sudden she *totally* switched sides and said that changing the school's initials was a really thoughtless idea because it was history, and we'd be *contaminating* an historical site, including her father's—grandfather's—Econ building, etc.

So I demanded to know whether she came from money or not, because I saw her parents' Jag, and if they lost all their money then why didn't she have to work, and why would she lie about that, because I didn't care one way or the other. And she said, "*Obviously.*" She said if I had any morals at all I'd never go serve meat and cheese at Bagle Finagle as a vegan, and I was probably not even a *real* vegan or even a vegetarian, which is *so* ridiculous! So then I told her that she obviously had a trust fund, which made it so stupid that she was running around preaching about only working PC jobs and she didn't have any life experience at all doing anything—

We were screaming at each other in the hallway. Really ridiculous. Mary Jo came out of our room and told us to break it up. We didn't, and were about to get into a cat fight when Mary Jo hauled me away like I was a stray cow. Slammed door behind us.

"Why do you even bother?" she asked me.

"What?" I asked.

"She was being so mean to you—I can't stand it!" Mary Jo said. "Do you know she was criticizing your idea the whole time you were gone?"

"Wh—what?" I said.

Mary Jo nodded. "She said it was stupid and counterproductive."

"Are you sure that's not what *you* think?" I asked.

Mary Jo shrugged. "Maybe I don't think your idea is great, but I don't *pretend* to support it while I go around telling everyone that it isn't. I'd never undermine you—or any friend—like that."

"So you don't think it's great," I said. "Well, I'm not surprised, but—"

"But I think the fact you're that passionate about it is awesome," Mary Jo said. "You obviously care a lot about this place."

What? I thought. What was she talking about? This protest isn't about making CFC a better place, it's about . . . well, anyway. Can't believe Thyme would desert me and our CFC protest now, after everything. Not a friend. But I didn't like hearing Mary Jo say it. I don't *have* any other friends here. Even though Thyme can be a jerk, what am I supposed to do? Toss her aside?

Mom called tonight when I got home from library, and she was so excited, it was great. She met some single guy at a banquet where Bryan was getting an award. His daughter's a cross-country star and so they really hit it off, because Bryan and his daughter also hit it off, so it was like stereo dating, they had tons to talk about, and well, did she mention he's handsome and a runner himself, etc., etc., blah blah blah.

"So did you ask him out?" I said.

"What? What do you mean? Of course not," she said.

"Mom!" She drives me crazy when she does this.

Peña was doing Tarot card readings in her room, so I grabbed a Fresca for her, went in, and asked her if she could give me some info on Mom. Like, will she ever date this guy?

The Fool card kept coming up. Not sure about that. I really don't want my mom getting involved with a jerk after all these years of celibacy. Peña kept saying the fool didn't mean an actual fool, but it did seem sort of coincidental. "Your luck is going to change soon, Courtney. That's what it means."

"For the better?" I asked. "Right?"

"Mm." She glanced up at the doorway. "Next?"

That doesn't seem good. Does it?

Called Grant to talk about the Bryan and Beth situation and my fight with Thyme and my big protest, which is only *2 days away*. But he wouldn't get into analyzing Beth and Bryan and wanted only to talk about Bugling Elk's Homecoming, which is this weekend. I felt like even though I was just there, all of a sudden we were living in parallel universes. Different worlds. Whatever. Him: stuck in Colorado, clinging to high school. Me: free-floating anxiety in Wisconsin. Living "so on the fringe."

"I can't believe you won't be here," Grant said. "It won't be the same without you."

"Make sure you say hi to everyone for me," I said. "And keep an eye on Beth. And take notes. I want to know how everyone's doing. And tell everyone I'm doing incredibly great here. You know. *Lie*."

Grant laughed. "You *are* doing great. Aren't you?"

"Sure," I said. "Actually, things are pretty good. I've got this huge thing happening on Saturday and—"

"Agh! Court, I hate to do this to you, but I've got another call," Grant said. "It's probably my lab partner, Melinda—I'm supposed to be meeting her to study for our exam tomorrow. Can I call you when I get to Denver?"

"Sure," I said, gulping for air. "Okay."

Lab partner Melinda??? Who is *that*? Why haven't I heard about her before? Suddenly very uneasy about everything.

11/10

OH MY GOD

Just got off the phone with everyone from home. *Everyone*. First the Tom called on his cell phone. The Tom! It was so fun to talk to him. Can't believe he's still at Bugling Elk, still working in Principal LeDuque's office to make up for money he embezzled last year. Still scoring with freshmen (fresh girls) even though he is now a Senior Plus. Disgusting pig. He totally made me laugh, though, because he kept describing everyone at the party and who had changed and who hadn't. And he said a million times how much he missed me.

Then he gave the phone to a bunch of other people who said hi, then Beth got on the phone. I kept teasing her about who she was going to pick up at the party, now that she was single again. Maybe the Tom? Who knows. Then she gave the phone to Grant. And it was just so cool to talk to him because I almost felt like I was there with him and everyone else.

I just love him and all those guys *so much*. I can't wait to see them!!!

Christmas seems like way too far away. I can't wait to see Grant, and Beth and even the Tom!

This is now the journal of Courtney Smith, Media Star.

This was me in front of TV camera today: "Yes, it was my idea."

This was the reporter (from world's smallest TV station, but who cares): "It's *very* innovative."

Watched her report tonight, and a lot of the coverage was actually about all the people who disagree with us. But this is just the beginning! Although I'm not sure how we'll get enough exposure now that football season is ending. Oh well. We'll think of something.

Final home game = biggest turnout yet.

We did our dramatic piece after Annemarie tapped into P.A. system, announced that the Not-Ready-to-Lose-the-Ozone-Layer Players would be performing "Why We Shouldn't Be Known as CFC."

(Okay, so we could have worked more on the title but we got all caught up in being psyched about our name.)

Half of us dressed in aerosol-can costumes made by these awesome new theater people. The other half of us were trees, the rain forest. A small rain forest, okay, but still legit. Cans ran around spraying the air wildly (with water); trees withered and died; lone iceberg in the show melted; Erik ran across field with his pale skin painted red, simulating intense sunburn due to no ozone protection.

Brilliant. Artistic. Some people laughed at us, but that was okay. Thyme even showed up at the last minute to portray a green shrub; we could hardly tell it was her. At first I was mad at her for being hypocritical, but then forgot and was so psyched about our performance that I hugged her once we got off field. We walked around in our wilting costumes, waving at the crowd whenever they cheered or jeered us. At one point Corny put his arm around me as we posed for the school newspaper photographer, and he pulled me really, really close, to where it was actually sort of embarrassing, but at the same time I sort of liked getting a bear hug from a cornstalk.

We all went out to celebrate tonight; spent hours and hours sitting in booths discussing philosophies of life, music, etc. We were having fun, and then we all got into a serious conversation about having divorced parents and reasons never to get married and how marriage was an overrated, outdated concept.

Gone all day. Got home and there were 5 messages: 3 from the Tom, 2 from Grant. What's up with the Tom? Did he get drunk and decide to hit on me after all these years?

Talked with the Tom this morning.

Not going home for Christmas.

Not going home ever again.

Beth and Grant. Tom said they were making out Friday night.

Complete, utter betrayal.

To hear it from the Tom, worst of all. Grant not home when I called (of course) so I got the Tom first.

So. That's why Beth and Grant both wanted to stay in Colorado for college. To be close to each other. Grant never got over their fling during junior year and has been pining for Beth ever since. Probably only dating me to kill time until Beth broke up with Bryan. God. I've been such a fool. It was so obvious.

So it all makes sense on some level. But logic doesn't mean I can stop crying. Why didn't I see this coming?

Hate them both.

Must call Jane now and tell her I lost the bet. Beth hooked up with someone before Thanksgiving. GRANT!

Will this day never end? Worst day of my life and it won't end.

Here is what Grant said. I think. I was so mad and hurt that my hearing was going in and out, like bad radio reception.

They were drunk at the Homecoming party. And after they called me, they drank more, and they kept talking about me, and how much they *missed* me and how *great* I was. And then they were drinking more punch. And Beth was talking about how much she missed Bryan, and . . .

Oh, ick. I can't continue to write this down in MY

journal. It's so . . . I don't know. Humiliating? Tawdry?

Mary Jo keeps asking if I'm all right. We ran out of tissues about two hours ago and my face is getting raw from using cheap dorm TP to cry into. No, I'm not all right, isn't it obvious?

She went out and came back with a pack of Twizzlers from the vending machine in the basement. "I'll call my brothers and ask them to beat up Grant. Okay?"

"No," I said. "Just leave me alone!"

Like licorice and farmers could help me now. I don't *think* so.

LATER . . .

Grant just called again to try to explain what happened. Mary Jo, Thyme, and Annemarie, who've been huddling around me for the past hour, all left to give me some privacy.

Okay, so. Grant and Beth were at Homecoming. I wasn't.

"Yes, I know I wasn't there, but if you even attempt to say that this is somehow my fault—"

"Courtney, I didn't say anything like that," Grant said. "I wanted you to be there, and you weren't, but I understand."

"Well I don't," I said. "I really can't listen to this." I hung up all of a sudden. Then I wished I hadn't, because I had to know the story and until I did, I was going to obsess endlessly. So I called him back and said "What?"

"Courtney, don't be so mad. Please, I can't stand hearing you so mad at me," Grant said. He started saying all these really sweet things and I started crying so then I had to hang up again. It's like I can only handle this 1 or 2 minutes at a time.

"So have you talked to Beth yet?" Grant asked the next time I called.

"No, and I don't plan on it," I said. "Why? Did you want to make sure your stories match up before you said anything to me?"

"There's no story!" Grant said. "Nothing happened, Courtney. Nothing serious. I mean, nothing at all. Not really."

How many times can you say "nothing" without having it become so incredibly obvious that it's SOMETHING?

"See, Beth and I—" he tried to say the next time.

188

"What? There's a you and Beth now?" Oh my God. I really needed some Pepcid AC if he was going to continue. A whole box of it. Maybe two.

"Courtney, come on. You *know* me. You know I'd never do anything—"

"Tom told me that you and Beth *made out* at a party, at Homecoming. You kissed her, you . . ." God. What had he done? Did I want to know? Wasn't it all over between us, anyway? If so, couldn't I hang up without hearing this?

So I did.

Grant called back. "Before you hang up, I just want to say that I'm not going to call you again tonight. But please, Court. You've got to forgive me! I . . . I'm so sorry, and it didn't mean anything to me. You're the one who matters, okay?"

I "matter?" What does that mean?

Hung up, opened door, let Thyme, Mary Jo, Annemarie back into room. I just want to wake up tomorrow and pretend today didn't happen.

11/13

6:15 A.M. Oh crap. Just woke up. It wasn't a dream.

8:00 P.M. Jane is here. She drove all the way from Madison and even skipped her classes today and is spending the night to help me deal with all this. (I called in sick to BF. Mark/Marc/Marque asked what was really wrong and I burst out crying, told him whole gory story.) Jane hasn't talked to Beth yet, but she said she doesn't believe anything serious really happened.

Over lunch, which I couldn't eat, I laid out the evidence. First you gather the evidence, then you prosecute. It was like being on *Law & Order*, except I was nowhere near as pretty as that woman lawyer with the dark brown hair, esp. with my growing-out crew cut. I had a feeling I needed her help on this case, but, oh well. I told Jane what I thought, and what I knew.

She nearly fell off her chair. "You know, maybe you're right," she said. "Not about any of that conspiracy theory stuff. But maybe they were still attracted to each other. Subliminally, you know."

"Jane!" I screamed. "Don't say that!" The woman is taking two psych classes and suddenly thinks she knows everything?

"But you said it," she reminded me. "And I think you're onto something. It doesn't mean that they actually *wanted* to betray you, but maybe they couldn't help themselves—"

I raised my eyebrow and glared at her. "Don't even start with that. They could have just, you know. Unlocked their lips and walked away." I dropped my head onto the table and started crying again.

"Courtney, it's going to be okay. You'll be fine. You're

190

strong. And look—maybe we don't know the whole story. I bet there's something we don't know."

"Like how I'm supposed to get on with my life?" I asked.

"I'll talk to Beth about it," Jane said. "Let's not rush to judgment."

"Oh, yeah, let's not do that. Just because my boyfriend and my best friend slept together . . . I wouldn't want to *judge* them or anything."

"They didn't sleep together!" Jane said. "It was a kiss, only a kiss. It was probably only a peck on the cheek. And we're getting our information from the Tom, remember? He exaggerates *everything*. I mean, some girl smiles at him, and he'll go around telling everyone they did it in the computer lab." She smiled uneasily. That's what happened to her when she first came to Bugling Elk.

She tried to get me to calm down by taking me on a drive through the country, past many many cows, and buying me a cute little basket of apples and a caramel apple and some honey. Then she insisted on going into cutesy gift shops and buying me cutesy barrettes to clip my hair with. Actually looks sort of stylish now. But who cares? Not Grant. Not me.

This morning after Jane left, I packed a duffel and went to the motel where the Greyhound bus stops. I have like $40 to my name and was prepared to spend it all. Turned out there were about 4 hours until the next bus. The lady behind the desk looked like she was about to phone the authorities because I looked completely unbalanced. But I waited. I don't know where I thought I was going. Something vague involving Phoenix, going to my dad's. Not that he'd be much help. I didn't know where to go. I just didn't want to be stuck at CFC and I didn't want to be back home.

So I sat in this really lame waiting area and after an hour, the lady behind the desk came out and started telling me about the Runaway Hotline, and gave me a brochure on suicide prevention, and I realized I really did have to stop sobbing in public. Very embarrassing. Also realized that I was turning into my dog, Oscar. Bolting at first sign of trouble.

I poured my heart out to this lady over a cup of instant decaf. I told her how I loved Grant and how Beth knew that, and how just because she was upset about not dating my brother anymore, she didn't have to choose Grant to get over Bryan with, okay so maybe they did have a thing before he and I got involved, but that was just physical attraction, and since when was that more important than love?

"I hate to tell you, honey," she said. "But a lot of times, it's *the* most important thing."

I asked for the suicide brochure back, and a refund on my ticket, and decided to walk back to campus.

The thing is that if I had a car, I'd be gone by now.

That's probably why Mom wouldn't let me have the Taurus, she knew something like this would happen. She's never believed in relationships working out. Why didn't I listen to her? Never gave her credit for being brilliant.

Why didn't I listen to myself? I was not supposed to get involved with anyone. I *swore* I wouldn't. But no, Grant had to force himself into my life, even though I made it totally clear I was not interested in seeing anyone. Such a *Grant* thing to do. Pushy, insistent, rude.

My favorite person in the entire world.

Formerly known as Superior.

Now known as Inferior.

Yes, so, okay, things can get worse. Not much I guess, but still.

I went to work this afternoon, but only so I could try and sneak in some phone calls to Mom, Alison, and Jane. Had only gotten to Alison (who was being really sweet and supportive) when Dean S. materialized beside my cubicle. He was actually carrying one of those paddleball things and whacking the rubber ball on a string all over the place.

I hung up the phone and tried to smile at him. "Hi, Dean Sobranksy."

"Courtney," he said, the red ball flailing wildly close to my head. "Your event on Saturday was really out there."

At first I didn't even know what he was talking about. I had completely forgotten about the fact I had even done something *fun* on Saturday, before I found out that what's-his-name and what's-her-name had ruined my life.

Dean S. started on this extremely-polite-yet-still-a-rant about how he certainly appreciated the creative process more than anyone, and that perhaps I didn't know that he was the Dean of Arts & Sciences at the college where he used to work, before this position became open, but couldn't I see that my friends and I were ruining what was a really fine year for Cornwall Falls in terms of academic and athletic achievements and—

The whole time he was talking, I was getting more and more choked up, because the last thing I needed was him yelling at me on top of everything else.

"I'm sorry!" I finally burst out. "But I'm not responsible for anything that happened last weekend!" Tears started streaming down my face. So embarrassing.

"But, uh, Courtney, you were there," Dean S. said. "You were dressed like a can of deodorant." Stopped playing with the stupid paddleball and started trying to edge away from my desk.

"I'm not talking about a protest, who cares about a dumb meaningless protest," I wailed, or something to that effect.

"Oh? Are you giving it up, then?" Dean S. started to get excited.

I shook my head as I mopped my eyes with Kleenex.

"But you might cut back. Is that what you're saying?" Dean S. asked hopefully.

"Can't you see that I'm upset?" I asked.

He didn't say anything for a minute. Then he asked if I heard about the weather front coming in—it might be very windy, so I should take care to bring an extra coat, did I have something that kept out the wind but also kept in the warmth, did I own any Gore-tex etc., etc., blah blah blah.

The fact that he refused to ask me what was wrong made me *want* to tell him more. The next thing I knew I was pouring out my heart to him, describing whole heinous scene of Grant cheating with Beth, Beth cheating with Grant, everyone cheating on Courtney.

Dean S. looked like he couldn't get out of there fast enough. So much for sympathy to student affairs. He didn't say one word in sympathy, or get me a new tissue when I soaked the last one on my desk.

But then he silently picked up all my assigned index cards for the day and distributed them to other people, and he said I could go home and asked if I wanted someone to go with me. Very nice offer, but I said no. Then, as I was leaving, I saw Wittenauer watching me. Gave him a pathetic little wave and ran out. Too embarrassing, because I would have told him everything, too, and don't enough people know already?

In retrospect: would I have wanted to hear Dean S.'s opinion? Probably not. He'd say something about how I was too "mat-oor" to be getting upset over a boy. I wish. Why must I always be getting so distraught over them, though? First Dave, now Grant. They end up stealing days, weeks of my life, because I become unable to do anything but mope and cry. Not worth it.

11/16

Dear Courtney,

I know you'll want to delete this as soon as you see who it's from. I don't know how I can make it up to you. I should never have kissed Grant, I should never have spent any time with him that night, I was too on the edge because of me and Bryan breaking up. So I made a huge mistake. And now I've ruined the best friendship I've ever had. It wasn't planned, and it's not anything that would ever happen again. We kissed, and that's it. Grant pushed me away and said, "This is wrong!" He's a great guy, he loves you so much. And I wish I'd never gone to that party. Love, Beth

Have to take down all the photos on my bulletin board. Especially the ones with Beth and Grant in the same shot. Have to take those outside and burn them in the approved smoking area.

LATER...

Not going to classes. Sitting in lounge watching *Montel*. Today's topic is "Teen Girls Who Remind Me a Lot of Beth." They're all backstabbing sluts who ruined other people's lives, like for instance sleeping with best friend's boyfriend.

Maybe I should write to Montel, see if I can get on the show. Not that I've ever enjoyed having my dramas played out in public. I mean, I got plenty of that in high school.

Which reminds me. Does everyone at Bugling Elk know about the Grant and Beth fling? Of course they do. The Tom does not know the word "secret" or "discretion."

Here is us on *Montel*, here are our running blurbs:

"Courtney: Won't forgive her ex-best friend even if she begs."

"Beth: Begging for forgiveness."

"Courtney: Still saying no."

Then Grant would come out after listening backstage and the audience would boo him. And he'd look shocked because he hasn't been booed in his entire life. (Except for when he was short and skinny when young and got picked on, but that's jeering, not booing. Anyway this is a fantasy, so who cares.)

Grant would probably wear the shirt I gave him for his birthday. He's *that cruel*.

Montel would hold my hand while I sobbed and spat out the details. One problem with this: I don't know the details. And I can't know them. Ever.

Ben and Marque—no, wait. New name tag today. Now
Marcus. Jennifer is furious because he's using up all
the label-maker tape. Maybe I'll change my name, too.
What variations are there on Courtney? Court . . . not?
Cortland—like the apple?

Anyway, Ben and Marcus insisted we go straight to a
party from work, as I was being far too much of a downer.
Marcus doing everything possible to make me laugh. Kept
grabbing customer comment cards and writing comments
about the customers on them, like: "Your shirt and those
pants? I don't think so."

"You know what would really cheer you up? A malt,"
Marcus said.

"It's like ten degrees out," I said.

"Yeah. Like that matters. I'll be right back."

"If you think about the temperature here, you'd never
go out and do anything," Ben told me while he was gone.
"Don't worry, you'll adjust."

Can I just say that I'm really tired of trying to adapt
and adjust?

Marcus came flying through doors five minutes later
with 3 giant cups from Koffee Kitchen, one for each of us.
"Oh, wait—you're not supposed to have milk, are you?" he
said as he handed mine over.

"Give me a straw," I said. "Now."

"Ooh, she's living on the edge," Ben said. "I've heard
of drowning your sorrows before, but did they mean in
frozen custard?"

"Technically, for her, this is worse than getting drunk,
because she's cheating on her diet."

"It's not a diet!" I said, laughing. "I just don't eat

dairy." I looked down at towering whipped cream sculpture atop chocolate shake. "That, um, often."

"Uh oh. Brain freeze," Marcus said when he finished his in record time.

"I've had a brain freeze for the past two weeks," Ben said. "I got a seventy-two on my last econ test because I forgot to study an entire section of my notes. Now my average is an eighty-eight, and I have to pull it back up to an A."

"I don't think I'm getting any A's," Marcus said.

We were talking about our classes so intensely that we didn't even notice some customers had come in and were waiting for service until one of them rang the bagel-shaped bell on the counter. Nearly gave me a heart attack.

After we closed up, I went home, where I received the second biggest shock of my life. 2nd only to Grant/Beth Shocker.

Joe is back. In Mary Jo's life. In my life. In our *room*. Help me.

"So, you and that guy broke up?" he asked. "How come?"

Mary Jo hit him on the arm. "It's personal."

"Oh. He dumped you, huh?" He got this stupid smile on his face. "That blows."

"Gee, that means a lot to me, Joe," I said. "And he didn't break up with me."

"He could have at least waited until Christmas break and done it in person," Joe said to Mary Jo, like they were having a conversation and I wasn't in the room.

Am going to kill Mary Jo tomorrow.

Went to work this morning. Afterward, came to library, like other unattached people do on Saturdays, especially when they don't want to be in their rooms. Supposed to be studying for sociology exam now. Students of the World, Unite!

Here are the key terms: Capitalism. Historical (Hysterical) materialism. Bourgeoisie. Exploitation. Alienation. Proletariat. Etc., etc., blah blah blah, *revolt*.

Forget Marx. There is a little-known piece of literature, soon to become famous, known as . . .

The Courtney Manifesto

1. A specter is haunting Wisconsin. Her name is Beth. Or maybe his name is Grant. It's hard to actually see a specter.

2. I must figure out how to react as a reactionary. What does that mean, anyway?

3. I must free myself by stopping harmful, low-self-esteem thoughts from entering brain.

4. There is strength in numbers, so . . . bring 5 fingers together to make a fist.

5. Use fist to punch specter(s) in the nose, mouth, anywhere painful.

6. Don't forgive specters. Never listen to anything they say again.

7. Become dedicated to the cause. Any cause, so long as it does not involve people in Colorado.

8. Think only lofty thoughts regarding future of society, not future of my pathetic little life.

Manifesto is impossible to live up to. I can't stop obsessing about what was happening 1 week ago today. Tonight. I keep picturing Grant and Beth. I don't care if it only lasted 5 seconds, like they said. 5 seconds is too long.

Everything is so impossible to deal with, especially long distance. Oh God. Dave, such a Dave . . . I totally underestimated him. He was right. This is why he broke up with me last year. This is why LDRs don't work, whether they're half an hour away, half a country away. I can see it all so clearly now. That weekend I went home? It had already started. That's why Grant and I had such a hard weekend. He was probably only hanging out with his grandmother because he didn't want to tell me he'd rather be with Beth. Grandmother Superior was faking her illness, in on the plot. All a giant conspiracy. It started back when we applied to colleges. The reason Beth & Grant didn't protest my going so far away was because they already KNEW they wanted to hook up. It was all a conspiracy to get me out of state of Colorado.

First Beth was going out with my brother. Then she's going out with my boyfriend? What kind of a best friend is she? Regret telling her anything.

So maybe Thyme can be annoying as hell sometimes. But at least she's a moral person. And at least she's *there* for me.

Just went to library pay phone to call Thyme. She said she didn't have time to talk to me because she and Kirsten

202

were going shopping at outlet mall. She also said that it was time for me to get over what happened and get on with my life.

What? Shopping with Kirsten? Has she lost her mind?

It's a sad day when Joe is actually looking like a better guy than Grant. Joe went to the cafeteria for brunch and brought back donuts and fresh fruit for me. Totally not like him. He's trying to win me over or something—maybe he realizes I'm not on his side and never have been, and suddenly it matters to him that I like him?

Or no. Probably just overestimated how much food he wanted and had leftovers.

Anyway, Grant called again this morning. We talked but it was completely awkward. He kept asking what I was doing for Thanksgiving, and if I was still meeting my family in Nebraska. I said no. I said I had to stay here and work, which isn't true, but I didn't want to tell him what I'm really doing—staying in the dorm with foreign students and other jilted students like self. Kept it vague.

It's snowing now. Hall is going sledding. Annemarie is threatening to drag me out the door in my pajamas, so I'd better get dressed.

LATER . . .

Got home and there was a message from Erik: "Courtney, where are you? We're ready to organize Phase Two but we need your help." Forgot all about Badicals meeting.

All for now. Hands are frostbitten and it hurts to write.

Life going downhill fast. I just looked up "finagle" in dictionary. It means "to obtain by trickery; swindle."

Stupid corporate office thinks it means some sort of hilarious caper or something. All those cute things about finagling. So stupid! How dumb of them to not even know they're blatantly advertising the fact that they *rip people off*.

There's this "regular" who comes in on Mondays. He always tries to flirt with me a little, and I always ignore it. But today—I just couldn't take it when he said, "Those new cranberry bagels look as sweet and delicious as you, Courtney." Stupid Thanksgiving theme. I mean is that rude and over-the-top or what???

"Actually they're really quite sour," I said. Like my mood. "Cranberries. They're like lemons."

That didn't even faze him. "You mean it makes your lips pucker? Now that I'd like to see."

Har har har.

So I made his bagel haphazardly (he orders *double* cream cheese so I gave him like a half ounce of cranberry walnut and that was *it*), didn't cut it in half neatly, didn't even clean the old chive cream cheese off the knife first, and didn't offer him a steal deal. He got his revenge by grabbing a customer comment card and covering it with comments while he ate his bagel, which couldn't have been so terrible, because he *did* finish it, and all he had to do was *ask* for more cream cheese on the side if he was so unhappy.

These customer comment cards are *so* stupid, and I'm not just saying that because I got all bad comments from this guy. "How was your visit?" Like it's a national *park* or something.

He kept glancing over at me while he was writing, like maybe he was sketching my portrait: *Still Life with Bagel Slicer*. Then he got up to leave and stuffed the comment card in the box. "Have a nice day, Courtney," he said. How *rude*.

I knew I had to get that card out right away. I ran around the counter and tried to pry it out, using the hot-bagel tongs. It took me a minute, tops. I really should have just put it in my pocket. But I had to see what the guy wrote.

Turned out that he filled both sides of the card with his insane ravings about poor customer service, plus he spelled my name wrong, plus he spelled "inconsiderate" wrong, plus I think he meant to say "snobby" instead of "snotty," plus his handwriting is really bad. I had just torn the card in half when Jennifer appeared. She grabbed both halves, read them, then asked me to come to her office, where she told me I was on BF "probation." "And what does that mean?" I asked.

"One more strike and you're out," she said.

"But that would only be a total of two strikes," I pointed out.

"Courtney, do you *really* want to have this conversation?" she asked.

Um, no.

"You know I value all your hard work. You know I trust you," she said. "But if you're going to be rude to the customers just because you don't like cranberries—"

"I love cranberries," I said. It's people I can't stand. Do I even want to keep working at a place that uses "probation"?

"All we have to do is write a bunch of really positive

207

customer cards for you," Marcus said afterward. "To offset the negative press."

"Jennifer will never go for that," Ben said. "You just have to sort of fade into the background for a while. Thanksgiving break is coming, the place is closed because no one will be around, so she'll forget all about it."

"And think of it this way. You're on probation, so you should wear these!" Marcus reached for the handcuffs dangling down over the cash register. "You're going to look *so* tough and dangerous. You'll get a new boyfriend in, like, days."

"I don't want a new boyfriend," I said.

"Oh." Mark and Ben looked at each other.

"I mean, I'm still with Grant. Sort of," I said.

"Oh?" They nodded. "Well, okay."

"What?" I asked.

"Nothing."

"Nothing."

I hate how everyone keeps saying that. I also hate the idea of being on my "best behavior" from now on. What if my standard is too low?

Went bowling with Wittenauer and the two Joes tonight. "The miracle isn't that we're bowling," he said. "The miracle is that you've lived in Wisconsin for three months and you *haven't* been bowling."

Wittenauer thinks he's so much better than me because he is a) a junior, and b) a decent bowler.

Anyway, I was really surprised when he came by my dorm room. Unheard of. I assumed he wanted to discuss our next meeting/protest, since I'd blown off the last one. I thought it was cool he came over, but at the same time I felt so weird about going out with him alone. Doesn't he know I travel in a pack? "Let's ask Thyme!" I said, and knocked on her door before Wittenauer could protest.

"*Bowling?* God, no," she said. "Anyway, I'm packing." Acting like a real snob all of a sudden.

Then I heard Mary Jo getting home so I ran back across the hall and mentioned it to her. Unfortunately Joe was in the room at the time, so it ended up: me, Mary Jo, Joe, Wittenauer heading off to Badger Lanes. All together now: why is Joe still in Mary Jo's life??? Topic for a much longer entry.

Badger Lanes: very smoky place with many neon beer signs and seriously overworn shoes. They were having a Turkey Special: for every game you bowled, you got one free (a game, not a turkey). So we played enough games to give me carpal thumb syndrome.

A very distressing thing happened when we were getting to our lane. We were sitting down to put on shoes and were entering goofy names on computer score thing, when somehow my Grant story came up. Okay, it was my fault. I mentioned that the last time I went bowling was after graduation with, uh, my, uh, boy, uh. Anyway.

"Dean Sobransky told me you and your boyfriend broke up," Wittenauer said as we were lacing up. "Sorry about that."

"Oh well." Felt my face get red. Then more red. Was probably blending in with hair color. "We didn't exactly break up."

"Did too," Joe said. "She doesn't even talk to him and she took down all his pictures and—"

"*Joe*," Mary Jo said sternly. "It's none of our business."

Yes, I agree.

Mary Jo kindly changed the subject to a discussion of her best game ever, how she and her brothers had their own team, how they taught her everything she knows, etc. Cast her a very grateful look as I shuffled up to select a giant pink ball.

Then Joe got all competitive with Wittenauer and they were arguing about rules. Mary Jo and I were sitting there awkwardly; felt like it was a double date that had gone terribly awry; but it was not a double date, it was just a very bad combination of people.

Also, Mary Jo can make even bowling shoes look cute. How can she get away with this? Tiny little 6 on the back of her shoes. Me? 9. Isn't there another way to keep track of shoes besides displaying the size? Not necessary on any *other* kind of shoe.

As I was bowling, I started to get a weird feeling (in addition to my sprained thumb). Started asking myself why Wittenauer wanted to take me out bowling. Has nothing to do with, like, anything we usually do. He asked what I was doing for Thanksgiving and I said nothing. I said I planned to just sort of hibernate in the dorm and

I was looking forward to time alone in my room without anyone else around. Unfortunately I was saying that when Mary Jo came back from picking up a spare. She wouldn't sit next to me at the scoring table and insisted on sitting on Joe's lap instead. She knows exactly what will get to me and does it anyway. She is even bringing Joe to her house for Thanksgiving, not realizing that he doesn't deserve it, and that he will be beaten to a pulp by her brothers. Or maybe they're too nice for that.

Anyway, afterward, it was really, really cold out, but Wittenauer and I stood outside the dorm and talked anyway. Then I was about to go in when Wittenauer sort of jogged after me and tugged on my jacket sleeve and asked if I wanted to go out again sometime. To do something other than in an organized group, or at work. "It would be like a very small, exclusive group," he said cutely. "No roommate, no Joe. Two of us."

"I can't. I mean, I'm, uh, still seeing Grant, you know," I said.

"Oh," he said. "I didn't know. I thought . . . Sorry."

"It's okay. I mean, I'm sorry," I said. Totally awkward.

"Hey, no big deal. I just thought . . . So, okay, well, good night."

Parted on really uncomfortable terms. I'm glad we won't be seeing each other for a few days.

2 P.M. Mary Jo just left. Joe went with her. Everyone gone. Dorm deserted. Krystyne just came by, doing her "clear-out" check, told me I was supposed to be gone. This dorm isn't heated during break, so I have to move into another one. What?

A person pays a price for solitude.

Maybe this wasn't such a good idea.

Is it too late to hitch to Nebraska to meet family like original plan? Maybe I'll call that motel/bus station, check schedules.

2:35 P.M. "Well, hello, *you*," woman at motel/bus station desk said. "How are things going, honey? I'm so glad you called to catch up."

"Actually I was hoping to get to Ogallala, Nebraska," I said.

She checked everything on the computer, and then came back and said she had some bad news and hoped it wouldn't plunge me into another dark depression. I had missed today's last bus. No bus tomorrow due to Thanksgiving. I could leave Friday, but wouldn't get there until Saturday. Etc.

"Sorry, sweetie. Why don't you come to my house for Thanksgiving?" She invited me for like ten minutes straight, I said no for nine minutes straight, and then finally the conversation was over. She made me write down her address just in case. I will now put it on now-vacant bulletin board. You never know when you might need a friend. With, um, bus schedules at the ready.

9 P.M. You won't believe where I am right now. Sitting in a farmhouse bed under a giant down comforter, cup of hot herbal tea on bedside table. Heaven.

Mary Jo came back for me!!! She and Joe and parents got halfway to her house, and then she made everyone turn around and come back for me. There wasn't going to be enough room in the crew cab pickup, so they dropped off Joe at a convenience store sort of near his parents' house and came back for *me*. She marched upstairs and said, "Look, Courtney, I don't even know why I'm asking you this, because you've done everything in the world *not* to be my friend. But would you please come home with me for Thanksgiving? Because I don't want to leave you here alone, I'm worried about you, and I think it would do you a lot of good to just get out of town for a few days."

It was quite the speech, and I was very touched. She chose *me* over Joe? I quickly packed a bag, grabbed my backpack full of homework, ran downstairs to the idling car. Mr. and Mrs. Johannsen are shy but so sweet. At their house, they have a sign out front with their names and all the boys' names on it. Can't tell all the brothers apart yet (except for my pal Ed). Too many twins spoil the pot. Also, one of them hasn't spoken yet and I can't remember his name. Very strange, because Mary Jo doesn't look anything like her brothers. They are very tall and strong and sort of thick-looking.

Mary Jo gave me a tour of the farm and told me about all the different kinds of cows you can have. Her family has Brown Swiss ones. They have really pretty coats, actually beautiful—color like elk antler velvet, sort of.

"I just can't thank you enough for taking me in," I said

to the family as we were gathered in front of a giant ham carcass. Words did not fit picture.

"God, Courtney. You make it sound like you're an orphaned pioneer or something," Mary Jo teased me. Hearty laughter from six boys almost put out the two tall pumpkin-scented candles on the table. "This isn't *Little House on the Prairie*."

"It isn't?" I asked. Then I started to laugh uncontrollably, too.

Orphaned Pioneer. That's how I felt, okay?

11/23 BEST THANKSGIVING EVER

Is it because for once in the past 5 years I'm not in charge of "all the breads" and don't have Grandpa hovering constantly at my elbow with a carving knife and a 25-pound turkey on a platter?

First off, this family does not even take off Turkey Day. I have never seen 8 people work so hard in my life. They are like this well-trained army of specialists. Milk division. They could start a dairy college and call it Milk U. Except that sounds vaguely obscene.

But what was so great was that they didn't *care* if I ate the turkey or not. I mean, they kept offering, like 10 times, and I kept saying, "No thank you," and that was just fine with them. Got the feeling they just enjoyed offering things again and again—ritualistic behavior that was part of the meal whether you ate turkey or not.

The mashed potatoes were completely lumpy and dreamy. They had a glass dish they called the relish tray, which wasn't filled with relish but with pickles and olives. When I ate everything on it, it miraculously got refilled, though I never saw it happen. Mrs. Johannsen made a green bean/onion-thingy casserole; MJ made fresh rolls; together they made 3 pies, all while I was still asleep. Only strange thing was the trademark red wobbly Jell-O sculpture, which I remembered from the day we met.

I love Mary Jo's family. They let me sleep until 10, they let me disappear into my room for hours whenever I want to, and don't get upset by it. Love it here.

Wonder how Grant is spending Thanksgiving. Wonder if he's having a good time. Probably watching endless football games with his dad. Probably not even missing me. He's home in Denver, and so is Beth. Best not to think about this, but to concentrate on positives in life. Like the fact there is leftover pie.

Just had the most incredible conversation with Mary Jo over breakfast!!! French toast. Yum. Forgot it was made with eggs and milk until 2 slices down the hatch. We were drinking the entire percolator of coffee, and conversation was flying. Mary Jo explained why she was back with Joe, even though she had ditched him for me for Thanksgiving; they'd already talked on the phone a couple of times. Which reminds me, I need to call Mom and tell her where I am so she doesn't worry. Anyway, Mary Jo was defending Joe.

"He's not that bad," she said. "He was really stressed about passing bio, and he still is. So he took it out on me. He apologized. Look, *we're* not the same, Courtney. So we're not going to like the same kind of *guy*."

Big relief. Because I thought she did like the same kind of guy—no—the same GUY, Grant.

So she told me how Joe never stopped saying nice stuff about her body now, and how stupid her extreme diet was, and how since she'd gone off it, she's been not even caring about weight anymore, which is the only way to be, I think. Of course I'm lucky in that, and probably shouldn't even talk about it, I said, because everyone in my family's sort of skinny. So then Mary Jo said, "My birth mother is really thin, you know. So I've got genetics on my side, too."

"Wait—your birth mother?" She has a birth mother? I mean, so do I, but—this was different.

"I told you I was adopted," she said. "Remember?"

She did? Gulp. Totally slipped my mind. I did remember her saying in our housing workshop that I never listened. This was really bad. "Oh, sure. And um . . . what about your brothers?"

"They're not. See, my mom really desperately wanted a girl, but she couldn't have any more kids after she had my youngest brother. So they adopted me."

"Right." I nodded. Had she told me that? And if so, when? "So um, do you know your birth mother? Or is this from pictures you've seen, or like . . ." LIKE WHAT, COURTNEY? I felt so clumsy and awkward with my lame questions, like I was drowning in quicksand and swallowing it at the same time. I suck. Haven't I listened to a word she's said? Well, no, not really. I've been sharing a room with her for almost 3 months and I don't know she's adopted? I *really* suck.

"Of course I know her," Mary Jo said. "She works at the town post office. We'll go down after lunch and I'll introduce you."

"That is so cool," I said. "I can't wait to meet her. I already love your whole family, you know, so I'm sure I'll like her." Pouring it on a bit thick, like the real maple syrup I was drowning my French toast in, because of a) sugar overdose, and b) guilt.

Snowing. Blizzarding. Trip to post office was called off. Everyone sitting around eating cold turkey leftovers. Mary Jo mentioned we could snowshoe to P.O., but then we realized her bio mom probably wouldn't be there by the time we got there. Ed said he could hook up horse and sleigh, which sounded awesome to me, but MJ said it was snowing too hard and we'd get stranded.

Instead sat around inside, first doing homework by the fireplace (a/k/a "napping"), and then watching TV. Very weird experience to watch *Sally Jesse* with 6 men looking over your shoulder. But I couldn't look away. The topic was Betrayal. The topic was Courtney's Life.

They were talking to girls whose former best friends had ruined their lives, while the "friends" waited in a secluded area. All of the guests reminded me of myself: and why is this topic on talk shows every time I watch them? Is it that common? And if so, what is the point of trying to find a new best friend?

The guest who was me kept describing everything that had happened to me. Little taglines floated at the bottom of the screen saying things like

Hates her best friend for stealing her boyfriend.
Says her best friend betrayed her and she'll never trust her again.
Says she doesn't want to be friends anymore.
Won't accept former friend's apology.
Can't stop reliving pain of phone call from the Tom.
Is sitting in a farmhouse for Thanksgiving because she can't face her family.

Once I started down this path, I had to run out of the

room because I was crying. Ed and Mary Jo came after me and took me out to the barn and showed me how to milk a cow. Found myself thinking that cows are cute, if large. Felt like a hypocrite as I enjoyed entire, bizarre process. Except that I really only brought one pair of boots, so they're outside in the snow now because they got too smelly.

Met Mary Jo's bio mom today. Her name's Patty, and she gave Mary Jo a big hug and told her how beautiful she was. They seemed really close and I thought it was amazing, considering the circumstances. I noticed she had tiny feet like Mary Jo and same hair also.

"Well, she *was* thin," Mary Jo said as we left the post office, which was actually a sort of desk thing inside the Stop 'n' Go. "Ever since she gave up her walking route and started sitting behind the desk, she's gained weight." Mary Jo let out a long sigh that was a white puff in the sub-zero air. It reminded me of when Beth used to smoke when we walked to school in the winter.

"Mary Jo?" I said. "No offense, but you have to stop looking at everything and everyone based on pounds. Okay? Because you look fine, you're doing great at school, and nobody really cares. Okay?"

She explained how she never thought about it at all, really—not until she came to CF. She grew up with all those brothers, and everyone always told her she was pretty, and she never really compared herself to her high-school friends. Then she got to CF and felt totally overwhelmed, and she was living with me, the health nut. And Joe told her she was too big, and it just pushed all the wrong buttons. I always forget that other people have buttons, too.

"So I'll try to change," she said. "I'm sure it's really annoying, listening to me obsess about it."

"No, it's not that," I said. "It's just . . . I hate worrying about how I look, and I hate when my friends worry about it even more. Because there's more to life. And anyway, you know what? Screw genetics," I said. "My mom likes everything I don't. And this hair color? It's like, where did that come from? Nobody else in my family is a redhead."

"Um . . . well, your cut's sort of starting to grow in nicely," Mary Jo said.

We went home and had lunch. Mary Jo showed me her wall of ribbons in the den, all for raising and showing sheep at fairs. Then she told me that when she was little and got lonely for not having a sister, she went out into the barn and slept next to a goat. "You're the first roommate I've had since Chipper," she said. Then she realized how dopey she sounded and we laughed so hard it was sort of embarrassing.

Mary Jo went to help with some chore, so I went inside and sat down next to Mr. Johannsen at the kitchen table. Brother who refuses to speak came in, nodded awkwardly at me, grabbed a sandwich and ran out of the kitchen.

I was trying to be polite, so I asked Mr. Johannsen about what it's like to have his own business and whether he knew about that bovine hormone.

He started telling me all about how factory farms are taking over; how thousands of family farms have closed or gone out of business in the last 30 years. He told me about how hard it is to make a living. (Man was just looking for an opening, apparently.) He told me about a famous historical milk strike, where farmers dumped out all their milk to protest the low prices, and how they were planning another one soon. Didn't have the heart to tell him that I've been on my own milk strike for years. I started feeling really guilty. Maybe people like me are the reason family farms are going under. I had him pour me 2 glasses of fresh whole milk and drank them right away.

Now Mr. Johannsen thinks I am a "great gal," and Ed is even more in love with me because I hit it off with his dad.

I, however, have stomach cramps.

Got back to campus tonight. I can't believe it. Grant was here while I was gone. He *drove* the whole way, hung out for 2 days waiting for me, and then left.

There are 7 increasingly despondent messages from Grant on the answering machine, and he left this very very sweet letter for me:

Dear Courtney,

I don't know where you are, and it's killing me. How can you not be here? I risked speeding tickets, I risked getting stuck in snow drifts, and I risked sleeping in the hallway of this dorm of yours that apparently has no heat.

[Good thing Grant keeps that sleeping bag in the car, the one with a tiger print on the inside that I'm always making fun of because he's had it since 4th grade? Or *6th* grade, as he claims.]

This campus is deserted and the whole town is sort of shut down. I looked for you at Bagle Finagle, but it was closed. Ended up having a turkey dinner at some place called Brat Wurstenburger, which I think you told me about once. The very nice people there all thought I was left on campus by myself for Thanksgiving and insisted on buying me dinner.

This campus (not including unheated Rankin Hall), despite 3-foot-high snowbanks, is pretty nice, actually—small, but old, nice brick buildings, lots of history, lots of trees. But with you not being here the place seems like a dump. Where are you? I finally tracked down your mom and Bryan in Nebraska. She said you went to a friend's at the last minute, but she couldn't remember which friend's. I didn't know if that was true, or if she was just mad at me, which is entirely possible. But you're obviously not here, and I've already filled up the memo board on your door, not to mention your answering machine tape, so . . .

So I'm left here sitting in the freezing cold hallway, with my Discman on, listening to the CD you made me, wondering: where are you? Why aren't you here? I missed you like crazy before. Now that I'm here, where you usually are—where you live and sleep every single day—I miss you even more. I've got 100 things to say to you. I want to make things right between us. I love you.

And I guess I have to leave today if I want to get back to CSU for classes Monday, which I *have* to do. I'm sorry. I'm sorry I missed you. It would have been great. Next time I'll call first, and next time you'd better be here. Please call me as soon as you're back so I know you're okay.

Love,
Grant

Read letter and collapsed on bed, woozy from emotion. Mrs. Johannsen ran to get me a cold washcloth from the bathroom, and Mary Jo fanned me with her bio textbook. "I'm okay!" I said. "Really." It's just that I forgot how great Grant could be. I'd been trying to forget. And remembering all of a sudden was a complete shock.

Mary Jo keeps pacing around the room, telling me I'm crazy if I don't call Grant this second, if I don't get back together with Grant immediately. Look at all he did, read that letter again, listen to all those sweet messages!

"Do you have any idea how much that means? What he did? Driving out here when he only has a four-day break, and I'll bet he had to take time off from work, and do you have any idea how much homework someone in his program would have over Thanksgiving break? And he risked it all to come see you, and then sat here in town and worried about you for two days straight and—"

"Okay, okay! I'll *call* him," I said. "Tomorrow."

Can't sleep. Very excited about the Grant letter. Very, very, very excited.

7:30 A.M. Just called Grant. Woke him and roommate Matt up. Told him how sorry I was that I left town without telling him where I was, told him about my trip with Mary Jo and what a good time I had. Told him I loved his letter. He sounded groggy but happy. Still tired from the drive.

All I kept telling myself while he talked was "Grant doesn't know how to lie." So he must be telling the truth when he says nothing really happened that night except a really dumb kiss. But no matter how many times he says it, I still have my doubts. And it's like, how am I supposed to trust them when they are living within an hour of each other, and I'm on the other side of Nebraska, and then some? But then Grant drove out here. So that means something. Maybe it means that he is extremely guilty. But no. Just looked at letter again. Seems to be an act of love.

Oh crap. Have to run—late for work now, and I'm still on probation.

10:45 P.M. When I got to work, Jennifer was standing by the door waiting for me. "Remember what I said? One more strike and you're out?"

"So how was your Thanksgiving?" I asked as I took off my coat, scarf, hat.

"Oh, uh, fine," she said.

Totally threw her off by being exceedingly polite. Trying to act like Mary Jo and her mom. I gave her a big smile, hugged Marcus, hugged Ben, put on my apron and immediately got to work.

"Three strikes?" Marcus said under his breath as we restocked cheese bins. "What does she think this is? Jail?"

"Isn't it?" I said, laughing.

"No, this is one of those hospitals for the criminally insane," Ben said.

Then funniest thing to date happened. Thyme came in. But I didn't even know it was her. She was waiting in line with her sister, both wearing lots of makeup, leather coats, skirts, leather boots, leather everywhere. But I honestly didn't recognize her until Ben said, "So Thyme. How was Chicago—uh, I mean Sheboygan?"

"Hello, Benjamin," she said. "Hello, Courtney. Mark." No emotion registering on her face. She had lipstick on. She had a purse dangling from gold chain with a cell phone hanging off it. Disgusting.

"Thyme?" I said. "Oh my God, how are you?"

More like: oh my God, WHO are you?

"Morgan, are you getting anything to drink besides a triple cap?" Her sister was down by the cash register, flashing a fresh 20, or maybe it was a 50. Tricia was making coffee drinks and chatting about the latest weather front with her.

"Would you grab an OJ for me, Thornton?" Thyme replied.

I was standing there thinking: Morgan? Thornton? What the hell? Thyme's ordering coffee drinks and a bagel with cinnamon cream cheese? I was unable to even speak.

"Did you guys hit the Anne Klein outlet yesterday?" Marcus asked as he prepared her bagel. "Or wait, maybe you have more of an Ann Taylor look going. Well, some Ann anyway."

"I was thinking Donna," Ben said as he looked at Thyme with this expression of complete disbelief.

"DKNY?" I said.

"More like DKWI," Ben said. I was starting to laugh.

"Or how about DWI," Marcus said. "Dressing while impaired."

Thyme narrowed her eyes at us. "Nice aprons."

Ooh! Cruel!

"*Morgan*. Your triple cap is getting cold," her sister said from a table by the window.

"Coming, Thornton! Talk to you guys later!" Thyme called over her shoulder.

Marcus, Ben, and I left standing there, stunned. Even Tricia came over and joined us.

"I *told* you she was a complete phony," Ben muttered.

"Does this mean she's going to shave now?" Tricia asked. "Because I really wish she would."

Then Jennifer came out, caught us all "clumping," and reminded us of company policy: only the batter is allowed to clump at Bagle Finagle!

I've got like 17 strikes now, but she is still allowing me to play.

Oh joy.

I heard Thyme saying good-bye to her sister this morning, so I immediately went across the hall to get the scoop. "So Thornton's gone, now. You can go back to being yourself," I said.

No response.

"Did your parents make you act like the way they wanted you to?" I went on. "Because I know how hard that can be."

Thyme just shrugged and gave me a bright smile. "This is me, Courtney. I don't know what you're trying to say."

I just stared at her long enough so that she did. "You used to lecture me about not staying true to 'the cause,'" I said. "You got mad at me for serving cream cheese."

"I was confused," Thyme said. "Anyway, I don't know who you're trying to be, but I'm embracing my roots. Did you see my new Honda yet?" Okay, that's not *exactly* what she said, but that was the gist of it. Apparently she had a breakthrough with her parents and has now decided to accept who she is, blah blah blah. I think it's more a case of: parents threatening to cut her off unless she toed their line. It's very disgusting. Instead of Zen Buddhist quotes, she now sounds like she's spouting lines from mugs with smiley faces. What happened to former best friend here? It's like she joined a cult. The cult of Economic Inevitability. I *knew* her family donated that econ building and that they never lost her money. Or else why did she never have to work, was able to spend so freely, etc.? Can't wait to discuss this with Annemarie, but she took an extra week of break to check out LA club scene. She picked a good week to be gone. My classes are impossible all of a sudden. Professors just realized that semester ends in 3 weeks and have shifted into some higher gear without warning. Papers due left and right, must read an entire book tonight.

Should have worked ahead like Mary Jo on Thanksgiving break. But was too busy watching TV with Ed, Eric, Dan, Peter, Jim . . . crap, still can't remember 6th name. Man Who Does Not Speak. Either Karsten or Horst or Soren or . . . Kierkegaard.

Saw Wittenauer tonight for the first time since bowling trip. Very awkward at first. He pulled me aside and said he couldn't stop thinking about one thing during break, it almost ruined his entire vacation back home in Iowa. I thought from the way he was looking at me, and the way he'd asked me out and I'd turned him down, he meant *me*. That he couldn't stop thinking about *me*. Got very uncomfortable and pretended that an alum was calling me back, grabbed the phone, etc.

But then he said, "I couldn't stop thinking about how I need to tell Dean Sobransky the truth. About how I need to out myself."

Nearly dropped my stack of index cards. Wittenauer is gay? I was thinking. I rejected him and now he is rejecting the female species? Or maybe he was *never* asking me out, and stupid me assumed, which was a very dumb assumption. "Well, yeah, there comes a time in a person's life, you know. Like my sister, Alison, she didn't come out of the closet until last year—"

Wittenauer rolled his eyes. "I was talking about coming out of the *costume*. I feel really guilty for hiding behind Corny. I feel like I'm being dishonest to Dean Sobransky, who deep down is a pretty good guy, by not telling him I'm behind the whole school change concept, plus I'm letting you take the flak, which isn't fair to *you*—"

Was trying to talk him down from the ledge, tell him not to stress so much, when Dean S. came into the offices. First he invited us all to an end-of-semester party at his house next Sunday night, the 10th, to thank us for all our hard work. Then he encouraged us all to make an extra push because people get more generous during the holiday season.

"Why don't you have us stand downtown in Santa suits, accepting quarters in a can?" I asked.

"Courtney, please," Dean S. said. "Do try to take this a little more seriously. Our future is at stake here. Alumni giving is down thirty-nine percent from last year." He pointed to the giant ear of corn on the wall that measures our fund drive. "The kernels should go up to here," he said, illustrating by pointing with a pool cue he was mysteriously carrying around. "They're way down here. What we have here is an undergrown ear of corn."

"Maybe it was genetically engineered," I suggested.

Everyone laughed—except Dean S. "This is a very serious matter. We need to up our endowment. Tell the alumni you reach that our endowment is slipping," Dean S. said.

"You want me to say that we're not well endowed?" Rachel asked. "You're kidding, right?" He wasn't.

Then he cornered me and said he hoped I had a nice Thanksgiving. And wasn't it nice that the seasons had changed, and football was over, and so that meant of course that my little protest group had ended for the season as well?

"But there's basketball teams, right? And hockey is really big here," I said. "Isn't it? Men's and women's teams? And then there's swimming—"

"Courtney! We're not changing the name of the college!" Dean S. cried, banging the pool cue against a file cabinet.

The whole time, Wittenauer staring at us, biting his

nails, racked by guilt, not helping.

"We don't want you to change the name of the college," I said.

Dean S. looked at me as if I had just kissed him and offered to bear his children. Ugh. "You don't? Oh, well, then what do you want?" Smiled at me and looked very greedy all of a sudden, sort of like the Grinch.

Suddenly I realized I had no idea. Have not been spending any time on this lately, and lost my train of thought. "We, uh, want, um, our voices to be heard," I said.

"That can be arranged. I suppose," Dean S. said.

"When?" I asked.

"Let me get back to you on that." Sounded very much like he did not mean that at all.

Later on, Wittenauer made me promise I will go to the Badicals meeting this Sunday and asked me to bring anyone I can round up—Annemarie of course, and even Thyme. Told him that Thyme had been transformed/morphed into Morgan, that she is wearing makeup over neck tattoo and getting French manicures and enrolling in business classes for next semester. I told him that when I asked her what's going on with her, how she can just turn her back on her entire personality, she said, "I realized I needed to be *in* the system to *fight* the system."

"How establishment is that? What *happened* to her?" I asked Wittenauer.

Thought he would laugh, but he didn't. "She's just like everyone else," he said bitterly. "You're really naïve if you think anyone actually cares about changing this place, or the world, or anything."

Whoa. Might go slip my Mental Health Resources

brochure under Wittenauer's door. Only I can't remember where he lives exactly.

Told him not to stress out so much, that obviously there are people who care. So we're a little aimless right now, but we'll pull it together.

Feel like everyone around me is cracking under the pressure of coming exams and massive amounts of work. Mary Jo and Joe are not speaking due to some notes-borrowing misunderstanding. Tricia snapping at a customer for taking too many pennies from the "Take a Penny!" cup. Marcus showing up at work in ratty T-shirt; Ben studying at every spare moment and getting all the orders wrong.

Good thing I cracked 2 weeks before now and am able to be there for people. Mostly this means they yell at me.

11/30

I have not seen the sun for days. Keep expecting to see polar bears on my way to class. Instead, layers and layers of fleece pass by. Largest coats I have ever seen. Boots also.

I don't understand how people ended up settling here, how they survived, unless this is warmer than Scandinavia? Or do they have different skin from me, like animals who have evolved, adapted? I have definitely not adapted.

Dear Mom,

In case you are wondering what I might like for Christmas and if you can take a break from chat room and have time to shop online, I could really use a new winter coat. Something large and thick and preferably not bright yellow or orange.

In all seriousness, I hope things are going well, and I can't wait to see you in a couple of weeks.

Love,

Courtney

Hi Courtney!

I was online when you wrote—not in a chat room, don't worry. It's so good to hear from you! I can't wait to see you at Christmastime. I hope we can spend *lots* of time together. How are things with Grant? Did you settle things?

Mom,

Everything with Grant is okay. I'm really too busy here right now to even worry about that.

Yeah. Right.
Grant emailed me from computer lab tonight, where

he and Melinda are working on writing some big report. Tried to tell myself this was no big deal, Mary Jo has a lab partner, too. Joe. And they sleep together, so, you know, what am I worried about???

Got Christmas card from Mary Jo's family today. Reminds me I still haven't sent thank-you note, and am in possession of world's worst manners.

December 1st. Christmas is coming up way too fast, like some high-speed bullet train. Usually it's the fallen-behind-on-shopping that gets to me. This year it's the . . . what is going to happen when I get home? Things with Grant seem okay, but we are not talking as often and I have flashes of jealousy when we do. Like for instance why does he *need* a lab partner? Melinda should partner up with someone else. Grant can do the work on his own, he's smart enough.

Perhaps Johannsens wouldn't mind 1 more mouth to feed at Christmas dinner, either. If they won't take me in, maybe Mary Jo's biological mother will. She might need help delivering all those Christmas cards and packages.

12/2

Spent the morning selling BF gift certificates and filling a display case with "Knockwurst Stockings" full of knockwurst treats for DOGS.

Need I say more?

Not now, because I already did at work. Tried to point out the contradiction this creates.

"You're saying that we're selling this prepackaged dog biscuit that is essentially made of the same things as our Knockwurst Knots, and this is supposed to send what kind of message to our customers?"

Strike 843 against me, but Courtney still not out.

Jennifer actually said, "Yeah. It's kind of gross when you stop and think about it."

Finally vindicated.

Not that it matters—we still sell the stuff.

Which is okay because I've got Oscar's Christmas present wrapped up now, for a discount.

Annemarie is back, and we went to the Badicals meeting today. It is our last one of the semester, because next Sunday is so-called Crunch Day, last day before finals begin. (Same day as Dean S.'s party. Why is he giving a party on a Sunday night before finals? Probably doesn't want a high turnout.)

At the meeting we talked about how we want to settle this whole CFC thing, and I said that Dean S. had promised to let our voice be heard. We made this list of our demands, and then decided to protest outside the bookstore on Saturday. They always give a lot of campus tours on Saturdays, for one thing. For another, everyone is jamming the bookstore now for study supplies, paper, highlighters, textbooks they never bought at the beginning of semester.

I think this is Crunch Month. I am going to spend the entire day studying. Annemarie, Mary Jo, Peña, and I are all sitting in the lounge, armed with pretzels and rice cakes, the low-fat study group.

Thyme just came by and asked what we talked about at our meeting. Annemarie said she should have come if she wanted to know. Didn't understand her hostility until she pointed out that we can't trust Thyme now. Morgan. Whoever. Because she's working against us now, and is only asking in order to infiltrate the group for her own good. That seems sort of unlikely. I bet she just misses hanging out with us.

12/4

Funny day at work. We put up more holiday decorations—garlands of lacquered bagels—and then discussed possible holiday specials. I said I wanted to do a Ginger-spread Gingerbread bagel. (This job is either growing on me—or growing in me, like a disease.) Marcus wanted to have something called New Year's Cheese. Ben wanted to have a Kwazy Kwanzaa Pizzaa, just for the visual of z's and a's. I don't think he was being serious, I think he was making fun of me and Marcus.

Anyway, Jennifer listened and seemed really interested and impressed. Then she announced that she had just received her shipment of the company's holiday menu items—on ice. She let out this sad sigh and brought out the tray with the things on it. First the Merry Carver: turkey rolled into a bagel. Then Rudolph's Roast Beef—meat, bagel, the usual, only more bloody. "What next—actual reindeer meat?" I asked. Then there were Sugar Cookie bagels, which tasted very rude. And the Kris Kringle Single, a nasty-looking green and white candy thing that was supposed to be a dollar bill.

"This stuff makes even the Bacle look good," I said, "which is saying a lot. I *really* don't think we can sell this stuff. I don't think *I* can, anyway."

I waited for the inevitable strike 3. Maybe I wanted it to come. Go ahead. Throw me out. I'll have more time to study for finals.

But Jennifer said, "I agree, these things look terrible. I bet we can come up with better ideas on our own."

"What? But we can't," Ben said. "We're not allowed."

"Wait—wait. Before we decide *anything*, are there holiday aprons?" Marcus asked.

Jennifer then announced a very amazing thing. Once every year, the managers are allowed to run their own specials. Jennifer said, "The time is now." She confessed that she's totally sick of answering to corporate headquarters, tired of all the unreasonable sales goals, tired of getting slammed with new products, etc., and was probably going to leave soon, but maybe this would revitalize her.

Then she insisted we work through the day, into the night, developing our ideas. Does she not understand the concept of burnout? But it was actually fun. When the store closed, we blasted music, made signs, experimented with recipes, etc.

Courtney's Gingerbread Spread. Coming soon to a non-chain near you.

Have been studying constantly, so I haven't been able to write in here much. However, 2 things are notable. The 1st one extremely notable.

1st Thing: Mary Jo broke up with Joe yesterday. For good this time, she promises. He kept showing up late or not showing up and then she saw him at the library with another girl and then he said he had to look at other options because she didn't care enough about him to bring him home for Thanksgiving, and she said if he couldn't understand why she did that then he'd never understand her, so what was the point? That I needed her more at the time. Whoa. As noted earlier: surprising amount of backbone.

2nd Thing: I got a Christmas card from Ed today. It was signed: "Love, Ed." "You didn't tell Ed any weird stories, did you?" I asked Mary Jo. "Like, that I broke up with Grant and I was interested in him?"

"No way," Mary Jo said. "But don't worry. He'll be totally infatuated with you for a few months, and then *poof*! He'll drop you and find someone else. He does this constantly."

Hope the infatuation ends soon. He's a very sweet person and all, but I don't really see myself ever liking him that way. Would have to get over my fear of flannel, for one thing.

12/8

Annemarie got me a spot on the radio today to discuss our CFC-logo cause. *Talking with Wauzataukie* is the show. Usually they pull some random person off the street and interview them. The DJ, named Paul, asked me to describe my pet issue.

"I don't have a pet *issue*," I said. "I do have a dog named Oscar, though, and I love him very much." Was supposed to just be a little joke, but we got into this lengthy discussion of our dogs and how weird Oscar is and how funny his Chihuahua is. Suddenly I realized my time was almost up and I hadn't done anything to promote our cause.

Might be fired as organizer of this thing. Managed at the last second to get in our plug for the protest tomorrow at the bookstore, but might have been cut off midsentence.

Oh well. Nobody listens to the campus station anyway. Right?

Attacked! I've been attacked!

Went to the CFC bookstore. There's this lobby area with lockers to stash backpacks—a couple of tables that are usually filled with people selling Guatemalan sweaters and credit cards.

Erik and I and a few other Badicals set up a table with signs, banners, posters, etc. We were sitting there greeting people and handing out a flyer about how we want new sweatshirts, new notebooks, new bumper stickers, etc. We had brought all these cans with symbols that said "no CFCs" to remind everyone of what a *negative image* we're promoting here.

We kept trying to grab people as they went in and out of the bookstore. This big group of students came toward us, and I got hopeful because there were a lot of Phish T-shirts and reggae colors and green army pants in the crowd. So I stepped toward them to make my pitch.

All of a sudden, out of nowhere, someone jumped right in front of me and sprayed something all over me. I was seeing red. I thought I was bleeding. "What are you doing?" I demanded, reaching for the sleeve of his jacket. "Stop it!"

"This is really lame and useless!" the sprayer yelled. "Why don't you work on something meaningful for a change? Fight for change that matters! Do something important!"

"I am!" I yelled, pawing at the wool ski mask the man was wearing—like half the people around here do just to walk to class. Not good evidence.

I wiped off my face and saw this stuff on my hand

that looked like blood. It turned out to be watered-down ketchup.

"People are dying every day, and you're arguing over *sweatshirts?*" he yelled. "Forget bumper stickers. Save someone's life!" He ran off, leaving us to get into a fight with bookstore staff over who should clean up the mess.

Protest over. Game over. We collected all our stuff and went home and everyone stared at me as I walked across campus as if I had been shot. Mary Jo clung to me when I walked in the door, ready to call 911, screaming, "Who did this? Who did this?" over and over.

Took a very long shower and thought things through. First I was very irate and mad. Sort of freaked out, also. Hate being criticized. Then I realized masked man is right.

It's not exactly a serious cause, but we had good environmental intentions at the beginning. We need to wrap this up and move on to another, more serious issue.

I wonder what group he was from. Or was he sent by Dean S. to break up our protest? I've got to ask Wittenauer about it tomorrow at the party at Dean S.'s house. If he goes. If I go.

Okay, so how many parties have I gone to that I shouldn't have?

Well, 1 good outcome. 1 very unsettling outcome.

First: Wittenauer and I tracked down Dean S. by the "nacho hot dish." Looked like nachos to me. He had lots of food and a giant bowl of cider on a table by the fireplace. Roaring fire, very cozy, festive, if you could ignore Wisconsin sports memorabilia clogging the living room.

Dean S. said he heard about the bookstore melee yesterday and that he wants to resolve this peacefully. "So do I!" I said. "So could we please set a date for us to talk to the administration?"

"You can bring all your concerns to the trustee meeting on January fifth," Dean S. offered.

"But classes don't start until the eighth. You're only scheduling it then because most people don't get back until the seventh!" I said.

"You can come back early," Dean S. said. "Of course, if you're not really committed to this . . ." He looked very hopeful.

I picked up another nacho, scraped some beef off of it, and ate it. "Oh, I'm committed," I said. Or I should be.

Dean S. turned to serve another guest some punch, and Wittenauer started to get this really antsy look. "I have to tell him. I'm going to tell him," Wittenauer said.

"Don't!" I whispered. "It's better if you work behind the scenes. Behind the helmet, I mean."

"Why is that better?" he asked.

"Because you can, um, get closer to people," I said. That came out entirely wrong.

"I can?" Wittenauer asked.

"You could like, infiltrate conversations," I said. "Stay friends with Dean S. and figure out what the administration is planning."

"But that would make me a spy," he said.

"I know. Isn't it cool?" I said.

Just then Dean S. turned around. "Well, Walter? What are you planning for your vacation?"

"Not much. But there's something I want to tell you before we all leave for break," Wittenauer said.

"Don't!" I said as I grabbed his arm.

Wittenauer smiled. "I was only going to tell him what an excellent fund-raiser you are. She's made a real contribution to the group, you know, Dean Sobransky?"

"Er . . . yes." Dean Sobransky obsessively filling cups with the exact same amount of cider. 30 cups teetering on the table. He did not realize the cider was sort of beyond its date and had morphed into an alcoholic beverage. Within the hour carols were being sung and Dean S. was nervously and discreetly arranging rides home for all of us.

Wittenauer walked me back to Rankin. We were standing outside and laughing about the stuff in Dean S.'s house and about exams starting tomorrow and how we were sort of tipsy.

Mary Jo walked by on her way home from the science library and glared at us as she went by. Apparently didn't approve of partying on nights before exams. Probably right.

"So Courtney? Have a really good vacation," Wittenauer said. "Don't forget to work on our arguments for the trustee meeting, and call me if you need any help. It was great hanging out with you tonight. And thanks for keeping me from confessing to being Corny."

"Well. You're kind of blowing your cover right now. You're being *very* corny," I said.

Wittenauer rolled his eyes. "Ha ha. Good night." Then he kissed me on the cheek. Felt very sophisticated. And I thought, Cool! That's what friends do in college.

But then he kissed me again—on the lips. For real. And the kiss just, like, blew me away, because I haven't kissed anyone that intensely since Grant. And it seemed very romantic because it was sort of snowing, little ice crystals were falling on our cheeks, and we were leaving for vacation, and we were standing there smushed up against each other and it felt warm—

Then I realized I was doing *exactly* what Grant did to me. Getting totally carried away by the proximity of a good-looking, opposite-sex friend and a couple of cups of turned cider!

"So, okay, good night," I said, bolting for the safety of the dorm.

"Courtney, would you *please* stop that?" Mary Jo just asked, interrupting flow of thought here. She is still studying. "You're humming. Or glowing. Or *something*."

"Sorry," I said. "I was just thinking about something."

"Like how you and Walter were making out? And how you're going to tell Grant about it when you get home on Friday? Or maybe you should call him now, and get it over with—"

Whoa! "We weren't making out," I said. "It was a friendly kiss. A kiss between friends. And his name isn't Walter."

"Please. I could see you guys from up here," she said.

"And if you're trying to get revenge on Grant or something by using Walter—"

"His name is Wittenauer!" I interrupted. "Only teachers are allowed to call him Walter."

"—then in a way you don't deserve Grant, who drove all the way out here to beg your forgiveness, and who's going to fail out of college if you don't totally forgive him soon—"

"So he fails?" I said. "So what?"

But the thought of Grant never becoming a D.V.M., never opening Superior Animal Hospital, is very upsetting. I don't want that. Don't want to make out with WW III again. I kissed a school mascot. *Voluntarily.* I really need to get out of here. Christmas can't come soon enough.

12/11

Exams start today.

I go home on Friday.

Wish me luck.

See you then.

Yes, I should tell Grant what happened.

But am too busy worrying. I mean studying.

12/15

On the plane right now. Direct from Milwaukee to Denver. Feeling very jittery. Spent last 3 nights awake due to 1) cramming for exams, 2) anxiety attacks, 3) camping out at library overnight last night so I wouldn't see Ed when he came to pick up Mary Jo for Christmas. Man does not take "no" for an answer, kept insisting I spend Christmas on the farm, Christmas riding horse and sleigh, Christmas as Mrs. Ed.

I'm writing to look busy because the 2 people next to me keep talking, trading "Best Christmas Ever" and "Worst Christmas Ever" stories. Since I'm thinking this year will be one or the other, I don't want to get involved.

Oh no. We're beginning our descent.

Funny, I thought I began my descent about a month ago. Ha ha ha.

I am so nervous. I can't even think about the fact I just took 4 finals and don't know how I did. I can't finish my soda and the flight attendant is getting really annoyed because he keeps coming by to get everyone's cups and I'm sorry but it's like *too much pressure* right now for me to finish my diet 7-Up.

All I can think about is that Grant is picking me up at the airport and I'm going to die when I see him.

LATER . . .

Home. In bed. Exhausted. Oscar's furry chin is resting on my shin.

Grant wasn't at the airport.

NOT AN OMEN NOT AN OMEN NOT AN OMEN

Bryan was.

He said that Grant called in a panic because he couldn't get out of work due to the holiday crush/rush and could Bryan please pick me up, he was really sorry blah blah blah.

I was starting to get furious by the baggage carousel when Bryan handed me a present Grant had dropped by the house already as a "Welcome Home" gift (a/k/a Forgive Me). I opened this little box and inside was a pair of silver earrings with little amber stones that match my hair. Beautiful. But does he think earrings will fix everything? I wondered as I lugged my giant Army duffel of Christmas presents off the conveyor belt. If I'd never bought all this stuff for Grant when I was still in love with him, I wouldn't have bounced checks and maxed out new credit card.

Am I still in love with him? You can't have these thoughts at airports under fluorescent lights while avoiding Smarte Cartes and listening to overhead pages.

Anyway, Bryan asked if I was hungry, which I was, now that I wasn't worried about seeing Grant tonight, so we went to Perkins on the way home. An amazing thing happened there. Over a pitcher of coffee and way too many pancakes, we had our first real, actual conversation ever. Mind blowing. He told me about Mom and his theory of why she won't date the guy in the book club or the guy from the awards banquet and will only write flirty emails to men in cyberspace. If they are actually men, and not a) 15-year-old boys or b) women.

He told me about this girl he's seeing now, Samantha, and his theory of why they're good together. Turns out he has many theories, even about me, Grant, and especially Beth. He isn't bitter at all. Not sure where he got that from.

But here is the mind-blowing fact of the evening: *he* broke up with Beth. Not the other way around. He said he was pretty sure she didn't see it coming, thought she could just treat him like he was always going to be there for her, no matter what. She was totally shocked and upset. So maybe that's why she made such a huge mistake with Grant.

I felt myself starting to forgive Beth, right then and there, in the middle of Perkins at 11 P.M. Or was it just the maple syrup going to my head?

"Are you guys ever going to get back together?" I asked. Because that would make everything a whole lot easier for me.

"We might," Bryan said. "But I doubt it. Not right now, anyway. I could see maybe in another year, you know . . ."

Danger. Little brother starting to sound like ex Dave, with time theories. Next thing you know he will want to be "free and clear."

Got home and really really wanted to call Grant. Everything here is about him, about us. Except Mom knocking on my door, constantly asking if I need anything else. Driving me crazy.

Saw Grant for the first time this morning. Got so nervous, I tripped coming down the stairs. Not the impression I wanted to make. We hugged, then stood in the hallway for a minute or two. Very awkward. Still 100 percent attracted to Grant. Grant seems to think everything is A-okay between us, like isn't it great I'm home and now we can spend the next 2–3 weeks together? I'm just confused.

We went out to lunch and talked nonstop about school, classes, exams, papers, anything but about us. Then out of the blue he said, "What do you want to do for our anniversary?"

Anniversary?

"Well, that won't be until, um . . ." Until I figure out whether you can count the last month or not, since weren't we technically not together???

"New Year's," Grant said. "Right? So do you want to go skiing at Breckenridge like last year, or . . ."

"Sure," I said quickly. "Sure. Breckenridge. Sounds great."

He gave me a funny look and then went ahead and ordered dessert. It was so good to be with him again, but I didn't know if I could sit through an apple cobbler without crying. Also, I kept thinking that I had to tell him that I fell off the wagon, too, kissing WW III.

Kissing WW III. Yet *another* great name for a band.

Should probably give up pursuit of poli sci degree and go into band management.

This working-things-out thing is so tedious. No wonder Dad just left, moved out of the house, started a new relationship without patching things up with Mom. Perhaps I don't give him enough credit for being smart.

12/18

Talked to Mom today about her perennial singleness. Kept tossing out names of potential suitors. "Whatever happened with that nice single guy you met at the awards ceremony? The father of that girl Bryan likes? You guys really hit it off. So why won't you go out with him?"

She beat around the bush for like 20 minutes talking about Christmas week/tree trimming/dinner plans. Then she finally said, "But he drives a Saturn. Two-door."

"*So?*" I asked.

"Well, I've never liked anyone who drove a coupe. Man or woman." She said this like it was logical.

Grrrr. She's going to spend the rest of her life all alone because she'd rather get involved with a sedan person? Or worse—another mini-van driver, to match her Caravan?

"So what *are* you looking for, Mom? An SUV?" I asked.

She wouldn't answer. She got all offended.

"Mom, come on, I'm worried about you," I said. "Alison and I are both in college, and Bryan's going to be soon—"

"So what are you saying? I'm old? Yes, I know I'm old, thanks for pointing that out."

"Mom, you're only . . . what? Forty-three?"

"Forty-seven."

"Oh." That seems old, but I didn't tell her that.

12/19

Totally embarrassing scene tonight.

Grant came over to get me so we could go Christmas shopping at the new giant mall in Broomfield. Went to our favorite stores but didn't buy anything. Felt really uncomfortable. Whenever he took my hand to hold it, I started thinking horrible things about how I kissed Wittenauer and hadn't 'fessed up yet. So there we were, strolling through the food court, when I heard someone yelling my name. Turned around and saw the Tom coming toward us. Agh! So humiliating. The last time I *saw* him was months ago, and the last time I talked to him, he was telling me how Grant and Beth hooked up. And like gloating about it.

The Tom came toward us doing his trademark saunter, like he didn't really *care* if we were there or not, even though he was shouting my name sort of desperately a couple of seconds ago. He had 2 girls with him, of course—never travels without at least 2. They looked like they might be high-school sophomores. Maybe. So he gave me this hug that was verging on pornographic, the girls looked mad, Grant looked pissed, never mind there's never been *anything* between me and Tom and never will be. Then he stood back and said "Hey, Superior," and then he said, "So you *are* still together." Sounded very shocked. Not that it takes much to puzzle the Tom, but still. Had he heard otherwise?

12/20

Stopped by T or D today to visit Gerry and bring him a block of Wisconsin brick cheese. Drove up to buffalo overlook first to visit old friends and prepare myself, just in case. Then I drove to Canyon Blvd. and sat outside in the car trying to establish that Beth was definitely not inside T or D, not in the storeroom, not in the bathroom, not out back smoking. . . . I must have been there 20 minutes. People kept going in and coming out with their smoothies and sundaes. They'd come back to their cars and see me sitting there, and I knew it was only a matter of time before 1 of them reported me for being a stalker.

Also I started to feel like a freak, sitting there parked outside my old workplace. Like I couldn't move on or something. Hey, I have moved on. I don't even live here anymore.

Finally got out of the car and went into the store. On the way in, checked out strip-mall sign that Beth had supposedly damaged. Looked fine to me. Went inside. Gerry wasn't there. Place was very crowded. Out of control. Beth working. Very flustered. 1 woman was complaining about her sundae having the wrong syrup, a boy was demanding a cleaner spoon, etc. Meanwhile there were about 10 people waiting for smoothies and cones. Beth caught my eye and her face sort of brightened. Her hair was all askew and she had 10 different fruits splashed on her hemp apron. I just felt so *bad*. We'd been in this situation together so many times.

So the next thing I knew I was dashing behind the counter, grabbing the apron covered with the Holstein cow pattern. "Don't you hate these balmy December days where everyone feels they just *have* to get out and enjoy frozen food products?" I muttered to Beth as I quickly washed my hands.

We got to work really quickly and didn't speak much for the next half hour. When I looked up and there was no line, I knew we'd have to talk. Busied myself making my own smoothie while I stalled. My old favorite, a CFS. That's CF for Coconut Fantasy, not Cornwall Falls. Not to be confused. Ever.

Beth came over to stand beside me. "Thanks for coming to my rescue. How did you know Gerry ran out for supplies right *before* the after-lunch rush?"

"I didn't." Because if I had, I wouldn't have come in here, I thought. But I had to be more "mat-oor" about all this. "Um, I just thought we should talk," I said.

"So, when did you get home?" she asked.

"Saturday," I said. "Well, Friday, but late." We made small talk for a while, about Jane, about Christmas plans, about exams. Then there was this gulf that opened up. I wanted her to bring up the Grant thing. I wanted a customer to come in and order 10,000 smoothies, so neither one of us would have to bring it up. But it was good to see her, even if my stomach was bubbling like overcooked hot fudge. You know when you take it off the burner but it keeps cooking. Like that.

"You never answered any of my emails," she finally said. "And that's okay. But I just—well, it's been killing me."

"Me, too," I said.

"I don't know, Court," she said. "I don't think you should forgive me. But if you could . . . that would be so great."

Just then Gerry barreled through the door carrying

packages of napkins and a tower of boxes of plastic silverware. He was panting and out of breath. He stared at me, did a double take, and then dropped one of the boxes. It opened as it fell, and 100 plastic forks spilled onto the tile floor.

"Now, what am I going to do with a hundred forks?" he muttered. "I can't believe I grabbed forks by mistake. Courtney? I don't know why you have an apron on, but a little help? Please?"

I went over and started collecting them into a heap. "You're going to have to wash these now, you realize."

"Not to mention come up with menu items requiring forks." He laughed. "How are you? When did you get into town?"

"A few days ago," I said. "I came by to bring you something, and, well. You know. The after-lunch rush was happening."

He stood up and brushed some chocolate sprinkles off his knees. "Well, I guess I didn't need to rush back. You guys have everything covered, as usual."

I helped him carry the stuff into the storeroom while Beth waited on customers. After we put the spoons and napkins on shelves, he stood there and stared at me for a few seconds, doing his typical Gerry "let me analyze you because I used to do this for a living" gaze.

"Your hair . . . you're different," he said. I had sort of forgotten about my haircut. Least of my problems lately. Also, I keep forgetting that I have these 2 separate lives now—home and school.

"Everything's going all right at school?" he asked.

"Um, sure," I said. "I mean, as well as can be expected."

That scared him. "You're not flunking out, are you?"

"No, of course not," I said.

"And you and Grant, you're doing well?" he asked.

"As well as can be expected," I said again. Trying to give him an answer without really answering. Only way to deal with prying questions.

"So. Everything going all right with, you know?" He tried to make a sly little head gesture toward Beth, who was still up front.

"Sure," I said. "I mean . . . as well as can be expected."

"Is that what you're going to say to all my questions from now on?" he asked, giving me the old G.C. look.

"Pretty much," I said.

Left with the promise to call Beth tomorrow and possibly meet her and Jane, who gets in tonight after trip to see new bf's band perform in Chicago.

I hope Beth and I can put this behind us and move on and be friends again. I have really missed her. Am crossing my fingers as I write this. With my other hand, dummy.

12/21

Spent a hilarious afternoon at Jane's house. Jane and I were telling Wisconsin stories to Beth, exaggerating maybe a little, but mostly true. Talked about stupid things we'd done at parties and said in class. Reminisced about senior year. I described seeing the Tom at the mall. Started telling Tom stories. We started giggling and couldn't stop. Perhaps it was because we were splitting beers stolen from the giant Nakamura beer fridge in the basement, while Jane played a tape of her new bf's music. I kept suggesting new names for his band but she wasn't impressed. I think maybe Brat Virgin stands a chance, though.

At one point I looked at Beth and realized I have to forgive her. Or I have already forgiven her. Like today. We have this connection. We have a history. It has nothing to do with Grant. Started thinking of how Mary Jo chose me over Joe, and how that talk show guest chose ho's over bro's.

And anyway, Beth spent like half an hour describing new guy she's seeing. So that helped.

I got home really late and Bryan said Grant had stopped by and called a couple of times and was looking kind of worried. We were supposed to go to dinner tonight. We were?

Alison got home yesterday. Very excited to see her. Spent all day and night talking. She has many valuable insights into . . . everything.

Why am I the only child in the family without insights? Is it because I'm the middle child? I'm too busy trying to convince everyone to get along to have insights. Despite insightful natures, however, Alison has only been home 24 hours and she and Bryan have already had 3 fights re: fabric softener sheets, folding stuff left in the dryer, and the lint screen.

Got a big package in the mail this afternoon. I thought it was from Mary Jo because of the return address, and I was completely shocked because we sort of exchanged little gifts before we left. But it wasn't from her. It was from Ed.

Grant happened to come over to get me just as I was opening the box and pulling out little red and green boxes with gold ribbons. (Really need to send those gifts back without opening them, but I wonder what they are.)

Grant looked very shocked. Stunned, actually.

"Who's *Ed*?" he asked in this really unhappy voice.

"Oh, just this guy," I said. "Mary Jo's brother."

"What? I don't believe you," Grant said.

"Look." I showed him the postmark and for a split second thought fondly of Mary Jo's bio mother, stamping the package. Pictured all the Johannsens, pictured the house, remembered the cows.

Grant misinterpreted my thoughtful moment as wistful pining. "Is that why you went to her house for Thanksgiving?" he asked. "So you could spend time with her brother Ed?"

"What?" I laughed. "No!" I started to describe how Ed and I got to know each other during Parents Weekend—

"You never mentioned that," Grant said. "You never said anything about Ed."

Then I realized how dangerously close we were getting to the WW III discussion, so I told him Ed was not important to me, it was a harmless crush, and that we'd better get going if we wanted to see the Wildlights at the Zoo.

Last year we kissed for the first time, okay actually sort of made out, at Wildlights. This year we stomped around in the cold with Grant not in a good mood, and I finally dragged it out of him that he found out he did not get all A's and actually got one B. Not even in his major, so who cares? But Grant cares. Obsessing about it. Tried to distract him with kisses. Was like kissing one of the metal giraffe statues.

'Twas the night before Christmas
And all through the house
Courtney was in big trouble

No more parties. *Really.* I mean it this time.

The big party was tonight. The Lebeau Mansion.

Last year I panicked and kissed the Tom. This year was even worse. Started out sort of fun, and also funny, because ex Dave showed up, home for Christmas. Gave him a huge hug and he looked confused. Didn't want to tell him he was right about LDRs being impossible, but he was. Not going to tell him that due to the rude way he dropped the bomb on me seconds before leaving town last year, that it was all over between us. Would never do that to anyone.

Anyway, here's what happened after that. Had some punch with Jane and Beth. Bryan and Alison were mingling. Grant and I then sat by the fire on this giant velvet sofa. Should have been very romantic but my mind kept wandering. I kept thinking about the fireplace at Dean S.'s house, our Fun-Times Funders party, and then I started thinking about Wittenauer, and my guilt about kissing him, and our trustee meeting coming up. Kept slugging punch. Grant and I went to refill our cups, and there was the Tom, hanging out with Beth. The Tom said something like, "Here comes the happy couple, back together again!" Beth looked like she wanted to die, and bolted for the front door. Didn't faze the Tom. He started teasing me all about how I was the forgiving type, and just his luck, he never got to go out with *those* kinds of girls. Then I told him that was because he only went out with idiot skanks.

Ran outside onto the terrace. Grant came outside

after me. I threw my cup of punch over the cute brick wall and told him that I wasn't over what happened, was never going to get over it, couldn't stand that he kissed Beth and that I kissed Wittenauer and—

"What?" Grant said. "Who's Wittenauer?"

"His name's Walter, okay? And he's also Corny. And he's also a three," I said. "And let's face it. He just doesn't sound as good as he is in person."

"What?" Grant cried again. "Courtney, who is this guy? Are you serious about him?"

"No! We're friends, that's all," I said. "And it didn't mean anything, we just got carried away by a Badicals project and we were at this party and he walked me home and it just *happened*."

"You've been home for a week, and you're just telling me now?" Grant went into furious mode. "Court, I called you the next day after Beth and I . . . you know. And that's only because I was waiting until it was a decent hour—"

"Like there's a decent hour to tell me that you and my best friend—"

"It was nothing! Nothing nothing nothing!" Grant insisted.

We got into this competition of whose slip-up/kiss error was worse, mine or his. Practically screaming. Completely ridiculous.

Went inside and got Bryan and insisted he take me home right away. The Tom overheard and volunteered to drive me.

"I have enough problems, okay? I don't need you mauling me in the car," I said.

"Like I would," the Tom said.

Not *this* again.

Still haven't heard from Grant since last night. I haven't called him, either. Christmas Stalemate.

Mom is losing her mind. Wonder if she has that seasonal disorder, because it seems like every winter she goes a bit berserk. Spending way too much money on Christmas. Last year she got us all cell phones, but then decided they were no better than traditional phones and returned them. This year she got us all new iBooks because the Internet is her life and thinks it should be ours, too.

"Hey, no complaints, I'll give my other computer to Mary Jo. But Mom. I'm sort of worried," I said. It's like she thinks this is her revenge against the phone company, to live through DSL. Not a life, I pointed out. Alison and I gave long lecture about perils of Instant Messaging with pedophiles. Or in her case, middle-age-o-philes.

There are always people on talk shows, where it's a 25-year-old dude dating a 50-year-old mom he met through Internet. Lives rent-free, giant scam. Sorry Mom, but we're the only ones allowed to live rent-free here.

We gave her a really hard time. We went on and on with endless examples of how she shouldn't trust anybody. Ever. Needless to say, I led the crusade.

Then she told us the guy she's going out with on New Year's is the guy in town, from the awards ceremony. And could we please just shut up? She learned her lesson already about chat rooms, and was only trying to give us these computers so we'd have the best advantage in school, in the world . . . Oops.

Alison gave me a cool sweater, Bryan gave me CDs, Dad sent cash. Typical Christmas, really. I'm sort of glad Dad & Sophia & Angelina & Bellarina didn't come, because last year it was so crowded. Grandma and Grandpa should get here tonight. I'm sure Grandpa will have a million questions about Cornball and I'll have to put my game face on, tell him I love it.

Well, at least I don't *hate* it anymore. There is that.

LATER . . .

Grant is back to being Superior.

I was sitting by the window, watching for Grandma and Grandpa, when I saw his car pull up. Nearly had a heart attack. Resisted urge to run upstairs and hide under comforter. Tried to be an adult and went to open the door. Grant came in. He started babbling apologies, and I started trying to counter each apology with one of my own. Then we just looked at each other and I started crying and we started hugging. Grant put his arms around my waist and started kissing my neck. And somehow everything was okay again. Like we're even now or something.

Ditched waiting for my grandparents to show up and went over to Grant's house. Very warm reception, parents and Grandmother Superior thrilled to see me. Then they disappeared upstairs so Grant and I could be alone. Christmas carols were playing softly on the stereo. We were holding hands, leaning against each other on sofa. Then suddenly Grant got up and kneeled down, on bended knee or however you say that.

I started panicking. He was going to propose! Mary Jo said we should get engaged if we were serious. But we'd only truly made up a couple of hours ago. What was I going to do, say, how should I react?

Then he scooted across the carpet. Turned out he was just getting down on the floor to pull my presents out from under the tree.

Gave me a new watch, very cool, with a note about counting minutes until we're together this summer. Gave me a coupon book with all these coupons he'd designed for my favorite things, like: One Chauffeured Drive to Buffalo Overlook, One Hot Dog with the Works at Mustard's Last Stand, etc.

Love Grant. Love love love him.

Am not going back to CFC for spring semester. Staying here, transferring to CU. Must stay with Grant. I could work full time. Make tons of money; ski every weekend; see Grant all the time. Beautiful plan.

12/26

"So you didn't make the Dean's List," Grandpa said when I got up this morning and stumbled downstairs for coffee. "Is that what you're telling me?"

"Um, well, I'm not sure yet, because I haven't gotten my grades." I did make Dean S.'s list of "People He'd Like to See Transfer from CFC." Did that count?

Then he cleared his throat and said he heard about my little protest idea to change the CFC "image." We got into a big debate, discussion, whatever. He said our idea was "needless nitpicking."

"But it's so simple," I said. "They could add graduate programs and become Cornwall Falls University. CFU. That would work," I said.

"Don't you get it?" Grandma said. "Initials aren't everything in this world, Courtney!"

This from the woman whose family gave me the middle initials V.D.!!!

Total cold war inside house now. He and Grandma are furious with me. Mom, however, is proud of me for being so involved. I guess she didn't know that I was actually having an impact. Never gives me credit for having an impact on anything.

12/29

Told Alison and Bryan I am thinking about not going back to Wisconsin next week. They told me I'm crazy. Alison said that would be like taking a giant step backward, because my credits might not transfer and I'd be a freshman next fall, and wasn't once enough? She had a billion arguments about how this would ruin my future academic life, my career, the possibility of me ever becoming Anybody.

Bryan took different tack. He said not to make any decisions based on love. (Has obviously been watching too many relationship experts on *Oprah*, which Mom *tapes* and watches during dinner, exposing her only son to dangerous airborne chemical: talk shows.) (I watch enough to know how they suck you in and ruin your own personal ozone layer.) He said I'd always feel I made a big sacrifice for Grant, and how I'd never be happy.

Hey, I can *be* happy, with or without Grant.

Wait a second. What am I saying?

12/30

Was being stupid and paranoid today and called Grant to ask him if our anniversary ski date is still on. Of course it is, and then he got mad at me for doubting the date, doubting him, me, etc.

"Okay, so I was thinking about moving back here for you, and you're going to get mad at me now?" I asked.

"What?" he said. "You were going to . . . ?"

"Never mind," I said. "See you tomorrow, okay?"

"How can you move back *here* when I'm planning to drive you back *there*?" Grant asked.

"What? You are?" (Is he trying to get rid of me?)

We discussed the plan—to leave on Tuesday, get there early in the morning on Wednesday. He doesn't have to come back until Saturday, so that will give us 3 days together. Plus he can be there for the trustee meeting.

So sweet of him.

But the idea makes me very very nervous. Like TV movie of the week: *Grant in Wauzataukie: When 2 Worlds Collide!*

Spent the day trying to convince Jane to drive back with me and Grant instead of waiting for silly first-class flight in a week.

"No way, I'm not going back yet!" Jane said. "Are you crazy?"

"But you do love Madison," I reminded her. "And Charles is there, right?"

"No, he's home with his family, too," she said.

"Oh. Well, aren't you getting tired of living under your parents' roof? I mean, it's driving *me* crazy, because I'm not used to having my mom watch my every move, you know?"

"My parents are cool. They sort of let me live my own life," Jane said. She took off her little rectangular glasses to clean them. "What's really going on here, Courtney?" she asked.

I shrugged. "Nothing. I just thought it would be fun, that's all. Road trip. Loud music. Windows down."

"It's winter," she said. "And you're still not telling me what's at the root of your question."

Does she *have* to major in psych? "I don't know what you mean," I said. When in doubt, feign ignorance.

"Why do you want me there? Don't you want to be alone with Grant?" Jane asked.

Busted. I twirled around on the kitchen stool. "Well, actually, um, *no.*"

"Courtney, you have to be alone with him sooner or later," Jane said. "He's coming to college to stay with you for a few days. Do you really think you can delay it by having me in the backseat? And anyway, what's wrong? Why can't you face spending sixteen hours in a car with him?

Is there something you haven't told me?"

So I told her about our big fight, and how I cheated with Wittenauer by kissing him. She was really excited about it, for some reason. "I don't understand. I thought you liked Grant," I said.

"I do!" she said. "But this means you've *individuated*. Which is what you have to do in order to move on and grow by yourself."

Don't know what she was talking about. I told her how we've worked through the problems and patched things up, but now I feel like one of those old roads with too many patched potholes. More patch than road.

She said I was being pessimistic, and that every relationship has problems, and the key is to get beyond the superficial problems (kissing others) to the root of the problem (mother issues). Well, sure. Anyone named Mrs. Superior is *going* to have issues. But does Grant have issues with that? Do I? Do I want to marry someone and be known to the world as Courtney Superior?

Wait a second. We are not discussing marriage, we are discussing a boring car trip on interstates. And anyway, Jane's had like 2 courses and thinks she can diagnose us?

"Okay," she said when I protested. "So what do you think? Is being exclusive going to work for you this semester any better than it did last semester?"

Did she have to ask that?

He's coming to pick me up soon to go out to dinner. I should really think about getting dressed up.

Grant and I had a great day skiing. Last night we went out for an expensive dinner in LoDo with our Christmas money. Very nice, but that's not the big story. The big story is *Mom's first date in 5 years*!!!

This guy, Bryan's girlfriend's dad (easier to just say "Michael"), came to pick Mom up last night. In dreaded Saturn coupe. It was dark, so maybe Mom was more inclined to overlook his car choice. Mom was more dressed up than I've seen her since my high-school graduation. Looked beautiful. I took pictures like it was prom.

She got home *after* me, for once. (Grant and I came home pre-midnight and watched the ball drop on TV; he left as soon as she got home because it was 1 A.M.). Her face was shiny and happy. She started telling me about the place they went for dinner and how nice it was, and how Michael was really interesting, funny, devoted to his 2 daughters, etc. Then she burst out crying.

"Mom, what is it?" I asked. "What's wrong?"

"I can't explain," she said. "You wouldn't understand."

Just like Bryan! Assuming I won't get it, when truth is I get *everything*, and more.

"What happened?" I asked. "Did he say something? Was the coupe too small? Did he kiss wrong?"

She shook her head and ran for a Kleenex box. "It was all perfect. It was great. I had a really good time."

I just stood there next to her for a minute, waiting for my brain to figure out what there was to cry about. Is Mom just sort of . . . unbalanced? Allergic to happiness?

"Tonight I realized what I've been missing," she finally said. "And it's wonderful. And it's horrible at the same time. You know?"

Agh! Why do relationships have to be so painful to everyone, like, all the time?

Why have one at all?

Tonight we are having a big family dinner: I leave tomorrow, Alison leaves Wednesday. Beth is coming over with Jane.

Sitting beside Grant in the car. Halfway back to WI. Landscape desolate and cold. We left at 6 A.M. so we can get there by midnight or so. Very hard saying good-bye to everyone last night. But not as hard as it was in August. It's better, I think, to know what you're about to get yourself back into than to get into it the first time. Like cold lake water.

Speaking of Lake Superior, I keep glancing over at Grant and smiling. I am so glad he's doing this with me? But in some ways, Mom was an easier traveling companion. Sad but true.

1/3

Agh! Disaster.

Grant and I slept late. We were finally heading out when suddenly Mary Jo arrived. She came back early to get a jump on her classes—of course. It was so nice to see her. We gave each other a big hug, and I was introducing her to Grant, and they were of course instantly hitting it off, laughing about his 2 trips out here, commiserating over each getting one B (tragedy).

So we were chatting outside our room as Mary Jo stood there with a suitcase in one hand and a new, horrid framed print in the other hand (a kitten and a puppy having tea) when Ed came down the hallway. At the moment, Grant was teasing me about something, like how I described this place as being *so* bad, but it was all I talked about while I was home, so he was sort of like pretending to give me a giant squeeze.

Before I knew what was happening, Ed ran up and punched Grant in the jaw! God. What a mess. Grant's already got one half-broken tooth. I could just picture another flying out of his mouth, and then I would be dating a hockey player.

Ed misunderstood the situation and told Grant to get his hands off of me. He told Grant he wasn't a real man because of what he did to me. (!) (Have never thought of Grant as "real man"—don't even know what that *means*.) Meanwhile Grant pushed him against the wall and was demanding to know why Ed was sending me gifts and what right he had to interfere, and Ed spat back that it was his right ever since I showed up at their house after Grant abandoned me.

The few girls on the floor who are already back came

running out of their rooms to see what was going on. Mary Jo was shrieking at Ed to stop hurting Grant. I was yelling at both of them to just shut up, the whole time thinking: This *isn't* my life. Guys *don't* fight over me.

Some guys from downstairs, including R.A. Kevin, overheard, came running upstairs to break up the fight. Kevin made Ed and Grant shake hands and asked if they couldn't just talk it out, or maybe they should go back to their dorms or to a conflict resolution workshop at the housing office—

At which point Grant and Ed both said at the same time, "Hey, I don't even *go* here."

And that was sort of funny so it broke the ice. So we all went inside and sat in the room and made small talk. Still very awkward. Ed was sad because I tried to return his Christmas gifts; he wouldn't take them; said I should keep them and think of him from time to time. (Sounded like a country song.) Then he left to drive home.

Grant was upset that his jaw is bruised, and upset that Ed feels that possessive of me, and made me explain 10 times that Ed means nothing to me. Mary Jo helped by explaining this habit of crushes Ed has. Mary Jo, Grant, and I went to Brat W. for dinner. Someone working there actually *recognized* Grant. Mary Jo and Grant really did have a ton to talk about. And every once in a while I'd catch myself feeling jealous and suspicious, and then I'd just hate myself for it. But I couldn't stop.

Mary Jo is being sweet and spending the night down the hall in Tricia's room. Tricia's back early because "I got like three Incompletes? And they want me to finish them before classes start on Monday?"

Tricia was very impressed with Grant, I could tell.

Wonders how someone "so on the fringe" could have hottie bf. I didn't *used* to be on the fringe. Or maybe there were just more of us on it back home and I didn't notice. Crowded Fringe.

Yes, another great band name.

Good night. I shouldn't be writing in here so much with Grant here, anyway, but he has been reading a textbook since 10, so who cares?

1/4

Went to Badicals meeting (mock run-through for tomorrow). It was sort of a shock to see WW III there. He was wearing this blue-and-red Nordic-type sweater, and he looked really, really cute. Forgot how blond he is. But never mind. I said hi and was really friendly, but I couldn't talk to him. I left before there was a chance of any alone time.

Later on Grant and I dropped by BF so I could pick up my paycheck and new schedule. Jennifer is running the place herself while everyone is on vacation. Said I had to start on Saturday. Or Monday at the latest. Monday, then. I asked how the holiday specials had sold and she said maybe there were some things better left to the Bagle Finagle main office.

Mmm. It is so nice to have Grant here lying next to me. But very crowded. Stupid single bed. Grant keeps insisting on coming to the meeting tomorrow to support me. I keep worrying about what will happen if Wittenauer is there.

This entry might need a parental advisory. Or there should be official notes about this somewhere taken by a secretary: not me. I should not be responsible for the official version. Too involved. Too many things happening at once. Agh!

All-day trustee meeting started at 10 A.M. Students wishing to make statements or requests had to be there at 1 P.M. I could not eat, and I drank too much coffee. Said good-bye to Grant and Mary Jo, who promised to come over and meet at the lecture hall and be there for my presentation. So Annemarie and I found the Badicals and we huddled outside the lecture hall, awaiting our turn. Wittenauer was not there and I was relieved. What if I botched the presentation in front of him? That would be awful, I was thinking. He'd lose all faith in me. Should have been the least of my worries. *Least.*

Dean S. came out at 1:00 to gather waiting groups. We went in. Waited our turn. I nodded at the long table of trustees on the stage and started to make my speech about wanting the college to not use "CFC" in any official capacity. I had 5 minutes and I filled it with important data so they'd be impressed. I also presented mock-ups of our new T-shirt design.

A minute or so later, Thyme/Morgan came in with some CFC 4-ever group, *including* Tricia (Incompletes? Complete lie!). I didn't even know Thyme was back yet. Turns out she was hiding out like a wealthy mercenary in a hotel suite, gathering her troops. She stood up and started presenting her argument to keep all the CFC stuff. "The CFC name has existed for over a hundred years, and it'll go on another hundred years, long past the day we're students here," she said, completely toeing the trustee line.

Then fur began flying. Whatever that means. She started pulling all this very familiar-sounding academic crap out of nowhere, about how it made sense we were doing this because it was a "rite of passage" to be "part of a counterculture," and how we were having a "role conflict" and we needed to be "resocialized," but the *sweatshirts* definitely didn't need to be redesigned.

"Wait a second," I interrupted. "Don't listen to her! She got that from my sociology notes! This isn't even an original *thought*!" Not only that, she was completely talking down to us.

Stupid photographic memory. I knew I shouldn't have let her look at anything of mine, ever.

She and I got into this screaming match about stuff, and she said I didn't take this seriously and had no convictions. She said she'd known I was a fraud ever since September because one time she counted the number of Slim Jims in a mug on Mary Jo's desk and Mary Jo was away for the weekend and yet the number of Slim Jims went down. Very embarrassing. "I didn't eat any!" I said. "I opened the package to see what it was *made of*."

Meanwhile another group had come in. Started telling us to get our petty concerns off the stage and get ready for a revolution. At this point, the trustees were looking worried. Caught Mary Jo and Grant sitting in the middle row of seats, also looking concerned.

"I'm sorry, but there are more important issues than this college's abbreviation," a guy at the front of his pack said.

Recognized his voice as the guy who had sprayed me with red stuff. Wanted to run over and punch him in the nose, see how he liked being sprayed with red liquid—only this time, actual blood.

"What is more important than saving what little is left . of the ozone layer?" I asked.

"So there's a hole, okay, the EPA is working on that," the guy said. "What about the problems of economic globalization?" He went on with very impressive list of world problems, like dairy cows being cloned, and genetically engineered foods, and chemical warfare, and human rights violations, and the fact the CFC shirts might come from a factory that used child labor and sweatshops—his group was checking into that.

I glanced nervously around at my group. Erik and Annemarie were kind of shifting around, looking uncomfortable. Spray Guy was very impressive and smart.

Trustees' necks turning back and forth as if watching a tennis match, as everyone in the 3 groups argued. One of the trustees started having a flashback to the sixties. "What will happen if this escalates? We can't have violence on campus. We can't have tear gas and firebombs and the National Guard!"

"Which is why you should let the name stay the same!" Thyme insisted. "It's so unimportant in the grand scheme of things."

"Exactly. Because wouldn't you rather save the wild Arctic refuges from being drilled by oil companies?" the guy said.

"Definitely. That's the largest breeding ground for pregnant polar bears!" I added, getting sort of excited. "I mean, um, before they get pregnant. Whatever." My group was suddenly frowning at me, as I had apparently jumped ship, and was sounding like an idiot as I did it.

"But, ah, to redirect this discussion . . . how does that affect *us* here at Cornwall Falls College?" Dean Sobransky asked.

"Everything affects us," the sprayer said. "We're the future, whether you like it or not. And we have a responsibility to the planet."

"That's what we're trying to say!" I insisted. "That's why we don't want to *cheer* for CFCs. That's why we don't want anyone thinking that CFC is a good thing that should be put on sweatshirts and bumper stickers!"

Suddenly the door opened and a giant stalk of corn came running down the steps. Wittenauer!

"What is Corny doing here?" I heard Dean S. mutter.

I started getting really nervous as Wittenauer walked up past me and onto the middle of the stage, right in front of the trustee table. "Hello, trustees," he said. Then Wittenauer took off his corncob helmet. "It's me, Dean Sobransky," he said. "I'm Corny, and I completely support the idea to get rid of any and all CFC merchandise."

"Wi—wi—Wittenauer." Dean S. got purplish. Started stammering about Wittenauer's "unmitigated gall." "You're breaking a one hundred thirty-seven-year-old tradition of Corny being a—a—secret. How could you do this?"

"Because it's time to stop hiding behind a cornstalk. It's time to stop keeping secrets," Wittenauer said. "I think Cornwall Falls has lots of great traditions—but this isn't one of them." He started to strip out of his costume.

Dean S. slammed down a pointer he'd been using to illustrate, well, some point or other. "What are you talking about?"

"It's an elitist tradition," Corny said as he peeled off a husk.

286

Suddenly I realized he wasn't wearing anything underneath.

"It means that only the same kinds of people get picked, year after year. I got picked by someone just like me, whose dad went here, who was like a third-generation Cornwaller Faller. We're all male. We're all white. It's not fair." Another husk came off. Soon he was standing there bare-chested. Then he reached for the "cornbelt" that circled his waist.

"Please, ah, Walter, be reasonable," Dean S. sputtered as some of the trustees studied their notes and some watched eagerly. "We can discuss this in private. Is this really necessary?"

"Who cares?" one of the older women said. "Keep talking, Corny, whoever you are."

"Walter Wittenauer." He smiled at her as he reached for the waistband of his green stretch pants. "The third."

Oh my God! I was dying. Was he really going to—?

Then he pulled off the pants.

Giant sigh of relief AND disappointment from the crowd.

He wasn't totally naked. He was wearing a pair of green-and-yellow CFC boxers. And he had put a red line through each little CFC logo.

"We need to change the abbreviation. We need to change the ways things are done," Wittenauer said. He turned to the More Radical Than Badicals group. "And yeah, we need to be more serious after this and work on bigger problems."

"Isn't he cold? Because it's like freezing in here?" I heard Tricia ask Thyme.

Dean S. cleared his throat. "If everyone could just

287

give us some time. We need to discuss this. It's a lot to take in all at once." He took off his blazer and handed it to Wittenauer. "Come back in half an hour and we'll have some decisions for you."

"Better make that tomorrow morning," one of the trustees said. "We have a lot to discuss."

We all went out into the hallway. Wittenauer was standing there in a leather-elbow-patches blazer and CFC boxers. I just looked at him and laughed and ran over to hug him. I couldn't help myself.

Then I remembered Grant was there. Oops. Because he and Mary Jo came up to hug *me*.

"So, this is, um, Grant," I said. My boyfriend from home? Even though I forgot he was here? "And Grant, this is Wittenauer."

"Walter, actually." He reached out to shake Grant's hand.

Is this what life is like for the Tom? Constantly introducing people he's kissed? I couldn't stand how nerve-wracking it was. Worlds colliding. Courtney freaking.

"Hi," Grant said. "Nice, ah . . ."

"Full Monty?" Mary Jo suggested.

We all laughed. I was actually impressed with the way Wittenauer and Grant were getting along. I admired them for it.

"So, do you think we have a chance?" I asked Annemarie as the group gathered around me.

"We didn't. Not until Mr. Maize here showed up." Annemarie checked out Wittenauer's muscular legs. "So. Been skiing much?"

Everyone went out for coffee, but I went back to the

dorm with Grant. I should be so upset he's leaving tomorrow. But I'm not. I mean I am, and then I'm not. And I
can't sleep. Too worried about what will happen tomorrow, next semester, next year, etc.

Grant is gone. I am crying, but for the wrong reason. I did the unthinkable today. I am regretting it already.

Grant was supposed to be leaving tonight, but he ended up leaving this morning. We got into this conversation over breakfast before our 2nd trustee meeting and the next thing I knew, I was telling him that maybe we should break up, because long distance relationships really didn't work. I said I couldn't help feeling jealous of him, when he was with Mary Jo, and I didn't trust him and Melinda, or him and Beth, or—or anything. So I didn't want to pretend that everything was okay being apart, because it wasn't. "When I come home this summer, we can start seeing each other again. But in the meantime, I don't think we should promise to be exclusive, because—"

"*You*, jealous? What? It's not me that you need to worry about. *I'm* so jealous of all the guys around you, I can hardly even breathe sometimes," Grant said. "Who is it? Is it that mascot guy? Is it one of those guys you work with—what's his name—Mark? No—Ben. Wait. Hold on. It's not *Ed*, is it?"

"No! I mean, they're nice guys. Great guys. But no, that's not it," I said.

"Then who?"

"It's nobody, Grant. It's me," I said. "I just can't. I feel like I'm living my life in these two different places, and I've got to choose one and just *go* with it for a while."

Grant looked so upset. Suddenly I felt like throwing up. What was I doing? What was I saying? I was throwing away Grant? The superiorest guy I've ever met (except for small slip-up) (still a factor, still bothering me).

"You're going to think about this some more, right?"

Grant asked. "I mean . . . God, Courtney. You're not *serious*."

"Grant, you know me. Once I decide something . . . well, it's pretty much set," I said.

"Like how you decided we'd make this long-distance thing work, no matter what?" Grant asked, sounding angry and sarcastic all of a sudden.

"The no-matter-what part sort of got to me," I said. "I didn't think no-matter-what would include what actually happened. But Grant, look. This summer, maybe we can work it all out, maybe—"

"You know what, Courtney? Forget this summer," Grant said. "I'll make my own plans."

Then he left. Left! Drove away. Left me standing there in a snowbank. Zero compassion.

I still love Grant. I love him to death. But I can't go through another semester like the last one. Especially not in this weather.

Spent the day on the phone with Alison, Bryan, Mom, Jane, even Beth. Even Dad. "You did *what*?" was the common response. Mary Jo thinks I'm insane. I begged her to not tell Ed I am single now.

Anyway, trying not to focus on the negative. Trying to enjoy the "New Year's Resolutions for Cornwall Falls College" that were published by trustees after meetings concluded yesterday.

> **RESOLUTION 16**: to phase out the use of the initials CFC and to spell out the college name on all official clothing, in all cheerleader chants, in all university publications, and whenever and wherever possible.

If I wasn't so depressed over kicking Grant to the snowbank-covered curb, I'd be happy.

Another Monday morning at Bagle Finagle. Another New Product Team. New Product: THE CHEESE SHOPPE. Located within the walls of BF. Cream cheese not enough. We're going to sell wedges of cheese. Cheese fries. Cheese curds (both deep-fried and fresh). Cream of Cheddar soup. I swear, I don't get it.

Who wants cheese fries with their bagel? Who would come to *us* for cheese when there are specialty shops on the same block?

But suddenly it was really funny, because we were all back there: Jennifer, me, Ben (best co-worker ever, just named Assistant Manager), and Marcus (missed him on vacation).

"Courtney? Can I rely on you to be the Product Lead?" Jennifer was asking.

"What? No," I said. "I'm going to be really busy this semester."

"Well, then . . . Marcus!" Jennifer said. "You can be Head of Cheese. Or . . . Head Cheese. Or Cheesehead! Ha ha ha."

Mark/Marcus shook his head. "You can make me Assistant Manager if you want. Of *Apron* Redesign." He pulled one of the new bright yellow ones over his head. It said "Cheese All That" in black letters. "Who comes *up* with this stuff?"

"You know, Jennifer . . . we're going to quit if you don't stop introducing new products to run local family-owned stores out of business," Ben said. "You took on Brat Wurstenburger, and Brat Wurstenburger won. They're *still* doing great. Take that as a lesson, okay?"

"And what does a cheese shop have to do with bagels?" I asked.

"It's market research," Jennifer said brightly. She was over her burnout, back on her warpath. "I thought you'd be glad, Courtney. I thought you'd embrace the lack of meat."

Marcus had picked up a plate of cheese fries Jennifer handed him and dug in. "Oh my God. These are really good."

I stared at the cheese fries, resisting them. But feeling very, very weak. I walked over to the Blue Cheese Bonanza and took a whiff, just to kill my appetite.

Later, we all stared glumly into the new refrigerator case.

"If she even suggests putting brats *and* cheese *and* cheese curds in a *bacle*? We're going to quit. Right?" I said to Ben and Marcus.

"Oh, definitely," Marcus said.

Ben nodded. "We are so out of here."

"Me, too." I started stacking the napkins with the BF logo facing out. Every once in a while, though, I stuck one in backwards or upside down. I'm such an instigator.

6 pages left in this journal. Should probably start a new one to indicate new semester. Really should. But don't want to waste paper. New group in Badicals is going to focus on enforcing campus recycling and on saving the giant oak trees that circle the oval near the admin building, and on saving all trees from being killed.

Hope they don't make me sleep in those trees or strip to draw attention to the cause. Very cold. 5 below. Even Wittenauer would not strip today.

I must set an example for new focus group by reusing all half-filled notebooks this semester. Also I really need to cut down on printing emails and sticking them on my bulletin board.

Phone just rang. It was Dean S. Calling about a new work-study job for me. "But—the Funders," I started to say.

"Oh, no, this is a much more interesting and exciting proposition," Dean S. said. Proposition? I was starting to get very worried. "Also, a lot more hours. You won't need to keep working at that bagel shop. Are you ready?"

"Um . . . I doubt it," I said. Leave BF? Leave Ben and Marcus?

"You're going to be assisting the deans' offices. You're going to assist *me*, Courtney," Dean S. said.

I was highly suspicious. "You're just doing this so you can keep an eye on me, aren't you?"

"Just the same way I like to keep an eye on all our Cornwaller Fallers," Dean S. said. "Report to me on Friday at 10 A.M. All right?"

Do I get a helmet with this job? I was wondering. Dean S. is very dangerous to be around, constantly flinging and throwing things around. Got kind of depressed about losing the funding gig. Called Wittenauer to tell him.

"That's okay," he said. "I got shucked." He's no longer the mascot. "It's *such* a stupid job. But I just . . . liked it," he said, sounding really down.

"So you'll get it back," I said. "We'll protest. Don't even worry about it."

"They said I defiled the image of Cornwall Falls College and they couldn't be sure I wouldn't do it again," Wittenauer said.

"Well, good for you," I told him.

We started laughing and then he asked if I wanted to go for a walk. Was feeling adventurous, so I said yes. We went to see the actual Cornwall Falls. We walked. It wasn't that far—2 miles, maybe. The falls were unfortunately frozen over, just like everything else here. At first I was laughing because it seemed pathetic. Then I sort of had to acknowledge how pretty it was, thick crystallized ice, frozen tundra and all.

"They're really beautiful," I said.

"Yeah. I know," Wittenauer agreed.

We stared at the Falls for a while.

"You know, polar bears trap warmth against the snow with their fur," I said as my teeth chattered, repeating some line I'd heard on a nature special I'd watched 50 times.

"Is that a fact?" Wittenauer said, teasing me. "Let's try it." So we both threw ourselves onto the snowy ground to try to trap warmth—kept missing it. Kept trying again. And laughing.

Then we started walking back to town. Worked up a humongous appetite on the way. Needed hot food, fast.

Ice crystals formed on Wittenauer's stubble. Sexy in an "Everest" kind of way.

First restaurant we came to was Brat Wurstenburger. Didn't even discuss it, just barged in past steam-covered windows and grabbed the table closest to the kitchen. I got the onion soup. Delicious with cheese on top. Forgot to tell waitress no cheese. Didn't care. At some point I realized this outing was sort of datelike, but not really. And then I realized I had a lot more guy friends than ever before, like maybe this was a "mat-oor" thing one does when one goes away to college. More guy friends, more weird friends, more friends who drink way too much milk.

So maybe there sort of could be something between me and WW III? But I'm not going to push it right now. Just because basketball season is starting up does not mean I should be Rebound Girl and leap into my next relationship.

"Oh yeah," Annemarie said when we were discussing it tonight. "Consecutive monogamous relationships make *no* sense."

Well, um, okay. So what else is there?

It's official. Mary Jo and I *both* have decided not to date anyone seriously this semester. Got too ugly and mixed up last fall. We're going to be single. Focus on classes (she was already doing that—I wasn't). Friendships. Checking account balances. We'll join more groups. Try out for some rec clubs.

"But you know, when all is said and done, I still think you should get back together with Grant," Mary Jo said as she chewed on a stale Twizzler.

"I know you do," I said. "But it's not going to happen."

"Yeah. Well, there's always my brothers. If it doesn't work out with Ed . . . you know. There's five more to choose from."

Threw Twizzler at her head. "Thanks. I'm sure Soren and I would be really happy together."

"Who?"

"Wait. Is it Kierkegaard? Or Hegel?" I asked.

"Who?"

"Maybe it's Wittgenstein," I guessed.

"I thought his name was Wittenauer," she said.

"Not *him*!" I said. "Your . . . never mind."

Still too embarrassed to tell her what I was trying to get at: name of 6th brother, who does not speak. Must sneak into her desk tomorrow and find out once and for all. If I can find her desk drawer handle under all the knickknacks.

Last page of a journal always makes me turn back to see where this all began. Started this journal missing Grant intensely. Still miss him. We made a pledge to stay together, to make our LDR work. Didn't know what I was getting into. Honestly.

How many pledges have I made and not kept? It's got to be in the hundreds by now.

On reflection, thinking about what I said to Grant . . . that whole "maybe by the summer" concept . . . I sounded exactly like annoying ex Dave with my stupid time line. Also I broke it off just as he was about to leave town, which I swore never to do.

Resolution: never sound like Dave again. Bad idea. Watch for Dave-isms in speech and seek to eradicate them.

And that whole thing with Mary Jo a couple of weeks ago about not dating anyone this semester. I mean, that seems *very* silly in retrospect.

Oops. That was yesterday.

Well, anyway.

Here's what I'd say to Grant if he could read this. But of course I don't want him to read this. Except for the last page. Which I could possibly tear out and send to him if I'm feeling adventurous and if this comes out halfway decently.

Dear Grant,

I was thinking it over, and maybe I was too hasty the other day. Not hasty, exactly. How about wrong? I don't want to be separated from you. Ever. And I don't know about this whole "exclusive" concept, but I'm willing to try again. I think.

What would you think of both volunteering at the humane society this summer? We could work together, and that way we'd get to spend more time together, which is really important.

See, I always kind of pictured us running this animal hospital, only I'm a real wimp about blood and body parts and singed fur and euthanasia.

But I could file, right? I'm really good with the alphabet. Remember: D comes before V except after C.

Love,

C.V.D.S.

P.S. In the meantime, how does spring break look for you? I was thinking maybe Cancun. Please get back to me ASAP.

Sundae My Prince Will Come

How do you say good-bye to a dream?

I've always wanted to start a journal like this. Really dramatic and over the top.

Wait. I think all my journals have started like this— dramatic and over the top. Oh well.

But this time, it's serious. And true. And heartbreaking.

Just when I finally get used to being away at college, just when I have found utter bliss with college boyfriend, I get the news:

Scholarship. Not. Renewed.

You. Are. A. Loser.

Soon to be an Alone and Lonely Loser.

"The thing is, Courtney . . ."

That's never a good start to a conversation. Trust me.

"Your scholarship." Dean Sobransky's hands were shaking as he tried to casually sip his morning coffee when he called me into his office as if it were any other weekday morning, but he slipped and spilled some on his lap, which made him yell, "Stupid! Stupid! One cream, I said!" He finally composed himself and managed to mutter, "Your scholarship," again.

"Yes?"

"It's . . . well . . . the economy. . . ."

"What are you saying?"

"It's over. Our endowment is plummeting. We can't afford to help all the students we'd like to, and . . . well, you're a sophomore and we have seniors who have been here three years so far and . . ." Then Dean Sobransky burst into tears and what could I do but try to cheer him up, because I'm, like, his assistant and that's my job, but the whole time I was thinking, what does this mean for me? And what good is it being the dean's assistant if he can't even save you? And if he'd left me to founder in the Cornwall Falls College Campus Funders, maybe I could have convinced alumni to give the school enough money to keep me.

Well, probably not. I kind of sucked at that job, unlike Wittenauer, best caller ever.

Oh God. Sinking in. Am going to throw up. I have to leave Wittenauer. I have to move back home to Denver. Because I called home and Mom said she had already heard from Dean S., and she was sorry but she couldn't afford to keep me there at full cost. Yes, she'd already asked Dad. Yes, she'd already appealed to my grandparents. Both sides.

"So you were just waiting for the dean to break the news to me? Thanks, Mom."

"I was hoping I'd come up with a solution on my own. I'm sorry, hon!"

("Hon?" Since when does she call me "hon"?)

Adding insult to injury, the school had already gone ahead and bought me a plane ticket home. That's how much they want me gone. (OK, so it's a voucher thingy and I can change it, but the way I feel now, I'm so mad I want to be gone. Except for Wittenauer! Not leaving Wittenauer. No way.)

This whole cancelation thing isn't even just about me, it's about fifty other scholarship students, too. Our generation is, like, bankrupt before we even get started. We'll be known as Generation B. They're ditching us and importing students with cold, hard cash. And trust funds, probably, so they'll spend lots around town and keep the town afloat, too.

It's like being kicked off Noah's Ark. "Sorry, but we actually *don't* need one of you."

Now I have to try to get into another college at home. Like I'll be able to. Whatever happens, I won't need this stupid CFC notebook that I bought for class, so it may as well be my journal.

I'll have lots of time to write in it because I'll be living *at home*. I can't even think about that.

So many things have changed since I last lived at home. Puny little brother, Bryan, is now a high school senior. A *senior*. He's the captain of the cross-country team at Bugling Elk, my alma mater. He gets college catalogs in the mail daily. He tweets. He has interests. He has, apparently, no girlfriend "right now" and says nobody does anymore, that it's not cool. That's code: It means he asked a girl out and got rejected.

We don't usually do well with the love connections in this family. Big sister, Alison, recently got dumped by Jessie, the girl of her dreams.

Beth, my best friend from HS and Bryan's former girlfriend (*ew*, still *ew* after all these years), is in Italy on a term abroad to study art history. Hate her hate her with intensity of 100 suns. Is it too late to fly to Italy to join her? Jane is still at UW and happy there. She constantly texts me about fun things she's doing. It's like . . . everything is still moving forward, everyone has moved on to something new and exciting. But not me. I moved backward. There was a board game and I drew the card that read "Go Back Three Spaces."

Dean Sobransky shoved this recommendation letter at me, begging me to take it, as it would help me get transferred somewhere else. Felt sort of like a foster child. Or foster kitten, anyway.

Is it because I was responsible for getting that amendment to the college constitution, stating that the CFC initials could not be used anymore because they kind of promote a pollutant, chlorofluorocarbon? I thought the trustees were over that. Apparently not.

There was a brief discussion among the campus Badicals about holding a protest over this drop in financial aid, but then we realized that half of us were on scholarship and would quickly need to pack up and move home, so we didn't really have time to be political about it. I mean, sure. Get rid of the politically active ones first. Stupid CFC.

Could they not have figured this out before August???

Friends are at door to commiserate. They have Ben & Jerry's. Must go.

8/28

Mary Jo, former roommate and now friend and again roommate, insisted on exploring every possible option to keep me here.

"What about loans? Can't you just get loans?"

We went downtown (not much of a downtown, but we still call it that). Of the three banks that used to be there, two are closed—completely—and the one that's still open is no longer making loans to students.

"Well, this is lousy," she said.

That's as close as she ever gets to cursing.

I figured I might have stood more of a chance if I hadn't bounced a bunch of checks freshman year. Maybe the banks would still be in business.

We went back to our apartment. On the way, Jane called. "What's going on?" she asked.

"Oh, not much," I said. "Just being forced to move home." Then I burst into tears. She talked to me the entire time I was crying about how she thought she had sophomore slump because she wasn't excited to be at UW, either, but it's not the same thing. She can suffer in place. I have to suffer in motion. And a thing in motion . . . stays in . . . whatever.

That's why I'll never take—or at least never pass—physics.

Jane said moving home wouldn't be so bad and would just be temporary. She tried to point out all the great things about Denver we'd both missed so much: mountains, sun, good shopping. "And I'll see you at Thanksgiving, or at least Christmas," she said. "Cheer up, Court. It'll work out for the best, it always does."

Easy for her to say.

Started packing up my stuff. All we need now are labels and packing tape for the boxes. Courtney Von Dragen Smith—return to sender. And all Mary Jo needs is a new roommate or else she's going to be stuck paying really expensive rent.

A bunch of our other friends came by later, threw me a going away party with pizza and last-minute gifts like bars of soap and travel-size toothpaste and tacky CFC sweatshirt: CORNWALL FALLS INTO YOUR HEART.

As we packed my stuff, Mary Jo insisted on my taking her clock that's shaped like a potato. Used to hate that thing. Couldn't stop crying.

Wittenauer came to whisk me away to his place, where I'm going to spend my last night. Would be a tad more romantic if he didn't share the house with four other guys. It's completely messy most of the time and smells like perhaps a dead mouse is under the sofa. (Well, they found one once, so it's not a far-fetched thing at all.)

Wittenauer had a blender and attempted to make fancy "adult" malts. (Ice cream with schnapps.) I was too upset to drink one. He's cleaning blender now. He's actually been in the kitchen for, like, hours, I think, cleaning. I think we are both panicking a little.

Somehow this isn't how I anticipated my last night being, but then again, I've only known about it for 2 days so at least I didn't get the chance to get my hopes up.

LATER

OK, let me backtrack.

Last time I kept a journal, I had come here for my first semester at college and was miserable. Then I was not miserable.

I finally started to like it, so much that I didn't even have time to lie around and write in a journal. Instead of bailing for home, I stayed for spring semester, and studied studied studied. I studied my butt off.

Over the summer, I stayed here and worked on campus, giving tours and doing fund-raising.

I probably sound like a butt kisser, but it was really all about me: I was seeing Wittenauer/Corny (not to be confused with Corny Wittenauer because he's not that corny at all) and I didn't want to leave him for the summer.

I was the ideal Cornwall Falls student. Wasn't I? I mean, I was. Really. I should have won an award. Instead, I'm getting kicked to the curb.

Wittenauer says not to worry, everything will be OK, something good will come of all this, etc. Such an optimist.

I hate optimists sometimes. So not realistic.

"What's wrong with having hope?" he said.

"Do you know me at all?" I said.

Optimist and pessimist that we are, we sit around, smiling, but glumly holding hands.

"Courtney. Courtney. Courtney."

The words were floating in the air above my head. I tried to wake up. My name was getting irritating, even to me, and it's my name.

"Courtney!" Someone was shaking my shoulder now. "It's time to leave for the airport."

I looked up and saw gorgeous boyfriend standing over me like a towering cornstalk.

Seriously. That is his mascot uniform for being Corny, the mascot for Cornwall Falls College, the place that is now apparently kicking me out until further notice. There is nothing corny about that.

Wittenauer was dressed for the CFC FFGP (Cornwall Falls College First Football Game Parade), something I'd dreaded but would now miss horribly, to the end of my days. He'd tried to give up being Corny and put it to an all-campus vote, but he ended up winning, so he's still school mascot. He gets to hand off the costume at the end of football season and supposedly has an understudy this year, otherwise known as Baby Corn.

This college has so many ridiculous traditions that I won't mind leaving behind.

Anyway, back to gorgeous boyfriend. Tall, blond, Norwegian-German. Strangely committed to eating black olives, onions, and sausage on every pizza, even though you've told him several times you don't eat sausage. Still, the kind of person who would give you his umbrella if it was raining. If he had one.

But guys don't usually carry umbrellas, do they? I need a better metaphor.

OK, say you were on a long bike ride together. Really

long, in the country, which had lots of hills. And you bonked because you completely ran out of energy and you couldn't make it back to campus. If he had one granola bar, he'd give it to you, even if he was really, really hungry, too. No questions asked.

Or here's another example. If you forgot about this ten-page paper you were supposed to write, OK let's say you didn't forget, exactly, but you just procrastinated until the night before it was due, and it was on Shakespeare, and you were kind of getting a B in the class but wanted an A . . .

Wittenauer (only his parents call him Walter) would bring you to that all-night breakfast place so you could stay up and get it written. And he'd be there but he wouldn't let you talk to him until you had 2 pages done and he wouldn't let you have pancakes until you had 8 pages done.

That kind of person.

For Valentine's Day, he went a little crazy and left a trail of three dozen roses from my dorm to his. A bunch of people stole some of the roses, and some got stepped on, but still. Very romantic. He was really sweet like that. Still, I resisted getting *involved* involved, because even though Grant and I were broken up, I didn't think I wanted another relationship.

Wittenauer kept doing everything to win me over. Still, I resisted. For about another month. Which landed at just the same time Grant and I were supposed to be giving our relationship another shot and going away together. I panicked. Well, can you blame me?

Probably.

So, anyway. Me and Wittenauer: a morbid good-bye

scene at the Milwaukee airport. Breaking down by the security line. Making out in public with a cornstalk.

"I'll come visit soon," Wittenauer kept saying. "Soon, soon."

More like: swoon, swoon. Security guard not sure what to do with me. She waved this packet of smelling salts in front of my nose that made me stumble even more, confused, down ramp to the gates.

Here I am. On the plane. Hating life. Hating everybody. Hating everything.

But loving Wittenauer. More than I can say.

Also, I keep trying but I can't stop crying. Annoying.

Is it weird that I still only call him by his last name? For a while I used "Witt" for short, but that sounded very pretentious, like an abbreviation for "Whitney." Walter's out, and Wally is not acceptable. *Wall-E* did nothing to make that name cuter.

Used to refer to him as WWIII, but he got tired of that. Tried W. Really, his name is impossible. What were his parents thinking? They are very nice people but did not think that through.

Of course, neither did Baroness Von Dragen.

Of all people, shouldn't she have had the power to change that dreadful last name? What's the point in being a baroness if you can't abolish bad names?

Home in Denver. Mom gave me generous, gigantic hug when I met her at baggage claim. That took the edge off for a few minutes, until we got home and I just sort of stared at bedroom walls for a few minutes too long.

Have talked to Wittenauer about 89 times today on the phone, but still can't stop missing him and crying.

Why did I have to leave when everything was just getting good?

Have friends there. Professors I know. A decent off-campus apartment. Hot, older boyfriend.

Do I really need to say this in a journal again? Long-distance Relationships. Do. Not. Work.

First boyfriend Dave broke up with me on way to college because of this.

Second boyfriend Grant and I broke up because of this.

Things don't look good for me and Wittenauer, third boyfriend.

Wow. I think maybe I've had too many boyfriends in the past couple years.

This is getting out of control. I was the one who didn't want to date anyone, and now look at this list. Insane what can happen.

What am I, turning into my best friend, Beth?

And speaking of Beth, what gives her the right to be in Italy on term abroad when I need her here? Normally I'd already be at her house. But no, she's learning about art and architecture. And Italian leather.

Me, sitting, staring at wall.

Wall not responding.

Learning about walls. American walls.

This isn't how it's supposed to be. Whatever happened to true love, anyway? Like, wasn't it supposed to be all perfect? Remember Snow White? She saw that prince guy once, and after a year he came back for her. Shouldn't Wittenauer be coming back for me any day now? Because I'm dying here.

OK, so Prince Charming went away for a year and let her lie there, half dead, which was not cool, but he came back.

Of course, she sang very well. To birds and animals who followed her. The only animal that follows me around is Oscar, my epileptic mutt.

And occasionally pigeons, when I have food.

8/31

Journals. Overrated.

Blogs. WAY overrated.

There was a period—a very *brief* period—when I kept a journal online. I created my own blog where I was known by my blogger name, Courtney Von Bloggen.

Several negative things happened, which I will keep brief—you, dear journal, will never turn on me like that, will you? If you do, I will shred you.

Anyway, here's what happened.

Current boyfriend read blog.

Ex-boyfriend read blog.

Courtney got hideously embarrassed.

Also, Cornwall Falls College started its restricted-access-blogs policy thanks to me, but I don't want to get into that right now. Involved certain photos of certain faculty members that no one could find on Facebook but were apparently screaming to be noticed once there was a link to my blog.

Link schmink is what I say. Links are chains that bind us to responsibilities, like being responsible for the downfall of Cornwall Falls College's Dance-a-thon. (And student blogs.)

(Don't drink if you don't want to see yourself on the internet in an embarrassing picture that will haunt you forever, I always say. It's a public service announcement waiting to happen. I mean, if you can't even uphold one of the most basic principles in life . . . !)

Anyway, here I am, back home in Denver.

Well. Uh. What can I say?

Ooh! IM from Beth! I'd emailed her the news that I was home.

shoe92gurrl: C, u there?

crtveg17: Beth, what am I going 2 do?

shoe92gurrl: IDK. I don't know what 2 tell u.

crtveg17: Well. *Something!*

shoe92gurrl: Enroll @Metro? DU? CU, CSU?

crtveg17: No. Stomach hurts just thinking about it. But maybe it's because I forgot to eat breakfast.

shoe92gurrl: Just had dinner. You won't believe food here. Gained 5 lbs already. OMG, I know. Come 2 Milan!

crtveg17: For the weight gain?

shoe92gurrl: Lol. OK. GTG. XOXOXO

I smiled. Maybe Beth couldn't actually help me with this, but just talking to her a little bit helped improve my mood.

First thing I've got to do if I'm going to live here is reclaim my bedroom. Mom has converted it into her personal workout center. Treadmill in the middle of it. Mom's gotten into good shape since I went to college. Now she wants to run a marathon with her new man-friend. A freaking marathon.

Forever and ever after she and Dad divorced, I wanted her to find a guy. Now she has. His name is Sterling. He's a triathleting consumer credit counselor. And she's become Ms. Luna Bar.

More like Ms. Lunatic Bar.

Anyway, the thing is that I am afraid to leave the house. What if I run into someone and, well, I don't know. I'm just so aimless right now. Without aim. It's like I got fired from a job or something.

And Grant? Where is Grant? Not too far away, actually. Should I call him? I should. But I'm so nervous. I haven't spoken with him much over the past six months. The last time I talked to him was . . . well, I don't know. I left him a message back in March. A couple of them, actually.

Agh. No idea what to do. Maybe an email, let him know what's going on and ask him for advice because I'm totally lost here and only he, cool calm collected type, might know how to help me?

Ew. Hands are too nervous and sweaty to type well.

Hey, Grant. Bet you didn't expect to hear from me. I didn't expect to, either. I mean, I didn't expect to write to you. I mean, not that I didn't *want* to write to you, because I totally did, but . . .

Delete. Babbling.

Hey. You won't believe what happened. Or maybe you will. I had to leave CFC because my funding ran out. So I'm home now. Nothing to do. Don't have a car.

Delete. Boring.

Hey, Grant. How are you? How's college? I'm actually at home now. In Denver, I mean. Oscar says hi. It's a long story but basically my financial aid was canceled so I had to leave—now I have to find a place near here to go. Any advice? I'd love to hear it. Plus, it'd be nice to get back in touch.

And sorry about being such an idiot about the spring break thingy.
CVDS

Man. My initials are hideously close to national drug-store chain.

Also, VD, but we've been through that before.

Not VD!!! Just the fact that my middle initials are unfortunate.

Crap. Can't put this off any longer.

Or can I?

Send.

Sitting here waiting for Grant to instantly write back.

Why would he answer me now, when he refused to before? Maybe he's over it by now. Maybe he no longer wishes I would be buried by an avalanche.

And you know what? If I have a BF, maybe he has a GF. So there's no reason why we can't be friends. That happens, right? All the time. People break up and stay friends. That's, like, the natural order of things.

Still nothing. No response. This was a big mistake. Am going to bed.

Just completed watching 13th consecutive episode of *Project Runway*. Marathon weekend.

Meanwhile, rest of family is *running* a marathon. Practically.

Oscar has been licking my feet for the past ten minutes. His epilepsy has clearly taken a turn toward scurvy or something; he needs the salt.

Why are my feet salty? I haven't moved enough to sweat.

Have talked to Jane (who says sophomore year still sucks and am I sure I want to be one), Mary Jo (who saw Corny at student center looking miserable), and Alison (who wants to know why I don't transfer to her college, when it's obvious, it's even farther away from W, and I'm not a musician).

Depression setting in. Must do something. Must get out of house.

Ooh—email just dinged. Hold on.

Mailer Daemon. Returned email. Addressee unknown. Address has permanent fatal error.

Well, that's not going to work.

Facebook? No, Grant once went on a rant about it *and* Twitter. "Why do I need to know what people are eating or listening to or how late they stay up and why they can't sleep and—"

Well, I had to cut him off. It was a seriously long rant and I had other stuff to do. Like, eat, listen to music, stay up late, and post about it.

#Courtneyfail.

LATER

Not sure leaving the house was the best idea. First, ran into strange neighbor across the street, the Broncos-obsessed guy who never stops working on his yard.

"What are you doing here?" Mr. Novotny paused mid-leaf blow to confront me.

"Excuse me?"

"Thought you were at college."

"I was. I mean, I still am." I coughed. "I'm transferring, I guess."

"Dropped out, huh? Why?" He didn't seem thrilled about the idea of me living at home. And why did he automatically assume I was a dropout? *I was on dean's list, Mr. Novotny!* I wanted to say, but that seemed like TMI.

"The economy?" I said. "And, uh, I didn't drop out. I was asked to leave," I said softly, realizing it didn't sound any better to phrase it that way.

"Stupid economy. You know that's the reason they got rid of Shanahan."

"Shana . . . who?"

"Mike Shanahan. Greatest coach in Broncos history. Surely you haven't forgotten him."

"No, surely not." I smiled and raced to the car. I hadn't had a car in Wisconsin—I hadn't needed one on campus. Now I have to beg and plead to borrow Bryan's. There is a certain amount of lost dignity involved when you're driving a Hyundai hatchback with a BOYZ WILL BE BOYZ bumper sticker.

Anyway, drove to Truth or Dairy to visit Gerry. A friendly face would cheer me up, I thought. Also, so would a Coconut Fantasy Dream smoothie. Perhaps a couple of them.

Got a funny feeling when I walked in.

One: no teen employees like me around. Just Gerry, former high school counselor and current owner of smoothie ice-cream shop.

Two: Gerry looked as though he had lost about 50 pounds, and while that is no doubt good for his health, it just didn't look right on him. I'm used to him being a friendly bear, not the Biggest Loser.

Three: He hugged me as if he hadn't seen me for 10 years, rather than a couple of months.

"Gerry. Everything OK?" I asked.

He reached into a bin and scooped a cupful of nuts. "Remember when we used to have pecans? You loved pecans." He handed me the cup. "Have a peanut."

"Um . . ."

"Pecans are just another unfortunate victim of the new economy. Premium toppings?" He made a slashing motion across his throat. "Oreos? History."

"Oreos are premium toppings?"

"You learn to make tough calls over the years." He hoisted his loose pants with his belt loops.

Rigggggghhhhht. "Are you, um, eating OK, Gerry?" I asked.

He laughed. "Fine. Just trying to get fit."

What's *with* everyone? Is the city of Denver giving people money to lose weight and get in shape or something?

And if so, how much does it pay and where do I sign up?

On my way back to the car, glanced over at the other stores in the strip mall. Pet Me was still there. Memory flashed back to the time I accused Grant of stalking me when in fact he worked at that store, that happened to be in the same strip mall where I worked. So. Embarrassing.

But he forgave me for being such a conceited twerp. And I started falling for him.

Then there was the time I went to apologize to him to try to win him back and he was so cold to me, because I hadn't been honest with him, and then I got upset and tripped over a fish tank on my way out.

But then we made up and he helped me organize this big fund-raiser where Pet Me gave our school half the proceeds from dog groomings and Truth or Dairy served up free smoothies. The perfect event.

Why did we break up, anyway?

Oh, right. Consequences of the Long-distance Relationship. He and Beth had a minifling. That was hugely awful at the time, but I decided I couldn't NOT forgive Beth, and now when I think about the two of them ever kissing it's almost laughable. Almost. If I'm in a good mood.

Anyway, the fact that they kissed meant that I didn't feel so bad when Wittenauer and I kissed. But basically, everything went haywire. LDRs. Hate them.

And that was freshman year, in a nutshell. Preferably a pecan. A premium topping. As if.

After using superhuman powers to turn off VH1, I rode my bike over to the University of Denver campus to look around. Even if Beth is in Italy now, it'd be fun to go to the same school when she gets back. Beautiful campus, students roaming around looking happy and not stressed. DU sounds a bit like "DUH," but is nowhere near as bad as CFC, chlorofluorocarbon, my previous school. Where, I'd like to announce, again, I made dean's list spring semester. Even if that same dean did call me to his office to tell me I was being cut from any and all CFC lists.

Am I obsessing about dean's list? Sorry. I just find it so ironic that it makes me a bit ill.

When Mom got home from work, I told her my brilliant idea.

She just chopped a leafy green and said it would be too expensive because DU is a private school, and that I need to go to a state school, for in-state tuition. "You know, Metro State." Chop. "Colorado State." Chop. "University of Colorado." Chop chop.

My stomach turned into a giant knot. Those are no doubt awesome schools. The problem is that I know people at two out of three of them. And by "people" I mean my two ex-boyfriends that I don't want to see because I kind of hate one of them, and one of them kind of hates me.

Probably I should be mature enough to not let that bother me. But I'm not.

Then Mom asked if I wanted to go running with her before dinner. Um, no. But I did go for a long bike ride. Since that's my primary mode of transportation right now, I'd better get in good biking shape. Can just see me riding round-trip to Boulder every day. I'd barely get there in time for my classes and would be a sweaty, disgusting mess. Mom would think that was so great. Classmates would think I smelled. And would be correct.

Have been talking to Wittenauer on the phone for two hours straight. Ear hurts. He wants me to move back to town even if I am not going to be in college anymore. Said he knew he was being selfish but didn't care. Said I could work for a year and then reapply for aid in the spring and in the meantime we'd be together.

"Where would I work?" I asked.

"I don't know. Bagle Finagle? Or you could wait tables somewhere."

"Right. Right! Definitely!" I said, though the thought of returning to BF made my shoulders slump.

Being a senior, Wittenauer has a different outlook on life. He's been thinking about "the real world" a little more than I have, which is to say, a little, anyway. He said I could wait and apply to wherever he decides to apply for law school and we'd be at the same college again, like at UW.

The way he described it, and us, sounded nice, better than nice even, but as I'm lying here thinking about it, that would mean postponing college. A whole year. And then maybe not even getting another financial aid package for the next year. "I don't want to do that. I want to finish college in four years because . . ."

"I'll be done with law school then," Wittenauer said. "I know."

Actually, it has nothing to do with him or his plans. I just want to be done in four years. I have my own goals, and the sooner I graduate with my degree, the sooner I can save the environment, animals, planet, etc.

Plus, I have this cousin, Karl, who has been in college for, like, eight years, and everyone complains about him all the time, and his parents have totally cut him off.

I'm on the bus to Boulder—Bryan claimed he needed his car today. I'm all in favor of public transportation, but this bus seems to run on an endless cloud of diesel fumes. Thought that Colorado had a zero-tolerance emissions policy. Or maybe that's a zero-tolerance admissions policy, so why am I heading to the University of Colorado?

Because Mom and I got into a huge fight. Huge. One of our worst ever.

She said I must find a new college to attend and move out. Me? Loser of financial aid? Now must be homeless?

"You know, when I was your age, I wouldn't have wanted my parents looking over my shoulder. You want to be free to live your own life, don't you?" she asked.

"Well, yeah."

"And besides, I need my privacy," she said.

"Hold on a second. Bryan still lives here," I pointed out.

"That's different."

"How is that different? Because he's a boy? Because he doesn't cook with tofu and isn't vegetarian? Because he's a runner, so that's OK because now everyone has to take some kind of running test to live here?"

"No. Because he's still in high school, he's under eighteen, and he needs me. And two, because he leaves the house occasionally to go to school," Mom said. "And you don't."

"Oh. Low blow, Mom. None of this is my fault."

"No, but if you ever want to graduate from college, you'd better start moving. Sprinting. Now."

Everything she says now has to have some sort of running connection. Annoying.

OK fine, I know that, and I'm the one who wants to stay in school and not miss a semester, but I still don't want to go to Boulder.

Too many unpleasant memories of visiting ex there and thinking we'd get back together when we so obviously weren't. Am getting off at next stop.

Phew. This bus is better. Much better. Less smelly.

Wait a second. Where is this bus going? Thought it was back to Denver.

Just asked overly cologned guy sitting next to me. "Fort Collins," he said.

WHAT? Totally misread schedule. No, no, no. Grant is there and I'm not ready to see him yet!

OK, so it's a big town. A city. And chances of seeing him are really slim. But I have just that kind of luck lately.

Or. Perhaps universe is sending me a signal. That I should ditch CU–Boulder for CSU–Fort Collins. But am I in any position to ditch anyone? Actually, this is more of a begging and pleading because my life is passing me by kind of situation.

Miles are going by. I should call Grant, I thought. I should ask him for help, tell him what's going on. But I don't want to see him, or at least, I'm dreading the first time I do. What would I say, anyway? "Remember when I asked you to go on spring break and we totally made plans, but then I freaked out at the last second and told you I wasn't coming and I was seeing someone else?"

Crap. Just spilled Diet Squirt all over my transcript.

Report from the Fort yesterday:

Took out my soggy Diet Squirt–soaked transcript and headed for the admissions building, which only took me, like, half an hour to find. Big campus. Very pretty oval.

I'd been here before, of course. To see Grant last year when home on break. But hadn't spent a lot of time here. Still, it gave me chills.

This nice admissions counselor was coming back from lunch and asked if he could help me. I told him my plight, how I needed to talk about transferring ASAP. Shoved my transcript in his direction. He looked at it like it was a dead fish.

If anything, coming from Cornwall Falls, it was a dead piece of bratwurst.

"What is *this*? You know, you can do all this online. Or, um, by mail," he said.

"Yes, but you see, my mom wanted me out of the house. Ever since I got home, I've been messing up her intense workout schedule." I rolled my eyes.

"And she is . . . ?" he asked.

"What?"

"Who is she?"

"Nobody. My mom."

"Oh!" He laughed. "I thought she was a big-deal athlete."

"She thinks so, too, I guess," I said.

We both laughed and after that he was really nice. He said I might have some issues proving I live here for in-state tuition, since my transcript from Wisconsin shows otherwise, but he'd actually heard of Cornwall Falls, and he helped me and they're going to review my materials and let me know if they have room for one more sophomore.

Do they have room? Excuse me. They have 25,000 students. What's one more?

He also said I'd be starting two to three weeks late, and asked if I was prepared for that, playing catch-up, and he said there wouldn't be a discount just because I missed a few weeks. I could just see Mom arguing that point. Ms. Frugal Goes to College. He also said I should get a job.

"For, like, backup? Just in case?" I asked.

"No. To help prove your residency. Plus, have you *seen* how much textbooks cost these days?" He chuckled.

Ha-ha. Very funny.

I walked around campus for a little while afterward. I was kind of hoping I'd run into Grant and dreading it at the same time. Call him, call him, I told myself. But he was probably in class. I didn't want to disturb him. He takes his studies very seriously, you know. Or, at least, he did. Back when we were not estranged. Estrangers. Whatever.

I went inside the student center to check out the bookstore and get something to drink; it was jammed. People at tables lined the hallway, trying to sign you up for clubs, sell you cheap jewelry, become your cable company and best friend. Tons of students moving slowly.

All of a sudden, around the corner, at this table selling newspaper subscriptions (like everyone our age doesn't read the paper online), I saw him.

Grant.

It's him it's him it's him.

That was the beating of my heart. Off the charts. Would he acknowledge me? Talk to me? Spit in my face?

First I wanted to duck, then I wanted to flatten myself

against the wall, then, before I knew it, my body took over. I pushed my way through the crowd. "Grant!" I shouted. "Grant!"

He didn't look—he didn't hear me over the din of other people yelling, selling, cajoling, high-fiving, etc. He turned to walk away, toward the exit, and I shoved a couple of girls with sorority letters on the back of their shorts out of the way (OK, so pledging there is now definitely out) and grabbed his elbow.

A very strong elbow.

An elbow not belonging to Grant Superior.

"Can I *help* you?" the guy asked, jerking his arm away and staring at me.

"Oh. No. Sorry. Thought you were, um, someone else. Sorry."

A Grant look-alike was the last thing I needed.

So are heart palpitations. I am so clearly between health insurance policies.

LATER (DUDE)

Wittenauer is so sweet.

Sweetest.

Ultrasweet.

But not NutraSweet. NutraSweet is artificial and therefore not genuine and original like Wittenauer.

Got home from watching Bryan's cross-country meet (he came in second) and there was a care package waiting. FedExed. Filled with items from Wauzataukie: brick cheese, cheese curds, chocolate cow, sausages (?), Bagle Finagle bagels, and a black Brat Wurstenburger tee that is fitted and actually looks kind of good except the name is too long to really fit onto the shirt and you have to read around my entire chest, which is probably going to make some people stare at my chest, which is not cool, and some Corny items. I don't mean just corny as in tacky and schmaltzy. I mean things made by CFC to promote Corny: a Corny cornstalk bottle opener, a Corny corncob pen where the stalk peels away when you turn it upside down (sexy), and a scarf that looks like a corncob.

Looks terrible on me—I can't wear yellow—but it only makes me miss him more.

Tears dropped onto cheese curds. Had to throw them out; got kind of gross.

Bryan ate all the summer sausage.

"How could Wittenauer not remember I'm a vegetarian?"

"I was wondering about that, too," said Bryan.

"It's because I'm supposed to share this stuff," I said. "I guess."

"So give me the chocolate cow," he said.

"No way!"

We started fighting over it, tackling each other, and the melted cow slipped out of my hands like a wet football.

Living at home is turning me back into a toddler. Must move out soon.

9/7

This is what I don't like about being home. Instead of being at Cornwall Falls Fall Blast party, outside on big grassy hill, I had to attend awkward Labor Day picnic at Mom's man-friend Sterling's house. With Sterling's extended family.

Talk about labor. Making conversation was impossible. Gave up and started texting friends. Then Mom yelled at me for being antisocial.

So Bryan and I played badminton with some elderly aunts and bratty nephews. I found myself struggling for the racket with a nine-year-old, fighting to the death, yelling, "Give it! GIVE IT!"

Well, better than knocking the eighty-year-olds to the ground, I guess.

I've got to find another place soon—and something positive to actually DO with my energy.

Classes have started everywhere. In a related development, Courtney V. D. Smith is falling further and further behind. And eating lots of Wisconsin brick cheese.

Well, the few scraps that Bryan didn't eat before heading off to school this morning. How can it be that I envy my little brother for going to Bugling Elk? I couldn't wait to get out of there. Now I'd like to just have someplace, anyplace, to go.

Enough slinking around. If I end up going to Colorado State, then I have to talk to Grant sooner or later. Besides . . . I could really use a friend right now. Mr. Novotny across the street doesn't count.

For some reason while Grant and I were dating, I got to know Grant's grandmother (Grandmother Superior, who I occasionally call Grantmother) better than his parents, even though they all live in the same house. I can't really explain why. Maybe because my grandparents, who I really do love, really drive me crazy most of the time? And she's just so refreshing. And because Grant was always such a good grandson, doing errands for her, etc.

Or, maybe it was because his parents never liked me much. Actually, I could never tell how they felt. But I'm guessing after the way I kind of vanished from his life they probably aren't Courtney Smith fans right now.

I figured they'd be at work during the day, while Grantmother might be home, and gave it a shot. Thankfully, she answered.

"Mrs. Superior? I'm so sorry to bother you, but . . ."

"Courtney. I'd know that voice anywhere."

"You would?"

"Well, that and we have caller ID and I don't know

anyone else with the last name 'Smith.' So how can I help you?"

"This is kind of bizarre, but—"

"You're looking for Grant?"

"Well, yeah. How did you know?"

"Why else would you call me? And, why are you calling from Denver? Shouldn't you be at school now?"

Man. Even Grant's grandmother is critical. I am soooo tired of explaining this to everyone.

Still, she gave me his new cell number. "Would you like me to call him for you?" she offered.

Even she knows the situation is dire. "N-no," I said. "That's OK."

But it was so tempting. Maybe I could ask Grantmother to do my dirty work. Call G for me, let him know I was seeing W, find out if he was with someone new. Etc. But that was probably asking a tad too much.

"But really," she said, "you just give him a call. He'll be so happy to hear from you."

"He will?" I asked.

"The boy's not heartless."

"So, um, how is he?" I asked, suddenly dying to know. You know when you don't think much about a person or see a person for a long time, you kind of forget about how they are, what they're like? And then when you do get to see them again, it's amazing because you were so close once? Just talking to Grantmother was flooding my brain with good memories of me and Grant.

"He's happy, and busy, and happy because he's busy. Trying to make a big dent in sophomore year." She said he works at a grocery store called Shop & Shop near campus, and told me where it was. I could track him down there, she said, and told me his schedule. "You know Grant. I mean, you could *try* finding him at home, I'd be OK giving you his address, but he's always either in class or at work."

That figures, I thought. Grant Superior. Reliable, hardworking, handsome, best boyfriend ever—

To someone else, probably. Not me. Now I am with W. And besides, I've changed, so I bet Grant has changed, too.

For instance, now I'm a college dropout. Kickout. Dropkickout.

Sitting in bathroom hiding from Mom and Sterling, who are being disgustingly romantic. Making out on sofa a little bit. Draping themselves in suggestive ways. Do they not realize they are middle-aged and not supposed to do that?

But then, think of my grandparents.

Or don't, if you want to spare yourself.

This family doesn't know how to have relationships but does apparently know how to kiss, etc.

I came in here to paint my nails, get ready for any future outings. Not just the one to possibly, maybe see Grant after not seeing him for eight months.

Eight months. That's, like, long enough that I could have had a baby in that time. Not that I *would* have, or even came close to having, because, you know, I don't do those sorts of things, but it's a point of reference, you know, nine months. And yes, I *would* know, because my stepsister Angelina-not-Jolie had a baby two years ago.

Babbling. Must pull myself together and stop contemplating the can of shave gel on the tub, which has line through CFC initials on back. CFC-Free. That's me. CFC with a line through it. Canceled.

And why does sensitive skin sound so much better in French? *Peau sensible.*

See, it's *sensible* skin I have—not rashy and allergic and sensitive. Just *sensible.*

Like *moi.*

Occasionally.

Am parked outside Shop & Shop grocery store on College Ave. The mountains off to the west are beautiful. I've really, really missed the mountains.

OK, I'm just delaying the inevitable freak-out.

Now, officially, freaking out.

So much for thinking that I've changed or am being mature. I'm a wreck. I'm stressed over the top. If I were a cheese, I'd be melted. If I were a bagel, I'd be toasted.

God. Can't believe I'm making *bagel* metaphors. I think I need to eat before I go inside and face Grant.

Like, an entire bottle of Tums. Well, probably they sell those at Shop & Shop, so at least I'm in the right place.

What if Grant won't talk to me? Won't talk back, I mean? What if he just stands there with that cold "like the lake" Superior glare he has sometimes? So disapproving. He'd just stare at me and mouth the words *spring break*, and I'd have to run out of the store with my tail between my eggs like Oscar.

Legs. Tail between my legs.

And think about it. How would I have felt if he suddenly showed up in Wisconsin and walked into the place where I worked, Bagle Finagle? I'd have freaked out. It would have made no sense, you know?

So he'll see me standing there and . . . how will he react?

Time to stop writing. Take deep breaths. And walk in there.

Wish me luck, dear journal.

LATER

Blood pressure: 300/200 at best.

Pulse: thready (learned that on *Grey's Anatomy*) and yet pounding.

I am recovering from Grant Encounter #1.

From a distance, customer service desk looked non-threatening.

Then again, from a distance even tigers can look non-threatening, like teeny tiny cute striped kittens.

I tried to camouflage myself by pushing a shopping cart. Then I put the closest tall thing I could find in front of my face to hide me; unfortunately the only thing that would work was a giant package of toilet paper, on its end. I was crouched over like a tiny older person with back trouble. Like I wasn't a mostly healthy, mostly vegetarian person with a love of calcium that strengthened my bones.

Up close, the customer service desk was a whir of activity. I hid behind the TP and watched.

It was him.

He turned around.

Same dark brown hair. Same eyes. (Why would they have changed? I don't know. I was just stunned by the sight of him, that's all.) Kind of stronger looking somehow. Older? I did see him in January, which isn't that long ago, but I somehow had forgotten a little about his hockey body. He's no towering cornstalk like Wittenauer. He's more of the strong, silent type. Not the tall, skinny type.

He didn't see me for a minute so I had time to study him, to peek.

I was slowly walking forward when my shopping cart slammed into someone else's that I didn't see. The towering TP tipped over.

Grant and I made eye contact. I wanted to run, but TP was in the way.

Grant looked a little pale and green, like he was going to throw up. Then I realized it was because he was wearing this green Shop & Shop employee vest. It was dorky. Not fashionable in the least. Almost embarrassing. Then he said, "You're not a very good driver, are you?"

"I'm a—a—fine driver," I said.

Then we both started laughing. "Courtney? What are you doing here?" He came out from behind the counter. "I'm so . . . stunned. I just can't believe you're here. Um, why are you?"

"I'm not sure," I said. My stomach churned. "I need Tums?"

There was an awkward pause while he adjusted a few packs of gum in a rack of candy. Big Red. Juicy Fruit. Stride. I stared at them, at his hands, to avoid making eye contact. He reached into the top rack, which was full of medicine that only *looked* like candy. "There you go," he said, handing me a roll of Tums.

"Oh. Thanks," I said.

Then I felt it. The chill. A polar ice cap descended onto the customer service desk, like every freezer door had been opened, which is funny, because Grant and I kind of hooked up over polar bears.

But then, the chill vanished almost as soon as it arrived. All of a sudden it felt really, really warm in that Shop & Shop. I wanted to run to the freezer section. My blood was running hot and cold. Any second now, I'd probably pass out.

Was I coming down with something, or was it just seeing Grant?

"Is that it?" he asked. "You drove all the way from Wisconsin for a roll of Tums?"

Maybe he thought I was there to try to win him back. Or apologize for bailing on him for spring break. Which I still needed to do.

"It's a long story. But not all that long, actually. I just found out that I, um, don't have financial aid for Cornwall Falls. So, I had to come home."

"Home?"

"To Denver. And I have to apply to transfer, and, um, CSU has great environmental classes and programs. . . ."

"So does CU," said Grant. "So does anywhere these days."

It wasn't exactly a welcoming hug kind of statement. What was he implying? "Well, right, I know. But I applied to transfer here."

He nearly choked on his breath mint. "Here. Really."

"Really," I said.

He didn't say anything. Not encouraging. At all. But I figured he was still mad at me from way back when, and so I'd have to really be convincingly nice from now on.

"So how are you doing? What's your job here like?" I asked.

"I'm responsible for customer service green team initiatives."

"Translation?"

"I'm kind of in charge of getting people to use reusable bags."

"Wow. Huge."

He smiled. "Shut up. I also handle customer complaints."

I raised an eyebrow. "That doesn't sound fun."

"I know. But it beats restocking forty-pound bags of

dog food at Pet Me." He shrugged. "Some of the time."
We both laughed and that kind of broke the polar-cap ice
a little more.

"The thing is, even if I do get accepted as a transfer,
I'll never find a place to live. I mean, everyone's already
moved in. But my mom wants me out, like, yesterday."

"Your mom wants you to move?" He looked really
uncomfortable.

"Oh, I wasn't asking—"

"I didn't say you were—"

"I mean that'd be really bizarre and—"

"Uncomfortable," Grant said.

"Uncomfortable?" I said.

"Sleeping on the floor. I mean. Obviously, *we're* fine.
That wouldn't be the problem."

"Of course not. Obviously."

Ha! What a joke. If we were "fine," then I'd hate to
see "horrible."

Fortunately, a customer came to the desk wanting
lottery tickets and I looked behind me and there was a
line that had formed. Because were we fine? Probably
not, unless I apologized for the spring break thing. But I
couldn't find a way to bring it up!

"Anyway. See you around?" I said.

"Call me when you find out what you're doing," he
said. "And, uh, if I hear anything about any kind of, you
know, openings . . . I'll call you."

"That'd be great. Thanks." I started to walk away.

"Courtney!" he called after me. "I need your number."

"Right. Right." I jotted my cell number down on the
corner of a brown paper grocery bag, then tore a piece
off and handed it to him.

"I could have added it to my iPhone," he said. "You just wasted a bag."

Stupid green team initiatives. I ran out to the car and started crying. So emotional. Nothing worse than getting corrected by Grant, Mr. Perfect.

Mr. Perfect Ex-Boyfriend.

LATER

Got home. Shaken and crumbly like a stale carrot cake muffin. Tried to call Wittenauer but he was heading into class and didn't have time to talk. Instead, called Jane. Told her that I'd just seen Grant.

"You're kidding!!! How is he? Tell him I said hi!"

"*Jane*. It wasn't like that. It wasn't a social visit."

"It wasn't?" she asked.

"No!"

"What was it, then?"

"I don't know. Awkward!"

She asked if I'd told him about Wittenauer yet, and I said, no, of course not, considering as how I only saw him a few minutes and we were in the middle of customer service. Did she really expect me to rub salt in an old wound the first time I saw Grant?

But *does* Grant know I'm still with Wittenauer? I wondered. Why would he? How could he? Well, that could wait until our next conversation. If we had one.

Jane and I talked so long that I was still on the phone with her when Wittenauer called back after class, and we talked for hours again. He still wants me to move back. Says he's miserable. I told him I'm more miserable. It was a contest trying to one-up each other on how miserable we are. I think I won, but is it considered winning when it's a contest for most miserable?

There is no "able" in miserable. Oh wait, there is. Able to feel misery. Lots and lots of misery. We are *Les Misérables*. We get very pathetic.

Do I move back to Wisconsin so I can be with Wittenauer? Or do I stay here so I can go to school, but only at a place where Grant is?

CSU has 25,000 students. Even if I do go there, and it's not guaranteed I could get in, it's not like I would see a lot of Grant. So that's not the problem, really.

The problem is that every day Wittenauer and I are not in the same zip code, I miss him. I get nervous about our prospects. And we risk splitting up.

And I hate splitting up. (See: Parents' Divorce.)

Mom proudly handed me a letter when I went down for coffee this morning. "Congratulations! You've been accepted as a transfer student. On behalf of everyone here at Colorado State University—your future—your education—" Blah blah blah—

I was still reading it, but I started crying. Mom and her man-friend wanted to know what was wrong. "I got in, all right?" I told them, sobbing.

"Hon, that's wonderful. Now all we have to do is find you a room or an apartment up there."

"Don't call me 'hon'!" I said through my blubbering.

"Wait a minute. I thought you wanted to live on your own," said Sterling. "Don't you?"

"Yes, but—that's—that's not the point." I shoved my chair back and went to the sanctity of my former room. Then I had to run back, grab my coffee, and vanish again. So much for dramatic exits.

Yes, I want to live on my own. It's not like I *want* to live in my mom's workout room forever. But this just all feels overwhelming and it would be nicer if I didn't feel like Mom is pretty much throwing me to the werewolves.

I called Wittenauer and we talked for a long time. He didn't want me to get accepted because he still wants me to return to CFC, but he said we need to take "the long view."

The long view: We both need to go to college. We both need to finish college. Then we can make decisions about what to do with our lives.

The short view: I have to start classes two weeks late, and will be living in my car.

Wait. I don't have a car.

So far I've spent the entire day looking for a place to live in Fort Collins.

Mom is so desperate for me to "gain my independence" that she went with me. We had searched every online listing first—then we drove around neighborhoods near campus looking for signs. Nothing. The places were terrible, or the roommates were horrible. As much as I wanted to move, I couldn't justify risking my life by moving in with someone who kept a pet boa constrictor.

"Mother, if you'd like to help, perhaps you could buy a house for me," I suggested. "You've been saving all that money for years, I bet you have a large nest egg, and it'd be a great investment because people are always going to need housing, plus, the market is, um, really soft. Or hard. Anyway, there are houses—"

"Why don't you call Grant instead, see if he has any leads?" she replied.

"You call him," I said. "I already asked him for help." The fact that he hadn't called me since I saw him didn't instill me with confidence. More like fear that he hated me and wanted nothing to do with me ever again.

"Ask him again," she said.

"Mom."

"Do it. Courtney, it's only Grant. Maybe you're not close anymore, but he's not going to bite. He'll probably do everything he can to help you out, hon."

She was bothering me so much that I decided I'd do whatever it took to find a place in Fort Collins. Forget that this was as embarrassing as, well, tromping all over campus with my mother in her workout gear, because she wanted to do some trail running after we settled this housing thing.

Called Grant. Initiated begging and pleading. "And I'm not asking at all to live with you, not at all, but I was wondering if you have any ideas or any leads, if you know anyone—"

"Court, I'm sorry! I've been meaning to call you but I've been so busy. Why don't you move onto my block?" he asked.

Whaaaa . . . t? "Your b-block?"

"Yeah, I just noticed there's a room for rent in a house on my block."

"Seriously?" Grant must not hate me too much if he was willing for me to live close by. Or was this a trick? Was he setting me up to live in a total dump, to get his revenge? But that would be so unGrantlike.

"Yeah. I can give you the phone number from the sign."

I called and talked to a girl named Shawna, who seemed really, really nice. She said they had a room left to rent because a girl who was supposed to live there had moved in with her boyfriend. It was a long story. I didn't catch all of it, partly because she talked a mile a minute.

She gave me directions but said she couldn't meet for a couple of hours, so I applied for a few jobs on College Ave., nothing too exciting, while Mom jogged. Wait. Here she comes.

Time to go. Wish me luck.

9/13 MOVING SOON—HOORAY!

When we got to the house, a cute little brick bungalow on a small, quiet street, a girl was sitting on the front porch waiting for us. When she stood up to greet us, she looked so familiar, I felt like I knew her already. But I couldn't place her. She had long, strawberry blond hair, a lot like mine, and was tall.

I started to introduce myself but before I got very far, we both realized that we had been in the same class year at Bugling Elk High School back in the day. We weren't really friends then—she was more of a jock, on the basket-ball team (coordinated, unlike me)—but we had definitely known each other, enough so that I knew she wasn't a hor-rible ax-murderer-type roommate.

"I moved away sophomore year," Shawna explained. "Colorado Springs. We had that, like, awful Spanish class together. Remember?"

"I've never been able to learn any languages since. Scarred for life."

She laughed and asked what I was up to, why I was starting at CSU so late in the semester and had no place to live. (She talked so fast that I just sort of guessed at some of what she said.) I told her the story of freshman year, and how I'd been sent back to Colorado and was now transferring to CSU. She was sorry that I had to transfer, but completely psyched I might be moving in. I asked if she was on the basketball team and she laughed. "No. Not exactly. I'm more into cycling and hanging out. You?"

"I'm more into, um . . ."

Just then her phone rang. "It's my mom," she said. "Calls twenty times a day. 'Scuse me."

The other housemate came home a second later,

pulling up in a French-looking car. Her name's Dara and she's very urban chic. She wears all black, has black-dyed hair with one purple streak in it, and wears these narrow glasses that somehow automatically made me feel stupid. She's from Seattle and is majoring in Poetry. "Well, technically English, but with a minor in Russian, I mean, it's obvious I'm a poet."

"Right." I smiled, thinking, Not exactly. And you're kind of intimidating, really.

"So, how did you end up here?" I asked.

She rolled her eyes. "Don't ask. I freaking hate the mountains. *And* the sun."

As if Colorado was such a terrible place to be? I mean . . . wait. Maybe she was just homesick. I remember that same thing happening to me when I mistakenly shipped out to Cornwall Falls last . . . fall.

From the Dept. of Redundancy Dept.

"So, do you want to see the room or not?" asked Dara. She struck me as the very impatient type.

"It's in the basement," said Shawna.

"Oh?"

"But it's huge. It's actually most of the whole basement."

We tromped down the stairs, and I found out she was right. It wasn't as bad as it sounded, and it had potential. If you like concrete blocks, that is. If you like a general bunker feeling to your life and like to be ready for the next millennium. There were enough bottled Starbucks Frappuccinos down there to last through another ice age—Dara mentioned she had a slight problem making it through the day without a few.

I did not want to live in a basement, but did I have a lot of choice? No. I had zero choice.

And there was Mom, grinning and standing beside me like wasn't it the most beautiful basement in all of Colorado?

"Shawna, are pets allowed?" Mom suddenly asked.

"Oh yeah, definitely!" Shawna said.

"Maybe," said Dara.

"Mom," I muttered, nudging her. Why do parents always ask the most embarrassing questions? Just when things were starting to gel between us, she has to ask about pets. "Why? I don't have a pet."

"I've been meaning to tell you, hon."

And I've been meaning to knock you on the head, I thought. Repeatedly. Hon.

"Sterling is allergic to Oscar, plus we want to travel to do marathons and triathlons and Oscar would just have to go to the kennel and he doesn't do well at kennels, you know."

I glanced nervously at Shawna, and even more nervously at Dara. "So I'm taking Oscar with me if I move. You're just telling me this now?"

"Well . . . please? Can you consider it?" she asked. "Because he's really making Sterling's life miserable."

It was the kind of thing I wished Grant was there to hear. How people put themselves and their feelings above their so-called beloved pets. If I had to rescue the mangy mutt, then so be it.

"OK, fine, I'll take Oscar. If they say it's OK." I glanced at my potential housemates again. They had moved over to the laundry area and were busy discussing the washer's flaws. "But it might not be OK and this is the only place we've found so far where I can live so this is not going to be a deal breaker, Mom."

She stared at me, looking stunned.

I was the one who was stunned. Mom was kicking out me, plus Oscar . . . I wondered if Bryan knew that he was living on borrowed time. I'd have to tell him to start asking his friends when he could move in. And if Alison was planning to move home after college, she could just forget about it, she might as well stay out in Oregon.

Mom used to go crazy by being too frugal.

Now she was in love, and instead of it being a good thing, it was horrible.

My dad was looking like a superhero in comparison. He moved away; he didn't make *us* move away.

When Dara and Shawna came back from checking out the washer, I asked them if it might possibly, maybe, be slightly OK if my dog moved in.

Dara shrugged. "I'm the landlord. My parents own the house. As long as your dog gets along with DeathKitty, it's OK."

"DeathKitty?" I sort of choked out.

She explained that she has a black cat named DeathKitty, which is the opposite of Hello Kitty, in that she's neither cute nor pink. I was thinking, shouldn't that be Good-byeKitty, when Mom chimed in again with her sales pitch: Take the dog.

"Oscar wouldn't hurt a flea. He's freaky, but gentle," Mom said.

Remind me to never have her describe me to someone.

"Wish I could say the same for DeathKitty," Dara murmured.

I worried for poor Oscar. "So we'll try it out and see?"

"Yup," Dara agreed.

"Well. I think this is going to be just great," Mom said

as we drove home to Denver. "You'll have a fresh start here."

"A fresh *late* start," I complained. I pointed out that I didn't need a fresh start, it's not like I started off really badly in college and this was my second or third chance at it. I'd aced college.

"All I'm saying is that starting over will be difficult. But remember, you hated CFC at first. And you and Mary Jo didn't get along right away and you ended up becoming great friends."

"True," I said. "But, Mom. What are you expecting me to hate?"

She didn't answer. Too busy thinking of how to turn my old room back into Workout Central, no doubt.

Now what. Do I call Grant and thank him?

Do I call W and give him the bad news? I was kind of hoping I wouldn't find a place and would have to move back to WI with him, whether it made sense or not.

I texted them both while Mom drove. What was the abbreviation for Parent Next to Me Driving Like Crazy Woman?

Oops.

Got distracted when Mom slammed on the brakes and sent my text to W to G's number instead.

Embarrassing.

Full of *x*'s and *o*'s.

What do you mean sorry you're going to csu and you're sorry you found a palace to live, Grant texted back. *I thought that was what you wanted.*

I didn't find a palace, I wrote back, trying to keep things light. *It's a basement.*

No response.

I added, *Please disregard former message, it was not 4 u.*

Ten minutes later: *Then who was it 4?* Grant wrote.

Um, Beth, I texted. *I was sorry she's in Italy and missing all this.*

Why so many x's and o's?

I miss her! Isn't it obvious?

You're crazy. That's obvious.

Then look out because your block just got a whole lot crazier, I replied.

No response.

No doubt regretting giving me housing advice.

So. Tx, I wrote.

Whatev. C U around.

Whatev? Since when did Grant use a word like that? I mean, *whatev*, Grant!

Packing up my limited stuff. Most of it I'd never unpacked from the boxes that I shipped here from Cornwall Falls.

Last night, told Wittenauer about finding a place and starting classes at CSU this week. I thought he'd be happy for me, but didn't sound that way at first. "CSU. Do you really think that's a good idea?" he asked.

"Well, why not? I mean, Grant does go there but so do twenty-five thousand other students, and—"

"I didn't mean Grant. He's the last thing on my mind. I meant, it's *far* from here, silly. Does it have a good rep? Does it have a good law school?"

"How should I know?"

"Court. You should know," said Wittenauer. "It's our future we're talking about here. The big picture. The long view. Remember?"

"Right, right. Uh. I'll find out about, um, all that." Wasn't it enough that I had to scramble to find a place for just right now??? Was I supposed to make everything perfect for both of us for all time? Who am I, Oprah all of a sudden?

Moved into the house last night with Oscar. Bryan drove me up after school, because Mom and Sterling had to do their "long run" after work today.

"Don't get me started," Bryan said when I complained about it. "This was *my* long run day long before it was theirs." He hoisted boxes from the trunk.

DeathKitty—largest, fluffiest black kitty I have ever seen—watched from the brick ledge on the porch and, as we approached up the sidewalk, started to hiss. Oscar put his tail between his legs and then lay down on my feet, which made it hard for me to carry boxes. Shuffled along the sidewalk with German shepherd mutt on sandals.

Fortunately or unfortunately I don't have a lot to move in. Clothes, bookcase, books, one foldable chair, assorted boxes of personal items.

On the way into the house, Bryan tripped and fell because DeathKitty ran out and got in his way.

"Omigod, you're, like, really hurt!" Shawna got a wet washcloth for his nose, which had started to bleed profusely. Onto the white living room rug.

"Gah, I'm so sorry," Bryan said. "I'm not usually a klutz."

Dara stared at the rug. "I kind of like how that looks, actually. Random drops of blood on white. Very Jackson Pollock."

"OK . . ." Bryan said slowly.

I had no idea what she was talking about, either. I wondered if that was how DeathKitty got her name, by taking out people, accidentally on purpose of course.

"We can replace the rug," I offered.

"No worries," said Dara. "If it cleans, great. If not, I

kind of hated it anyway."

Down in the basement, Bryan helped me put up some wall shelves and a desk and generally get settled. Then, as much as I kind of really didn't want him to leave, it was time for him to go. It felt like Cornwall Falls all over again. Being abandoned in a strange place. Even if it was in Colorado, I still didn't feel like I knew anyone or actually belonged here.

"I'll miss you, buddy." Bryan hugged Oscar by the front door while Shawna and I watched.

"Look at them. That's so cute," Shawna said as Oscar rolled over to let Bryan scratch his belly.

Oh no. Not my brother and my friend again, I thought. Not that it was on par with Beth and him, because I'd only just met Shawna. Or re-met Shawna. Or whatever. I still wasn't interested in seeing history repeat itself. "OK, well, Bryan has to go now," I said, and I shuffled Bryan outside as quickly as I could.

Shawna followed us out to the car, carrying her mug of chai. "Do you, like, have to leave right now? Because I was going to cook dinner, and if you want to, you know, hang around."

"You're cooking?" asked Dara, standing on the porch. "Since when?"

"Um—that sounds cool—" Bryan began.

"But unfortunately, he does have to leave now, he has to be home early, because he's still in high school," I said.

Bryan looked at me like he wanted to ram me with the car. "I'll be up to visit soon," he said. Not sure whether he meant that for me, or for Shawna, or for Oscar. Or all three of us.

"Like you have any actual homework in high school,"

Dara said. "As if it isn't a complete joke."

"I know, right?" Bryan said. And then he gave me this two-second hug and got into the car and drove off.

Oscar and I went down to the basement and I started arranging my stuff, trying to make the place look homier. Oscar followed me around as I put up some pictures, a poster, magnetic bulletin board, and unpacked books for my bookshelves. I put up my little chili pepper lights around the short basement windows to give the place a little more warmth and atmosphere.

Oscar loves lights. He's drawn to them.

But tonight, Oscar just let out this big, long, sad sigh as he settled down on the rug beside the bed. And I started leafing through all my new textbooks.

I knew exactly how he felt. What were we *both* doing here? I missed everyone I'd ever known in my entire life.

Then I realized: I could call people to cheer up. Oscar couldn't.

He could, however, drool on my socks while I talked to Wittenauer.

9/16

Made it through first day of classes. My Monday-Wednesday-Friday classes—Art of the Essay (which Dara calls Art of the Easy) (and which they are making me take as punishment for missing Freshman Comp), Sociology of the Environment, and Psychology of Social Change—are mostly big, like their names, and stopping by TA desks to talk about my late enrollment was no big deal. They gave me the syllabus and said I could email them to get the missed class info, lectures, handouts, etc. I'll have some makeup assignments to do, for sure.

Got a call back about a job I applied for. The Smoothie Stop. It's close enough that I can walk to it. I'm not sure why they are still hiring, when every other place seems full. Someone must have quit. That doesn't bode well, does it?

Neither does a cat named DeathKitty staring at me while I write in here. I expect to find this journal shredded one day and used as cat litter.

I hear Oscar outside, making funny, whimpering sounds. Must go investigate.

Hm. Didn't find anyone or anything. Oscar only makes that whimper sound when he's happy. Is he so happy to be living here? Well, makes one of us.

Time to call W.

Tuesday-Thursday classes not quite as smooth.

First, Oscar followed me out the door before I could close it, and I couldn't catch him. He kept running around me and following me at the same time. Eventually I had to grab him and drag him back to the house, and he whimpered the whole way like I was a horrible dog owner, so I was wondering when my neighbors would come out and call the ASPCA on me—

Anyway. So, I was late to my first class of the day, Journalism 210. (No flashy name there. Because it's hard-hitting journalism, y'all.)

In my second class, Environmental Activism, which I was late for because I got lost on campus and found myself outside the Potato Building (which, of course, I had to take a picture of with my phone to send to Mary Jo, the original Potato Clock owner) and which I had to beg to be let into because it was already at capacity (half of the guys in the class looked like they'd be totally willing to torch a ski resort for Earth First!—if they hadn't already), the professor looked at me as if I had made a wrong turn.

"May I help you?"

"Is this Active Environmentalism?" I asked.

He chuckled, while the rest of the class just laughed loudly. At me. "No, but you are close," he said. "This isn't a phys ed class. If you're interested in that, the gym is due west—" He lowered his glasses and pointed toward the mountains.

I cleared my throat. "I'm Courtney Smith," I said. "I just—I'm a late addition to the class."

"Late. I'll say." He glanced at the clock. "Find a seat promptly, Ms. Smith."

I had to slink across the front of the room to the one empty seat, then I had to wait for the two guys who were using it as a footrest to move their feet.

Let's just say they both needed a fresh pair of dude sandals. Mandals?

After class, could not even reach professor to talk to him. Giant crowd surrounding his desk would not let me in. Felt like I was at a casting call for Environmental Idol and he was Simon.

I was crossing Mulberry on the way home from class when a dude on a bike went past me so quickly that it left a breeze behind. Then he stopped on the other side of the street and just stood there. Waiting for me.

Great, I thought. Now what?

Then he took off his helmet. It was Grant.

Panic attack began.

"What's up?" he asked when I got closer. Like we saw each other all the time.

Deep breath, deep breath, shallow breath, hyperventilating. "Not much," I kind of exhaled. *I'm only struggling to get settled into a new school and living in a place I only found because of you, when rightfully you could and should hate me.* "You?" I asked. All casual-like.

He told me that he was headed home and that because we live on the same block he was waiting for me so we could walk together. I'd been here 4 days already and he hadn't come by to see how I was yet. If he hadn't nearly run me over with his bike, would he have made a point of stopping over, or not? I wanted to ask him that, but knew I couldn't.

"So," I said, and I thought I had a follow-up line to that, but I found out that I actually didn't. "Nice . . . street."

"Yeah. It is. You know, it's close to campus, but it's pretty quiet. Unless all my housemates are home."

"Uh, which house *is* yours?" I asked.

"Um, that one." He pointed to a brick house. Which was actually right beside the brick house where I was living.

"You said you lived on the same block. That's not 'on

the same block.' That's next door!"

"Sure, but that's a minor technicality." He shrugged and looked kind of embarrassed. And then he laughed and looked slightly mortified.

"Grant! How could you not tell me this before now? How did you not come over and help me move in? And what about Oscar?"

"Oscar?"

"He moved in, too, or are you deaf?"

"Seriously?"

See, Grant and Oscar used to be pals. In fact, when Oscar went missing, as he always does, Grant was the one who helped look for him. Grant was the one who usually found him. He'd drop everything for that silly dog.

Now they were neighbors and he hadn't even noticed? Where had he been? Or had he felt too awkward about us to come over?

"I guess, you know, I've been working later, studying late and stuff. I really hadn't heard him."

I can't figure this out. Did he want me to live next door to him? Of all the places in town? Or did he have to think it over? Was he ever going to tell me? If I hadn't called him back, would he have called *me*?

Was he embarrassed because he wanted me to live next door, because he never got over me? Or was he playing hard to get, kind of?

My head was spinning with questions as we got up to the house. I opened the door and Oscar bolted out of the yard, right into Grant, almost knocking him off his bike. He started making that funny whimpering sound—Oscar, not Grant, I mean—and it suddenly dawned on me. I'd heard those sounds before! It meant that Grant had stopped by before. He'd visited Oscar but not me. And that hurt, like, a lot. And the fact he was even kind of lying about it—wow. Things were very strained.

While Oscar was licking Grant's face, a bit too lovingly I might add, I ventured, "Just so you know, I'm, uh, still seeing Wittenauer."

Grant stopped snuggling with Oscar long enough to give me a look that could stop traffic, whatever that means, and said, "Just so *you* know, I still don't care."

Ouch. How long had he been saving up that line? Since last March? "Oh?" My voice warbled.

"Because we're just friends now."

"Friends. Right."

Not sure how I am supposed to adjust. But I don't get that feeling around him that I used to get, like a hundred ants were running up and down my body (not in an annoying way but in a good way), so I guess I am doing OK.

Suddenly my phone started ringing. Not just any ring. The CFC fight song.

Grant stared at me because I wasn't answering it.

"It's, um, Wittenauer," I said.

"Don't let me stop you." He stood up, gave Oscar one last rub behind the ears, and wheeled his bike over to his garage.

Weird. We have never lived this close to each other. Now we don't date anymore and we're next-door neighbors. The kind that probably need a fence between them.

Forgot about Grant and talked with Wittenauer.

Practically made out on the phone.

Some calls are best taken in the privacy of one's basement bedroom.

Got back from brunch with Dara and Shawna (cinnamon-roll toast = yum) and found a dead bird on my bed.

Thanks, DeathKitty. Thanks so much.

This is how my weekend is going, in case anyone is wondering. Which they're not. Because they're all having fun watching Wittenauer aka Corny leap around and cheer at soccer game. I heard.

Well, at least I found out how DeathKitty got her name.

She used to have a sister kitten. (I'm not sure if Dara was joking about this. She has a weird sense of humor.) Also, she's taken out several birds and about a dozen mice. No doubt she's working her way up to defenseless mutts with epilepsy. Killers don't discriminate.

Maybe I need to get Oscar a dog sitter, someone to check up on him while I'm gone, because it's not like I can stay inside the house all the time—I'll miss college.

On the other hand, I should be realistic. How is a 15-pound cat going to bring down Oscar? By hissing?

Found out how Dara and Shawna became friends— they were roommates in a quad last year. They were supposed to be sharing this house with their mutual friend Tobie, but she moved in with her boyfriend in an apartment two weeks before school started. So that's how I ended up getting her spot.

Shawna wants to major in Elementary Education. Dara is majoring in English and minoring in "getting out of here in three years."

"What's so bad about this place?" asked Shawna at brunch. "You've been saying stuff like this for, like, a whole year. Getting annoying."

"What's so *bad*? Look at that woman over there. She's wearing *Wranglers*. I mean, what even is a Wrangler? And what's with his cowboy boots? And look. Agh." She sank down in the booth. "That guy has a horseshoe pattern vest."

"Maybe you should major in fashion?" I suggested.

"It's the West. People have, like, ranches here," Shawna said. "Get over it. Get over yourself."

Dara looked completely shocked that Shawna had stood up to her.

"So," I said. "Who wants more coffee?"

Years of dealing with my parents' arguing have given me special skills.

Met with Smoothie Stop manager yesterday. First thing he said was "Hey, I remember you from Truth or Dairy."

"You do? Me?" This is weird running into people who knew me from Denver. Was it a good thing or a bad thing? Felt kind of like a celeb.

"Yes, don't you remember me?" he said.

I stared at him for a second. He looked like he was about 25, wearing a ball cap with the Smoothie Stop logo, and a T-shirt and jeans. He wasn't good-looking; he wasn't bad-looking. He was slightly generic, if that makes sense. In other words . . . forgettable. At least, to me.

"I used to work day shifts before you came in the afternoon after school," he said. "I was in night school. Business administration." He held out his hand for me to shake. "Guy Nicollet."

"Right, right!" Now I remembered. What I remembered was that he usually left before I got there and Gerry would get mad at him because it was not the smooth(ie), painless transition he wanted. Sometimes he'd leave half an hour early, and that was eventually why Gerry fired him.

"So, how's it going, Courtney? What finds you here in the Fort?"

Wasn't it obvious? "Here for school," I said, and as I explained what had happened over the past few weeks, I looked at the menu and surveyed the place to see if it was somewhere I'd want to hang out for 15–20 hours a week. After my experience at Bagle Finagle last year, I can't be too careful about accepting another part-time job. That one had been way too challenging, at least when you factored in personality disorders.

I couldn't help thinking that lots of things were similar to Truth or Dairy, from the smoothie recipes, sizes, and combos to the frequent sipper cards to the cups and even the store's logo.

Plus, Smoothie Stop not only offered smoothies but also had a menu section called Sundae Stop—just like Truth or Dairy. (Beth and I used to fight over those dumb cowhide print vs. green hemp aprons.) The freezer case was divided between healthy fruit options and the high-fat gluttony of chocolate-chocolate chip. It was torture for a person who couldn't decide if she wanted to be a health nut or a high-in-fat pecan nut.

A person like me.

But since when have I ever shied away from torture? (Besides not running with my mom and Sterling.) I dive right into difficulty. Conflict is my middle name. Which is a lot better than Von Dragen.

We talked for a while—I guess technically it was an interview—and he asked if I could start next week. Which I can, so I will. If it doesn't work out I can always bail, right?

On the one hand, I don't want to condone the fact that it seems like he stole all his ideas from Gerry, and Gerry should probably be getting a cut of the profits. On the other hand, I need a job unless I want to get by on my so-called allowance from Mom, which is a mere pittance.

Guy said he might need me to work the late-night shifts. They're open late, like midnight, for the late-night study crowd. (It's not far from the library.) He said they usually get a rush on energy-boost drinks, and showed me some questionable-looking prepackaged brownies that felt like bricks. "Top sellers with the late-night study crowd. Maximizing our profit percentages," he said.

I probably ought to be *in* the late-night study crowd, trying to catch up in all my classes, instead of selling them snacks.

9/21

Wittenauer and I spent all day—all day—on the phone or messaging.

He brought me to a meeting.

I brought him to the library.

We shared lunch.

It was a virtual date, but with actually zero contact. Did not enjoy that aspect.

He said the cutest thing, though. He said he was thinking about transferring *here*. As if Corny, Mr. Legacy Student, could transfer in his senior year. But he laid out the whole scenario and made it sound like it could happen. He said he's always wanted to be a snowboard hound since watching the Olympic half-pipe.

"It's not like that every day," I reminded him. "That's, like, vacation."

"It could be every day," he said. Then he mentioned he was not doing very well in his classes so far. That he was thinking it might be time to take a leave of absence.

"What? It's only September. You have months to pull your grades up."

"You would think so," he said, getting all distant for a second.

Wait a second. He was distant the whole time. He was 1,000 miles away.

9/22

Freezing cold today. Snowing in the mountains. Went out for lunch (despite impending financial doom; we are Generation B after all) to this place called the Pythagorean Theorem Café. Bunch of equations on the walls. Shape mobiles. Sandwiches named after, well, mathematicians, I guess? Like I would know. But it was a near-vegan's heaven. I could get anything I wanted. I could pay $12, which would kill my food budget for the week, but it would be lovely vegan food and fresh-squeezed organic juices.

"They put *sprouts* on everything. I hate sprouts," Dara said while we were in line. She was wearing her hair in little miniponytails on the back of her head, and cool eyeglasses. She always wears dresses with leggings and boots or ballet slip-ons. I look hopelessly boring beside her.

So she hates sprouts. What does she even like? I haven't found out yet. I know she doesn't like:

Mountains
Fresh air
Exercise
Sunshine
Non-bloodred lipstick
Colors
Sandals
Fleece
Lending me her car
Green tea
Ramen noodles
Fruit
Fruit smoothies

Oscar
Sprouts
Me, possibly

"So, why don't you just, like, order something without the sprouts?" asked Shawna.

"Because when I asked them to hold the sprouts last time, they gave me this look, like, look at the freak, like I'm unnatural," said Dara.

"That's because, like, you *are* unnatural," said Shawna.

"Shut up," said Dara. "And stop saying 'like.'"

"Just because you don't, like, *like* the word *like*, or know how to even like anything, that's not my fault," Shawna said.

We ordered and found a table. Place was jammed with students and also some professor-looking types (they had facial hair, which seems to be a requirement). A few minutes later I heard my name.

"Courtney!" the guy working behind the counter screamed at the top of his lungs. Sounded like kurt-kneeeeee. "Sandwich up!"

I hurried over to the counter for my basket of sandwich and corn chips. When I turned around, I almost bumped into Grant, who was walking over from the cash register. Flustered flustered flustered.

"Grant, I hate to say this again, but, um, quit following me." He stared at me. I pushed him gently. "Joking."

He laughed. "Who's following you? I'm meeting my vet sciences study group here."

"Oh?" I coughed.

"We've been meeting here long before you moved to town."

"Oh. Vet studies. Interesting. You're still majoring in, um, veterinarianism?"

He stared at my sandwich. "And you're still failing at vegetarianism? Isn't that turkey?" Then he smiled. "Just kidding. And it's called veterinary science. Actually."

"Well, this is called vegan cheese. Actually."

We kind of laughed, awkwardly. He stared at my sandwich. "Really? That's fake cheese and not turkey? OK, here's one thing I don't get. Why not just give up cheese?"

We got into this conversation about the merits of vegan cheese. We so had nothing real to talk about.

"GRANT!" the guy behind the counter yelled, nearly splitting my eardrums.

"Yell much?" Grant commented to me under his breath.

"Didn't need that ear anyway," I added as we both picked up our baskets of food and headed away from the ear-shattering counter person.

Grant stopped by the table to say hi to Dara and Shawna on the way to his own table, which he was sharing with a few other students, one guy and two girls.

"So, I see you met our next-door neighbor?" asked Shawna.

That was the understatement of the year. "Um, yeah."

"He's totally nice, don't you think?"

You want to see nice? You should kiss him, was the first thing that popped into my head. What? I nearly slapped my own face. I was about to tell them that Grant and I went way back, when Dara said, "Nice? Maybe, but I think he's kind of a clueless dolt."

"Who—Grant?" asked Shawna.

"Yes. He's doltish. Doltesque."

Shawna shook her head. "No, he's not. He's, like, really sweet."

"In a dolty-like way." Dara brought up the time Grant had broken the window moving a couch into the house, but Shawna said that was his housemate Cody, who really, apparently, looks just like him but *is* a bit on the dumb side.

Another Grant look-alike? (A Grant-alike?) I'd have to meet him. I wondered if Grant was good friends with him, and the rest of his housemates, and I wondered who his best friends were now. Did he stay in touch with anyone from Bugling Elk? Did he ever see that group of friends that once used to include Dave, other ex of mine? What about his roommate from last year, the one I ended up talking to sometimes when I called—Matt, right?

And as I was sitting there, mid–sandwich bite, a hundred questions went through my mind. I can't remember them all now, but if I was to try to reconstruct them, they included things like:

What did Grant do all summer?

Where did he live last year? I couldn't remember the name of the dorm.

Boxers or briefs? (JK.)

Did he still think it was OK to wear that striped polo shirt that made him look like Where's Waldo?

Did he go through the Taco Bell drive-through anymore, and if he did, did he ever think of me?

I'm a hopeless romantic. I know.

I felt like I had to say something, or I'd be dishonest not to mention it. "So, back to Grant. I actually knew him from before. From Bugling Elk."

"Bugling what?" asked Dara, making a face as she

pulled a stray bean sprout from her roast beef sandwich. (If anything, she should take out the roast beef.)

"It's our high school," Shawna explained to Dara. "Well, I was only there a couple of years. I never knew him then, but I, like, wanted to."

"Yeah. Well. I kind of, sort of, like . . . dated him."

They both shrieked. Really loudly. And often.

I ducked down, hoping Grant wouldn't see or hear—he had to know what we were talking about, but still. My new favorite place to eat in town was rapidly becoming a place I could never set foot in again. At least not on Tuesdays during vet sciences study group.

"Seriously? You and him. Was it, like, serious?"

"No. We were only in high school, you know. Seniors. No big deal." It only made my senior year the best one yet at high school or anywhere else. Until Wittenauer, of course.

"So what made you break up?" asked Dara.

"Well . . ." College. I went away, and he kissed Beth, and then I kissed Wittenauer . . . and then it was too far away . . . and we sort of got back together but not really because I didn't trust him . . . so then . . .

"Hello. Earth to Courtney."

I suddenly realized I hadn't said anything out loud. "Oh, I don't know, really. Lots of things. Typical, you know, breakup stuff."

"Hooking up with other people." Shawna nodded.

"Existential angst." Dara nodded.

"Pretty much." I glanced over at Grant's table and noticed his study group hunched over their notebooks and laptops. "I, um, went away last year and things just changed."

"In other words, you hooked up with Witts-his-name," Dara said.

"Not exact—"

"This is major," Dara interrupted. "A major development. We're never going to look at you the same way again."

"You're not?" I asked.

They both shook their heads.

I couldn't tell whether they meant that in a positive or a negative way, but I didn't have time to ask because Tobie, their former roommate, walked in, and they all started talking about party plans.

I ate my fake cheese and wondered why I was eating it. Maybe Grant had a point. Besides, would a slice of Munster really kill me? Sure, I'm slightly lactose intolerant, but what about Swiss? The holes would not contain any lactose at all.

I need a new cell phone plan. Have spent approx. 1,500 anytime minutes talking already this month, which is about 500 too many. Had to call Dad to appeal to his sense of guilt; he agreed to add me to his family plan but only if I start keeping control of my minutes.

My minutes are out of control, apparently.

It's not like my *life* is out of control or anything. . . .

Crap. Have to write my first essay for Art of Essay and can't think of anything.

We're supposed to write about something we feel passionate about. Well, obviously, I'm not writing about Wittenauer. I mean, that is way too personal.

Maybe the TA doesn't mean passionate that way. Maybe he means an issue that really concerns us?

Wait, I know. I have something very current: "The Evildoers: Phone Companies and the Overcharges." But that subtitle sounds like a band. Besides, I believe my mother already wrote that story when she took on the giant MegaPhone corporation.

I do *not* want to copy my mother. Especially when it comes to cardigan sweaters.

Near disaster in Environmental Activism class today.

First of all, I found out Dr. Bigelow knows my name now.

Second, halfway through what was a slightly boring lecture, I thought I saw Grant go past in the hallway and I kind of, sort of, leaped out of my chair. I was so happy to see a familiar face.

See, at a small school like CFC, occasionally it gets old running into people. You sometimes wish you didn't see someone you knew everywhere.

But then here, it's the opposite. And I'm new. So I hardly ever see anyone I know.

"May I help you, Ms. Smith?" Dr. Bigelow asked. "You're already starting three weeks late. Now what?"

"I just . . . excuse me. Sorry." *I saw my ex-boyfriend go past and, uh . . .*

"Are you feeling all right?"

"Yes, yes, fine. Sorry. Leg twitch. Cramp thing."

"Maybe you should see a doctor about that. But in the meantime, let's keep our focus."

"Sorry." I stared down at my notebook, feeling like I was about eight years old.

"Oh, Superfund. I lost my place." Dr. Bigelow shuffled through his notes. He glanced up to glare at me.

I couldn't slouch any lower without landing on the floor.

9/25

Is it my fate in life to always have crappy, part-time food-service jobs?

Because that's how it's starting to feel.

Oh, wait. I'm in college so that I *won't* have to do that. When I feel like giving up, I must remember that. I am avoiding having my career stop at the Smoothie Stop.

Fortunately, Dara and Shawna dropped by to visit, which made working with Guy Nicollet, SuperZero, better. Dara hates all things fruit but had a hot fudge sundae, and Shawna opted for an Orange Immunity Blast.

You can learn a lot about people by what they order.

But usually, you really don't care.

Grant's house had a party tonight. Yesterday night, since it's now 2 A.M.?

Whatever. I had too many energy drinks at the party next door. Great for mingling but not recommended if you plan on sleeping. On the plus side, I can chat/IM with Beth in a few hours. Or now, maybe.

Grant wasn't there at the beginning. Which was actually kind of nice and relaxing and gave me a chance to meet other people.

"What's the occasion?" I asked the Grant look-alike, Cody. Except they don't really look that much alike. Cody is a cargo shorts/flip-flop/T-shirt person. Every single day, as far as I can tell. That's not really Grant's look. Grant's more of a cargo shorts/tee/flip-flop person.

Wait. That's the same thing.

Anyway. "It's Saturday night, dude," Cody said, as if he didn't need a reason to trample the grass, rent a keg, blare music, and annoy the neighbors.

"Well, yeah. Of course it is," I said. I clinked my can of Rockstar against his cup of beer. "Party on."

"Right on," he said, nodding.

Sometimes those of us in tragic long-distance relationships lose track of things like parties and fun and weekends.

I sat down in a webbed chair to watch some volleyball. Game was kind of boring. Meanwhile, I kept texting W. We talked a few times and I held the phone out so he could hear what a Saturday night party in Fort Collins sounded like. Same as it does anywhere, just at slightly higher altitude. Does the air being thin make the noise louder, or softer?

Eventually met some people, including Matt, Grant's roommate from last year. We talked for kind of a long time, just small talk, naturally. I was wondering how much he knew about me and whether he loathed me for the way I'd acted toward Grant. "On behalf of Grant Superior, I'd like to punch you . . ." could easily have been his greeting.

But he was just a nice person who seemed to be genuinely interested in my life and felt bad about the fact I had to transfer but was glad to meet me, etc.

I was talking with Shawna about a million different things, like people we both knew from Bugling Elk sophomore year, for hours. I think we ate three bags of tortilla chips. Jane called and she totally remembered Shawna, so they talked for a while. Jane pointed out something I already knew: I'm so lucky that even though I moved to a new place, I live with someone I already knew, totally nice Shawna. (Then Jane complained about her own housemates for a while.)

Finally Grant showed up. Said he'd been at work. Man, whenever I think I have a bad social life . . . Grant is working at a grocery store on Saturday nights. I hate to say it, but . . . that's slightly loseresque. Wonder if he is steering away from vet science into food science. Only explanation for his devotion to customer service desk and green team initiative.

We talked for a couple of minutes. I told him about the Smoothie Stop, and my classes, and how I'm already on Dr. Bigelow's hit list. I told him about the time I thought I saw him walking by the room and how I jumped up and got in trouble. He laughed a lot but told me not to worry, that everyone starts out there and has to earn their way up. He started to tell me a story about what happened to him freshman year, until the guys started setting fireworks on the street.

When there was a pause in the action, I heard this howling sound coming from somewhere. Then I realized. It's Oscar. Poor Oscar. Scared to death of fireworks.

I ran home and Oscar was running in circles around the room. He had started to wear a path in the basement rug. I crouched down to catch him, midlap, and got him to stop by giving him a bear hug. He was shaking all over and kind of whimpering.

I'd been hugging him for a second when there was a knock on the door. I looked up and saw Grant, just as another firecracker whistled into the sky. Oscar and I both must have looked pathetic and helpless, or maybe he only cared about Oscar. Anyway.

"I'll take care of it," Grant said in this deep, somewhat manly voice. He was off, up the stairs, back outside. A minute later, he got everyone, even the really drunk people, to stop doing fireworks. He made some argument involving post-traumatic stress disorder and its effect on animals. He was Oscar's hero. Again.

When I went out to thank him, a thought occurred to me: There was another favor I needed. "So I have a kind of strange question to ask."

He looked very nervous.

"Can I borrow your car tomorrow? I have all this stuff I need to get and—I can't drive Dara's because (a) it's too expensive, and (b) it's a stick shift, and (c) she refuses to lend it to anyone—"

"Say no more. Sure. Of course you can. But I hope you drive a car better than you do a shopping cart."

"What? You've driven with me, like, a thousand times!"

Suddenly, we started arguing about driving, and I said then I wouldn't take the car, and Grant said, yes, I would, he'd leave me the key tomorrow night, and I said, don't bother, and he said, no, it was no bother—

Then someone threw him a glow-in-the-dark Frisbee and he was gone.

As we went inside our house, Shawna had a kind of singsong taunt going. "You guys used to date, you guys used to date . . ."

I dragged her off to the kitchen for some ice cream.

Now, sitting here, wide-awake with a gut ache.

Should see if Dara wants to use that line in any of her poetry. It's golden.

Dara, Shawna, and I were sitting outside having coffee and doing homework on the front porch when Grant came out and headed for his car.

"Hey, Grant?" I called over to him. "Thanks again for last night!"

Dara nearly spit out her coffee and she slapped me on the leg. "Who says that? You don't just *say* that."

"What?" I said, completely innocent.

Grant walked toward us and Oscar immediately jumped up and ran over to him. "What for?" he asked, rubbing Oscar behind his ears.

"Calming down Oscar. Getting your friends to stop the fireworks," I said.

"Oh, so *you're* the one who, like, killed the party," Shawna said.

"Sorry." Grant shrugged. "But it's Oscar. Sometimes animals have to come first."

Right. It *was* all about Oscar, of course.

"I still can't believe your mom made him leave home. I mean, that was sort of cruel, don't you think?" asked Grant.

Don't get me started, I thought. First I had to go, then Oscar. A person should never get caught up in someone else's midlife crisis. For that matter, neither should a dog. "Totally. He's not the kind of dog that can just move around and adapt to new environments."

"No. I'm glad I can help. I mean, if I helped at all," Grant said.

"Definitely." I smiled at him, and he seemed a little startled—or pleased, I couldn't tell. Or maybe just late to his volunteer gig.

"You didn't ever move Oscar to Wisconsin, did you?" he asked.

"Oh no."

"Good."

"Why? Wisconsin would've been nice to him. What do you have against Wisconsin?" I asked.

"Nothing!" Grant laughed. "Well, except it made you leave. I mean, Colorado was hurt. For a long time. States have feelings, you know."

"States?" Shawna asked. "They do?"

"He's kidding, obviously," said Dara.

I wondered. Was he just trying to be funny, or was he talking about . . . him?

"See you, guys." Then he headed off to the Humane Society, where he volunteers every Sunday.

I should volunteer there, I thought. I love all animals. I remembered thinking once that Grant could open a vet clinic and I would do all the filing and receptioning. But maybe there was somewhere a little less smelly and barky to work?

We were joking and laughing but at the same time it all seemed kind of flirty and serious.

"Wow. He really loves Oscar, doesn't he?" Dara said, looking slightly dreamy. She had this soft, sweet expression that changed her entire face.

"It's not just Oscar. He used to work at a pet store, and he's volunteered for the ASPCA and the Humane Society. And, I mean, he loves all animals."

Just then, DeathKitty leaped up on the ledge and hissed at Oscar, taking a swipe at his eyes.

"Well. Almost all," I said.

Even Dara had to laugh at that.

I thought about how obsessed I used to be with Animal Planet. Why did I stop watching? When did I stop caring?

Maybe it was when I got too much homework. Like now. I'm at least 3 chapters behind in everything. I hate Sundays. Hate them hate them hate them.

9/28

Grant left his car key in our mailbox today so I took his car to Target. I needed stuff for my room, plus my grandparents had sent me a Target gift card that was burning a hole in my pocket. Grandparents understand what it's like to be kicked out by Mom. She once made them spend the night in their RV in our driveway because she had turned what had been the guest room with a futon into her home office. She has a history of being a bad host.

Yes, I'd love to always ride my bike or take public transportation, but there are some things you just can't put on your bike or the bus. Like trash cans. Beanbag chairs. And large bubble mailers to send W care packages of CSU Rams T-shirts (RAM 'EM!). And "feminine hygiene products." And this really cool new kind of mascara that is clear but also brown/black so you get this double coating action thingy going on.

Sitting in Grant's car again was weird. Really strange. It was the same car that we'd driven around, you know, *around* around when we were seeing each other. We drove to school, to prom, to graduation, ski trips. Things had happened in this car. Important things. Kissy things.

That was when I had to slam on the brakes because I hadn't seen the truck in front of me stop and I nearly crashed into it. Whoa. Nearly totaled Grant's car.

Anyway, lots of memories were in this car. Mostly good ones, but a few bad ones, like when we'd driven it back to Wisconsin together, at the end of Christmas break last year, before we broke up.

Probably it was a mistake to borrow it, because it was acting sort of like a time machine on my emotions. It even smelled like Grant. I think it's his deodorant.

On the way home, the sun was in my eyes so I folded down the visor.

A note fell down.

I knew I shouldn't read it, but I did.

Because that's the kind of person I am. Nosy.

It was written on a napkin from a coffee shop near campus and read, "Hey, Grant—nice talking to you last night. Have a good day." There was a picture of a cat with a smile drawn on it, and the word *Meow* in a small bubble over it.

What? Who wrote this? When was this written?

Just as I was about to analyze the handwriting, the light turned green, I accelerated, and my bottle of juice spilled onto the napkin. The ink ran a little bit and the napkin turned slightly orange.

I quickly waved it in the air, turned the AC on full blast to dry it off, then put it back where I'd found it. Drove with fingers crossed on both hands the rest of the way home that it was just a silly memento from a long time ago and he's completely forgotten about it. Made it hard to use steering wheel.

Don't crash don't crash don't crash, I told myself, thinking of Grant's shopping cart comment. If I crashed, he'd find the note for sure. That was my twisted logic. Not that I or someone else might get hurt.

When I brought the key back, Cody answered the door and told me to go ahead down the hall to his room. Their house had the exact same setup as ours, and Grant's bedroom was on the left. I peeked inside. Grant was lying on his bed, headphones on, studying. I stood in the doorway for a second, just watching him, waiting for him to notice me.

We used to do this thing where we'd lie end to end so we wouldn't talk and we'd tickle each other's feet if we dozed off. I don't know what came over me, but I leaned down and touched his bare foot.

He nearly hit the ceiling.

So did I, because he kind of kicked me. I coughed. "Sorry, just wanted to give you the key."

Grant asked if everything went OK with the car. "Sure. Fine," I said. Then I told him that I had used reusable bags instead of plastic ones.

He said, he actually said this, "Courtney, I don't care what you do."

Ouch.

I guess he could tell how hurt I was because he said, "I mean, with your bags. Shopping bags."

OK then. I hurried home. Confused. Not that there's anything new about that.

OMG. OMG. OMG.

Went to Shop & Shop for groceries just now.

Was innocently pushing a cart down the middle aisle, where I had a dead-on view of customer service. Saw Grant standing off to the side, talking to a girl. She had short black hair, very cute. Looked familiar.

Then I realized—vet sciences study geeks—that was where I'd seen her before, at the Pythagorean Theorem Café. I also thought maybe she'd been at Grant's house party, but I wasn't sure—it had been kind of crowded.

I thought I'd march over and introduce myself, but then she snuggled up close to him.

And he didn't resist. In fact, quite the opposite.

He snuggled up close to *her*.

Then they started kissing.

Abort, abort! I thought, making a U-turn, steering in a completely opposite direction. Abandoned my cart in the cereal aisle. Ran out exit door.

Crashed on my bike on the way out of parking lot. Have giant scrape on my leg. All Grant's fault. I have W. Why do I care if Grant wants to snuggle with some girl at the Shop & Shop?

I don't. Really.

Really.

Up early due to lack of sleep due to not being able to sleep. Just IM'd with Beth. Told her about Grant having a girlfriend.

> shoe92gurrl: Really? And he didn't tell you before now? Why?
> crtveg17: ???
> shoe92gurrl: what did she look like?
> crtveg17: cute
> shoe92gurrl: well, I guess that's it then, you both moved on
> crtveg17: I guess

Now, reflecting. Pausing before I call Mary Jo, Jane, Alison . . . That's what journals are for, right? Reflecting? On what dumb things we do and how we can maybe, possibly not do them again? But then we do them again anyway and have to throw out a journal and start over and pretend like this was the first time and we didn't know better, in case someone someday finds our old journals and, like, calls us to task on what we wrote and supposedly learned—

Anyway. Why was that whole Shop & Shop experience so incredibly hard?

Why did I run away?

Why didn't I just walk over and say in a low, sultry, completely calm voice, "Well, hello there, you must be Grant's new girlfriend. I'm his previous girlfriend, Courtney. You've probably heard a lot about me."

We'd laugh uncomfortably and look for similarities in each other. We'd trade stories about how cute Grant was and didn't she just love that scar of his on his cheek and did she know—

Well, anyway. That's NOT what I did or how I acted. I ran. Like a petite, frightened mouse that has just spied DeathKitty coming its way.

So, OK. I guess I just can't face that yet, the idea of Grant with someone new. Why not? I don't know. I mean, I guess I was wondering if he ever got over me. And I kind of wanted him to and kind of didn't.

OK, I guess in an egotistical way I wanted him to pine for me forever. But he isn't pining. At all. He's moved on, like I have. Which is so apparently mature of both of us that it feels funny. Not ha-ha funny. Bizarre funny.

Here I was, thinking he rigged this housing situation so we'd live next door because he wanted to, I don't know . . . get back together with me?

He doesn't, though. He has no interest in me that way anymore. Just like he said the other day: He doesn't care about me or what I do.

And maybe the truth is, I never got over him, because I feel so horribly jealous I could throw up. Or maybe it's because I ate some fake-crab salad samples at Shop & Shop before I saw him and her.

There's a her now.

A her that is not a me.

What am I so upset about? I'm with Wittenauer now. End of story.

I think I'm upset because I gave him the perfect opening to tell me about whatever her name is. I told him about W, and he said how we didn't have to tell each other everything. I was brave enough to tell him my own dating status. And was he? No. He let me find out by reading notes and crashing supermarket carts.

I definitely need more Band-Aids for my scraped leg.

Ended up borrowing some from Dara. They are skull-and-bones pattern. I look like a wounded biker.

Grandma came for a visit, wanting to see my new place, and once she met Shawna and Dara, she invited all three of us to lunch. Wouldn't take no for an answer. She insisted on eating at Perkins because of her senior discount. She also kept saying she was going to the doctor for a brain density scan.

"I think that it's called bone density," Dara said. She read over the menu and uttered under her breath how she hated Perkins and bread bowls.

"They're checking everything," she said. "What's really important is to maintain sexual health into your sixties and seventies."

"We'll work on that," Shawna said, and giggled. And then I laughed, and then even Dara snickered and soon we were all cracking up and Grandma V. D. was shaking her head and saying, "Girls, girls, pay attention. These are the best years of your lives."

That's pretty much how it went. Grandma Von Dragen giving advice on how to go to college based on her experiences in the 1960s. She was into free love then; she's into free love now. She has no idea what that even means anymore, how much trouble a person might get into. She's like the antiabstinence voting bloc.

She started talking about Thanksgiving in Nebraska and how we all have to go. . . . I've been hearing this my whole life, I've been *going* my whole life. Is it really something we need to discuss at length? Turkey and trimmings? Anyway, I only care about the trimmings. She should know that by now.

Hated, dreaded words: "There's someone I want you to meet."

But let me backtrack. First, I was coming home from getting back my first Art of the Essay essay, which was not that artful, according to TA David.

"You didn't do the assignment correctly. You need to work on this makeup assignment. You don't know how to describe in depth. Go back to the first five assignments for this class—think you missed them."

TA David is very good at describing, in depth, what is wrong with my writing.

As if I don't write really great essays. Hello, I'm almost a journalism major. Or at least, I *thought* I was going to be one.

Maybe I'd written that one too quickly. Or maybe that was the paper I sort of wrote while I was on the phone with W. Maybe I'll never catch up here, I thought. Maybe I should just give up. It was all too much and I started crying on the way home.

Which wouldn't have been so bad if I hadn't run into Dara, who said, "Art of the Easy? You're failing *that*?"

"I'm not failing! I just have to do some extra-credit type stuff."

Dara says she can help, as a poet. She's always starting sentences by saying, "As a poet, I . . ."

I told her it had nothing to do with poetry.

We got into an argument about what counted as writing. She said I had no idea how hard poetry was; I said she had no idea how difficult writing articles was. And even *that* wouldn't have been so bad if I hadn't walked home and seen Grant sitting outside his house, so I had to go say hello even though I didn't want to. I tried just waving, but he beckoned me over.

"Hey, uh, Courtney? There's someone I want you to meet."

Then I noticed there was a girl sitting with her back to me and she turned around with this nice, friendly smile. Gah. Blindsided, completely blindsided. The girl from Shop & Shop. What am I saying? The *girlfriend* from Shop & Shop.

I mean, not that she lives at S & S or even works there, I just mean . . . I saw her there. In Grant's arms.

"This is Kelli Barber," Grant said, his face turning red as he introduced us. And I could see how hard it was for him, too. That made it better. Then he said, "Kelli with an *i*." As if that mattered, like I was going to be sending her mail or something.

We exchanged awkward hellos.

But, sadly, how nice she is. How kind. How impossible to hate. Still, I manage.

Because I'm just that immature.

Felt too tall, too red-haired, too skinny, too everything around her. We made small talk about our majors, Grant's housemates, and the weather. She went to camp in WI for a couple of summers. She thought that meant we had something in common. Besides the obvious: We have both spent lots of time with Grant.

Emailed Beth and Jane to give them the report. Jane wrote back, "No offense, Court, but I think you should probably be telling W this, not us. It's not a secret that you once dated him, and it's normal to have these feelings."

Nothing at all feels "normal" about this. Just ate an entire pint of Häagen-Dazs while writing this.

Felt dumb because the more Kelli and Grant talked, the more I realized (a) they do have a connection, and (b) I know absolutely nothing about being a vet. Although I do a damned fine job of giving Oscar his meds every day. Oops. Think I forgot this morning. Gotta go.

Art of the Essay Description #1: Kelli

Grant's girlfriend has short black hair that has just the right amount of swishes and flips. But she can still curl it around her cute little ears. Her hair is the color of licorice whips. The color of a black car that is kind of new, you know, and shiny.

Not the color of a cat with evil eyes that stares at you every time you write in your journal and sometimes has green eyes, sometimes yellow, and that creeps you out.

Not that. Very very beautiful. As beautiful as a sunset over the mountains.

OK, so that IS a cliché. She's pretty. She had on a silver necklace with a purple stone. Her birthday must be . . . I don't know, but it's amethyst.

She is petite but not wimpy. Skin a nice brown hue. She could be a Title Nine/Athleta model, which I only know from Mom's current catalog collection.

Tank tee and jeans. The kind of toned shoulders that could probably go rock climbing with Grant, whereas I have the kind of shoulders that are good at scooping ice cream (which reminds me, I have to go to work soon). Where I am biceps, she is triceps.

She wears Keen sneaker-sandals, the kind with a bunch of openings and rubber soles you can wear anywhere and climb rock faces with.

Her tank top was purple, like grapes.

Her eyes are dark, dark brown, like black olives that come in a can.

Her smile is as sweet as a bowl of cake batter ice cream.

I think I have to go eat.

I am as hungry as a meat-eating lion in a vegetarian jungle.

As hungry as a person who forgot to pack snacks for an eight-hour plane ride.

As hungry as a celiac disease sufferer in an all-wheat-gluten world.

I don't know why I have to do this extra-credit work. Obviously, I know how to *describe* things. Even new girlfriends of old boyfriends. I dare anyone else to try doing that without becoming catty.

Speaking of cats. DeathKitty attacked Oscar today when he tried to drink water out of her bowl. She sliced a chunk of fur off but drew no blood. That probably only made her madder. Oscar has been hiding under the bed. Must lure him out with hot dog in order to eat hot dog with embedded pill.

No wonder he needs to drink DeathKitty's water. Hot dogs = sodium on a stick.

I should know. I only gave them up a year ago. Mostly. May have had a corn dog at Wisconsin state fair.

Ooh, speaking of WI—Wittenauer's calling!

LATER

First, almost got hit by freight train in middle of town. Riding bike, late to class.

Then had to wait for train. Was late to class.

Then, class sucked because we had to do an in-class writing exercise and then some people got picked to read theirs out loud and I was one of them and mine was not very good.

Well, come on. Who can be inspired by the setup: "What if an Alien Walked into the Classroom Right Now?"

After I read it, the teacher just sort of looked at me. Was it that illogical and uncreative to suggest that the alien might not decide to stick around and would instead head to the Pyth for lunch?

At least I didn't suggest the alien shoot up the place and take us hostage, like someone else did. I mean, was that supposed to be original? Anyone can put a gun in a story.

Then, Dara was supposed to give me a ride to work but she didn't show up, so I had to ride my bike. It's not that it's far—it's just the idea that I was waiting for her, and then had to scramble on my own to get there in time.

And then? Well, it was not a good night at work. Things were sort of slow, so Guy left. (That's Guy as in Guy Nicollet the owner, Guy being a French name, not as in some guy.) I said, "You can't, like—leave me here. Alone."

For one thing, it's not safe to have one person working in a retail place anytime, never mind ten at night. For another, our rush starts around quarter of eleven. So there was a line out the door and just me to ring everyone up, make smoothies and sundaes, etc.

Now there's a lull so I'm sitting here recovering. Crowd has died down. Or actually, crowd is too busy eating and drinking and shouting to need me. Occasionally someone staggers up to the counter for a refill, apparently thinking we give free refills, which we don't, only I'm so pissed at Guy N. right now that I feel like giving everyone free stuff.

This is, like, the worst week of my life so far. Sure, Bagle Finagle sucked, but this sucks more. It's like a bad rip-off of Truth or Dairy and if it is doing well, it's only succeeding because of stealing ideas.

I should have stayed at CFC. I should have written a bunch of IOUs to pay for college, like they did in California when the state ran out of money. CFC, I O U about $40,000. Give or take a thousand.

We are Generation B, for Bankrupt. We know how to make alternate plans.

Dear journal, I've missed you. But not that much.

Long story short: Worst week ever ended up being best week ever. Blissful. Kissful.

Friday night I got home at one in the morning, and W was waiting for me on the porch. Can you believe it? Well, you're a journal, you have to believe everything I tell you. (Don't you?) But still. It was so unbelievable that for a while now I've been wondering if I dreamed it myself. But no.

So there he was, like a vision. Just sitting on the brick wall on the porch. "You missed curfew," he said.

"Shut up," I said, running over to him. "Why are you here?"

Naturally we hugged and all that.

"Where have you been?" he asked, kind of into my hair.

"At work! Oh my God, what are you doing here, why didn't you call me?"

"I just got here," he said, "like, five minutes ago. And I was kind of worried when you weren't here, and nobody else was home. Figured you were out partying."

"Yeah, right. But—what about the football game tomorrow?" I asked.

He shrugged, looking unconcerned. "I got a sub."

"There's a sub for Corny? No. Impossible."

"Sure. Baby Corn, remember? The understudy."

I attempted to not roll my eyes. I mean, of all the ridiculous things about having a mascot . . . "How did you . . . what did you . . . fly?" I asked.

"I drove."

"You *drove*? I talked to you and you were probably on

the road and you didn't even *tell* me? Why didn't you tell me?" I shoved him and he nearly fell over the wall and off the porch.

"Ow! It was a surprise. Why didn't you tell me Grant lived next door?"

"I know! It's not a very good neighborhood, is it?"

"That's not funny."

"Well . . . yes, he does live next door. You must have seen him?"

"He just got home," Wittenauer said. "Right before you."

"Hm."

"With his girlfriend," said Wittenauer.

"Right. His girlfriend, Kelli." This was all so mature of us that I almost could have puked. "So, you can obviously see, he and I are friends. That's all."

"Friends with benefits?" asked W.

"What? No! The only benefit at all is that he let me use his car once."

"His car."

"Yup."

"Sounds serious."

"Nope. He has a girlfriend and I have a boyfriend and it's all very normal and boring."

"Right. Wait a second. You have a boyfriend?" he asked.

Then we started kissing.

Fade out.

No longer *Les Misérables*.

Le Sigh of Happiness.

Art of the Essay Description #2: Walter Wittenauer, aka "Corny," aka Ultrasweet Boyfriend

When he is asleep, he looks like a Norse god.

OK, I don't know anything about Norse gods, so perhaps I should choose another comparison.

He looks like someone who should be cloned for his cheekbones alone.

His skin looks like the color of this really yummy bread they sell at the co-op that's called, like, Boulder Valley Wheat, but it's a light wheat, a Scandinavian wheat. Or perhaps it's called potato, not wheat. Anyway. Light golden like sunlight on a, um—

You know, forget it.

What I can say for sure is that he snores like a freight train.

He snores like a train loaded with freight in the dark of night, going around a curve. In the French countryside. The train drowns out the birds that are chirping in the French trees but every once in a while you can hear one.

A dog barks.

If a dog barks in the French countryside and nobody hears it, does it still bark?

Further hated words: "We should all have dinner together."

This was Wittenauer's idea of a good time last night. He called it Supper Club. His plan involved me, him, Kelli, and Grant.

I'd rather be stuck with pins and put on the campus activity bulletin board.

"Let's just go for coffee," I said.

"Why?"

"Kelli doesn't eat much. She's tiny."

Wittenauer laughed. "Thin, athletic people eat, too, Courtney!"

What was he saying? That I'm not thin and athletic? I think I'm insulted. Doesn't he realize I walk or bike everywhere? I haven't been in this good shape since, well, forever.

He explained about his Sunday night supper co-op back at CFC and how it's not necessarily about eating, but more a way to get everyone talking.

I said, "Yeah, but you can't form a co-op because you don't even live here," and he said, "No, not yet," and I was so busy trying to convince him not to have this dinner thing that I didn't even have time to react to that. Writing it now, I'm wondering: What was that all about? Is he planning to move here?

How cool.

But how weird.

More cool than weird. We could get our own place! No more DeathKitty!

But who am I kidding? One, I couldn't afford that, and two, my mom would never let me live with a guy, not yet.

So then what? Wittenauer would move in here with

the 3 of us? No, never. Wittenauer would move in next door with Grant? No, never.

Anyway. Back to real life. I distracted him from the whole supper club idea by pointing out we should spend our last night together, just by ourselves. Dodged that bullet and had fun while dodging. It was, as they say, a win-win situation, and normally I hate that expression but not last night.

Le sigh.

Wittenauer left this morning. There is his bio textbook that he forgot, right there on my desk. I will have to get out of bed soon and take it somewhere to ship overnight because he really needs it.

Anyway. It's evidence.

I cannot get out of bed. Lying here under comforter, not willing to move on with life. Skipping all my classes today. Or at least the first two. And if I skip two, why not go ahead and skip all three? It's not like anyone will notice me. Besides, I can work on my descriptive powers at home. I have a lot of reading to catch up on, anyway.

Or, I could call Wittenauer.

Or, since I started the semester 3 weeks late, I probably should get my butt out of bed and get to class.

Ha! This will show petty Art of Essay teacher. Today, I, Courtney V. D. Smith, possessor of bad descriptive whatevers and weak argumentative skills, got a job at a student zine.

Moi!

I got the job while procrastinating writing papers yesterday. See, I can be productive while also being a sloth.

But get this—I even have my own column!

There was an ad on a student discussion site for this new online journal, and I mean, who knows about journals more than I do? So I proposed the idea to the managing editor and she got back to me today and said it's a go.

My proposal: a column called "Holding Court." It will appear every Friday. Sort of like a student blog, but whatever—it counts for my resume. I will be published!

Which is cool, because I always wanted to be an attorney and am now considering going into environmental law. Will use my powers to bring down environmental villains. At least, that's what I promised in my proposal—a look into local companies and where they can improve on lessening their impact on the environment.

Where do I begin, though? The list is long. The resources are few.

Plus, the new *Project Runway* is on.

How green are fashion designers? Couldn't they be greener? What about TV? Shouldn't TV be more environmentally friendly?

Man. I wish I hadn't just thought that. I'm going to have to stop watching.

Art of the Essay Description #3: DeathKitty

A black cat of approximately 15 pounds

Approximately 3 years of age

Eyes that can vary in size from round saucers to thin slits

Eyelashes that are so pretty, they make death seem glamorous

Black whiskers the size of a petite broom, the kind you use to whisk up the sweepings into the dustpan

Personally responsible for culling the bird population

Especially fond of sparrows

Enjoys leaving carcasses on comforters

Attitude that life is not worth living unless you are pouncing on something

The unviolent life is not worth living

Leave no stone or dog bone unturned

Live free or die

Etc.

Environmental Activism took a strange turn today.

Dr. Bigelow went on a rant with about five minutes left of class, about how our generation (Gen B for Bankrupt) knows nothing about sacrificing for the greater good. He insisted we all plan something big and have the guts to carry it through. Then, he insisted he wasn't officially sponsoring anything illegal or dangerous and if any of us spoke to the authorities, he would find out who told and fail those students.

After class we all kind of looked around the classroom at each other, like: What are we supposed to do?

Would he fail us all if we didn't come up with something good? Would we all get kicked out of school if we did?

This is a little intense, even for me.

Talked to Wittenauer about it and he said I should be able to think of something, thanks to experience as a campus Badical. True. I've protested before, I can protest again. Maybe not involve the board of trustees this time, though.

I went to Shop & Shop after class, on bike, and saw Grant there. Told him I was kicking around ideas for my blog and thinking about writing my column. "I could expose Guy at the Smoothie Stop," I said.

"Um . . . what?"

"He's an environmental nightmare, and I work for him. So what do I do? Quit, or bring him to justice? Well, not that I have the power to do that . . . but what if we listed businesses around town that were not environmentally friendly?"

"Sounds great," Grant said, and returned to work.

I'm pretty sure he wasn't even listening to me at all.

However, it's the first time so far I've managed to see Grant at Shop & Shop AND leave store with actual groceries. Yes! Score!

Running tally: Maturity: 1
Immaturity: 97

Homecoming at Cornwall Falls. Giant parties. Big game. Wittenauer is out cheering. Mary Jo, everyone having fun, hanging out with alums, parents, etc. Meanwhile, I went to work. How much does that suck?

As I stood there making order after order, it hit me that (a) this is not where I want to end up in life, and (b) I should probably let Gerry know he's been hacked.

T or D item Coconut Fantasy Dream (my fave) = here, called Dreaming of Coconuts

T or D item Hot Fudge Fudgorama = here, Fudgorama Diorama

Sunrise Strawberry Supreme = Sunset Strawberry Supreme

Banana Splitsville = Banana Splitsville = Blatant Rip-off

I mean, this makes it really, really easy for me to work here . . . because I know all the recipes by heart . . . but I feel like I'm cheating on Gerry somehow.

Wait, that came out wrong. Not *cheating* on him, just cheating on Truth or Dairy.

Do I sabotage my own job by cluing in Gerry to what's going on here? Or do I assume that most smoothie and ice cream places offer the same items and just move on?

"You kind of borrowed a couple of ideas, didn't you? From Truth or Dairy?" I asked Guy very casually during a very casual moment. I smiled. Casual-like.

"What?" He acted like that was an insulting, way off-base question. "I came up with all the concepts myself. It took months," he said.

Guy is not very bright.

Anyway, so much for the so-called late-night study

crowd, seeing as how I was working on a Friday night. More like late-night drinking crowd, from the nearby bars and fraternities. People staggering in for smoothies and energy drinks, trying to sober up. Or maybe just trying to get the energy to stay out later. Or at least to have the energy to be happy drunks.

Last weekend Wittenauer was here.

This weekend, it's Bryan.

He came by the Smoothie Stop to pick me up from work at midnight last night. He's sleeping on the floor beside my bed, and Oscar is practically sleeping on top of him.

I can see DeathKitty's eyes glowing in the light from my book light. She's sitting over by the stairs. She won't let any of us move without knowing about it.

Bizarre cat. With violent tendencies.

I'm not normally this close to Bryan so this is weird, but maybe our relationship is changing as we get older. He's been begging me for the chance to get away. "Please, Courtney. I *really* don't want to be around Mom and Doofus right now. Plus, I miss Oscar."

How could I argue with that?

Still. Bryan's been spending *way* too much time making Shawna laugh. Insisted on all of us going up to Poudre Canyon for a hike—Dara came, but she would only hang out by the car and wait for us to get back. Then Shawna insisted on all of us biking around town afterward.

Dara rode her one-speed cruiser and got left behind on the first little hill. I think she actually just was planning to ride to the coffee shop anyway. Couldn't wait to get rid of us.

Then, Shawna went to work, and Bryan insisted on visiting Grant next door. No amount of arguing and complaining from me could stop him. I was still telling him that maybe we should call first when he was out the door, stopping Grant and Kelli in their tracks.

Then, just like old times, it was the four of us sitting

around: Me. Bryan. Grant. Oscar.

And Kelli.

Whoops, I guess that makes five of us.

"Come on, Bryan," I said after a little while, under my breath. "Let's go. We're like the third, fourth, and fifth wheels here."

"What?" He gave me a clueless look.

"Hey, who's up for badminton?" asked Kelli. She was so nice. So incredibly nice.

So then it was me and Bryan against her and Grant. Nothing like a Saturday night with your brother. Playing badminton, which is not fun even in the best of circumstances, against your ex and his new GF. And your dog trying to chase down every single badminton bird thingy and chew it to bits.

Well, at least that made the game a short one.

Nightmare of epic proportions. Talked to Shawna tonight while we were studying in living room. We were talking about me and Wittenauer when all of a sudden she said, "Your brother is, like, so cute."

I shook my head. "Not really." Despite the fact we didn't look all that different, I had to protest.

"He is, he is." Shawna sighed. "And the sad fact is that I'll never meet anyone like him."

"Probably not. You should just forget him and others like him."

She frowned. "Why do you say that?"

"Because he's too young for you! Because he's my brother!" I nearly yelled.

"I didn't say I wanted to go out with him. Someone *like* him. God. What do you take me for, a cradle robber?" she asked.

It was then I had to explain to her what happened with Bryan and Beth.

"Well, yeah," Shawna said. "Beth was always kind of a little too, um, friendly. With guys."

I wanted to defend her, but that wasn't too far from the truth. Even though Beth is in Italy and has settled down a lot, she can't escape her HS reputation.

That kind of sucks.

Does that mean everyone will remember me as a bad class vice president who let the president steal all the money in the treasury? And gave a very poor, very embarrassing speech to get elected? And slept on the roof of a school to raise money but was not even touched by the infamous player Tom "the Tom" Delaney?

There's so much to live *down*.

No wonder it's a good thing to go away for college. Far, far away.

Anyway, Shawna and I plotted a strategy for her to find someone more appropriate to lust after. She claims that she never meets anyone, but I don't get it. She says guys don't approach her because they assume she already has a boyfriend. On account of being kind of beautiful.

Which she is, but still.

Working graveyard shifts at a copy shop is not helping her. She only meets strange, stressed grad students. We made a list of every guy she knows and is slightly interested in. I was shocked when she wrote down "Matt from next door."

"Oh yeah, he's really nice," I chimed in.

"Grant from next door," she wrote next.

"But he's, um, seeing someone," I pointed out. Not to mention that he's my ex and that would be horribly awkward.

"I know," she said. "But it probably won't last forever."

Dara walked in the door just as I was saying, "No, you're right, I guess."

"Right about what?" asked Dara.

"That Grant and Kelli are, like, on borrowed time," Shawna told her. She talked about her ex, who decided he didn't want to be tied down to just one person. "And I was like, later. Have a good life. Why would I want to waste my time with someone like that? You either want to go out and be serious or you don't. But then I think he's kind of right, you know? That we're too young to be settling down with one person. I mean, like, look at Tobie, who's living with Bradley, and all they do now is fight about the dishes, and then there's you, who's tied down to Wittenauer and he's a hundred miles away," Shawna went on.

"I'm not tired down," I said. "And it's a thousand miles."

"Tied down," Dara corrected me.

"Whatever. I'm not."

"Sure you are," said Dara. "You're not agreeing to see other people, are you?"

"No."

"Then you're tied down," she said.

"But what's wrong with that?" I asked.

"Nothing! If that's what you like. I just don't, I'm more of a spontaneous free-spirit-type person when it comes to going out," said Dara.

"In other words, lonely," said Shawna.

"No, actually, no. I'm not. And what's more lonely? Being alone, or missing the person you're tied down to?" she asked.

Ooh. Check. Mate.

I was going to call Wittenauer and ask if he felt like he was too . . . tied down, or up, or whatever. But that seemed like something only a tied-down person would do.

What a horrible expression. Picture bound wrists.

Of course, some people like that sort of thing.

Doorbell rang this morning while I was finishing breakfast. Opened the front door and saw Grant and Kelli
standing there. "We have kind of a weird question to ask
you," said Grant.

I braced myself.

"Do you think we could borrow Oscar?" Grant asked.

I narrowed my eyes. "Borrow him? For what, a walk?
Because I already took him on a long walk—"

"No, it's for Wednesday morning, actually," Kelli
added. "Do you think that would be OK?"

"Well, what for?" I asked.

"We're sort of having a show-and-tell in vet sciences,"
Grant said.

"Aren't you a little old for show-and-tell?" asked Dara,
holding DeathKitty in her arms, stroking her neck.

"The professor asked us to bring in any pets we have.
Since I—uh, we—don't have any—"

"Then why don't they call it *pet* sciences?" I asked.

Grant laughed, but Kelli didn't. I could tell my humor
didn't amuse her.

"That might be stressful for Oscar. Why not take
DeathKitty instead?" I suggested.

"That's a great idea," said Dara. "She loves the spotlight. And maybe you could ask your professor why it feels
like she's gained ten pounds in the last month."

"It's because she's been eating Oscar's food," I said.
"It's not a mystery. Add that to all the calories she gets
from killing birds—hey, you could talk about her love of
the kill," I said to Grant.

"But I don't know her. I know Oscar. I'm familiar with
his issues," said Grant.

He sounded just like a vet already. That, or a therapist.

"Fine. Take him. But if he freaks out in front of all those people, don't blame me," I said.

"If he has a grand mal seizure that would be so cool. A great *learning* opportunity," said Kelli.

I just stared at her. She actually *wants* him to have a seizure. She has a cruel streak.

"Well, he won't have one," I said. "He's been doing really well lately."

I don't know how to break it to Oscar that he's about to be a scientific experiment.

I'm obsessing over the fact that Kelli and Grant want to take Oscar to class. I can't say why, but that feels wrong. Grant and I bonded over Oscar. He's, you know, *our* dog, or at least my dog, who has a very small circle of friends. Not for Kelli to interlope with.

Especially not if she's looking forward to him seizing up and freaking out.

I called Wittenauer to talk it over. "What kind of person wants that? Is that the kind of cold, scientific personality you have to have in order to become a veterinarian? I mean, imagine if she wanted to be a doctor. She'd walk around wishing people would fall ill right in front of her so she could *learn* more. She'd be like, 'Would you mind breaking your leg so I can learn how to set a cast? Would you skip your insulin so I can watch you go into a diabetic coma?'"

"Courtney? Courtney! I have to write a paper, so . . ."

"Yeah, OK. Bye." He wasn't that interested, but why would he be? Still, he could have faked it. Everyone has to fake something sometime.

Made a bit of a scene today. Am probably unbalanced and need a B-12, vitamin D, every-kind-of-vitamin smoothie boost. This is embarrassing to write down even *here*, where no one else will read it.

First, when Grant and Kelli came over to pick up Oscar this morning, I insisted on going along. Never mind that it meant I had to skip two of my own classes, and never mind that sitting in a classroom where animals are potentially . . . dissected . . . or operated on . . . at some point or other, made me feel sick to my stomach.

I told them that Oscar would freak out if I wasn't there because he's had so many changes lately, and he has this fear of abandonment, which he's had since he was a puppy, and Grant nodded, saying, "That's good, that's good, I'll talk about that."

He was petting Oscar when he suddenly said, "Where's his rabies tag?"

"I'm not sure. In Denver?"

"Don't you have *any* tags for him?" Grant turned his collar around, checking.

"I'll get them, OK? What's the big deal?"

"You know what you should do? You should get him chipped," said Kelli.

"Right," I said, thinking it must hurt an animal or she wouldn't have suggested it. "Well. Can we go? Because I have my own actual classes later."

"You don't *have* to come along," said Grant.

"I do. I really do," I said. "Come on, boy." I clipped the leash to Oscar's collar and we went outside. The 3 of us crammed into Grant's little car, with Oscar sitting in the backseat next to Kelli.

Well. That's just how it worked out, I mean, she got in first, and Oscar clearly can't sit up front. Air bag and everything.

The vet buildings are on the far south side of campus. As we drove there, Grant was grilling me for details to refresh his memory of how we got Oscar (he was abandoned), and how Oscar got the way he is (he was abandoned).

So we get to class, which consists of, like, fifty people sitting around and some random pets. Everyone gets to go up on this little stage/podium thing and say something about an unusual behavior their pet has that no one has seen, heard of, or even read about.

In other words: monotonous and boring after the fifth pet. (Though I did see that student with the room to rent, the one who had a boa constrictor.)

OK, so it wasn't that bad. But ferret behavior is just not something I'm interested in. Or Siamese cats. DeathKitty would have been the superstar. (Or, she would have taken out a couple other pets.)

Oscar cowered under my legs as we sat in the third row of long desks in the lecture hall. So. This was what it was like to be a vet science major. Sit around and watch a pet parade.

Well, and eventually cut them open.

Finally, it was Grant's turn. I offered to go with, but Kelli said that wouldn't be necessary. I glared at her. What does she know? Is Oscar her pet? I mean, really. They went up onstage, Oscar walking behind them, tail between legs, acting scared.

Grant had just started to talk about Oscar's epileptic hopes and fears when someone's cell phone rang—really loudly—and Oscar freaked and started running in circles, howling.

"Well. Like he was saying." Kelli shrugged.

Everyone started to laugh, and although Grant looked a little uncomfortable, he didn't do anything to stop it.

I thought: Are these the people who will be vets in the future? Since when is it vetlike to laugh at a dog's personality flaws?

"And for my next act . . ." Kelli joked.

"It's not funny, OK? It's not funny!" Before I could think about it, I was on my feet and running to the front of the classroom. "He's not even your dog, he's my dog." I grabbed Oscar's leash and crouched down beside him, trying to calm him. But all he wanted to do was stand next to Grant.

"Are you sure about that?" asked someone in the front row.

I glared at him. "We didn't laugh at your parrot. Or your stupid ferret," I said to the student beside him. "And your pet rat? Well, that's just disgusting. I mean, who keeps a rat anymore? This isn't the Dark Ages."

"Rats are very intelligent," the rat owner shot back. "Unlike some people."

"Oh really, and it's intelligent to *keep* a rodent?"

"All right, all right—everyone settle down." A professor-looking type (in other words, he had a beard) who'd been sitting off to the side finally got up and intervened. He lowered his eyeglasses and peered at me. "And you. Where did you come from? Are you even in this class?"

"No. *They* just borrowed *my* dog," I said. "Which is not cool, when you think about it. Besides, I'm an Environmental Studies major. Well, I haven't declared a major yet, but I'm pretty sure, unless there's a way to major in Journalism and then minor in the Environmental Studies thing, but there's no way I could ever cut up an animal, I mean, I don't know how you guys are going to handle it but I couldn't. I don't believe in eating meat, either."

Everyone looked very awkward for a minute.

"OK then," said the professor. "I think we've seen enough of your furry friend—"

"And of me. Understood. We're leaving," I said.

I marched up the steps to the exit with as much dignity as a highly insulted person who had just babbled her entire life story to a roomful of strangers could have.

After class got out, on the way home, I sat in the backseat with Oscar. None of us said a word for a while.

"Well, uh, do you want to go get a coffee or something?" asked Kelli.

"Um, no thanks. I'd better get home with Oscar. Take him for a walk. In fact, you guys could drop me right here and we'll walk the rest of the way."

"But don't be silly," said Grant. "You know we have to go right by your house to get to my house—"

"Oscar needs the exercise," I said. "It'll help calm him down."

Unfortunately, Oscar was sort of asleep when I said that, tired out from all the stress, so it made no sense. Anyway, Grant pulled over and I wrestled Oscar out of the backseat onto the curb. "Well, um, thanks," said Grant. "Hope that wasn't too traumatic."

"Oh, he'll be all right," I said.

"I meant *you*," he said.

I wanted to jump back in the car, take the wheel, and

run over him at that point. What did he know about me, about anything?

"Yeah. Thanks a million," said Kelli, leaning out of the passenger seat.

I gave her a fake smile, a fake wave, and started to walk as they pulled away from the curb. It was then that I really paid attention to where we were.

Didn't realize how far from home we were. What a hike.

I'd acted like such an idiot. Why did I have to act like that? How juvenile was I? What was wrong with me?

Almost started crying on the way home, it just hurt so much to see Grant with someone else for real. (Plus, I was getting blisters from my ballet flats, which are not designed for walking two miles.) That note I'd found over the visor? It was probably still there, he'd save it forever and put it in their memory book. Scrapbook. Whatever.

Why couldn't things have stayed the same?

Why couldn't anything ever stay the same?

I must have PMS or something. This is ridiculous.

Called Wittenauer. Didn't tell him everything that happened yesterday as that sounded stupid, but did tell him this wasn't my best week. He was really, really sweet. Made me wish I'd stayed in Wisconsin. Well, that and the fact I'd made a complete idiot of myself yesterday. He reminded me that he's a mascot who once stripped down to his shorts in front of the board of trustees. He got me to laugh at myself, relax, and think about next year.

"Next year?"

"Yeah. I'll be done with school here, and we'll be together."

"We will?"

He laughed. "Of course we will. Don't worry, I have a plan."

Well, good. At least one of us has a plan. Me, I'm more worried about *this* year. Who's to say CSU won't raise their tuition rates and I'll end up transferring even somewhere else?

Is it possible to homeschool for college? Probably not if you don't want to actually live at home. Besides, imagine the social life. Nightly dinners with Mom and man-friend.

Speaking of which, Mom's been calling and asking me to come visit this weekend. Like I want to spend my Saturday night with her and Mr. Man-friend?

Maybe I don't have anything better to do.

Ack!!!!! Must join a club or other extracurric ASAP. Like, "Sophomores Whose Moms Are Infatuated at an Advanced Age." This is a big school. They'll have *something* like that.

I'm published! Sort of. If you count student blogs, which I swore never to do again.

"Holding Court" by Courtney Von Dragen Smith is up on the web. (Debated a long time whether to use my middle name or not. Has embarrassing V. D. initials, but is more distinctive than just using "Smith.")

My first column, "Bring Back the Silver," is about how many places still use plastic cuttery.

That doesn't sound right.

Cutlery. Yes, that's the word, just went back in to edit.

Anyway. I listed several of them by name. Yes, to-go orders are challenging, but in-house orders should use mugs, not plastic cups; stainless forks, not plastic.

I was going to suggest that restaurants and coffee shops quit giving out napkins, but that seems a little impossible to achieve. What would people use?

Instead, I urged restaurants to compost all paper products, such as recycled napkins, and food waste.

Not sure where compost goes, but I've heard of it.

Perhaps should check into how stainless is made. Does it involve strip-mining? Is there such a thing as strip-mineless stainless steel?

Anyway, I wonder if a project like this is big enough for the Env. Activism group thing Dr. Bigelow talked about. If we took it to a slightly bigger scale, maybe? Then again, do I want to be the person spearheading any kind of protest? Look where it got me last time. Last year. Was hated by CFC sweatshirt wearers around the globe when I demanded we stop using harmful initials on college gear.

Then, somehow, lost scholarship. They claim no connection, but can't help thinking otherwise.

K OS.

Utter total K OS.

Just when you think things won't get worse, after you humiliate yourself in front of your ex, his girlfriend, and an entire classroom of people and animals . . . well, they do.

So on Friday night, Grant asked if I wanted a ride to Denver—he was going to visit his parents and grandmother. I said sure. Mom had asked me to visit, anyway, so I was doing the right thing. Shawna promised to walk Oscar a few times and generally keep him out of trouble while I was gone.

Besides, I thought it'd be cool to spend a little time with Grant and make up for the way I acted on Wednesday. I was glad he was still talking to me.

Of course, they probably were only taking pity on me. They. Because of course Kelli was coming along. Why wouldn't she? They're boyfriend and girlfriend after all.

I was minding my own business in the backseat when I heard her and Grant arguing a little outside the car, something about "why would you ask her" and Grant saying he felt sorry for me and was only trying to help. . . .

I was about to bail when they both climbed in, closed the doors, and we were off to I-25.

"So, is this the first time you'll be meeting, uh, the Superiors?" I asked Kelli, trying to make pleasant small talk.

"Yes. How do I look?" she asked. "Is this too much?" She was wearing a dress that looked like it had come from that cool, expensive shop in Old Town . . . can't remember the name of it. She looked like she was going to a wedding: had on heels, fancy necklace, makeup.

"No, it's perfect," I said, thinking: Why would you get dressed up to meet someone's parents? They're only . . . parents. They don't know what's in, or out, of style. All they care about is whether you're a nice person or a psycho killer.

Besides, Grant's mom's idea of dressing up was matching her T-shirt to her Birkenstocks.

Kelli turned around and rested her chin on the headrest. "I should totally get notes from you. Tell me what they're like."

I just sort of smiled, feeling very, very uncomfortable. Why was I in this car again? Fool me once, shame on . . . me? "Well, they're very nice," I said, glancing at Grant, who was glancing at *me* in the rearview mirror. "A little bit intense, though. They'll grill you about everything."

"What?" asked Grant.

"Oh yeah. You don't know because you weren't there," I said to him. "But they get you alone, see. They'll find some way to get you alone and they'll just grill you. Be ready for the third degree."

Kelli suddenly didn't look very confident. I think her hair literally wilted a teensy tiny bit from the fan vent in front of her. "What kind of, um, questions?" She fiddled with the vent, which was blowing right at her.

"That one doesn't close," Grant and I both said at the same time.

That was so awkward that I said, "Excuse me a sec. Have to check in with Wittenauer."

I made a point of talking to him for a little bit while we rode down, just so it was clear that we'd all moved on. But he couldn't talk long because it was a football game, so that figured. Of all times to be Corny. I kind of pretended I was on the line longer than I actually was, to be honest. Kelli was squirming with nervousness and I have to admit I was enjoying it.

They dropped me off and Grant idled at the curb, waiting to make sure I got in OK. He always did that. I always loved that he did that. Some other people would just take off, like Dave.

Anyway. Got to the front door, rang bell. No answer. Had my keys, and attempted to unlock the door.

My key didn't fit in the lock. WHAT? I felt ridiculous. How embarrassing. Locked out by own mom. She changed the locks!?!?!? (This *was* a trick!)

But I couldn't let them know that, so I just waved and said, "I'm in!" as they drove off and I stood there, waving and pretending to open the door.

I pounded on the door. Then I tried calling Mom, and it went straight to voice mail. "Mom! How could you not even be here?" I cried.

I called Bryan but his cell was off. I called Wittenauer to vent, but his phone was off, too. Had to rely on my own devices. I remembered that Mom usually kept a spare key under this brick on the side of the house, so I ran to get it.

Guess what? No hidden key anymore.

Trick.

I gave up and sat on the steps for a while. Somebody would have to come home soon, right?

Wrong. Instead, neighbor across the street, Mr. Novotny, came out and started talking about the Broncos with me. "Big game Monday night against the Chargers." He had no ideas for me to get into the house, but he did tell me a lot about the strategy the Broncos would need to use, and their defensive backfield, whatever that is, and other key points of the game.

As I sat there trying to rely on my own wits, and listening to more about football than I've ever known or cared to know in my entire life, I suddenly remembered that we had this one window screen that was always sort of loose—Alison had started it, just in case she ever got home past curfew. It was in the back of the house, off the den.

Of course. Brilliant.

I excused myself for a minute and went around back. I found the loose screen, which didn't seem quite as loose as it used to be. I pried it off and tried pushing at the window. It wouldn't budge.

As I was standing there, I remembered coming home late one night last spring, senior year. . . . Grant was helping me to sneak in at about one in the morning, but we got kind of tangled up trying to open the window and ended up falling on the ground, and, well . . .

Suddenly, I heard sirens.

Getting closer and closer.

Since when was it illegal to have risqué memories?

I went around front and saw a white security company car pull up in front of the house. Two seconds later, a police car rounded the corner and stopped behind it. Next thing I knew, a male security guard and a female police officer were walking toward the house—and me.

Talk about not being welcome at home.

"May I see your identification, please?" they both asked at the same time.

"See, the thing is, I used to live here, but—"

"ID, please."

I grabbed my bag from the front steps and desperately searched for my wallet. It had dropped into some crevice that would not release it. Or had I just forgotten to put it into my bag because I was tired?

"How are we coming on that ID?" asked the police officer.

"Not, um, good," I said. "But can't you look me up on your onboard computer or something?"

She glared at me.

"Ma'am?" I added as a sign of respect. "Ma'am Officer? I really do live here. Well, I used to live here." I ran through the story of everything that had transpired lately, how it came to be that I would be standing here with the wrong key and trying to enter illegally.

Mr. Novotny had been standing there and watching the whole thing. Finally both guard and officer turned to him. "Can you vouch for her?"

"That depends. How much do you need?" Mr. Novotny regarded me with a wary expression.

"Is she who she says she is?" asked the police officer.

Mr. Novotny shrugged. "You never know with teenagers, do you?"

I rolled my eyes. I swear. Ageism.

Fortunately, Mom and Sterling finally showed up, in Sterling's football field–size SUV. They went out to brunch. *Brunch*. Who eats brunch?

They said they turned off their cell phones so they could have some real together time with no interruptions. Stupid romantic ideas of old people. There's nothing *wrong* with interruptions when they're important, like your daughter is ABOUT TO BE ARRESTED.

"You got the locks changed?" I yelled at her once the law had left.

"Bryan lost his keys—"

"And since when do we have an alarm?" I asked Mom.

"Sterling worries about me living here by myself."

"You don't. Bryan lives here. And Oscar did, too . . ."

"Oscar's no guard dog," she said.

"That's because you never believed in him. You never did!" And then I started sobbing and turned into an emotional wreck. I seem to be good at that lately. "You know what? Just take me back."

"Courtney, don't be ridiculous."

"Take me back, or I'm hitching a ride. On the highway."

She used to work hard on this mother-daughter stuff. Now she could not care less. She's forgotten all about book clubs and Oprah. Instead of O magazine, she now subscribes to *Running Fanatic*.

Running Frantic is more like it.

Wait, that's my life. Or perhaps Oscar's.

Not speaking to Mom.

Got back last night; Gerry drove me. I know, of all people. But Bryan had a meet, and I was not on speaking terms with Mom. Or Sterling, for that matter.

If it weren't for Sterling's allergies, Oscar wouldn't be living with me. If he weren't living with me, then Grant and Kelli wouldn't have borrowed him for class. If they hadn't done that, I wouldn't have embarrassed myself in front of 50 pre-vet students. All Sterling's fault. Most everything that's going wrong can be traced directly back to him—and Mom, by the transitive property.

I had dropped by T or D Saturday afternoon to show Gerry a menu from Smoothie Stop, and he got very riled up and said he'd have to come see for himself. But as we got closer to Fort Collins, he seemed to lose his nerve.

"I hate confrontation," he said as we pulled into the Smoothie Stop parking lot. (Where there are some very dumb red stop signs with the store name on them.)

"Tell me about it," I said, thinking of my argument with Mom. "But, Gerry, you used to be a counselor. Didn't you have to know a lot about conflict resolution?"

"Yes. But I still hated it."

"You could just be friendly and nice today," I said. "Just take a look around and see if you agree with me, that he borrowed your ideas a little too liberally."

"OK. Today, I just look."

We went inside and Gerry stood behind me, trying not to be noticed, I guess. Of course, Guy immediately saw who it was and came out from behind the counter and started shaking Gerry's hand and saying all these compli-mentary things about how he never realized how hard it was to be a store owner, and how it was great employees like myself that made a great shop, etc.

Total snow job.

Guy seemed to think it was strange that Gerry and I drove up together. Couldn't understand why. When I told him that it was a long story, he seemed to think that was even weirder.

Whatever. Probably doesn't understand the concept of friendship. Probably has never had a friend.

"Guy Nicollet. Never liked him," Gerry muttered as we walked to the car.

"He worked for you for, like . . . two years," I reminded him.

"Oh, I know. Believe me, I know."

"So why didn't you fire him sooner? Oh. You really don't like conflict, do you?" I said.

He smiled sadly. "Not at all."

"Well, that's OK. You can let your lawyer do the confrontational stuff, like suing him."

"Right, right." Gerry started the car. "What lawyer?"

"You'll find one."

"Sure, sure. They don't cost much, right?" He smiled nervously and ran his hand through his thinning hair.

Right before he dropped me off at my house, he said, "You know, Courtney, instead of lawyering up, maybe you could help me instead. You've already gathered the evidence. Now, as part of your journalism major, you could write about it. How he stole all of my ideas." He was sounding a little delirious. "I can see it now. The truth will set you free."

"The Truth or Dairy, you mean," I joked, trying to get him back to reality.

"No. No! The smoothie will set you free!" he cried. "Will you do it? Please?"

"I'll think about it," I said.

"Please!" he said. "Think of the great publicity this would bring me. Maybe even enough to save the store."

"The store . . . it needs saving?" I asked.

"In a big way," he admitted, looking down at the steering wheel.

"OK then. I'll do it," I promised.

Not sure what I can do. Not sure what I've gotten myself into.

10/19 MONDAY NIGHT FOOTBALL AT GRANT'S

"You could have called me, you know."

"What?"

"When you were locked out," Grant said as my roomies and I walked into his house.

I frowned. Stupid housemates do not keep secrets. At all.

"Oh, it was no big deal," I said, still a little embarrassed by everything. "It worked out. I spent some quality time with Mr. Novotny."

"Mm hm. And the Denver police?" he asked.

"You were arrested?" gasped Kelli. "You didn't tell me about that. When?" She looked excited about *that*, too. She loves it when people and animals are in trouble, apparently.

What does Grant see in her? I thought she used to be nice and sweet but now I'm starting to wonder. She was like a wolf in sheep's clothing. Although she looks nothing like a sheep. She was a tiger in a striped sweater. . . . OK, that makes no sense at all.

TA is correct. I cannot describe things sometimes.

I took a seat on the sofa next to Shawna. "Thanks for keeping my story to yourself."

"No problem," she said.

I punched her arm. "I wasn't serious."

When the game started, I found that I actually cared what happened. "If Orton doesn't have a good night tonight, they don't stand a chance," I said.

And then, "Their defensive positioning is all wrong," I said.

And then, "What they need to do is get the running game started so that the passing game involves the defensive backfield—"

"Um, do you have any idea what you're talking about?" Grant interrupted.

"Of course. I'm completely in the know."

"No!" Grant started laughing. "It's that neighbor guy, isn't it? Isn't it?" he asked, leaning over and squeezing my arm.

"Stop it!" I was laughing, too, and Grant was quoting Mr. Novotny and—

Then I realized everyone was looking at us. Kelli was giving me the evil eye, like she wished I would have a full-on seizure. Not the kind I could recover from.

Awk . . . ward.

We tried to explain who Mr. Novotny was, and why it was so funny, but it didn't seem to be funny to anyone else.

When we got home, Dara said, "Courtney? I think you were having, like, too much fun over there. One, it's football, and two, you and Grant—"

"Since when is it possible to have too much fun?" I asked.

"When you're laughing that hard with a guy who isn't your S.O.!"

"S.O.?"

"Significant Other," she said.

"I laugh that hard with my friends all the time. Grant's a friend."

"Mm hm."

"I never laugh that hard with Wittenauer, and he's my significant other. So there," I said.

Dara arched her eyebrow, the one with the piercing. "I don't see how that proves anything, but I've got, like, a hundred pages of Brontë to read. Why did I let you guys talk me into going over to watch football, anyway? I hate football. It's so . . ."

"Fun?" asked Shawna.

"Violent and pointless. Hey, that sounds like a good title for a poem." She was off and running to her bedroom.

Shawna and I stayed up watching TV and kind of, sort of, like, studying. I fell asleep on the living room rug next to Oscar. Woke up and there was rug wool and/or dog fur stuck to my face. Think it's time for one of us to buy a vacuum.

10/20

Mom did an impersonation of Shawna's mom and called me about 20 times today. I ignored her. Still not over the whole invite-me-to-visit-and-then-ditch-me-and-then-nearly-get-me-arrested thing.

10/21

It's Wii-dnesday at work. Which means Guy sets up a Wii and anyone can play.

Which means it gets kind of sweaty in here.

Which I guess means people order more frozen things.

This is how the brilliant business mind of Guy Nicollet works. At least that's one idea he didn't steal from Gerry. Gerry wouldn't be that stupid.

The night was going along fine, or at least wasn't horrible, except I felt that Guy was hovering around me, like an annoying dragonfly. Finally, he asked, "So. You and Gerry. You're close?"

"What? No."

"Really? You seemed close."

"No. We talk every couple of months."

"Is that so? But you mentioned he gave you a ride up from Denver, so . . . would just anybody do that for you?"

"Well . . ." I didn't want to get into details, like, "It's because I was telling him you stole all of his ideas and should probably give him a percentage of the profits here," so I just said, "Well, nothing."

"Right. Nothing." He nodded, looking at me as if it was anything *but* nothing.

I helped the next person in line. Why did he care if I was friends with Gerry—the only reason he would is if he felt guilty for being caught plagiarizing the T or D menu. Guy didn't strike me as the kind of person who felt guilt, though. Or many other emotions, for that matter.

Maybe he was an alien. It would explain so much. Especially the bad hair.

Dr. Bigelow, I presume.

"Do you want to make a difference or do you want to sit around and watch the continental shelf drop off into the Arctic Ocean? To be responsible or not to be responsible. That is the question."

Wow. This guy is so full of himself. Talking like Hamlet. (Yes, I got an A in Shakespeare.)

Still, I wanted to tell him that I was taking responsibility by writing my new blog, encouraging local businesses to Green Even More (GEM).

So I stood by his desk after class. But the thing is, there's always a swarm of people waiting to talk to him, to get his take. He's like the green guru. He has groupies. I have waited a few times already, and I never get any closer than second in line.

I waited about ten minutes and then I had to leave for work.

Tonight, composing my next column: "What Does Animal Cruelty Have in Common with Antienvironmentalism?"

Where do I begin?

No. I mean, seriously. Where the hell do I begin?

"Holding Court"
by Courtney Von Dragen Smith
What Does Animal Cruelty Have in Common with Antienvironmentalism?

This is a question that a lot of people don't think about. Even I didn't think about it, until the question was raised in a class of mine. One student was arguing that saving the environment was the most important issue in front of mankind at this moment. Another student argued that if we didn't save animals that are threatened, both domestic and wild, we didn't deserve to inherit the earth in *any* form, damaged or otherwise.

But if we think about it, saving one is a win-win for both.

Saving the environment preserves a livable habitat for animals.

Being kinder to domestic animals and pets helps save the environment. How? Let's take a look.

- Fewer court cases involving abused animals leads to less paper usage, which means reduced use of trees
- Less driving around by animal control to rescue abused animals minimizes carbon footprint
- Fewer dead animals in landfills

Sorry to be so disgusting. I guess a lot of the unwanted ones get cremated, anyway.

Sorry. Again.

Maybe the real question is: Which comes first? Saving animals or saving the environment?

Well, can't we do both?

Saving habitats = saving animals.

So, I guess the environment is the egg, and the animals are the chicken.

Without egg, no chicken.

Or without chicken, no egg.

Which is it?

And should we even eat chicken or eggs? I think not.

Oscar is missing.

It was only a matter of time, I guess. He runs off at least once a season. We were due. Still, he's been missing since last night. He got out while I was at work. Somehow. (Ahem. Clearing throat.) Not saying who. (Clearing throat.) (Dara.)

Overnight! He's hardly ever been gone overnight before. I didn't even get to pack him a lunch. Or his pajamas.

Shawna, Dara, and I just spent hours driving around in Dara's car looking for him. After we searched campus, we headed for the mountains.

"Who knows, he could have felt the pull of the mountains. His, like, wolf instincts kicked in," said Shawna.

"You've been watching too many Coors commercials." I shook my head. "They've never kicked in before. You know what he likes? Bright lights and pasta."

"So we're looking for an all-night Italian restaurant," said Dara.

"Want to hit Olive Garden?" asked Shawna.

"I said *Italian* restaurant," Dara said.

I didn't think he'd be all the way up in the mountains, but then again, he has strayed pretty far before. "Maybe he saw the big *A* in the hills and headed for it, thinking it stood for, I don't know . . . Animals?"

"I've been meaning to ask," said Dara. "What *is* that giant *A* all about, anyway?"

"This is an ag school. Agriculture," I said. "That's its background."

"Oh. I always thought it stood for athletics," said Shawna.

"I thought it stood for altitude," said Dara. "'Cause, you know. It's up on the mountains."

"Why would they label a mountain that . . . never mind," I said.

Since we were all the way up near Horsetooth Reservoir, we decided to scout that area as well. I didn't think Oscar could run that far, but he'd escaped once in Denver and we found him all the way at the zoo.

"So this is that Horsetooth place? OK . . . it's a horse's tooth. Really? It doesn't look like one," said Dara.

"How many horses did you ride back in Seattle?" Shawna asked.

Dara shrugged. "None. Why?"

"Just wondering."

"Let's go home. Maybe he's there by now," I said, feeling strangely, falsely confident for some reason. But he wasn't. I mean, he isn't. Here yet.

I don't want to say anything to Dara yet, but I can't help thinking DeathKitty is involved, that she lured a bigger, meaner dog to the yard and then somehow got Oscar to go outside. How many times can you tell a dog not to talk to strangers without feeling ridiculous? Um, one.

I called Grant to ask if he could help look, but he's working tonight.

"You have the magic touch. Or eye. Or whatever," I argued.

"But—I can't just take off, Courtney. This is my job," he said.

"Right. You're right. OK, fine."

"Don't be hurt—" he protested.

"No, I'm not, I'm not—I get it. It's not your responsibility—it's mine."

So, I just called Bryan and told him to drive to FC ASAP.

Wait a second.

What about all those stories and movies about animals that walk, like, 1,000 miles to get back to their original homes?

Oscar must not be as happy as he's seemed.

Tragic vet science class experience.

He has begun the long, lonely trek south to Denver. Only explanation.

I didn't get a chance to tell him that Mom changed the locks.

Called Bryan back and told him to stay there, just in case.

LATER

Oscar's home. Major drama involved. Grant got a container of pasta salad from the ready-to-eat cooler at Shop & Shop as he left work, and we met in Old Town, which is this old section of town (*duh*) with brick buildings, restaurants, bars, shops, etc.

We called and called Oscar. Nothing. Some street people asked us for money and we may have attracted the attention of a couple of shopkeepers.

Finally, we spotted him.

He was sitting outside this great restaurant called the Rio Grande, which has a big, lit-up margarita glass in the window. He seemed to also be eating a taco, which can't be good. I gave him a hundred hugs and squeezes, but all he wanted to do was lick Grant and make happy whimpering sounds at him. Like I didn't exist.

A waiter came out and explained how everyone felt sorry for this poor, lonely dog. He'd been seen wandering around Old Town and he was so skinny, but whenever someone tried to help him, he'd run away—

"OK, it's only been, like, a day, and he's not that skinny," I said.

"So then animal control tried to corral him, but that didn't work. And did you know his collar has no tags?" the server asked.

"Well, I—"

"Courtney!" Grant said. "You told me you were going to get tags!"

Just then my phone rang—it was Wittenauer.

"I'm with Grant and guess what?" I said. "We just found Oscar!"

Wittenauer was not impressed. "Is it me, or does it

seem like you're spending every spare minute with Grant?"

"But I had to find Oscar. And Grant's really good at finding him," I said.

"Maybe you shouldn't have let him run away in the first place," said Wittenauer.

I was getting so exasperated with him I didn't know what to say. "Of course I didn't *let* him!" I said.

"Didn't you?" He hung up abruptly.

Agh. I was getting attacked by both sides.

I gently clipped the leash to Oscar's collar, thanked all involved, and started walking home. Next thing I knew, Grant was walking beside me, eating from the little bowl of pasta with his fingers as he walked.

I kept stealing angry glances at him. Looking so smug. He hadn't even really *helped* find Oscar. I mean, maybe he was a good-luck charm, but that was it. And now Wittenauer was mad because I'd asked him to help, and he hadn't even really helped.

"You know what?" I said. "This has to end."

"What does?"

"This!" I cried. "You and your potato salad walking me and Oscar home—"

"It's pasta salad," Grant said. "And it can't walk."

I knew he was trying to make me laugh. But I couldn't. My life was getting really sort of out of control. It was a Saturday night, and instead of being out with friends, Wittenauer was a thousand miles away and mad at me, and I was wandering down a Fort Collins street with Oscar and Grant.

He touched my sleeve. "Hey. I'll help you get Oscar's tags," said Grant. "There are some forms at the Humane Society—"

"I don't need your help," I said.

"Well . . . yeah, you do. Or why else am I here?"

"I don't know!" I said. "OK? I don't know! Maybe you shouldn't be."

"Well. I'm headed to my house, which is right next to your house. I'm not going a different way."

"Fine," I said.

We walked the rest of the way home without talking. He went into his house. I went into mine. Oscar trotted to his food bowl, where DeathKitty was in the midst of eating. I glared at her. All her fault. Or was it my fault, for asking Grant to help? But what else could I do, and Oscar was home now, so all's well that ends well, right?

Probably not when it ends with your boyfriend not speaking to you.

10/25

Wittenauer made up by text, but make-up text is not as good as some other things that may possibly rhyme with it.

Wittenauer: You need to get away. Come visit me. Come on, please.

Me: But who would watch Oscar?

Wittenauer: Your roommates. Please, he's not an exotic pet who needs special attention.

Me: Yeah, but . . .

Wittenauer: But nothing! Ask Bryan, then. He'll pick up Oscar for the weekend.

Me: K.

10/26

Went to about twenty travel sites last night, until I found a flight even I could afford. Going this weekend. Will only be there two nights, but it'll be great. Wittenauer and I can snuggle for 48 hours, I'll see my friends (so maybe we won't snuggle for 48 hours straight), I'll be there for Halloween, which should be awesome. . . . I emailed flight confirmation info to Wittenauer sometime around 3 AM, and this morning a van pulled up with a flower delivery from him.

Note said: "Sorry, just having a really hard time. Love you and can't wait to see you soon! Xxooxxoo W."

Soon, soon.

Swoon, swoon.

10/27

Dreamed that I got on this giant plane to Milwaukee but halfway through the flight, the pilot announced we'd be landing in Fort Collins.

"No!" I cried.

I ran up to the front of the plane to protest that the airport was too small for a 747, but before I could get there, a hot-looking vampire stepped out of first class into the aisle. Told me to stop making trouble. Attempted to bite my neck.

I was just starting to enjoy it when he opened the emergency door and threw me out.

I was falling through the sky. Saw lots of cool things on the way down to imminent death. I was hoping I'd land on a snowy mountain when a giant eagle swooped from the sky and—

Sometimes I really hate dreams.

10/28 WII-DNESDAY

It's definitely time to go away for a few days.

Shawna, Dara, and I are not getting along. At all.

We keep arguing about everything: dishes, cleaning, DeathKitty and her dead birds, Oscar and his pacing, the fact that one of them keeps letting Oscar out.

Dara says I never clean the blender after I make smoothies. What? I always do. And how would she know? She's never even used the blender. She's just reaching.

Shawna says Dara doesn't know what clean is, because she hasn't ever cleaned the bathroom since we moved in, while she has cleaned it, like, twice a week.

Which makes me feel bad because I've only cleaned it twice, ever.

I told Shawna she keeps me awake when she studies all night and listens to the TV for "background noise" but blares *The Daily Show*, so then I want to get up and watch it, and then I oversleep—

And then Dara said she can't write here because we're both too loud, and she should have gotten her own place instead of sharing it with us. Somehow it's all Tobie's fault for moving out, and all my fault for moving in.

So I told Dara not to plan on taking me to the airport on Friday, that I'd take the shuttle van.

"Oh no, I'll *take* you to the airport," Dara said.

Clearly she wants me to be gone as much as I want to leave.

Still . . . kind of rude, don't you think?

I left the house to go to work at the same time Grant

was outside, headed to his car. We waved at each other. I thought he was going to offer me a ride, but he didn't.

Rudeness. It's going around sort of like a viral YouTube video.

Just started snowing. Stupid snow must not get in the way
of my trip. I need a break from the Fort. Even though I
have made up with roomies, tension lingers, like smell
from litter box.

In class today, found out that Dr. Bigelow's call to
action was answered. Not sure with what, though.

"So, it's been planned," the guy next to me in class
whispered.

"Right." I looked around. "*What* has?"

"Our big statement," he said. "Our end of semester
project."

"And?" I asked.

"And what?" He seemed confused.

Typical stoned, overly-committed-to-the-environment
mandal-wearing guy. "It *is* . . . ?" I urged, waiting for him
to fill in the blank.

He looked around furtively. "Oh. Well. I can't talk
about it here."

Suddenly, Dr. Bigelow was approaching us. "Is there
something you'd like to share with the class, Ms. . . . oh,
Superfund. I'm drawing a blank."

"Smith. It's Smith," I said. Then wanted to kick myself.
Why stress my last name when it was not for a good thing?

"Right, of course, Ms. Smith. Is there something you'd
like to share?"

"Well, actually, I . . . I mean, it wasn't me. . . . He said
something about a plan?" I said. "I actually don't know
anything. I mean, about it."

Great. Now I was admitting I didn't know anything.
"Smith, Third Row, Doesn't Know Anything" he was probably jotting down in his notes.

I never did find out what the big plan is.

And it's still snowing. I like snowboarding as much as the next person—maybe even more. Wow. I actually live in a decent place to snowboard again. The world is like . . . my oyster. My snow-covered oyster.

IM'ing with Beth.

> crtveg17: Have been up all night. Nervous about the trip.
> shoe92gurrl: Why?
> crtveg17: Idk. Just am. Stomach hurts. Haven't seen W for a month.
> shoe92gurrl: So it'll be fun!
> crtveg17: Seems like we argue on the phone.
> shoe92gurrl: Do u still love him?
> crtveg17: Sure. Sure I do.
> shoe92gurrl: Then don't worry. It's just the stress of being apart.
> crtveg17: Like u and me. Like how we fight. ;)
> shoe92gurrl: Constantly. ☺ Ciao.
> crtveg17: Ciao. Easy 4 U 2 say.

Snowing again. Airport claims to be open though—flights not canceled. It's been snowing since last night. Dara wants to leave now—extra-early, just to make sure. Fine. Will write more from WI after I get there. If I get there.

Gave Oscar a hug. He walked in circles by the front door.

"If Bryan can't make it here, for any reason, ask Grant, OK?" I said to Shawna before we left.

"Don't worry, it's going to be fine," she said, squeezing my shoulders.

"Maybe I shouldn't go."

"What? *Go* already," Shawna argued. "God. If someone as hot as, like, Wittenauer, was waiting for me, I'd fly myself."

"How would you do that?" Dara asked.

Shawna glared at her. "It's a saying. And you know, if you want to catch a flight anywhere like Seattle while *you're* at the airport, feel free. I have a ton of studying to catch up on."

Outside, Grant was attempting to shovel the sidewalk. Asked where we were going. "Uh, the airport. Going to Cornwall Falls for the weekend."

"Oh. Wow. Well, good luck," he said.

"Is that all he has to say? 'Good luck'?" I complained to Dara when we got into the car.

"What do you want him to say?" she replied.

I don't know, I thought. Don't leave? Don't risk your life? I love you madly?

But that was wrong.

TWO HOURS LATER

It's snowing. A lot. Not sure we will make it. Not sure airport will be open if we do make it. Traffic moving at one mile per hour. Every once in a while, someone comes along going faster than that, has to put on brakes, and slides off into median or down into ditch.

Trying to reach DIA to find out about flight. DIA? More like DOA. Dead on Arrival. Or, lack of arrival.

Cell service not working.

Radio talking about winter weather advisory. Upgraded now to blizzard warning.

Our arms collided as we both went to grip center armrest in fear.

Barely moving. I keep trying to make small talk that dies instantly. Kind of like we might.

We've made it about a mile so far, I think.

Cars in ditches.

Windshield wipers caked in ice.

Radio is advising everyone to stay home. Well, uh, kind of late for that.

"I don't want to die!" Dara just screamed as she put on the brakes and we slid sideways.

God. So dramatic. It's only a little skid.

BACK HOME

I ended up making Dara trade places with me, and I started driving because I know how to drive in snow. Well, so does she, but she had a case of temporary insanity.

We got off I-25 finally and ended up in a diner in Loveland, which is normally, like, a 15-minute drive from here; took us 3 hours.

We ate pie and gathered strength to drive home. Thought I was going to have to give Dara a good-natured slap in the face and yell, "Snap out of it!" Girl needed to breathe into a paper bag to keep from hyperventilating. She who is so cool about everything. I felt bad for her.

Couldn't get through to Wittenauer to tell him I can't make it because flights are all canceled; airport is closed. We came home and for some reason, Bryan was here. He and Shawna were watching a movie together when we walked in. They seemed surprised, but not all that surprised, to see us.

"OMG, what are you doing here?" asked Shawna. "Are you guys OK?"

"Didn't you watch the news? People are dying out there!" Dara said.

"And how did *you* get here?" I asked Bryan.

"I left really early," he said. "Grant's been over here twice to see if we heard from you."

"Oh?" I asked. So he did care, at least a little bit. "Well, uh, what's the bag for?" I asked Bryan when I saw his duffel sitting by the door.

"Well. Thought if I was coming all this way, I should be prepared to stay over," he said. "With the weather and all."

Warning lights were firing in my head like shooting

stars. He and Shawna. They were hooking up. It was déjà vu all over again.

"But I was gone, as far as you knew," I said, narrowing my eyes at him.

He nodded. "As far as you knew, yes."

I had to puzzle over that for a while.

"Courtney! You asked me to take care of Oscar. You didn't say *where*."

"I didn't? Well, wasn't it obvious?" I said. "At home."

"No. Not with Sterling and his allergies, no."

"Courtney!" Shawna yelled. "Don't you appreciate what Bryan did? He drove through a blizzard to get here. For Oscar."

Bryan nodded. "Yup. Plus, Grant posted something about a party at his house tomorrow night—"

"Hold on, hold on!" I cried.

"What? You didn't know about the party?"

"No, not that. You just said Grant *posted* something? Where?"

"Twitter. Didn't you know that? You should totally follow him. He's funny," said Dara.

Grant posting something? Since when?

"You should go tell him you made it back," Shawna said.

"Right. Right." I opened the front door and Oscar bounded outside after me. We made it halfway there before I thought to myself, What if Kelli's there? What if I walk in and they're snuggling together in front of the fire? Not that they have a fireplace. I actually don't know.

Turned and went back inside to text him.

So I made it back.

He responded a couple minutes later.

Grant: To WI?
Me: No, next door.
Grant: Why r u texting
Me: Might get lost in blizzard walking over.
Grant: O. So. No cheese curds.
Me: No. Sadness. If u want to come over, everyone's watching a movie.
Grant: What movie?
Me: Um . . . I love you, man
Grant: ?
Me: I mean, the movie, "I love you, man."
Grant: Right. Well, maybe later.

Aha! I was right. He was busy.

I tried to pour myself a cold glass of ener-juice, but my hands were still shaking from the scary drive home.

"Whoa, Courtney. Little less caffeine tomorrow, OK?" Shawna said.

I faked a smile. I was disappointed over the trip falling through . . . and uncomfortable about the fact that I'd just invited Grant over, like, what was I thinking? And I still needed to call Wittenauer to break the bad news about the canceled trip.

When I did, he wasn't surprised. He'd seen it on CNN. He said we'd reschedule, we'd figure something else out.

And then everyone just snuggled in to watch the movie, while the snow kept falling outside.

One good thing about Bryan being here: He can help us shovel tomorrow.

10/31 HALLOWEEN PARTY

"I wasn't supposed to be here."

That's what I told Grant aka Scarecrow from *The Wizard of Oz* when I walked into the party at his house, meekly following Shawna, who was wearing a plastic Twister game costume covered in polka dots, and Bryan, who was dressed as a vampire.

Me, I was wearing a Snow White costume. "I'm wearing this ironically, just so you know," I said.

"I hope so," said Grant. "That looks small."

"It was the last costume even near my size, OK?" I pulled down the sleeves of the Youth XL I was wearing.

"Right on," said Cody, nodding, dressed as the Cowardly Lion. He nods a lot, as if this is communicating. "It's all good."

"Nice to see you," said Matt with a smile, his Tin Man costume creaking as he bowed in greeting.

And there was Kelli, little Dorothy with a gingham dress, to complete the costumes.

It was so cute that I almost wanted to puke, but that could have been all the candy corn I ate while I was costume shopping.

Bryan was across the room, mingling with Shawna. I must tell him. No matter how cute he can sometimes be, no one in college would ever seriously date a high school guy. Ever. I really need to talk to him. Why is he so clueless? What about his friends at home? Don't they miss him? Don't they tell him he is a nerd for coming to hang out with his sister? And what's wrong with the girls at Bugling Elk? Sure, they're not as hot as they were a couple of years ago, when I was there . . . LOL.

Dara swept in, dressed like a punk rocker (not exactly a

costume or a stretch for her), and informed me that Oscar was having trouble with all the trick-or-treaters coming to the door, and told me it was my turn to babysit him.

Gratitude for saving her life yesterday? Gone.

I happened to be standing next to the tortilla chips when she was talking, and so was Grant. "I'll go with you, maybe I can help calm him down," he offered.

"Are you sure?" I asked. "And where's the Wicked Witch?"

"Shut up," he said. "Sure I'm sure. Hey, maybe we can dress Oscar as Toto and bring him back."

"Um, how about no," I said. I went home to keep Oscar company, and Grant followed me. Even in stupid costumes, felt strangely close to him. We talked about the drive to the airport, and Bigelow's class, and how pretentious he is, and how you just have to survive it by any means necessary, and he talked about the big project his class did the year before, how Bigelow gives the entire class the same grade depending on how it goes, which seems a tad unethical to me. Or at least unnecessarily mean, considering half the people in the class are airheads.

"Or maybe they're not, they just act that way," said Grant. "You never know."

"True," I said.

The whole time, I kept absentmindedly handing out candy to kids who came to the door, but I guess I wasn't really paying attention because I dropped some chocolate bars on Bryan's foot when he showed up on the doorstep. He didn't have a bag. Well, was that my fault?

"You guys have been here awhile. Everything OK?" he asked.

"Sure. Have a Milky Way."

"Because, um, people over there are, um, looking for you." Then Bryan disappeared before I could ask him to take a shift watching Oscar (which he was supposed to do all weekend, anyway).

"Oh yeah—I'm hosting. I should be there." Grant slid off where he was perched on the arm of the sofa.

"Hold on a sec, Scarecrow," I said. "Your straw's falling out."

"Shut up, it is not," he said. "Snow White."

"Hey, I told you, it's supposed to be ironic. I didn't even *want* a costume," I said. "Right here, your sleeve, all the straw's coming out—where did you get all this straw?"

"Hey, cut it out. . . ." He grabbed my arm just as I was pushing some straw down his back.

There was a loud knock at the door, which was still open. "Trick or treat!" I turned to see who'd be so bold to just walk in.

Kelli was glaring at us. Wishing we were having life-ending seizures, no doubt.

"Hi, uh, Dorothy," I said, still clutching a clump of straw in my hand.

She didn't say anything. Oscar barked at her.

"So, let me guess. We're not in Kansas anymore?" I joked. "Right?"

Complete. Utter. Silence.

"If I only had a brain . . ." Grant said under his breath before he ran out after her.

Good thing I am not trying to hook up with anyone here who I'd then bring to my room, because Bryan would seriously be in the way. I tripped over him, like, five times last night. He sleeps lying one way across the room, Oscar sacks out the other way, and it's like a trap.

This morning I was peering at Grant's house out of basement window, at feet going past, trying to identify them. Boots going back and forth on snow and ice, crunch, crunch. Whose boots were they and why were they making so many trips?

"What are you looking at?" Bryan suddenly asked from his spot on the floor, in his sleeping bag.

"Oh!" I gasped, because he nearly gave me a heart attack. "N-nothing. Just checking the weather. Look, Bryan. You—you can't keep coming up here."

"Why not, am I ruining your love life?"

"No! I have no love life—not here, anyway."

"Could have fooled me," Bryan said under his breath.

"What's that supposed to mean?"

"It just seems like you and Grant are still kind of, um, close," he said. "Like last night?"

"We're still friends," I said. "Is that so wrong?"

He folded his arms across his chest. "You tell me."

"It's not. And anyway, we're not talking about me, we're talking about you. It's time for me to give you some advice."

"And advice versa," Bryan replied.

"OK, quit it with the cute comments. You have to stop sleeping over in my room. In this house. You need to get a life at home!"

"I *have* a life at home. I just like it here. Anyway, why am I telling you? It's not like you'll get it. You don't get it. Nobody gets it."

I groaned. Bryan's trademark phrase. Hadn't heard it in a while; apparently he'd been saving it up so he could repeat it three times. "What am I trying to *get*, exactly?" I asked.

He wouldn't say.

"If you think something's going to happen between you and Shawna—"

"No! Of course not. It's not Shawna. We're friends, that's all."

Hm. Sounded familiar. I ran through all the possibilities in my brain. "Wait a second," I said. "Are you, uh, gay?"

"No. You'd know by now if I was, don't you think?"

"Yeah, but Shawna's really, really cute, and if you're not attracted to her and only want to be friends . . . then why else are you coming up here all the time?" I heard heavy footsteps above us, on the ceiling. Boot footsteps. Dara's. I looked at Bryan. He shrugged. "It's not her?" I asked. "Because she doesn't even talk to you."

He just shrugged. "Talking is overrated."

"It's not her. Tell me it's not her. Bryan, it'll never work out!"

"You should know all about unrequited love," he said.

"What's that supposed to mean? Bryan?"

He didn't answer. He just walked upstairs. When I got there, he and Dara were seated at the breakfast table, reading their texts, checking email, etc., both drinking black coffee but not speaking. Wondered if I should tell

Bryan his hair was sticking up.

Wondered if Dara liked that, because he looked slightly punk.

Unrequited love. My brother and Dara. As if.

11/2

Due to events beyond this reporter/blogger's control, I am working on "Holding Court" a few days late. This week's topic: "How Can We Make Snow Cleanup More Environmentally Friendly?"

There's only been one comment on all of my blog posts so far: "*I'll* hold you, Court." Signed, Anonymous

Creepy stalker.

Figures.

Crap, someone at door.

Not crap, Wittenauer is here!!!!!!!!!!!!!!!!!

Love having Wittenauer here. He caught a ride with someone who was headed to Denver. Ride-share. Walked me to every class and met me afterward. He and I took Oscar for a walk. He went to coffee shop with me and sat there for a couple of hours while I wrote my snowplow blog, a few days late, and worked on homework.

I kind of like the attention, but at the same time, feel like I'm not famous enough to need a security detail. But it's Wittenauer! And I get to be guarded by a very famous cornstalk.

One awkward moment as we were coming back from Smoothie Stop: We ran into Grant, naturally. For some reason, Wittenauer ended up doing most of the talking.

"How's Kelli? What's she up to?" he asked.

"Oh, she's, uh, uh, at, visiting, the library," Grant stammered. "I think. In fact, I'm supposed to meet her . . . see you around!" He took off on his bike and didn't look back.

He is a horrible liar. Something is up. Are he and Kelli done?

11/4 WII-DNESDAY

Wittenauer was not impressed by, basically, anything happening at the Smoothie Stop. And who can blame him, really? Though he did play several Wii games against random customers.

"So this is what you do on Wednesday nights," he said after an hour. No doubt bored out of his skull.

"Yes?"

"And it's fun."

"Yes? Don't even try to tell me that the social life at CFC is better than this," I said.

"Um, Courtney?" He coughed. "It's better than this."

In the midst of talking, Mom called. She was adamant about the fact that we needed to talk and said I couldn't keep ignoring her forever. (Maybe not, but wouldn't it be fun to try?)

"It's about Thanksgiving," she said.

I sighed. When *isn't* it about Thanksgiving? She starts planning months in advance for a holiday that lasts 3–4 hours at most. Not counting digesting.

"Mom, I don't know if I can make it this year. I started out late this year, three weeks late, remember, and I could use the time to finish all the unfinished assignments and . . ."

"No, Courtney. This year it's really important that we all go. Like every year," she said.

"Mother? I came down to visit you recently and you weren't even *there*," I reminded her. "What makes you think I'm going to fall for that again?"

"Alison's even flying in. I just want to put it on your calendar," Mom went on.

Alison's coming? Good, haven't seen her in a long

time. "Well, I can't talk now," I said. "Wittenauer's here."

"He is? Oh good. Do you mind if I talk to him?"

He'd been studying for the LSATs, but he was willing to talk to her. Next thing you know, she'd invited Wittenauer to meet us in Nebraska for Thanksgiving and insisted on his being there.

If that doesn't ruin our relationship, what will?

Honestly.

Wittenauer following me everywhere is starting to get on my nerves. Feel like I need a can of Static Guard spray because he's clinging to me. A *big* can.

This morning over coffee I asked, "So don't you think you should be getting back?"

"Oh no, it's cool. We have this weeklong break," he said as he lounged on the sofa, holding his LSAT prep book. I was attempting to get the reading done for Bigelow's class this afternoon.

"Wittenauer. I *went* there, OK? I know that's not true," I said.

His face turned a mottled shade of red. "Fine. I'm taking some time off, then. A, um, what's it called? Sabbatical."

"But you can't take one of those, whatever it is."

"Why not?"

"Because! You're a student, not a professor. And you have to at least finish the semester! You're going to graduate soon!"

"I know, that's why I'm studying for the LSATs. But I have a lot of flexibility at this point. Hey, you know what would be a good idea?" he suddenly asked. "Why don't we go down to Denver later so I can meet your mom?"

I sighed. "You're just trying to change the subject."

"True."

"I really think you need to be getting back," I said.

"Wow, Court. You really sound like you want me to go."

"No, I—I don't, but . . . I don't want you to flunk because of me, either. And I don't want to fail out because of *you*. I mean, long view. Long view Wittenauer. That's you, right?"

He laughed. "Yeah, true. But long view, I want us to be together, and the rest will sort itself out. That is, if I get into law school." He leaned over the practice questions again, raking his hands through his hair.

So, everything is sort of OK again, or at least he knows how I feel. He couldn't stay here forever. It was a visit. He wasn't moving in.

I wasn't ready for that. Especially not if he was going to move in here. I didn't know how many more awkward waves and nods I could exchange with Grant.

Wonder how Grant is doing, if he and Kelli are together or not.

11/6

Didn't hand in assignment for Art of the Essay, as Wittenauer and I went to movies last night instead and then bowling. Skipped classes today. Also, didn't write my blog this week.

No time to write in here when BF is constantly hovering at my side, in my bed, etc. Hours formerly known as private time no longer exist. He's sleeping beside me. My bed is not all that big.

Basement feels crowded. Not big enough for me, Wittenauer, and Oscar.

Someone whose name ends in *r* has to go. And not the one who has fur and likes to run away.

Is it possible I'm falling out of love with W? Or am I even *in* love or do I just really like him a lot?

No. Just stressed. It's one thing when we both have classes and homework; that works.

We went to Estes Park to visit Rocky Mtn. National Park, and Wittenauer is convinced he must move here immediately after getting degree, if not sooner.

Have I mentioned he snores?

Am going to check ride-share postings on Craigslist and other places.

Maybe I really like him, but I'm not in love with him, because maybe if I was truly in love with him, I wouldn't feel this way, like I need more of my own space.

Maybe I need to burn this journal, right now. Or at least find a better place to hide it.

Feel guilty, terrible. Broke Wittenauer's heart this morning.

Over coffee, took a deep breath and told him he had to go home, that I couldn't get any homework done, that we'd never last this way, that I'd found a ride for him on a ride-share board.

"Yeah, but—"

"But nothing. It's not a sabbatical. You're just avoiding reality. I should know, OK?" I reminded him of how unhappy I'd been the year before, until I just bit the bullet and started enjoying where I am. Was. Whatever. "This works better if we're both in school. You know?"

"OK, OK. You're right. Maybe I'll sign up for some classes."

"No, no!" I shook my head. "You're not dropping *out*. I think you're depressed. I know because I felt that way last year when I left Grant behind." I coughed nervously. Perhaps this wasn't the best way to make an argument. "You're Corny. You need to get back to campus and be Corny."

"Depressed and corny. Wow. Sucks to be me," he said.

"Seriously! You're about to get your degree. You have a semester and a half left. That's it! I mean, look at me if you want to get depressed. I'm a transfer student, a sophomore, and I work at a nasty smoothie place."

"I *am* looking at you. That's the thing. I don't want to leave." He was standing there, his face a bit scruffy, looking adorable in his faded blue Milwaukee Brewers tee.

So naturally we had to make out. It all seemed so romantic now that I knew he was leaving. I was crazy about him again.

Or, just crazy again.

"I'll see you in a few weeks," I said when we finally unlocked lips. "At Thanksgiving, remember?"

"Right. Thanksgiving." He kissed me again.

"It'll be a nightmare. I'm warning you."

"What are you talking about? It's only your family."

"Have you spent any time with my family?"

"Not a lot, no."

"Brace yourself. Oh, and there's the fact that my mother and I aren't speaking. But I'm still expected to go." I groaned. "On second thought, take me back to Wisconsin with you. Right now."

Shouldn't have said that. He thought I was serious and I had to talk him out of it.

Wittenauer left at 4 A.M. Feel lonely without him but also not pressured to entertain him. I am so far behind in my reading, I must set aside personal writing in order to . . .

Dozed off for a second there. Textbook on environmental history is so boring. And you know, why did they print it on paper in the first place? Probably should have been an e-book.

But then people would fall asleep over their computers or e-readers and bash faces into keyboards. Giant fluffy textbook pages make for softer landings.

Sterling came to take me to dinner. On his own. Claimed he was on business and just wanted to treat me to a more nutritious meal than pizza. Highly suspect. I don't even eat pizza due to my cheese issues. Much.

Sterling asked me, like, ten trillion questions about school, and how things are going with Wittenauer, and whether I needed any groceries and stuff like that.

He is totally trying to win me over. He even insisted I have the flourless chocolate cake for dessert.

But it takes more than that. Like, a to-go box, maybe. An entire cake to share with roomies instead of just a piece.

I have to know he is a decent person who will not let my mom down. She might be annoying but deserves to be happy. Is Sterling the guy who makes her happy?

Probably. He's really into statistics. She's all over that. She likes Excel spreadsheets better than 400-count cotton sheets. They probably sit around and plot graphs together.

Then again, maybe not. I have seen them kiss for minutes on end. Well, I looked away, but I could still *tell*.

What if she was to get . . . like . . . I can't even write it. Married to Sterling?

And what if they, you know. Decided to have children together? Because I think technically it could still happen, Mom's age might be an issue but it wouldn't be impossible. And then I would have a one-year-old brother or sister at my graduation, no doubt screaming and crying? Oh, that would be embarrassing.

Well. It's not going to come to that. I mean, that would just be ridiculous.

On the plus side, I did find out some interesting facts

about Mom's man-friend.

One, he is younger than her. By a couple years.

Two, he has kind of a good sense of humor.

Three, as a corollary to two, he likes Judd Apatow movies.

Four, he partied too much his freshman year in college at CU. He flunked out. His parents made him take time off, work, get his act together (what act?), then go back for his degree later, paying for it himself. Warned against that.

Warning taken.

Art of the Essay Description #4:
Sterling Vickers

Your average man, I guess.

Middle-aged, forty-something.

Nice. If you like that sort of person. I guess I do.

Genuine? Maybe.

Short. Not his fault.

Drives a large SUV. His fault.

Is a consumer credit counselor. Helps bankrupt people. Not bankrupt them, he helps them after they become bankrupt. Bankrupted people?

After a while that word looks very weird. Bankrupted. (Bless you.)

Turned to running as a way to get discipline in his life. (Hey, he said that, not me. To me it sounds like an ad for the army.)

Agh, I can't write tonight.

Well, I can, but. Not when I really don't care what I'm writing.

What is artful about it when it is forced homework?

Mom called to see how the dinner with Sterling went.

He'd acted like it was last minute and unplanned, so this was confusing. Which was it? Impromptu or a setup?

Then she informed me that Sterling is coming with us to Nebraska for Thanksgiving. In fact, Sterling is driving.

"Good, because he has a nicer car," I said.

"Is that all you have to say?" asked Mom.

"Yup, except, what breads is he responsible for bringing?"

"He's not."

"No?"

"He's bringing the pies," said Mom.

Well, he may as well be exposed to her Thanksgiving nuttiness before things go much further between them.

LATER

Took Oscar for his late-night walk and ran into Grant, who was just getting home. Alone. Naturally, he had to spend some quality time with Oscar. Wondered if Oscar had seen him during the time I hadn't . . . like, illicitly. The way he did when I first moved in.

Haven't seen Grant in a long time. He asked what was up, and since I wasn't going to talk about my week with Wittenauer, I immediately started complaining about my mom. Suddenly, I stopped. There were other things I wanted to talk about with Grant. "Why am I telling you all this?"

"I don't know, I guess because I kind of know your mom," he said.

"Right, right. The thing is, *I* don't even know my mom anymore. The woman who wouldn't spend twenty-five cents to buy a newspaper is now splurging on hardcover books, and that's just the tip of the iceberg."

Grant gasped. "Wow. She really is *out* of *control*," he said in a sarcastic tone.

"Shut up. She is! For years we had to put up with her being a miser. Now she's throwing her money around."

"What money?"

"Hm. I don't know, I guess."

"Maybe because you're all getting older, she has more money of her own," Grant guessed.

"Yeah—since she made me leave CFC and come here, she has more money, you mean," I said.

"There's nothing wrong with this place. Besides, you were nearly on a full scholarship there."

Stupid logical Grant. Hate him sometimes.

"You're not very grateful, you know. People sacrifice

stuff for you and you don't appreciate it."

I just looked at him. "People?" What was this about?

"I totally sacrificed my A in Chem for you last year," he said. "I went from an A to a B minus because of you."

And then I knew. "Am I, uh, is our chemistry that bad?" I asked, trying to get him to lighten up.

"I failed my midterm because of you. You dumped me when I was ten minutes from taking my exam! Who does that? Who does that by *text*? I mean, come on."

"I called," I said in a small voice.

"Yeah, after I called you to ask what was going on, where you were, why we all of a sudden weren't going to Cancún on spring break together. Then the second I turned off my phone for the exam, you call back and leave a message—a message? Like, a five-minute message about how you can't go to Cancún, which was your idea, and the tickets are nonrefundable but you'll send me a refund?"

Oscar started to whine. Not a happy whine. He, like Gerry, hates conflict.

Shivering. Cold, November wind.

"I really felt terrible about that," I said. "Not sending you the money."

"I didn't care about that. I didn't want a refund! It's that you never even said why, where you went instead," he said.

"I didn't go anywhere, OK?" I said in this quiet, pathetic voice.

"Then why did you all of a sudden have to break up? I hated you for doing that. It was so weak. If you weren't OK with going and you were with Wittenauer or who-ever, why didn't you tell me before it was the day before we were leaving and I had midterms, or didn't you have midterms at that junior college you went to?"

"It's a good school," I said through slightly gritted teeth. "And I didn't know what I wanted! I mean, I just couldn't make up my mind."

"Yeah. I know. You can never make up your mind and stick to anything. Vegetarian? Sometimes. Dairy? Maybe."

"If I'm such a horrible eater, why are you even still talking to me?"

"I don't know. I don't know sometimes. I mean, I must be crazy, right?" He shook his head and walked up the sidewalk to his house.

"It takes two. To be crazy," I said.

Grant looked over his shoulder. "Since when?"

Oscar was running from one of us to the other, back and forth, as Grant headed for his house and I headed down the street. He was trying to herd us together.

Grant slammed the door shut. On me, on Oscar, on the whole awkward, horrible night.

How long had he been waiting to say that? Since March, I guess.

Clearly, I haven't apologized enough. I mean, I did send him a long email about it. Or did I? Maybe I forgot to hit SEND. Which you can add to my list of tragic errors involved with Grant.

Feel like crap about what Grant said yesterday. He's right. What I did, when I did it, how I did it, is, like, unforgivable. So why has he even been tolerating me lately? Because he is the nicest person, kind of guy who visits his grandmother, helps animals, and doesn't hold childish grudges. And what kind of person am I? The opposite.

Had to get out of the house, away from the neighborhood. Went to a poetry reading of Dara's and other poetry students tonight. She writes morbid poems about failed love. Why am I not surprised? Still not sure who she is pining for, though. Someone in her past? Hopefully not Bryan.

Her final poem she dedicated to me. It was called "Snow Struck," about trying to get to DIA that night. It was confusing as it had nothing to do with me.

"Snow Struck"
by Dara MacDonnell

Crystals
Falling
Whisper thin
Piling up
Into solid mass
Nothing can break you now.

No hurtling SUVs
Or skidding sports cars

You mock two-door Saturns, while
Smart cars disappear inside your

Fluffy
Warmth.

Like whisper-thin feathers
And squeaky packing peanuts,
You fall, quietly,
And we duck and cover
And find ourselves stranded on the beach of your massive
indecisiveness.

To fall
If we fall
As you fall

There can be no forgiveness tonight.

I-25
Will your pavement still hold me
If I make a U-turn?

Dara's poetry has inspired me.

OK, not really.

Still, at the Pyth, eating a sprouts sandwich and finally writing my blog about Smoothie Stop and its suckingness. Dara is opposite me, having plain grilled cheese.

Grant and his vet pals are here. However, Kelli is not with the group. I can't think about that or about what I might have done to contribute to that. Am having a bad enough week as it is, consumed with guilt and self-hatred.

What was my problem? Why did I back out of spring break trip? Was it that I still hadn't forgiven Grant for making out with Beth that one time? Maybe I need to talk to her about it. Or even better, Jane.

Tapping pen against desk while listening to iPod and attempting to write on laptop.

Just looked up to gaze around the room for inspiration. Caught Grant's eye and we exchanged awkward waves.

Yeah, hi. How's it going? Remember last time I saw you? Yeah. You yelled at me. Reminded me of what a crappy thing I did to you. So, I'll just sit over here. Yeah, OK. Please don't throw anything in my direction.

Impossible to concentrate when one is aware of all of one's flaws.

"Holding Court"
by Courtney Von Dragen Smith
When Is Recycling a Crime?

By now, we all know the three R's: Reuse, Reduce, Recycle.

Right?

Recycling is a great concept, but where does recycling end and where does copyright infringement begin?

A certain smoothie stop in town that shall remain nameless has recently been seen by this reporter to be copying a venerable establishment in Denver known as Truth or Dairy (Canyon Boulevard Shoppes location).

The setup is the same: Each offers smoothies, wheatgrass shots, and ice cream dishes such as sundaes and milkshakes. Perhaps that is not such a surprise, as other shops have tried this before, but let's look at the names of smoothies, the menus, the sundae descriptions:

(Here is where I inserted photos, in a slide show, side by side.)

Only one of these shops is original.

The other is a copy, and should rightly pay for basically being a franchise with no original ideas of its own. Otherwise, recycling and reusing have become nothing less than hijacking.

11/14

Crap, just visited my blog to see if there were any comments yet. Realized I wrote a certain smoothie "stop" instead of a certain smoothie "shop."

AGH!

Seconds later, cell rang and caller ID was store. Freaked out.

Turns out Guy only needs me to work; slammed with visitors to campus, final football game of season, etc. I said sure. I'll get hours as long as I can. I expect to be unemployed soon. . . .

Last night was unbelievable.

Dara got dropped off at home by a friend, who warned us that Dara might be a little tipsy. No sooner had she gotten out of the car than Dara immediately made a bee-line for wrong house. Grant's. We tried to get her to come back. She kept insisting she had to see Grant, it was now or never.

"What's now or never?" asked Shawna.

"Him. And me," she said.

"What? But he's—he's not your type," I stammered. "Not even close. And besides, he has a girlfriend, Kelli."

"No. He's single now," Dara said.

"He is?" I asked.

"Sure. Kelli, like, dumped him a couple weeks ago," said Shawna. "You knew that. Even Bryan knew that."

"It's probably *your* fault," Dara sort of slurred. "He probably won't care how I feel because he's pining for you and you are totally stringing him along."

"I am?"

Shawna nodded. "You're, like, a first-string stringer-alonger."

"You know, I left him a note in his car, and he never even wrote back," Dara complained as we got her to sit down at the kitchen table. I quickly made some coffee for her, and remembered the cat drawing on the note I'd spilled juice on—I'd always assumed that was from Kelli.

"But he's not your type," I just kept repeating. The thought of Dara and Grant together was just . . . unthinkable. For my brain. It made me feel as dizzy and ill as Dara looked.

"What's my type?" Dara sobbed. "My type doesn't exist."

Shawna was all business. "OMG, you should not drink wine. Ever. Look at you." She got some cold water and a washcloth, and we started trying to sober up Dara, made her go on a walk around the neighborhood. She kept babbling about how pretty the mountains looked, when it was too dark to actually, really, see them, or much of anything.

Turned out she went to some graduate student's poetry reading and stole the wine.

No doubt she'll be writing a poem about that when she recovers.

But now I have so much more to worry about. One, what if Dara does actually tell Grant how she feels? Would he like her, too?

And two, what about Bryan? When he finds out Dara likes Grant, and not him, he'll be devastated.

Well, serves him right.

Maybe he'll stop poaching my friends then.

But isn't that just like stupid love? It's all twisted. And am I stringing along Grant? How?

Maybe we'd been spending too much time together trying to be friends, but not since he finally yelled at me the other night. We hadn't exactly spoken since then. What else was there to say?

Interviewed Grant at grocery store today for my column. Not stringing him along. Just interviewing him. There's a difference.

I thought maybe doing a story on him would make him forgive me. Win-win. I get good blog material and attempt to repair bad relationship at the same time. I'm profiling him, Shop & Shop, and the green team initiative. Grant seemed pleased.

"We're trying to get away from plastic completely, but as much as that's not possible, we strive to collect every bag we give out by urging customers to return bags for recycling."

I really made him sound smart!

"Of course, we can't retrieve every bag. Some end up in landfills. But we try. There's no way we can control everyone's behavior. Some people are thoughtless—and some people are just dumb," Grant had said.

The article practically wrote itself as I sat at a nearby coffee shop post-interview. I was feeling so fabulous. The week wasn't out yet and I'd already gotten blog done and set it to post automatically.

Then I got home, and there was a certified letter from Smoothie Stop. I have been "terminated."

Like a rodent. Wow. I am really screwing up at everything these days. Wittenauer hasn't even returned my call. I probably insulted him somehow, too.

Mystery solved. Did some searching on the web. My article about Smoothie Stop was everywhere. It got picked up by one blog. And then another Twitterer. And then another.

One was even titled: "Stealing Is BAD! Smoothies Are Good."

And it's shades of Cornwall Falls and Courtney Von Bloggen all over again.

Everyone knows that I think Guy N. at the Smoothie Stop stole many, many, if not all, ideas from Truth or Dairy and did not even attempt to cleverly rename them.

Why did I start a blog again?

Why do I swear to never do things? I always end up doing them anyway and then paying the price.

Need a job.

Horrible newspaper article today: "Smoothie Shop Strikes Back."

Blog war has taken to traditional media outlets.

Guy N. says that I was jilted by him, and that's why I am writing bitter article. He says I have made a history of becoming involved with smoothie store owners.

What? As if!

Article has a picture of Gerry.

As if, people!

And a photo of me—the one from my student ID. And Guy N. claims Gerry and I are having an affair.

OK, if I was having an affair with Gerry (again—as if, people!), why would I pursue Guy N.? Dude makes no sense. He is so stupid!!! And why am I even making this rational argument?

Ludicrous! Nightmare!

Someone just called for an interview.

Crap.

Must I now blog in order to refute vicious, offensive (possibly slanderous) claims?

Phone rang again. This time it was Mary Jo, calling to ask in general how things were going. I gave her an earful of all my current problems. Made it funny, though, so she laughed. Sure, it's funny to *her*. It's not *her* picture with Gerry.

After that, I asked, "Have you talked to Wittenauer lately?"

"I've seen him," she said. "That's why I was calling."

"Doesn't he look OK?"

"He does," she said slowly.

"I'm going to see him at Thanksgiving. In, like, a

week." I told her about the grand grandparents' plan in Nebraska.

"Sure you don't want to come to my house again? That was a lot of fun last year."

"You came to my rescue," I remembered.

"Anytime," she said. "So, I'm sure you'll talk then."

"Right." What was she getting at? Didn't have time to find out because housemates ran in, carrying all the copies of the *Coloradoan* they'd managed to buy around town. Fewer for sale = less humiliation for Courtney.

Second article in newspaper today. When interviewed yesterday, I explained about blog and how I'm trying to write about ways to make the city greener. Reporter pointed out that slandering Smoothie Stop does not save the environment.

Stupid reporter.

Anyway, it's not slander. That's for serious writers. This is just random musings on a random blog that nobody is supposed to read.

Dr. Bigelow gave me a strange look in class. Oh no. Don't tell me. Here I am just getting closer to making a good impression on him, and this article hits.

He thinks I am a sleazy go-getter.

That I like older men with hair loss and questionable fitness. Authority figures.

Realized as I was standing there in line at his desk after class, waiting to tell him about my upcoming Shop & Shop post, that he was rushing through other people's questions to finally get to me, after all this time.

Seemed like it wasn't a coincidence.

"Wait! Wait up, Ms. Smith!"

"Must catch a flight!" I called over my shoulder.

Fled classroom.

Can't wait for Thanksgiving break.

Kept a low profile today. Was packing for Nebraska. Wondering if I should just pack everything and not plan to return. But then I think, No, I'm not going to let stupid Guy Nicollet ruin my life. Any more than he already has.

Dara had already left for Seattle, and Shawna's parents had picked her up, so it was just me and Oscar and DeathKitty in the house. (A neighbor is feeding her while we're on T-giving break.) (A brave neighbor.)

Suddenly, there was a knock on the basement window and I nearly freaked. Peered up anxiously and saw Grant standing there. "Let me in," he said.

I met him at the back door, wondering if he came by to see if I needed a ride to Denver. Bryan was picking me up, but—

"You drive me crazy, you know that?" He slammed the door behind him.

Ooh. This was kind of exciting.

Oscar kept leaping all over him, whimpering, and licking him. "Not now, buddy." Grant actually pushed Oscar into the kitchen and closed the door, then went downstairs into my basement hovel. "I could lose my job because of you!" Grant said.

"What? What are you talking about? I only wrote good things," I said.

"You call this a good thing?!" He quoted the part about not being able to get every bag and how that was just unrealistic, and people being dumb.

"Well, you did *say* it," I reminded him.

"And I trusted you to edit it and make it sound better!"

"I thought you sounded great. I think the program sounded really, really good," I said. "And anyway, what are you worried about? Nobody reads what I write."

"I read it, OK? I Googled you."

We were standing very close. There was a really short, really embarrassing pause. I felt a little glow inside me, like I was a toy with a battery inside me. Like a doll with a belly button that lit up when it was happy and had a bottle.

He's going to kiss me, I thought. Or I'm going to kiss him, or something. And that would be really, really great. And really, really wrong.

"How could you forget? Thanks to your attack on the Smoothie Stop, everyone's reading your blog now, OK?"

"Really? Cool," I murmured.

"No, it's not cool. Because all it takes is one person to show that piece to my manager and I will be toast."

"Whole wheat or sourdough—"

"Courtney! This isn't funny. This is my life. This is how I support myself!"

"OK . . . OK! I'm sorry. What do you want me to do?"

"Take it down. Tonight. Before anyone else sees it," Grant said.

"OK, but once something is on the net, it's on there forever—"

"I know, but just *try*."

"OK. I'll do it right now," I said.

"I'll watch," he said.

"Like I'm not going to do it?" He had to stand over me and make sure that I followed through, as if I was completely unreliable and incompetent.

I started to get that hot and cold feeling as he loomed over me, watching me type my username and password. Like, he shouldn't stand that close to me. I have a boyfriend! I have a boyfriend! But somehow I still can't resist Grant. If he makes even one move toward me . . .

"Um, did you write that 'I'll hold you, Court' comment?" I asked.

"What?" asked Grant.

"Nothing. Never mind." I tapped away. I was taking my best article down. This was a crime. But I'd do it for Grant. I'd probably do anything for Grant, if he asked.

Suddenly, there was a commotion upstairs: I heard DeathKitty screeching, and Oscar barking. The pets were killing each other.

"Just—stay out of my life, OK?" Grant asked. "Whenever you're around things get messed up."

"Fine, I will."

"In fact, maybe you shouldn't have transferred here," he went on.

"And maybe *you* shouldn't have had me move in next door!" I shot back.

Sparks were flying. Upstairs, fur was no doubt flying.

Through it all, found myself wanting to kiss Grant so badly. Which was a great and horrible feeling.

He stopped in the doorway and said, "Just for the record, I still haven't forgiven you. For the blog or anything else." And then he was gone.

Woke up at home in Denver with a vague, blurry memory of Grant and me, lips locked. Did I dream that, or did that happen?

Then I remembered: That wasn't real life. In real life, Grant is furious at me, and I'm not so thrilled with him. I'm meeting Wittenauer in Nebraska on Wednesday night. *That* is what I'm excited about, not Grant.

However, in the meantime I have been accused of having an affair with Gerry. G-E-R-R-Y.

Had to talk to him. Drove over to Truth or Dairy, THE ORIGINAL, I don't mind saying. Put on my trademark wool ski hat and Mom's hideous pink down jacket for camouflage.

Business was slow. Gerry was sipping coffee and tapping his feet, looking very anxious. Talked to him about how we can defuse this situation.

"Gerry, look. You have to make another statement. You have to tell everyone that there's nothing between you and me. People are coming out of the woodwork with pictures and stories—"

"I've tried telling them, Courtney. But do you really think coming by here was the best idea?" He quickly blended a large Coconut Fantasy Dream for me and shooed me out the door as if I were just another customer. A poorly treated customer, at that.

As soon as I walked out of Truth or Dairy: snapping photos. Paparazzi!

OK, maybe it was only one guy and a large flash on his camera, but still. One is all it takes. Now my picture will be everywhere: in newspapers, online somewhere, fraternizing with Gerry AND wearing Mom's horrendous pink jacket.

Wonder if we can leave for Nebraska tonight.

I've never written that before.

11/22

Went outside to get newspaper on the stoop.

Outside, Mr. Novotny had no leaves left to tend to. The trees were bare. He was sitting in his garage with the TV on.

Looked over at me. "So. That's why you came back?"

"What?" I asked.

"You and ice cream guy," he said.

"What? No!" I slammed the door.

Ice cream guy? Is this how everyone's going to know me now? Well. Maybe better than fruity guy, but still.

Opened Denver section and there was Gerry's face. "Smoothie War Blends into a Frenzy."

Blends. Ha-ha. So clever.

Hate journalism and all journalists.

Plus, I will never have, or make, a smoothie again in my entire life.

Was in the car, picking up Alison at airport, when Grant
sent me a text.

> Look, that was weird Friday night. Sorry. Just worried
> about job. I don't want you to think . . . Anyway, so have
> a good Thanksgiving. Don't run off the road again.

I didn't! Argh! When is everyone going to forget about
that?!?!

And what does Grant mean, "Have a good
Thanksgiving?" Isn't he here in Denver and couldn't I talk
to him before then? Or see him at Jane's party tomorrow
night? Or is he still mad at me, or did he go somewhere
else for Thanksgiving without telling me, but why would
he do that?

All this was swirling in my head and I was trying to
reply but I couldn't decide what to say. Then Wittenauer
chimed, and then I was driving and texting and nearly
smashed into a nice family of 4 standing outside baggage
claim.

Went to a party tonight at Jane's house. So happy to see her.

She had a party for the old bunch home from college for Thanksgiving break. Seemed like I should be safe from paparazzi and annoying questions there. Everyone knew me, really knew me, and also knew Gerry, and knew nothing would ever, ever happen between us.

Jane and I found a couple minutes where we could talk in private, and I told her about the fight with Grant and how he was furious at me again.

I thought Grant might show up, and I could apologize again for misquoting him, even though I didn't, and possibly getting him in trouble at work, but he wasn't there. Still hating me, apparently. Fair enough.

"There's something I don't get. Why doesn't he just ignore you?" Jane asked.

"Gee, thanks."

She laughed. "No, I mean—if someone really got under my skin as badly as you apparently get under his, wouldn't you just walk away from the whole thing? Leave the situation? Instead he lives next door, visits your dog daily, and comes over to talk to you—like, more than once." She shook her head. "He doesn't know what's good for him. But that's—that doesn't sound like Grant."

We were talking about her life in Madison when we were interrupted.

"Courtney." The Tom (last name Delaney, nicknamed after a tomcat) gave me a big hug.

Seeing him again, I was feeling glad that we'd run student council together senior year, but that it had been the extent of our relationship. "What's the deal with you and ice cream smoothie dude?"

"Nothing. *Nothing.* There's no deal," I said. "It's just— a long story. But we're definitely not involved in any way at all, except that I used to work there. Used to!"

"Tone it down, Court," Jane said. "You sound a little too defensive."

"OK. So he's not your sugar daddy. Then you're still single?" he asked, stepping back to give me a once-over. Or, more likely, knowing the Tom, a twice-over.

"What do you mean, still single? I have a boyfriend. Why, was I supposed to be married?" I joked.

"Some people settle down by now," he said, looking proud of himself.

I raised an eyebrow and looked at him. "You're not telling me *you're* married."

"No, but I'm engaged."

"Really." This I found hard to believe. From the person in our senior class voted "Most Likely to Cheat"?

"Yeah. Great girl. Great, great girl."

I smiled. Also, invisible girl, it seemed. Imaginary, maybe?

We briefly exchanged stories—why was I home, what happened to being in Wisconsin, some details about my boyfriend, that the Tom was thinking about majoring in Econ (which is hilarious considering he once stole all the student council money)—and I was wondering if he'd actually kind of sort of reformed into not being a total player when he stepped closer to me again and said, "Courtney? Why did you and I . . . why did we never . . ." He sort of pointed to himself and then to me and then back again.

So much for being "engaged."

"The timing was off," I said. *As in, you weren't the last*

507

man on earth. When you are, get back to me . . . or not. I looked around for a different, not-so-friendly face, and headed back over to Jane, my safety square. Was so wonderful to see her and hang out.

But it felt weird to be at a high school reunion thing without Beth there, or Grant there.

Of course, despite friendly text, Grant hates me now. He really does.

You know those "three strikes and you're out" programs for criminals? Well, I'm out.

Which is OK, I guess, because I'm going to be seeing Wittenauer in two days, and did I mention I can't wait to get out of town?

On the road to Ogallala in Sterling's silver SUV. Me, Bryan, and Alison crammed into backseat. Sterling and Suzanne plus three.

Just your average family of five, with one very neurotic dog.

Oscar can't settle down in the back. Keeps doing that turning around three times, lying down, then gets up right away and turns around three times again.

Sterling keeps sneezing and wondering out loud if Oscar wouldn't do better in a kennel for the long weekend, and Mom keeps saying, no, Oscar wouldn't, and he should just be patient and wait for his Zyrtec to kick in.

Meanwhile, *I* can't quit making comments about the low gas mileage.

"If I could afford a hybrid, I'd get one," said Sterling. Then he sneezed.

"This is a very useful family car," Mom said. "And it has four-wheel drive so we won't get stuck if it snows. Remember two years ago?"

How could I forget? Stranded on the side of the road, and Oscar trying to run away.

"Courtney swerved into a snowbank," Mom told Sterling.

There goes my chance of ever driving this car. "It was a blizzard!" I called up to the front.

Beside me, Alison is composing music on her computer. Bryan has iPod on and is working on his college application essay. Me, I should be studying, but have middle seat and can't concentrate.

Isn't that always the way? The middle child gets the worst seat?

"Would anyone like some cheese?" Mom held up her infamous Ziploc bag of cubed Monterey Jack.

How. Many. Times. Do I have to tell her that I do not eat cheese anymore???

Ooh, text from Wittenauer.

Wittenauer: Did u leave yet?
Me: Oh yes. On 1-76. Windy. Bored.
Wittenauer: Lucky u.
Me: It's a nightmare. When do I see u.
Wittenauer: 2nite.

11/26 THANKSGIVING—5:00 A.M.

Just woke up with a start.

Where is Wittenauer? Why isn't he here yet? He was supposed to be here.

Ran down to the kitchen. Grandma was putting the turkey in the oven. At 5 A.M.

I was tiptoeing out when she saw me and asked me about my "beau," whether he really was coming or not, and complaining about men and their broken promises.

Found my cell on kitchen counter and there was a message from Wittenauer that his parents were forcing him to stay overnight but he'd be here by noon.

Went back to bed. Can't sleep though.

11/26 THANKSGIVING—8:00 A.M.

Mom, Sterling, and Bryan are dressed for the annual Ogallala Turkey Trot.

The turkeys don't trot. The people do.

They are making me get dressed so I can go along and cheer. "Dress for the fun run," Sterling urged me. "You can always jump in at the last minute."

Well, it sounds better than making gravy.

This Thanksgiving . . . it's going to go down in history. And not just because it started raining 24 hours ago, mid–turkey trot, and hasn't stopped since.

We had an awkward meal. Grandma and Grandpa only talking through other people, like "Would you please tell your grandmother to pass the sweet potatoes?" and "Would you please tell your grandfather to stop being such a conceited ass?"

Wittenauer came in right when we were all sitting down to dinner. We gave each other giant hugs and he sat down next to me.

"You're just in time for the toast," Mom told him.

"Funny. I thought we'd be having turkey," Wittenauer said.

I squeezed his hand under the table. He squeezed my leg back.

Mom continued, "I'm thankful for my healthy parents, my wonderful children, and for Sterling."

"And I'm so thankful for all of you coming into my life," said Sterling. "Even Oscar." He laughed.

I swear, Oscar was glaring at him. He was resting his head on his paws and just looking up, like, "Dude. You made me move to Fort Collins and live with a killer cat. Not thankful. Unless you pass me some of that turkey under the table."

"We have an announcement to make," said Sterling. "One that makes us very happy, and we hope will make you happy as well."

I coughed on a sip of cranberry juice that went down the wrong way.

"Courtney? You OK?" asked Wittenauer.

"Sure, sure."

He rubbed my back and I looked up at him, eyes watering. An announcement? That could only mean one thing. I cleared my throat and looked up expectantly, trying to smile even though my lungs were failing me and I wasn't breathing correctly.

"I'm sure it will come as no surprise to you that I've asked Suzanne to marry me," Sterling went on, "but the *big* surprise is that she's graciously accepted."

"M-marry?" asked Alison, looking as stunned as I felt.

Mom held out her hand, displaying a sapphire-and-diamond engagement ring. It looked beautiful. *She* looked amazing, so radiantly happy that she was almost glowing. Or else it was that the house was *really* hot from having the oven on all day.

"That's great, Mom. I'm really happy for you guys." Bryan went over to hug her, and Sterling hugged him, too, giving him the man-friend's manly clap on the back.

"Well, how long is the engagement?" asked my grandmother.

"Not long at all. We're having a Christmas Eve wedding," said Mom, beaming, beside herself. "Can you believe it? We're getting married!"

"That soon? I have nothing to wear!" cried Grandma Von Dragen. "And my hair—"

"Nobody cares about your hair," said Grandpa, busily carving the turkey.

Grandma smiled, then looked down a bit sadly and took a bite of cranberry jelly.

Alison and I each hugged Mom, then Sterling. Then I hugged Grandma, for good measure. Seemed like she could use it.

After dinner, while others were cleaning up, watching football, Wittenauer and I were sprawled on the sofa together.

"So I've been thinking," said Wittenauer.

"So have I. I've been thinking how I shouldn't have had any stuffing. At all."

"No, seriously."

"I am being serious," I said.

"I think we should move in together, in June," he said.

"What?"

I'd been so overwhelmed by Mom and Sterling's news that I hadn't even had a chance to put my own thoughts and feelings together. Where was I on all this? How did I really feel about Wittenauer?

"It only makes sense. Let's definitely find a place of our own," he said. "I'll go to law school, you'll be a junior—"

"But, Wittenauer."

"But what?"

We really weren't "on the same page," as the saying goes. We weren't even in the same chapter. I felt my pulse kind of speeding up. "Have you really, um, thought this through?"

"Yes. It's perfectly logical," he said. "It's the only logical solution."

But you don't live together to be logical, I thought. You live together, maybe, possibly, because you're in love. And because you're going to make a commitment and be, like, a married couple someday.

Was it because I was a so-called child of divorce? Was it because I was at heart really against my mother getting remarried? Was it because I didn't actually respect Snow

White for just getting off that glass coffin table and riding off with the prince, no questions asked? I mean, she totally ditched her friends, Grumpy, Dopey, etc., which was not cool.

"Um, OK. Let's not do anything rash. Let's talk about this," I said.

Then I passed out.

I knew I'd had too much stuffing.

Woke up to grandparents, rest of family, Wittenauer hovering over me.

Grandpa was waving a little sack of balsam fir under my nose, so all I smelled was Christmas-tree scent, which was confusing, because wasn't this Thanksgiving holiday?

Not that he usually waits more than 24 hours after T-giving to chop down a Christmas tree and haul it in.

"Courtney? What's going on? Are you pregnant?" asked Grandma.

Wittenauer's eyes widened. "Are you?"

"WHAT? No!" I said. "I just . . . it's hot in here."

"Oh. Well, I could let the fire go out, I suppose." Grandpa started fiddling with the fireplace.

"You always put too many logs on," Grandma said. "You have no impulse control."

They started bickering again, just like they had all during dinner. They clearly weren't getting along the way they had been these last couple of years.

"She's fine. She's just got stuffing in her veins." Wittenauer scooped me up in his arms and carried me over to the front door so I could get some fresh air. "You OK?" he whispered. "For real?"

I told him that it was just a lot to take in—the idea of Mom getting married and maybe us living together.

"What do you mean, 'maybe us'?" he said, sounding a little disappointed.

"Maybe you what?" asked my mom, craning at me, putting her palm to my forehead. "Courtney, you feel cold and clammy. Are you sure you're all right? You can tell me, you know. You can tell me anything."

"I'm fine," I said. "I just got . . ." Overwhelmed. Freaked out. Scared. "A bit hot," I said. "That's what I'm trying to tell you."

"Was it my news—our news?" Mom asked. "It was our news, wasn't it? Oh, I knew you kids weren't ready."

"No, Mom—it's—that's fine. And we're not kids anymore, right?"

I found that I was dying for a minute by myself so I could call Beth and Jane about it, and even Grant. I couldn't wait to tell them. They'd never believe Mom was getting remarried. And they had to come to the wedding—all of them.

Wait a second. That could be awkward.

We all settled down at the table for a game of Von Dragen Boggle (you make words using the letters in bad family names) and leftover pie.

Should not have had that second piece of apple. I will never sleep again.

11/28 MORNING

Phew. Finally, we had to leave to drive back to Denver, and Wittenauer had to go back to his parents. Still driving, cold, nasty rain. Fortunately, Sterling's massive SUV insulates us from entire rest of world.

This will give me and Wittenauer some time to think. Hopefully, he will come to his senses.

I don't know if he needs time to think, but I do. Moving in together sounds so serious. That should be part of the long view. Looooonnnnng. Not the next year.

We didn't even really get a chance to talk about it, because we never had any time to ourselves. I did manage to tell him not to tell anyone else right away, to just keep it between us.

"Why? I mean, of course. Of course! But why?"

"Why? Because my mom will pitch a fit. Because they'll say we're too young." But mostly, I was thinking, because I have no idea if this is something I really want to do. I mean, it sounds nice, and Wittenauer's nice . . . but it would mean choosing each other, like, seriously. Settling down. With a cornstalk.

OK, so he'd be done with college and the costume.

If he moves here, would he try out to be the Ram? Do you think there's more than one? Because one does basketball games and has all these skills—

Anyway. I know I'm only obsessing about mascots in the car because I don't want to face the real question: Do I want to live with Wittenauer? Or not?

11/28 NIGHT

Spent the morning at the Cherry Creek Betrothal Boutique for our so-called final fittings. Felt more like a week.

"Mom, do you really think a big wedding is a good idea, at your age?" I asked as I pulled the strapless, cranberry-colored bridesmaid dress over my head.

"What's wrong with my age?" she asked. "And it isn't a big wedding at all—just a hundred people."

Alison and I walked out of our fitting rooms at the same time and cracked up laughing. We looked so . . . seasonal. And identical. "Who schedules bridesmaid dress fittings two days after Thanksgiving?" Alison commented. "Like I don't feel fat enough?"

"What's the problem?" Mom said, admiring us. "When I ordered them, I used the measurements from your prom dresses. That wasn't so long ago."

"You *kept* those?" I asked.

"I'm a math geek, remember? I have a file."

"And what is she talking about? You didn't even go to prom," I said to Alison.

"Yes I did. I just didn't have a *date*," she corrected me. "I went with everyone from band."

"Oh. Well, no wonder you don't bring it up much," I teased her. We started poking each other in the arms, trying to push each other over.

"Girls. Girls! Knock it off!" said Mom, sounding tense, and it was like we were 10 and 12 again, instead of 19 and 21.

"What does Bryan have to wear?" I asked. "A cranberry leisure suit?"

"Don't be ridiculous. A black tuxedo. He's one of the groomsmen," said Mom. "There's an even number of bridesmaids and groomsmen—besides you two, there's Sterling's sister, Abigail, and my friend Heather is maid of honor. . . . For groomsmen we have Bryan, Sterling's brothers—"

"Gold and Platinum?" asked Alison, and the two of us started giggling again.

"Drake and Andrew," Mom went on, ignoring us, "and his nephew Nick, who's going to be the ring bearer."

That's when I first glimpsed that Mom was losing it. She, the queen of accounting, hadn't come up with an even number at all.

"And I'll need to know ASAP if you're bringing dates so I can get the seating chart done. Oh, and I'm inviting your father," she added, almost as an afterthought.

"*What?* Mom, isn't that going to be weird?" Was she trying to freak us out about all this? Could you take a kind of strange situation and make it even stranger, Mom?

"No, it won't be weird at all. Sophia will come, and hopefully your stepsister," added Mom.

One big, happy, bizarre family. "Speaking of Dad. I mean, aren't you sort of, um, old to wear white?" I asked.

"I'm not wearing white. It's cream. Ecru," Mom said.

I look at her and it's not that she's 45 and I'm not. Although that helps. I just know that no matter what Wittenauer thinks, we're so not ready to move in together and take things to that next teetering, scary level.

"Courtney, you look funny," Alison said, sometime around then—I don't remember, exactly.

"I know. I don't look good in red," I reminded her. Plus, I am feeling undecided, confused, and, frankly, a bit nauseous. Which does nothing for my complexion.

"It's not red, it's cranberry," Mom said.

"Whatever it is, it's not a good color on me," I said.

"What? It's beautiful, hon. You're beautiful."

I turned to Alison and rolled my eyes. "Mom doesn't have rose-colored glasses. She's looking through cranberry-colored glasses."

Later, after we changed back to normal clothes, Alison asked what was going on with me and why I seemed so stressed.

"It's me and Wittenauer," I said.

"What's wrong?"

"Nothing. It's just hard sometimes, living apart." And, uh, thinking of living together. And has anyone seen Grant around lately?

Shawna and her mother picked up me and Oscar and we came back to the Fort together. They talk a mile a minute and drive even faster. Got here in record time.

I sort of snuck into the house as soon as we got home. Not ready to see Grant right now, and definitely didn't want to see any reporters. But maybe the story died over Thanksgiving and there's more important news to report.

DeathKitty was sitting on the sofa, batting eyelashes, looking innocent. Downstairs, found my blanket shredded on my bed. Upstairs, Shawna's entire collection of perfume and beauty products were knocked onto the floor, some broken.

Dara got back at one in the morning; I was in bed, reading. Went up to say hi, then figured it was morning in Milan so I'd try Beth to tell her about W's plan—seems like she's the only one I can tell truly confidential things to, besides you, dear journal. You can't talk, and she's halfway across the world.

shoe92gurrl: Why do u not sound excited?

crtveg17: Idk.

shoe92gurrl: Id.

crtveg17: What?

shoe92gurrl: I *do.*

crtveg17: Tell me.

shoe92gurrl: It's 2 soon!!!

crtveg17: Right. Exactly.

shoe92gurrl: And we're supposed to get a place together after college.

crtveg17: Right!

But that wasn't quite it. It was that: If I'm living with W, how will I still see Grant???

I am a bad person. Very bad.

I was eating lunch at the Pyth when I saw Grant and friends. Slouched down in booth, wearing a ski hat, but he recognized me anyway. (Have taken to wearing a ski hat in all situations. You never know when another embarrassing article featuring my photo and an old man's photo will appear in the newspaper.)

"Hey, what's up?" he asked as his friends left to find a table.

You have no idea, and I don't think I can tell you. "Not much. Just, you know. Lunch."

"That looks like turkey. Is everything OK?" Grant knows I only give up the veggie ghost during stressful times.

"Oh yeah. Fine." I nodded, covering my mouth while I chewed.

"Nice hat," he said.

"Thanks. Trying to not be seen."

"Oh right. Anything new there?"

"No."

There we were, making small talk like the last time we saw each other hadn't been really intense and exciting, like we hadn't stood so close to each other that sparks flew and I was afraid we might start making out.

"So, ah. How was Thanksgiving? The Von Dragens?"

"Great. Fine. Filling," I said. "My mom's, um, getting married."

"Really?"

That was all he was going to say about it? "Really. And how was your Thanksgiving?"

"Fine. You know, boring. I studied the whole time."

"You should have gone to Jane's party," I said.

"Everyone missed you."

"Yeah? Everyone?" he asked.

"Oh yeah. The Tom was there."

"Hm. Some people you don't necessarily stay friends with after high school, and that's a good thing."

And others, I thought, looking up at him, you think maybe you're over, but then you're falling for them again, which is really inconvenient. "Well. See you," I said.

"Yeah. See you."

When he walked off, I felt like I was having one of those bursts of adrenaline you get after you nearly have a car accident and you're relieved you're OK but at the same time you realize what almost happened. Fatal accident. Fight or flight.

I chose flight. Tossed the rest of my lunch in compost collection can and bolted.

I may not eat much chicken, but I'm definitely 100 percent chicken.

After Env. Activism class, Dr. Bigelow started moving toward me in the crowd. For most people in class, this would be thrilling. Private audience with genius. Groupie heaven. But for me, no. Frightening. Everyone else seems to have forgotten about my supposed affair with ice cream guy Gerry, but apparently not Dr. Bigelow.

"You. Ms. Smith," he said, pointing at me.

"Um, me?" I was trying to avoid the herd and move toward the door.

"Yes, you. I need you," he said.

I groaned. Oh, great. Here it came: the professor proposal. He'd give me an A if I slept with him, etc. "You don't necessarily know the whole truth—"

"I need you to meet with the advisory committee. I think you need to stage a coup, take it over. Their ideas so far are completely bogus." He cast a disparaging glance at a couple of my classmates that I'm sure they didn't deserve.

"M-me?"

"Yes, you. I've read your blog. A colleague tipped me off. I like your work, though you're a bit random and you need a decent editor."

Up close, even though he was saying somewhat insulting things, he seemed a lot nicer than he did when he was giving lectures and tirades.

"So you mean you didn't want to talk to me . . . because of me and that ice cream guy . . . ?"

"I really have no idea what you're talking about. Just help them. Talk some sense into them. We have zero time left here. Could you come up with a decent idea for the class project?"

"I thought they'd agreed on an idea," I said, although I still hadn't figured out what it was. So much for my skills at investigative journalism.

"It's brainless, which will reflect on all of us. *All* of us," he repeated. "I may have tenure but I'm not immune to criticism. If you save this project, I'll be indebted to you."

So, I set up meeting time, place, and recruited more volunteers to attend. Dr. Bigelow is right. My blog *isn't* horrible, and can make a difference. They can't hold me down. I refuse to let Guy Nicollet ruin my career in journalism by censoring my blog.

Got home and tried to share the exciting news with Wittenauer. Don't think he was really listening to me. He kept talking about Baby Corn and how hard it was to train a new person. How it wasn't working out at all and they'd chosen the wrong person entirely and how they were supposed to go to the annual holiday bash at Dean Sobransky's house. . . .

Honestly, I could have dozed off if I didn't have to stay up tonight and plot my idea for the committee. Not interesting in the slightest.

12/2

Breakthrough. TA David says I am totally caught up. He even said, "You've really improved, thanks to your careful exploration of detail and word choice. I'm glad I could help you."

Sure. *He'll* take the credit. I did all of the work.

Mom called about wedding plans. Went on and on about menu, napkins, flowers, favors, and how everything has to coordinate. She forced me to call Wittenauer to make sure his suit will coordinate with my cranberry dress by wearing something called a cranberry cravat.

Excuse me, but I need to get back to my real life now? Meeting tonight with EAC. Will report.

Turns out the EAC is very, very small. Consists of three dudes and one girl. No volunteers in sight. Here were their ideas:

One guy's idea of massive campus activism protest was to use pipe bombs. (Will need to double-check his last name and report him to campus security.)

Another idea was to stage massive nude protest. (Not interested.) (Not in a million years.)

One was to create a rain forest for people to walk through and enjoy, and then ruin it with machetes and take it down.

Or idle cars on student center plaza and see how poisonous the air could get and how long it would take.

I sat there and thought, and thought, because if our grade was based on this, and Dr. Bigelow's performance . . .

We needed something shocking, attention getting, but not illegal and idiotic.

"Well?" They all stared at me, like I was going to be a guru and just say something brilliant instantaneously.

"I'll think about it," I said.

"We don't have much time," the other girl said, and I nodded.

"Yeah, time is, like, totally running out. On our project and on the environment," Pipe Bomb guy said. "And the whole world, really."

Have to remember to contact security about that guy. Don't want him near any of us.

Walked out of student center and was looking down to text Wittenauer with the report when I ran smack into Grant. Oops. I told him about the meeting and how I was supposed to report back tomorrow. While I talked,

I was vaguely aware that my phone was vibrating with Wittenauer's reply, but I quickly reached into my pocket and shut it off.

"I feel for you. I hate oral reports," he said.

"It's not a report!" I snapped.

"Sorry!" he said, holding up his hands.

"No." I laughed. "I'm sorry. It's just . . . Bigelow, you know? He's so intimidating. My brain freezes up when he talks to me. And this committee . . ."

"You'll think of something," Grant said.

I rolled my eyes.

"You will!" Grant insisted. "What time is class, again?" he asked.

"Ten thirty," I said.

"You've got twelve hours to be brilliant. You'll come up with a great idea. I mean, you're Courtney Von Dragen Smith, right? You always do."

"I do?"

"Do I have to make a list? Because I can make one," he said. "Except right now I'm late for a study group. Good luck. See you!"

Just like that, he was gone. Flying off. Like a superhero. Way better than that wimpy Prince Charming, anyway.

So Grantlike. He was always the one talking me up, giving me confidence when I had none. Even though I've been a total cretin to him at times, he still does it. Superhero or angel. Not sure of his status. Single?

Despite Grant's confidence in me, I showed up for class with nothing. I walked into the room at the last second, nodded at my classmates, and took a seat.

Dr. Bigelow strode in two minutes later and dropped his heavy briefcase on the desk. I was hoping he'd launch into one of his usual lectures, but no. He turned directly to me. "Well, Ms. Smith? What do you have?"

A *nervous feeling*. "We, uh, discussed things," I said. "And we're getting there?"

Dr. Bigelow sighed. "Courtney, I expected more from you."

My heart sank. "We, uh, well . . . we're thinking of something maybe on the plaza outside the student center."

"Something?" He made air quotes. "Such as?"

All of a sudden, a face popped up in the door window.

It was Grant. He was hopping up and down. And waving. And jumping. And smiling.

I cracked up laughing, and for some weird reason, that's when I realized it. I'm definitely in love with him again. (Still?) Absolutely, totally in love with him. I can't ignore or avoid it any longer.

He's so thoughtful. He doesn't forget anything. I told him about this once, how I thought I saw him, it was months ago, and he, like, *remembered*.

"Ms. Smith, is there a problem?" asked Dr. Bigelow.

"No. No, not really." I coughed. "I just, um, thought of what we could do for our big class project," I lied. Because I didn't totally have it, yet.

"Enlighten us. *Please*. Time's running out."

I reached for my notes and nearly knocked over my cup of herbal tea that I'd bought in order to try to calm myself. Suddenly, I had a vision. An idea. I looked around the room at the cups and bottles on everyone else's desks. (This is a two-hour class, and you get thirsty and/or sleepy.)

If we were all in this class because we were really concerned about the environment, and even *we* were still using some Styrofoam, plastic, and insulated cups . . .

Well. That's how I found myself making something up, on the spot, for the entire class's grade.

Poor Bryan. Because Dara doesn't get it.

He emailed her a poem, trying to tell her how he felt, and she wrote back and said it was hopelessly simple and displayed a complete lack of visual imagery and tonal structure. She showed both emails to me.

Ouch. But I'm not sure what she means, exactly, by showing it all to me. He was going to come up this weekend but now is not. Which may be for the best, because Shawna is trying to ask out Matt next door—

Oh. She's back. He said no, sorry, he didn't, like, like her that way, and said he thought she was dating Bryan, anyway, because of all the time they spend together and how much fun they seem to have.

Disaster.

Shawna and I both tried calling Bryan, for different reasons, but he isn't taking either of our calls. "Did you have to be so mean to him?" I asked Dara.

"I wasn't mean. Just truthful," she said.

"He's young, so he doesn't know how to write poetry, he was only trying to impress you," said Shawna once we'd explained what was going on.

"Well, it didn't work. And why would he be interested in *me*? I'm so not the right person for him."

"But how do you know that? I mean, how do you know who *is* the right person?" I said. "Remember when things went haywire before? In my life?"

Shawna nodded. "When Beth and Grant, like, whatever?"

"Whatever. Yes. That," I said. "Everything feels kind of crazy like that right now. I mean, I'm supposed to be living with Wittenauer next year and I can't even get him to talk to me, and—and—Grant's, like, being the nicest he's ever been, and it's like history repeating itself except it's switched—"

"Wait a second, wait a second." Shawna waved her straw in front of my face. "What did you just say?"

"You and Wittenauer are moving in together? When? Where? And when were you going to tell *us*?" demanded Dara.

"What is it, like, about us?" Shawna said, laughing. "We end up making people move in with their boyfriends."

"You won't get the security deposit back," said Dara. "Oscar's ruined the hardwood floor."

"What about DeathKitty? She's trashed—"

Dara started to cry. "Don't bring her up. She's missing. I haven't seen her in forty-eight hours. You know what that means," she sobbed. "She's not coming back."

Did I imagine it, or did Oscar's ears prick up when she said that?

The night ended with all of us watching *The Hills* marathon and eating popcorn. I love other people's problems. Even when they're fake.

"Holding Court"
by Courtney Von Dragen Smith
Is Getting Married
Environmentally Sound?

When I get married, my wedding will leave zero carbon footprint.

How do I love thee, environment? Let us count the ways.

The wedding dress. You can find one that's been refurbished or restored, or choose something unusual that you can wear again. Like, for instance, a rain barrel.

Your bridesmaids should not have to buy new shoes that are dyed with environmentally unfriendly harsh chemical dyes. And are cranberry colored, no less.

The invitations—use email. Come on. No one's going to save the fancy invites but you. Print one for yourself and frame it. Done.

Flowers—forget it. Carry only sustainable crops.

The food for the reception must be locally grown or at the very least grown in the U.S.A. Stay away from beef. Just good common sense. Everyone likes finger food best, anyway.

The napkins—please. Use recycled, and avoid getting your names plastered all over them in harmful, environmentally unfriendly gold ink. Look for soy ink.

The cake—make it vegan and gluten-free. Your friends will thank you.

The limo—no, thank you. Take a train, bus, or bike to the wedding reception!

The photos—store online.

Finally, the honeymoon. What can we do to lessen

our carbon footprint? Well, we can probably skip flying to Maui.

If and when I get married, I will make sure I leave no trace.

12/5

DeathKitty is still missing. Dara is getting frantic, you know, like how she did during the blizzard.

We keep telling her not to worry, that cat can clearly take care of herself. She's survived on mice and birds.

"But that's the thing," said Dara. "I'm worried because she hasn't caught anything in weeks."

I thought about it. There had been a distinct lack of carcasses on my bed. "Maybe she's reformed?" I suggested.

"She's probably trapped in someone's garage and will come out soon. Don't worry," said Shawna.

We have opened three cans of tuna with no luck.

Hope she will return soon. None of us likes tuna salad that much.

12/6

Dara and I went to the Humane Society to see if DeathKitty had shown up, if she's been picked up for loitering.

Grant was there volunteering, working behind the counter. I could say that I'd forgotten he volunteers on Sundays, but that wouldn't be true. It was actually my idea to go look for her there, but I mean, why did no one else have that idea? It's because I've had to deal with a missing pet. Frequently.

We toured the cat room with Grant, checking all the cages for DeathKitty. No luck. So many cute cats and kittens, though. We went back out to the reception area so Dara could file a report, and while she did that I wandered back into the cat room to look at a family of black-and-white kittens I'd fallen in love with. I can't adopt a cat, I know that. I already take care of a crazy epileptic dog and live with a psycho killer cat. It wouldn't be fair. Or nice.

Still, they were so cute!!!!!

When I came back out to the main area, Dara and Grant were leaning close to each other, whispering. "What?" I asked.

"Nothing," said Dara. "Just telling him how upset I am." She sniffled.

"Here. I've been meaning to give you this," said Grant, shoving a small, brown envelope at me. "Make sure he wears them or you'll be here one day looking for him, too."

Engraved Oscar ID tags. Grant didn't forget. He doesn't forget anything.

Need a new grocery store. Stat.

Was shopping at Shop & Shop, staring at the Tofutti options through a foggy freezer door, when phone rang. It was Dean Sobransky, of all people. Figured he was calling to check on me, but he said right away he had great news. "Guess what, Courtney? Some money has been freed up in our scholarship program."

"Dropouts?" I asked.

He coughed. "Improved budgeting," he said. "We'd love for you to come back to Cornwall Falls if you're interested. I can fax or email you a revised financial offer. . . ."

I felt excited and sick at the same time. "You're asking me *now*?" I cried.

"Uh, yes," he said. "We've run through all the numbers. Had all-night budget meetings. We've come up with a way to invite select students back for spring semester and we're just thrilled."

"Thrilled," I repeated, half in a daze.

"So you'll do it?"

"Wait! I'm thinking," I said. "I mean, this would have been a dream come true back in, say, September," I said. "But I've kind of settled in."

"Well, you don't need to decide today. Think about it. What school will give you a better opportunity to grow, change, and affect the future of the world?"

"Oh, is *that* all," I said.

He started laughing. "Ah, Courtney, I've missed you."

"Oh, I miss you, too, Dean Sobransky." He laughed. "No, really," I said.

"So what do you think? Can Cornwall Falls win you back?" he asked.

"I'm going to have to think about it before we go any further," I said. "I really—I don't know. But can you keep this confidential for now, Dean Sobransky?" I needed time to think it through on my own, before anyone else—like W—knew about it.

After saying bye, I slipped my phone back into my pocket. Then I heard someone clear their throat behind me. Guy Nicollet was lurking. And smirking.

"So. That's one smoothie store owner you've had an affair with, one college dean . . ." He used his fingers to count. (Probably doesn't know any other way.)

I glared at him. He still owed me my last paycheck. "Are you following me or something?"

"No, I'm here for supplies, obviously." He had a shopping cart full of giant 5-quart pails of ice cream.

I narrowed my eyes at him. "You're supposed to sell premium ice cream. Not store brand."

"What are you going to do . . . sue me? Oh, never mind, you already trashed my reputation. But you know what? It hasn't hurt sales at all. Not one bit. There's no such thing as bad publicity."

What is it about him that makes me want to punch him?

On the way out of store, ran into Grant at customer service desk. I ended up blurting out about the call from Cornwall Falls. I wanted him to say, "Don't go" and "How could you even think about it?" But all he said was, "Well. Sounds like a plan."

A plan? "But I'd have to leave." For spring semester. And every semester after that.

He shrugged. "Might make things easier. You never know."

How would it make things easier? I wondered. What was he talking about? "Well, I haven't said yes or no yet. He just called. I'm busy working on this huge project for Bigelow's class right now. I'm kind of committed to stick it out for that," I said, trying to sound important and wondering why he was being so cold and rude to me.

"Hm. Well, good luck."

Grant wants me to leave. That's all I can think. Really?

I'm finally ready to talk to Wittenauer, to tell him what happened, how Dean S. called and what he said. I know he'll be excited and at the same time, I know this might change things. Or, change everything. The thing is, now that I'm ready, I can't reach him. Which is weird.

I don't know if I can handle transferring again. Feel like a Ping-Pong ball. Live here, no, live there. Live at home. No! Live next to Grant. Move in with W. No, don't. Move back to Cornwall Falls.

I think I should at least talk it over with him, but since I can't seem to reach him, I talked about it with Mary Jo instead. Mary Jo = voice of reason, except for that brief but all-too-long period when she was seeing that loser Joe.

"Have you seen Wittenauer lately? I keep calling him but all I get is voice mail," I said.

"Um, not really. How are things?"

We talked about classes, finals, Mom's wedding, et cetera, and then I told her about Dean S.'s call last night.

"Wow. What a tough decision," she said.

"Yeah," I said. "It is. I mean, three months ago—you know, I'd have jumped at it. Maybe even two months ago. But now?"

She was quiet for a minute, then she said, "I miss you like crazy, and things would be a lot more fun if you came back, but in a way, I don't think you should transfer."

"Why?" I asked.

"Um. Lots of reasons. Because you'd have to retransfer. Because if I were you, I'd be mad at the school. Plus, there's a good chance they'd screw up the finance package again, you know?"

All those things were very true. But were they the reasons I wasn't calling Dean S. back immediately and saying, "Yes, see you in January"? Probably not.

12/9

All spare time being spent on project—we're doing this on Friday, no time to waste.

Ha-ha. Pun. No time to waste. Maybe I can use that somehow on posters.

Mom just called with umpteenth wedding update and schedule. Reported that it may be a tad uncomfortable at the ceremony because her parents are getting a divorce. Then she brought up the seating chart.

"Again, Mom? Again with the seating chart?"

"What?" she asked innocently.

"Mom, there are other things going on besides your wedding, OK?"

"What's going on?" she asked.

"Only everything," I said. "Only my entire future!"

"Again?" she said. "Again with your future?"

Touché. I guess.

Working on project. Want to put all personal-life crap out of my mind and just focus on getting an A.

You know how in September they put a wrecked car outside, on the plaza, to show everyone how drinking and driving kills? Which it does. And which is a much worse problem, heartbreaking, serious problem, than what we're doing.

But we're using a similar theme: drinking and discarding.

Everyone who takes a plastic or paper cup out of Lory Student Center will get a sticker on their back (or backpack): neon orange, but made with recycled stuff:

The sticker says: I (GOT) WASTED TODAY!

Naturally, we're too late to order stickers, so we're writing and/or printing them all out ourselves. We each have hundreds of sheets of neon stickers to prepare.

Unfortunately, our printer is out of ink. Fortunately, Shawna and Dara are helping me.

Today we staged our Env. Activism protest in front of Lory.

Anyone who used a reusable coffee tumbler or water bottle got a gold star.

Anyone who didn't got the I (GOT) WASTED TODAY sticker on their shirt, back, or cup.

All the disposable cups were tossed into a giant Dumpster that we rented, and by the end of the day the Dumpster was nearly full. We took pictures to post online to increase awareness—I just put up some on my blog, actually. A reporter from the *Coloradoan* was on campus for another reason and snapped some photos, too. (Naturally, I kept out of them, hiding behind Dumpster.)

The event was a major success, in that some people got really insulted and yelled at us. Which means our message was getting through.

Dr. Bigelow congratulated us many times, said he is giving the class an A for final project. Said he's excited about working with me on my thesis when the time comes.

Afterward, I called Dean S. and told him I'm not coming back. He wasn't in the office. I took the easy way out and left a message.

That is so like me.

Feel strangely calm about my decision.

That is so *un*like me.

Time to make some more decisions.

12/12

Just when we had given up all hope, DeathKitty is back!

And guess what? She's not alone.

Her so-called weight gain from eating Oscar's food? A myth. She was pregnant and has returned to the house with 3 kittens.

DeathKitten 1, DeathKitten 2, and the runt of the litter, DeathCutie.

Dara swears she will give up those temporary names and let us help name them. So far she calls one Sylvia, short for Sylvia Plath, one of her fave poets.

She's so wrapped up in those adorable kittens that I had the window of opportunity to sneak out and put a note in Grant's car.

Yes, I could call him (but I am 100 percent chicken, remember), and yes, I have texted him, but he hasn't gotten back to me. Decided to do something old-fashionedly romantic.

The old note was *still* above the visor, which made me think he had never used the visor. So, I put my note on the driver's seat.

Dear G,

Thanks for the Oscar tags and thanks for making me laugh in Bigelow's class that day, and giving me confidence to do project. Did you see it yesterday? What did you think? Please call me, or come by, I <u>really</u> need to talk to you!

—C.

When I went back inside, kittens were all crawling on Oscar and he was licking them like a good mom cat would, while DeathKitty ate.

No call from Grant. He has to have seen the note. He has to. So what is the deal?

Finally tracked him down, via info from his house-mates, at the vet science library. Walking in, I thought I saw the ferret owner from the class Oscar and I went to. He gave me the evil eye. Also, I thought I saw Kelli. Kept walking. Finally found Grant sitting at a desk by a window. When he looked up at me, I saw sheer panic in his face.

Tell me about it.

I pulled up a chair and sat down. "I really have to talk to you. Why are you avoiding me?"

"Look, I really need to study. Don't you?"

"Yeah, but . . . this is important. Potentially life changing."

"Sorry. So are my grades."

"I know, I know. I really have to talk to you, though."

"OK." He sighed. "So talk."

"So, um." And all of a sudden I had no idea how to begin, or what to say. I bumbled into some explanation of what happened at Thanksgiving. How I didn't tell him because I didn't know what to say, how I'd been trying to figure out what to do.

"I didn't know what to say—I was so surprised—but I don't want Wittenauer to move out here, much less live together. I mean, I think we're kind of, well . . . I just don't think we should."

"Why not?"

"Because of you." *I'm back in love with you.* I couldn't say that, though.

"Me? And what did you say to him about . . . me?" Grant asked.

"Well, nothing, yet," I admitted. "I wanted to talk to you first."

He seemed to be getting more aggravated by the minute. "Listen, Courtney. Don't hedge your bets."

"What?"

"It means—"

"I know what it means!" I cried.

"Shhh!" somebody said.

"But I'm not doing that," I said in a whisper. "I'm not hedging anything."

"Aren't you?" He raised his eyebrow in this attractive arch that I seriously don't think any human female could resist. "I mean, why are you even telling me about this? What are you asking me, exactly?"

I felt like I was in the glare of a police detective's light. This was it. My moment to confess. And I couldn't.

"I don't know. I—I have to go." I grabbed my book bag and bolted for home. By the time I got there, I was freezing cold and wet. It wasn't raining or snowing. I'd been crying the whole way.

I blubbered the story to Shawna, who is, like, ALWAYS there for me and also for Dara, and never brings any of her own drama to the table, which is so damned likable. Anyway.

"Hold it, hold it," she said. "Why would you have one of the most important conversations of your *life* at the *library*? Like he's going to talk there."

"And he probably loves Dara anyway, and he doesn't want to tell me," I sobbed.

"He doesn't. She asked him out and he said no."

"Oh? Really?"

Suddenly, my phone chimed with a message.

U drive me insane.

It was Grant.

Me: Sounds intriguing. Do tell.

Grant: Y would u have such a big convo @ library? Not the place.

Me: So name the place.

Grant: Not now. Not finals week! Anyway, it's your decision to make first, not mine.

Me: Y me?

Grant: You're with someone. I'm not.

When he's right, he's right. How come I never get to be right?

12/14 FIRST DAY OF FINALS WEEK

Finals finals finals . . .

Good-bye for the next few days, journal.

On second thought. Don't leave me. Stick around. I will need a place to vent after I fail my exams.

Oh crap, someone's knocking at my window.

It's Grant.

LATER

Recovering now. Sort of.

First thing he said was that he's known for days that Wittenauer and I were going to move in together in June. Days! Dara told him at the Humane Society last Sunday. EIGHT DAYS AGO!

And he was so mad at me because he was waiting for me to tell him, but I just acted like nothing had changed, nothing was different.

Well, it wasn't—yet! And none of this was my idea!

Second thing he said is that it's crazy for me to talk to him about me and Wittenauer and ask what I should do.

"I've grown up, I've changed. After what happened with you . . . when I temporarily lost my mind and kissed Beth that one time, I decided I'd never do that to someone again. So when you moved back here and I started having feelings for you again, I broke things off with Kelli."

"I thought she broke up with you," I said.

"No. Wrong. And since you obviously have feelings for me, too, you could do that. But no. You refuse to make up your mind. You just avoid things and people and hope the problem will go away. And then you tell me you're moving in together and you don't want to be—what am I supposed to do with that? Do you want me to call him for you? Why would you say yes?"

"OK, but, Grant, you don't understand."

"Clearly."

"He didn't *ask me*, ask me. He just started saying we should do it, that it would be cool, and logical, and a good plan. The plan! I never said that was the plan."

"It takes two to . . . plan," said Grant.

I couldn't argue there. I mean, I could have told

Wittenauer no, right away. So why didn't I? *Was* it the stuffing in my veins?

"And now you're leaving me notes trying to get me to tell you how I feel, when you won't tell me how you feel? I mean, seriously. What are you going to do, wait until he's almost finished packing the U-Haul and then tell him? The way you treated me at spring break? I'm not going to be part of that. I hardly know him but I wouldn't let you do that." He shook his head. "Man. How can you be so mature when it comes to certain things, and so immature when it comes to others?"

He looked at me like I would have an answer for that. Am I suddenly a Psych major? "Uh . . . Grant. Look. I . . ."

"Are you ready to say how you feel, or aren't you?"

"The thing is . . . I . . ."

"See, I knew it. You're not sure you want to choose. Even though you know how great we are together and how—"

"We are great together. But I'm scared. Is that so wrong? I mean, look at what happened last time."

"Yeah. But we're older now, we could handle it better. Or at least, I could."

Can't stand his superior Superior attitude!

"You know what? I don't even know what I'm doing here. I've got two finals tomorrow."

He was about to leave, and then all of a sudden he turned around and came back.

Then we had this really passionate, absolutely hot kiss that I was still seeing stars from when he headed for the door again, saying, "Call me when you get it figured out. But not before. Don't leave me any more cute notes, don't text me, don't visit me at work! Don't even eat at the Pyth,

OK? That was my lunch place before you came to town."

So what does that even mean? My heart is still pounding and it was, like, half an hour ago.

Why was he talking like a western sheriff in an old movie?

Oh, and *he* has two finals? What about me? I do, too.

12/15, 12/16, 12/17 AN ETERNITY OF FINALS

My love life has been temporarily suspended.

Must pass all of my classes.

Still, can't stop thinking about Grant.

Am I ready to be with him again? Am I ready to break up with Wittenauer? The fact he's been strangely quiet, and everyone is in finals hell, means I may have a few days to just do nothing. Which I'm very good at, so, cool.

I mean if I tell Wittenauer now and he's upset . . . it'll be just like how I ruined Grant's A in Chem, or whatever that was.

If I tell him now and he's *not* upset . . . I'll probably be upset.

And if I even think about seeing Grant, I'll be too distracted to find the building for Final #1.

Agh! Focus. Not here for the love connection. Here for the bachelor's degree.

Sexist term. Bachelor's degree.

12/18

Done. I am done. I have handed in my 2 papers and taken my 3 finals.

I am done with school until the middle of January.

I don't have a job.

I am headed home to Denver to be in Mom's wedding.

I've broken up with Wittenauer—

Oh, wait. Knew there was something major left on my to-do list.

Everyone is doing it by Twitter these days.

Can't I just do that?

No. OK. Try to be brave, like Grant said.

I was kind of waiting until we were ALL done with finals. Now I have no excuse. And that's too bad, because I so love excuses.

Well, things could be worse. I could be driving to Seattle with DeathKitty, Sylvia Plath, and DeathCutie in a cat carrier. (The white one has been adopted by a poet friend and named Frosty, for Robert Frost.)

LATER

I did it. I've done it.

I drove up to the buffalo overlook, my calming place up on I-70. Called Wittenauer, who was in the midst of Christmas shopping with his folks. He slipped off into a coffee shop so he could have some privacy. From his parents, anyway.

I hated to have to break his heart like this over the phone. During the Christmas season, no less.

"So, uh . . . there's something I have to tell you," I said.

"Oh, me, too, me, too," he said, sounding all excited.

Started feeling like world's worst person, or at least, Colorado's. "I'll go first," I said. Because if he was going to tell me he was coming out earlier than for Mom's wedding, or had bought *me* a ticket to visit him over the long winter break, I wanted to squash those ideas ASAP.

"I've been thinking about it, and I don't think you should move out here after you graduate, and I definitely don't think we should live together," I said.

"Really?" he asked. He didn't sound crushed. He didn't sound thrilled, either.

"Yeah. I don't think we're ready. And actually, I don't know if I'll ever be ready. The thing is, Wittenauer, I love you, but . . . well . . . I guess I need to break up with you. Actually. Because I think I'm kind of *in* love with someone else."

My heart was pounding a million times a minute, hands shaking, etc. Meanwhile, complete and utter silence on other end.

Then he finally said, "You're not."

"Well, maybe. I mean . . . yes," I said, trying to be a little clearer. "Evidence suggests."

He laughed.

Laughed?

"Grant?" he asked.

"I'm really, really sor—"

"That's OK, Courtney. That's *totally* OK. Because, um, I think maybe . . . I'm in love with someone else, too. Or at least I have a serious crush."

"What?" After the anguish he'd put me through, insisting we make a commitment when I wasn't ready, now HE wasn't ready and wanted to break up, too?

"Remember Baby Corn?" he said. Then he laughed. "She's my apprentice. I spend a lot of time with her."

"Yeah, but—that's crazy. Why did you talk about moving in together at Thanksgiving if you were already falling for her?"

"Did I talk about that?"

"Yeah, you said it was the plan," I said. "The logical plan."

"I thought we were just kicking around ideas. Weren't we?"

"*Just kicking around ideas?* I want to kill you," I said.

"So probably we shouldn't live together," he joked.

And then I started laughing so hard that I was doubled over. I could tell he was, too.

"I just thought—you know, that's what you're supposed to do when you graduate," Wittenauer said. "And you were so far away and so unhappy that I wanted to save you."

"But I wasn't," I said. "Unhappy."

"Oh. Well, maybe I was then," he said. "I missed you a lot. And I really like Colorado, and I'm still going to apply to law school at Boulder. But, like, the minute we talked about it, and I went back to campus, I knew I couldn't do it; I'm not ready. That's why I've been avoiding you. I felt so guilty for, like, leading you on."

"You didn't have to feel guilty," I said. "I was just as confused."

"The thing is that I'm probably not ready to settle down because I seem to have this awful habit of falling for someone new every November. Did, uh, Mary Jo tell you?"

"Tell me what?"

"She saw us. Holding hands. We acted like it was nothing, but I thought she knew."

"Oh. She might have tried to tell me," I said. "So, um, do I know Baby Corn? What's her name, anyway?"

"Let's not go down that road. I mean, you've moved on and all."

"What's the big deal? I'm not going to *call* her," I said. "Just tell me."

He let out a loud sigh. "Her name's Courtney, OK? But it starts with a *K*. And don't give me a hard time about it, just *don't*."

We talked a lot longer—more serious stuff, not joking around, about how much we meant to each other and how we wouldn't regret anything and how much fun we had. I knew I should mention the part about Dean S. calling to offer me the chance to come back, but it just didn't seem relevant. Whether I got the offer or not, I still wouldn't be going back.

So weird. I'm free and clear. And the first person I want to tell is Grant, but I can't. Not yet.

We picked up our bridesmaid dresses yesterday morning, then went to a fancy restaurant in Cherry Creek for a so-called ladies' luncheon. Mom gave us all little mementos, a pair of silver ski earrings that I will probably not wear in a hundred years, but I appreciate the gesture because presents are always good, even when they're not your thing.

"Why do we have to do all this?" I asked.

"It's tradition," said Mom. "When is Wittenauer meeting us?"

I bit my lip. Here came the uncomfortable parental questions. "Um."

"Um, what?"

"He's not."

"Courtney!" Mom yelled. "If he doesn't come, then the whole seating chart will be messed up!"

"Mom, I think it's a little bit more important what's going on with your daughter than what happens to your perfect seating chart," said Alison. She scooted closer to me. "What's going on?"

"We broke up," I said. "Yesterday."

"I know the feeling," said Grandma Von Dragen. "Completely heartbreaking."

But it's not, I thought. Not for me.

"Well, do you think you can find another date by Thursday?" asked Mom. Not even asking how I was feeling or doing.

A mental image of Grant in a tux flashed through my mind. He looked good, even in a mental image. But that would mean contacting him and asking him. "I'm not sure, Mom."

"Well, could you decide by tonight?"

"What do you want her to do, hire an escort? Get real," said Alison.

"An escort?" Mrs. Vickers, Sterling's mom, started laughing. "Oh, that would be rich."

Suddenly, our conversation turned to whom we'd choose for an escort. Dream companion for wedding. Mrs. Vickers gave quite the monologue about George Clooney. Grandma said she'd have to get past her first. But then they moved on to some younger contenders, like Zac Efron and Robert Pattinson.

Cougars! Every last one of them.

12/21

We're in Breckenridge for the weeklong wedding celebration. Today is ski day. I can handle that. Unless Mom and Sterling get married on the slopes.

We're not that far away from Denver, but it feels like we are.

I can't stop thinking about Grant's parting words, how I have to be completely sure before I contact him again.

Don't text me, don't visit me . . . etc.

But DO kiss him?

What?

Has he ever heard of the term *mixed messages*?

LATER

Skiing over. Have windburn on face but feel good, exhausted.

We're staying in this cluster of rented condos, where pets are allowed, so Oscar does not have to be abandoned yet again. Tonight a bunch of us got together to watch movies. Tonight was Mom's choice: *The Graduate*.

Very old movie about a guy who goes home after college and is totally alienated from parents.

Hm. Familiar.

"Men," my grandmother complained when Dustin Hoffman started sleeping with that pretty girl Elaine's mother, Mrs. Robinson.

12/22

Had a dream last night after watching the movie.

Instead of Dustin Hoffman racing to the church to stop the wedding, and pounding on the window, it was Grant, shouting "Courtney!" instead of Elaine. "Courtney!"

In the dream I was getting married to the Tom, in a hideous, cranberry-colored wedding dress with a dozen ruffles and bows.

And instead of escaping on a city bus, Grant and I went flying down the slopes on skis.

But then we ended up skiing on the highway and getting stuck in the Eisenhower Tunnel and after that skied right into a rock slide.

12/23

Rehearsal dinner tonight. Dad and Sophia flew in from Phoenix.

Why would an ex-husband go to his wife's wedding? Why? Insane family of mine. Mom said it's for us, the children. The children are now, respectively, 17, 19, and 21 years old. Think we could handle it.

Still, it was nice to see Dad, even though occasionally I get annoyed, remembering that if he hadn't left in the first place, I wouldn't:

Have so many freaking issues with commitment;

Be wearing a cranberry dress tomorrow night because Mom wouldn't be getting remarried;

Have to make awkward small talk with yet another set of relatives, including stepsister, Angelina;

Be getting a manicure at ten.

Wait. It's not all bad.

Alison and I were hanging out together, while Bryan was keeping to himself, writing dark poetry he wouldn't let us see.

During dead part of dinner, while various people made various obnoxious toasts, I texted Grant:

Please rescue me. Please.

I even gave explicit directions to the condo.

No response. Not even allowed to text him. Forgot.

12/24 CHRISTMAS EVE

I'm going to do it.

I'm skipping the Frozen Fingers 5K this morning that everyone is supposed to run in as a sign of solidarity and support for Mom and Sterling.

I'm not going to wear the WATCH STERLING AND SUZANNE RUN TO THE ALTAR T-shirt that I'm supposed to wear at the after-run brunch.

Because you know what? I don't run. It's too cold to stand around and watch a 5K. And I don't even like brunch.

But also because I can sit here all week and wait for Grant to come rescue me from a disastrous wedding . . . or I can go find him myself, tell him I love him (gulp), and see where that takes us.

Because in real life, unlike in the movies, your prince does not come. Dustin Hoffman doesn't show up. Neither does Prince Charming. You have to go get him.

Even if you have to drive your little brother's car that has a BOYZ WILL BE BOYZ bumper sticker.

Wish me luck, dear journal.

Not that you've ever helped me before, but who's keeping track, really?

12/24 LATER CHRISTMAS EVE

There's something really, really challenging about having romantic conversations that start off with, "Hello, Mrs. Superior. Is Grant home?"

Gah. Should have done this in Fort Collins where we at least live on our own, sort of, or at least with peers. Had to sit around with Grant's parents and Grandmother, snacking on gingerbread cookies and fruitcake (bluck) and admiring Christmas tree and other holiday decorations. Had a feeling Grant liked watching me squirm. Parents seemed to be evaluating me a little too closely as well. Making note of every crumb I did, or didn't, eat. Watching me sip coffee.

Finally, Grant asked if I wanted to see the new mountain bike he was getting for Christmas. Kind of question a ten-year-old boy would ask. But it worked.

We went into their attached garage. Grant closed the door, but I still pictured his parents and grandmother leaning against door to kitchen, listening.

"So, Grant," I said as he wheeled his new bike out for me to look at.

"Check out the front suspension," he said.

"Yeah. Great. So, listen. I broke up with Wittenauer. About a week ago," I said.

"And it has twenty-eight gears. The lowest ones are really intense," he said.

"Is that so," I murmured. What was with him? "Anyway, the thing is, Grant. I'm ready. I mean, I've made my choice. I'm making it right now."

"It has fenders so that I can ride in really wet weather—"

"And it's blue! With silver accents! OK, OK, I get it!"

I grabbed Grant's arms and the bike dropped and leaned against his parents' sedan. "Grant! I really, really want to get back together. I love you! I never stopped, I don't think! And I want to be with you and no one else, ever, and I want you to come back up to Breckenridge with me for the wedding!"

He arched that eyebrow, the one that kills me. "You're not suggesting a double ceremony, are you?"

"T-tonight? No." I shook my head frantically. I did love him, but I wasn't ready to discuss anything like that.

"Not that I wouldn't want to marry you. Eventually."

Eventually? I thought. Ooh, I like the sound of that.

"But not at the same time as your mother. I mean ten, fifteen minutes later, I'll be ready." He smiled, then picked me up and gave me a big hug. He started to swing me around but my heel nearly gouged the sedan, so we moved to the edge of the garage where all romantic garage encounters must occur.

By the rakes and shovels.

Grant kissed my neck, my shoulder blades, behind my ear . . .

Had forgotten how much I love the way he kisses.

Had forgotten my name at that point.

There was this vintage sign on the wall by the tool bench behind him, showing a guy watching TV and drinking a beer, with his feet up. It read: WHAT HAPPENS IN THE GARAGE STAYS IN THE GARAGE.

Which was probably a good thing, considering what Grant and I were doing.

"If you ever, ever back out on spring break plans again . . . or any plans . . . that's it, OK? We're done," he said, still kissing me.

"I wouldn't. I mean—I'm sorry." He backed away and just kept looking at me, waiting for more, I guess. "I'm really sorry. I don't expect you to forgive me for a while yet. I won't ever hedge my bets again. Unless of course we go to Central City and gamble sometime."

"I think I've gambled enough lately," he said.

"I hear that," I said. "But sometimes it pays off, right?"

And we started making out again, right by the wrench collection.

"We're going to have to, um, go back in the house," he said, and we tried to tear ourselves apart from being entangled. Again.

Complete and Utter Bliss with Superior Boyfriend. There's just this feeling between us that I've never had with anyone else.

Now must dress for wedding. Can't count how many times Alison, Mom, and various others have knocked on my bedroom door to tell me it's time to get ready.

I *am* ready. But it's Grant that's still fixing his tie.

12/25 WHAT. A. CHRISTMAS.
SCENE ONE: THE WEDDING

Grant and I ran down the snow-covered street to the church, me in my bridesmaid dress with the high-heeled shoes that were dyed to match. I kept slipping in the snow and the dye was starting to run, so I was leaving this pink-red trail behind me.

Grant picked me up and carried me the last block, and when we got to the church, Bryan was standing outside on the steps—with Shawna, of all people. We squealed like we hadn't seen each other in months, instead of just a week.

"I knew you guys would end up together, from day one!" she said.

"And I knew *you* guys would," I said.

"Oh. We're just friends," said Bryan.

"Yeah," added Shawna, nodding.

"Right. And so are we," I replied.

Grant squeezed my hand a little too tightly. "I mean, good, good friends," I said.

He kept squeezing.

"Quit it! We *are*," I said.

"Which is why he's *carrying* you," said Bryan. "Come on, let's go in."

There were only a few minutes to prepare ourselves before the music began, then we slowly walked down the aisle, bridesmaids and groomsmen, just like we'd practiced. The bridal procession music started. Mom emerged in her ecru gown, looking gorgeous, although I thought I saw her running shoes peeking out from underneath her dress.

It hit me. This was really happening. Mom was really

getting married, again, and she was so happy, she looked about ten years younger.

I was about to cry when I saw Grant sitting in the church, watching me.

Then I really started sobbing. Grant was here. With me. I was so happy!

"Pull it together, Court," Alison said from out of the corner of her mouth. She shoved a Kleenex at me.

And so, I did.

Pull it together, I mean.

SCENE TWO: THE RECEPTION

"Well, you just look like a prince in that suit." Mom gave Grant a warm hug in the receiving line.

The ever-polite groom held out his hand to Grant. "Sterling Vickers. Nice to meet you."

And, I thought, they'll probably be seeing a lot more of each other. This is all good. I think.

Best Christmas Present Ever: back together with Best Boyfriend Ever.

"Sorry I messed up the seating chart again," I said to Mom.

"Oh, hon," she said, crying as she hugged me tight.

It's her special day, so I'll tell her I don't like being called "hon" another time.

Later, Mrs. Vickers stopped by our table, just as Grant and I were about to get up and dance. "So. I see you got yourself an escort."

"Well, I had to. Seating chart and all," I said.

She and Grandma Von Dragen kept eyeing him the whole time we danced.

"I think they're Googling you," I said.

"Ogling, you mean."

"Call it what you want. If I were you, I wouldn't go anywhere alone right now."

"Wasn't planning on it," he said.

I looked around the small ballroom while we danced. Despite all her protests, Mom had actually incorporated a lot of my ideas into her reception. It was the Green Party. No plastic cups were used—only glasses. There were cloth napkins (with no initials). The party favors were reusable coffee tumblers, and inside each tumbler was a pair of rolled-up cotton running socks with Mom and Sterling's initials and a little slip of paper that read WE'RE A PAIR NOW.

Except for endless running references, everything in the universe seemed slightly OK.

I was with Grant. Bryan was dancing with Shawna, as *friends*, they kept insisting, and at least that made a lot more sense than him pining for Dara and writing bad poetry. Alison would be home for a few weeks, and we were starting to be close friends again. Dad hadn't made any scenes and, in fact, I'd seen him and Mom's parents laughing and reconnecting.

When Mom threw her bouquet of fresh herbs, Alison caught it, which means she will have to find a state where same-sex unions are allowed. Which is another family drama I hope doesn't happen for a while.

As they left the reception and walked down the steps to Sterling's waiting SUV, we all threw snowballs at them. Little teensy ones, so nobody got hurt.

Then Mom and Sterling left for a two-week honeymoon trip to Maui.

SCENE THREE: THE AFTER-PARTY

We all went back to the condo for an after-party.

Well, five of us anyway.

After-party consisted of changing out of stuffy clothes and into swimsuits, and going to condo's heated outdoor pool.

Love being in a pool, looking at snow and stars.

We made plans to see friends in Denver tomorrow: Beth, who's FINALLY coming home from Italy, and Jane, and some of Grant's friends, and Shawna might stay for a night or two—as a *friend*—and we're going skiing, and—

"Uh, Courtney. Where are we going to do all this?" asked Grant as I listed all my ideas.

"Isn't it obvious? Since Mom and Sterling will be in Maui, we'll be using our house for party central for the next two weeks," Bryan said.

"OK," I said. "But do you think Oscar will be able to handle it?"

"Well, at least he won't feel abandoned. And that's another thing," said Grant. "What was with you that day we brought him to class?"

"I'd rather not talk about it right now," I said. "Or ever. If that's OK."

"Fine. But if you're going to try to save the animals, like you used to, you can't be so rude about rats and ferrets."

"Does *every* animal need to be saved?" I asked.

I/I MOST ROMANTIC NEW YEAR'S EVE EVER

Grant picked me up from home and said we had to go up to Fort Collins to feed roommate Cody's cat. I never knew Cody had a cat, but he said he had adopted it right before Thanksgiving. I actually hadn't been to Grant's house in a long time; what did I know?

On the way, Grant drove up to the Smoothie Stop. "Check it out," he said, pointing at the door.

CLOSED, it read.

No surprise there. "It's New Year's Eve," I reminded him.

"Keep reading," he said.

"UNTIL FURTHER NOTICE!" I read out loud. "Yes!"

Apparently, Grant had read about the store closing in the *Coloradoan* but had saved it as a surprise for me. He'd helped alert people to the fact that Guy was buying cheapo ice cream at Shop & Shop, like the day I saw him there, and apparently Guy was also several thousand dollars in debt. So maybe in the end, I had nothing to do with Smoothie Stop going under, but I still felt proud. Maybe I'd saved Truth or Dairy.

When we got to Grant's house, it was decorated all in white: white flowers, other snowy things. Grant had bought chocolate soy milk that he heated for hot chocolate. Then he got me this white square of chocolate and held it in front of me, offering it up as if it were a jewelry box.

"I have something to ask you," he said. "Would you—"

This whole setup. It could only be leading to one thing. I felt my heart tense up. I couldn't breathe. "We're too young—" I started to say.

"—like to go see the polar bears?" asked Grant.

I let all the air out of my lungs. Phew. "You mean, go to the zoo tomorrow? Sure."

He shook his head. "No. Go see the polar bears in Alaska. Next summer."

"Seriously?" I smiled. "Thought you'd never ask."

"Are you kidding?"

"Pretty much. Do you really mean it? You're inviting me to go to Alaska? For real?"

He nodded. "It's a cruise—"

That wasn't exactly how I'd pictured it, but OK.

"—with my grandmother and parents."

That was definitely not how I'd pictured it. "OK . . ."

"Well, seriously, do you think I could afford it on my own? They said I could bring a friend."

I looked up at him and crinkled my nose. "*Are* we friends?"

"Well. Kind of." He leaned toward me and kissed me on the cheek. "We're very close friends."

He pulled back and played with a strand of my hair, twisting it around his finger, then curling it back behind my ear. I thought I was going to die of anticipation. If Oscar weren't lying on my feet, I would have tackled Grant on the sofa right then.

"But, Courtney. The thing is . . . there are these tiny cabins on the ship, and you sort of have to have two people to a cabin, so . . ."

I started to get this sexy yet cheap feeling, but then I realized what he was talking about. "I have to room with your grandmother, don't I?"

"Yeah." He smiled, a little sheepishly. "She doesn't snore . . . much. I mean, it's not as romantic as maybe you'd want it to be—"

"No," I said, scooting closer to kiss him again. "It's perfect."

Well, that's it. The whole scoop.

Snow White I'm not. But I'm happy to be me, in my situation, and not keeled over after a poisoned apple waiting for a magical kiss from someone I barely know.

I wouldn't want to live in a castle, anyway. Drafty. Probably full of mice. No decent vegetarian meals.

No more boyfriend drama. Just me and Grant, back to normal for now, and maybe for a long time.

I won't say ever after. That would be a jinxing thing.